# THE BOOK OF GOOD LOVE

# THE BOOK OF GOOD LOVE

*by*
Juan Ruiz

*Translated by Elisha Kent Kane*

*Introductory Study by John Esten Keller*

*The University of North Carolina Press* • *Chapel Hill*

# PREFACE

When Elisha Kent Kane published his now famous translation of the Spanish *Libro de Buen Amor*, by Juan Ruiz, Archpriest of Hita, he gave to the public—the educated non-academic public as well as the scholarly public—the results of a long labor of love. The many years spent in translating some of the most difficult passages in Spanish into his own language; the considerable artistic skill expended in rendering the lines of the original poetry into English lines while preserving the medieval rhyme schemes; the arrangement for private publication at his own expense in days when the book in translation seems to have been considered a forbidden item; the use of excellent paper and deluxe binding; and the inclusion of many ribald and comical illustrations drawn by the translator himself all testify to the love that went into this work. Certainly Kane succeeded in making enjoyable, and even reasonably reliable, a book which had previously been available only to those who could read Spanish, and medieval Spanish to boot.

That Kane wrote for humanity and not solely for the erudite is made most evident in his famous "Translator's Preface," a kind of classic itself in its humorous attack on pedantry and scholarly ambiguity. There is, too, a section following the Preface entitled "The Life and Work of Juan Ruiz," in which Kane seeks to portray the Archpriest as a writer of wry but human as well as humane character. Here he pokes more fun at professorial theorizing about the book and its author, which, in his day, was at the point of running riot, and in our own time is so proliferated as to be beyond the scope of most scholars. Even Kane's footnotes, all of which have been retained in this edition reflect his scorn for the duller aspects of scholarship.

The great volume of subsequent research published by innumerable critics and theorists may possibly prove Kane in error in some of his views. But even this statement can be questioned, and one can detect in the most up-to-date criticism agreement with some of the ideas Kane supported.

To date no other English translation of the *Libro de Buen Amor* has been published, although, as can be seen in the bibliography, short passages have appeared from time to time. This is not surprising since the translation of the entire *Libro* runs to over six thousand lines of verse. Kane's work, then, is a notable piece of scholarship, as well as a delightful presentation of Spain's outstanding medieval masterpiece. In its original form, a limited edition printed in 1933 and now advertised only occasionally in rare book catalogues and at very high prices, it is greatly sought after. This second edition, it is hoped, will fill a need long felt.

I should like to thank Mrs. Elisha Kent Kane for her kindness in providing me with the pertinent biographical data on her late husband and for her permission to publish this second edition of *The Book of Good Love*.

JOHN ESTEN KELLER

*University of Kentucky*
*Lexington, Kentucky*
*December, 1967*

# CONTENTS

# ELISHA KENT KANE
## 1894–1959

Elisha Kent Kane III, son of a famous surgeon, Evan O'Neill Kane, and Blanche Rupert Kane, was born in Kane, Pennsylvania, on March 18, 1894. He was graduated from Kane High School in 1913 and entered Roanoke College in Salem, Virginia, from which he received the degree of Bachelor of Arts in 1917. In 1919 Harvard University awarded him the Master of Arts degree; this same institution also granted him a Shattuck Scholarship and, in 1926, the doctorate. Later he attended classes at the University of Madrid where he gained valuable insights into Spanish life and customs while he steeped his mind in Spain's venerable past—an indispensable preparation for his translation of Juan Ruiz's great book.

Elisha Kane began his teaching career in 1920 when he joined the faculty of the Department of Romance Languages at the University of North Carolina at Chapel Hill. After several years of teaching, research, and writing there, he joined the faculty of the University of Tennessee in Knoxville where he was made Chairman of the Department of Romance Languages.

A veteran of military service in major Allied offensives in World War I, he distinguished himself as an officer and a marksman. Even after long years in the classroom he could not divorce himself from military service, and after the War, he renewed his association with the military by joining the Reserves and, in 1930, completing a course at the Command

and General Staff School at Leavenworth. During World War II he served in the Pacific Theatre where he took part in the fighting at Guadalcanal, the Bismarck Archipelago, and on Luzon in the Philippines. His decorations included the American Theatre Ribbon, the Victory Medal, the Philippine Liberation Ribbon, the Defense Medal, the Navy Distinguished Badge, and the Bronze Star.

Professor Kane's hobbies were mountain climbing, hiking, camping, oil painting, and of course, reading and researching.

He died on February 28, 1959, at St. Petersburg, Florida, from a cerebral hemorrhage.

## Kane, the Translator

Elisha Kane's scholarly works are sound. His excellent critical study, *Góngora and the Golden Age*, published by the University of North Carolina Press in 1928, is still read with profit by those who wish to understand the art of the Swan of Cordova, and his scholarly articles in learned journals are still consulted. But it is his translation of the *Libro de Buen Amor* that most actively keeps his fame alive. Constantly cited by scholars who must quote the Archpriest of Hita in English, read with affection by those who own copies, and carefully guarded in the rare book rooms of many libraries, his translation remains his *magnum opus*.

Kane's powers and skills as a translator were truly considerable. Entire pages of the English so closely parallel the Spanish in meaning and in tone that one can consider them all but perfect literal translations. Line by line he translated the poetry into English verse, even preserving the exact rhythmic patterns of the original, and this in the face of the numerous rhyme schemes employed by Juan Ruiz. However, as is the case with all who translate verse from one language into another, Kane encountered problems. At times, in the interest of preserving the original rhythm and rhyme, he simply had to sacrifice exact meaning. Occasionally he was compelled to insert concepts not present in the original—even figures of speech—and to suppress concepts in the Spanish in order to make the English versified line run true to meter and rhyme. In certain passages he allowed the Archpriest's suggestions of bawdiness to carry him beyond the author's ideas, although this is rare. Even so, and in spite of change, substitution, and even downright creativeness on the translator's part, there emerged an English rendition—for it is a rendition as well as a translation—that catches the spirit of Juan Ruiz and of his times so surprisingly well that we can scarcely hope for an improvement in our language. Few professional poets could have accomplished more.

Kane was regarded among colleagues and acquaintances as a man of wry wit, quick humor, scathing critical opinion, and perpetual impatience with stodgy scholarship or dullness in the classroom. This is, as has been suggested earlier, quite apparent in his "Translator's Preface," a piece of writing which, perhaps better than anything else, reveals Kane as a translator and helps the reader to understand his purpose, his method, and his art. Without this preface one cannot truly understand the spirit of the man or of his work, and I have therefore included it here.

Nothing could be more Kanesque than this short piece of writing. The fact that he flayed certain great scholars of the time, venerable gentlemen who could not possibly have been damaged by his facetious words, should not be taken seriously. No doubt those "flayed scholars" themselves laughed outright when they read what he said about them. The famous "Translator's Preface" runs as follows:

A translator should make the past live in the present. When a poet, like Juan Ruiz, has been dead for six hundred years the difficulty is obvious. It is necessary to keep the historical perspective, to present the local color in all its narrow picturesqueness but at the same time prevent its antiquarian impedimentia from obscuring the author. I have tried to make my bard speak as clearly and as naturally in America of the twentieth century as he spoke in the Spain of the fourteenth but at the same time to leave no doubt that it is always the Archpriest of Hita and not Hamlet in knickers or Helen of Troy jazzing up her private life for modern sophisticates. When Juan Ruiz prayed, or wrote hymns I have used King James English for I understand that is still the custom today when people pule. Where he has been racy and colloquial, I have endeavored to be the same. When he used slang and thieve's cant I have done likewise. At times Juan Ruiz is obscene; I have not soft pedalled such passages nor uttered them *sotto voce* with smirks but let them ring out *fortissimo con amore* for the greater glory of God and the shivering delight of old ladies of both sexes— hence this private edition.

My translation has been a labor of love, and if I have occasionally been unfaithful to the poet in one of his weaker moments let me reply that infidelity is a natural concomitant of love—particularly for one who has been wedded to a work so many years as I. Nevertheless, as they say in matrimonial circles, I have never quarreled with Juan Ruiz all the time I have been married to him, but have loyally loved, honored, and obeyed him, perhaps not according to the Pharasaical letter of the law, but certainly according to his spirit.

A preface seems to be the conventional place to render oblation and thanksgiving to persons who have assisted mentally, immorally or financially in the printing of a book. With this in mind let me sincerely and gratefully but with becoming modesty accord first place to myself. "Without his unselfish labor, without his constant, friendly, and un-stinted faith, etc., etc., this work never could have been completed." Second glory I accord to Professor J. P. Wickerbottom Crawford of the University of Pennsylvania for no particular reason at all except that he flayed my last book because I had unfortunately neglected to burn due incense to him in the preface and I do not want this to happen again. Third prize goes to Professor Keniston of the University of Chicago who has earnestly offered very good advice which I have con-sistently not followed. I don't know whom to accord fourth honors, but it really doesn't matter. Perhaps Professor N. B. Adams of the University of North Carolina should have it. He was my friend, not-withstanding that we were neighbors, during the dark days of my pedagoguery, and I feel that I should make some public profession of the good rye we kept buried under my dog kennel. I also ought to mention Professor S. E. Leavitt of the same university because he put up with me for three years as his colleague and I still like him—the same goes for Professor Huse, and Professor Learned, his friend. Last but least I want, particularly, to offer homage to all good book re-viewers who speak praisefully of this work.

> Blest be he who spares these bones
> But damned be he who stirs my stones.

The section Kane included immediately after his "Translator's Preface" is entitled "The Life and Work of Juan Ruiz." It is, of course, pure speculation, but so is 90 per cent of contemporary scholarly writing about this famous author. No one really knows anything about Juan Ruiz, and even though many scholars assume that his book reveals his character and his life, we cannot accept this as unquestionable fact. Perhaps the very paucity of information, coupled with the enormous amount of scholarly speculation, often bordering on statements of proven fact with no justification, influenced Kane to speculate, tongue-in-cheek, on the poet's life. The same sort of speculation has often been made about a good many other famous authors of whom little is known—François Villon, for example, whose mysterious life has even become the subject of fiction and opera. The brief character sketch of Juan Ruiz Kane presented, then, is admittedly pure conjecture, but it is certainly within the pale of reason and might very well express Kane's true opinions. It is reprinted below because it reflects important views held by Kane and offers a convenient and even advantageous point of departure into the criticism and theory of greater and more recent scholars. As one reads what the accepted authorities have been saying of late about the *Libro de Buen Amor* and its author, one comes to realize that Kane's opinions, ideas, and theories and theirs are not at great variance:

### The Life and Works of Juan Ruiz

*Si non e vero e ben trovato*

#### THE AUTHOR

Almost nothing is known of the life of Juan Ruiz. He was born, perhaps in the eighties of the thirteenth century, perhaps in the nineties, perhaps not. His native town was, perhaps, Alcalá de Henares, perhaps Guadalajara, perhaps not. Most of his life seems to have been lived in New Castile. It is certain that he became Archpriest of the village of Hita not far north of Guadalajara. For unknown reasons he was thrown into prison—unjustly, he claims, as all prisoners do—and there he languished some thirteen years. His book was finished, perhaps in 1330, perhaps in 1343, perhaps not. He appears to have died about the middle of the fourteenth century, but then again, perhaps not.

So much for scholarly precision and exactitude; now for unscholarly conjecture. Ruiz was born of poor parents, the love child of a strolling beggar and small town prostitute. Certainly his affection for old bawds dabbling in sin like his reverence for the spotless virgin bespeaks a childhood fixation. At a very early age the precocious gamin was corralled from the gutter by some discerning ecclesiastic. Within the walls of a monkery, he received, as an embryo clerk, a formal education in reading and writing and an informal one in the infinite debaucheries of various theological confraternities. There he first observed life; there he learned how to write it down.

Despite the advantages of this liberal education, as the unruly youth grew older, he tired of the religious life and felt the lure of the open road. Running away from the church when its restraints, punishments and penances became intolerable, he endured, like Pablo and Lazarillo, the vicissitudes of a vagabond. He starved and feasted, begged and stole, loved and lechered, with many a sturdy picaro. He listened, fascinated, to strolling jongleurs, now singing their songs in crowded taverns, now telling their tales upon the lonely highways. Little by little his own genius began to develop. At first he composed careless doggerel for blind beggars and riff-raff students. Then he began to embroider, with mocking realism, upon romantic pastourelles. In his hands, fables, proverb-laden, took vigorous and spontaneous form. Love songs, too, he wrote and infused them with a fervor and naïve beauty hitherto unknown. In those years of wandering his heart widened with his horizon.

But as time went on the vagabond's thoughts returned again and again to the church which had nurtured him. Sleeping in filthy hovels, or in rainy ditches, along the endless highways, became too much for his aging bones. He began to see the hardship if not the error of his ways, and like many a better man decided to consecrate to God the Devil's leavings.

The Devil had left much. Shrewd in the wiles of men, his right reverend ability soon won him the position of Archpriest of Hita. There, cynical and tolerant, grizzled but virile, he must have been a popular confessor to the opposite sex. It is easy to imagine what delightful penances he imposed upon the erring ladies of his district. It is easy to understand how the unhappily married, and the happily widowed, would come to him for consolation, and it is quite certain that they received as sweet solace as that which he freely gave. That was a season of refection and reflection. He wrote little, but the wine of his experience aged and mellowed.

*The Book of Good Love*    [xiv]

Then, alas, into his paradise came a snake—the worst of snakes—an intolerant religious master. In 1337 the arrogant, bellicose Cardinal, Don Gil de Albornoz became Archbishop of Toledo. Hardly was he there a day before he clapped the Archpriest into prison for being Juan Ruiz—a very good and sufficient reason. Those were great days when right triumphed over wrong without justice.

While languishing in prison, in order to beguile the dismal interminable hours, he began and finished his famous *Book of Good Love*. Recalling his Aesopic fables, he embedded them, like so many proverbs, in appropriate portions of various longer episodes, as for example, in the tale of the seduction of Lady Sloe. Poems that would not logically fit in, he left simply helter-skelter upon the very thinnest of sequential frameworks. His work, therefore, resembles a sort of diary, with jottings quite incongruous in matter, and in spirit. Occasionally the gloom of his dungeon overpowered him and he wrote hymns; occasionally the bleakness of mediaeval night darkened his mind and he moralized, but usually he managed to keep a stout heart. Stone walls were no prison for his fancy, iron bars no cage for his gay satire. His heroism was unquelled alike by the narrow prison of life and the straiter prison of Don Gil.

Juan Ruiz was a wise man with little learning. Smatterings from the pseudo Ovid gleaned from Pamphilus undoubtedly he had; bits of Cato and tags from the Scriptures he drags in. But the mere mention of Flower, Tristram, the Speculum, Guy's Rosary, and other mediaeval clutter are no more evidence of genuine familiarity than with us the mention of Einstein. The wisdom of the Archpriest came from his observation of life. Yet even here the poet learned much and missed much at the same time. Like most Spaniards, he possessed the faculty of living among things without seeing them. Whatever did not directly concern him he did not perceive. On the other hand his concentration and engrossment in his own milieu, his Ptolemaic orientation of everything with himself, gave him a certain narrow strength and glowing intensity which marks his work unmistakably. Here, however, the poet projects his life upon his work and it is in the *Book of Good Love* that one must look for a fuller knowledge of the author.

### THE POEM

"The most powerful book ever written in the Spanish language," the eminent critic, Cejador y Frauca, calls the *Book of Good Love*. With scholarly restraint he continues, "Our literature presents three summits which reach up to the stars and tower over the loftiest productions of the human mind. The *Quixote* in the novel, the *Celestina* in the dramatic, and the *Book of Good Love* in the lyric, satiric, dramatic—in all genres because the surging, creative genius of this solitary poet combines them all as he lifts up his powerful voice in an environment half warlike, half barbaric." Indeed, were it not for fear of damning Juan Ruiz with faint praise one might cite further encomiums of the sober Cejador like the following: "In strength of fibre, in fluent artistry, in tumultuous vitality, unembarrassed sincerity, and openness of heart, the Archpriest of Hita surpasses all the artists in the world." Spanish critics never fully appreciate the greatness of their poets and so one finds them belittling Juan Ruiz with titles like, "The Spanish Homer," "The Spanish Boccaccio," "The Spanish Chaucer," and "The Spanish LaFontaine."

Of course, the Archpriest is no Homer. He lacks the profound, prophetic strength of the author of the Iliad although he preserves much of his rough, elemental vigor. He is no Boccaccio; he does not possess the terse artistry or breadth of the Italian raconteur withal his power as a story teller and his understanding of frailty. He lacks the dignity and comprehensive breadth of Chaucer but is full of his gusto and gay humor while he surpasses him in frankness and realism. It would be better to call Ruiz the "Spanish LaFontaine" except that he writes for the saloon rather than the salon and has a much deeper and wider range of feeling. "The Spanish Rabelais" would fit the Archpriest still more appropriately, reducing the humanism of the sixteenth century to appropriate proportions for the fourteenth. Ruiz is amused with "sin," his preachments against it are mere excursions into professional ecclesiastics. He delights, like Rabelais, in exposing the corruption of clerical circles, yet he does it without the Frenchman's vitriolic hatred of sham. The Spanish bard is too tolerant even to become intolerant of intolerance. He loves life; its hawks and its hens, its grubworms and its great ones fascinate him. Like Rabelais, Ruiz may seem indecorous but his indecencies are merely the excrements of wit, evacuated somewhat copiously, to be sure, from a robust and hearty nature.

However, such comparisons are of value only in orientating this great but little known poet among other more familiar geniuses. The Archpriest's work has an individuality, a strength and nobility quite as remarkable in its way as any of the more familiar classics of Europe, but it is so intensely Spanish that it must be judged by quite a different set of standards.

A French proverb says, "Africa begins with the Pyrenees." Certainly the physical peninsula of Spain is so shut off from Europe as to be a world by itself, and this also is true of its literature. It is as full of contrasts as the land; grim and harsh as the arid central plains, glowing and sensuous as its Arabian valleys, lush as its strips of green, austere as its snowy peaks. Like the people, too, the poetry is passionately individualistic; restrained yet extreme, religious to the point of fanaticism, and voluptuous to sensuality. It is savage and gentle, sorrowful yet light-hearted.

In this strange contrasting character of Spanish letters lies much of its strength and, to us, most of its weakness. The work of Juan Ruiz to a very high degree embodies these national characteristics. Furthermore, like all Spanish art, the *Book of Good Love* is hasty and full of holes. It has no artistic unity and less coherence. There is much improvisation but even in this there is much charm. Ruiz, like Skelton, makes a careless, unexpected use of rhyme which is brilliant and startling. His poetry is often garrulous and padded like mediaeval hauberk, but as in a hauberk, this padding lends it a sort of thick strength. There is dull moralizing tacked onto sprightly fables, but this gives his work a striking chiaroscuro effect like a painting of dazzling and exuberant reality upon a sombre background of a grim, impossible dream world. On the whole, however, there is a singular gayety of spirit for one who lived so much within the gloom of a dungeon and beneath the blacker shadows of the church. Doubtless, because of this, throughout the Archpriest's poetry there seems to be a continual wrestling between an angel of darkness and an angel of light, an incoherent struggle, producing a work with an absolute lack of plan or formal unity other than that of the personality or rather the dual personality of the poet.

But what Juan Ruiz lacks in unity and coherence he makes up for in vigor. The heterogeneous kaleidoscope of songs, hymns, tales, and fables is animated with his powerful individualism. Although he takes over, as did Shakespeare and Molière, tales, almost entire, from earlier works, and although he leaves them still in their patchwork structure, he nevertheless infuses them with his tremendous creative genius. Just as Ezekiel's God breathed over the valley of dry bones and skeletons became living men, so the Spanish bard transformed lifeless mannequins into beings with convincing characters. His work thus becomes intensely dramatic, a trait of most Spanish classics. Notice, for example, the irresistible psychology in the old bawd's seductions (stanzas 711 *et seq.*, 1344 *et seq.*, 1480 *et seq.*), and witness how vivid and how lifelike is the hesitation of the woman on one hand and the persuasiveness of the venerable pander on the other. The poet draws his characters with bold, sure strokes. With sharp irony he portrays to perfection the dregs of the low life he knew so well. At the same time his work is inspired with the sweeping beauty and tragic poetry of passion. He records with supreme power the fatality of love and lust but at the same time with engaging cynicism, verve, and merriment. It is difficult to believe that much of this was written by a man lying in prison; it is hard to conceive that flashes of clever modern sophistication could have come from a dark and troubled land in a dark and troubled cen-

[xvii]    *Elisha Kent Kane—1894–1959*

tury. Juan Ruiz is a paradox and his work is a paradox, but the work will survive as one of the classics of all time, and the author within that work as one of the world's great literary geniuses.

Elisha Kent Kane gave some twenty years of his life to the task of giving English readers the translation of Spain's most famous medieval masterpiece. The proof of its greatness lies in its use and citation by present-day Hispanists and students of comparative literature.

# INTRODUCTION

## Unity and Content of the *Libro*

The previous section has presented Kane's speculations concerning the life of Juan Ruiz and his opinions about the *Book of Good Love*. His literary criticism and evaluation of the *Libro* are in general acceptable, but in one matter at least I must differ with him. I cannot agree with Kane when he states that the *Libro de Buen Amor* is "a work with an absolute lack of plan or formal unity other than that of the personality or rather the dual personality of the poet." Too many great scholars have seen and described the *Libro*'s unity—Martín de Riquer, María Rosa Lida de Malkiel, Anthony Zahareas, Menéndez Pelayo, Menéndez Pidal, and Felix Lecoy, to name a few. The plan is well defined, indeed, and even "formal" in its unfolding, although admittedly there is, at the same time considerable lack of unity of presentation and an over-all haphazard quality which greatly obscures the mechanics of the Archpriest's plan for the *Libro*. But unity is present. I make no polemic, therefore, for this unity, now almost universally accepted, but I feel that the unity should be both stressed and treated in considerable detail. The general reader and possibly the Hispanist who is not a specialist in the art of the *Libro*, might, if left only with Kane's introductory remarks, fall into Kane's own error, thereby failing to note an important element of Juan Ruiz's work and losing sight of his purpose. Either of these contingencies would be regrettable and would seriously hinder the reader's understanding of the structure and even the very art of the Archpriest.

To the medieval audiences who either read the *Libro* or heard it recited, and who knew a good deal more about the work than we do today, or were at least more closely linked to it in thought and philosophy, unity was apparent. Even though Juan Ruiz patched together a great many episodes seemingly unconnected or unrelated, he nonetheless kept in mind a definite unity of plot and did not stray very far from this unity. One must remember that if there are three redactions, or one original and two redactions extant, there may have been other versions, and indeed, the manuscript now regarded as the original may not indeed be the true one. Who can state with certainty that the lost original, if a version prior to the three extant versions actually existed, was not more unified than the extant forms? Today scholars have been asking the same question about the *Iliad* and the *Odyssey*. Many believe that Homer—whoever he was—and the other bards who recited and sang the great epic poems never in their lives presented them in exactly the same way or with exactly the same content. Albert Lord has enlightened us greatly on this point in his *The Singer of Tales* (Cambridge, Mass., 1960), showing that today in the very land of Homer where long, narrative folk or epic-like poems are still being created, the bards compose as they recite and sing, since each audience is receptive to a different rendition or presentation. Lord thinks that when at last Greece was ready to have her great epics set down in writing, perhaps to compete with the written epicry entering Hellas from abroad—the *Epic of Gilgamesh*, for example—some minstrel perhaps, probably a lesser light, was asked to dictate both the *Iliad* and the *Odyssey*. People who dictate, whether they are folk poets or their erudite brethren, tend to include all they know about a subject. If this could have been true of the Greek epics, couldn't it also have been true of the work of Juan Ruiz? Perhaps his original poem was more carefully worked out than that set down in the extant manuscripts, for he was a writer of great artistic talent and broad knowledge. It may be that he himself had written several versions or even several different poems, dealing with quite different subject matter. Perhaps, when the time came to set his great poem down on parchment, or on paper, he collected the various poems or the several versions, together with a great many shorter pieces he had written, and either dictated them or wrote down all he had created or collected into the *Libro de Buen Amor* we know today. No one, of course, can prove any of these speculations, but what had happened before might well have taken place in the life and work of Juan Ruiz. With this in mind, one might feasibly see in the *Libro de Buen Amor* a definite structure and unity of plot at times very clearly defined and at times half concealed in verbiage and interpolated material.

Through all the kaleidoscopic diversity of theme and form, then, there runs straight and clear, if one will only watch for it, a kind of biography, or perhaps an autobiography, of a young man learning the mysteries of love, of a searcher after romance. This theme helps to make coherent what at first glance must appear to the reader as a vast hodge-podge of everything available to Juan Ruiz that was even remotely connected with literature, daily life, and folklore. This biography, or pseudo-biography, actually saves the book from chaos, thereby permitting the *Libro* to rise above the well-known Spanish literary sins of haste, of striving for quantity, and of producing writing that is imperfect, unpolished, and haphazardly planned. As the reader may recall, at times even Cervantes suffered from some of these faults, and an over-all or central theme improved his masterpieces.

The theme of the *Book of Good Love* enables one to see that Juan Ruiz envisaged his creation as a work divided into roughly three separate divisions, each dependent upon the other. Each division is a phase in the life of a young man of the Castilian middle class whom the author gives the names Don Melón de la Huerta or Don Melón Ortiz, both of which may be translated in all their bourgeois plainness as "Mr. Garden Melon." We suspect that Mr. Melon is none other than Juan Ruiz himself when he was young, for from time to time, through careless slips or by deliberate intent, he allows the reader to hear Mr. Melon addressed by the name of Hita.

In the first general division of the book we meet Mr. Melon and learn a bit about him. He is clearly of the middle class, he is young, he is eager for love and romance, but he is ignorant and inexperienced regarding the refinements and courtly techniques of love, and before he is able to receive the proper instruction, he bungles his courtships like a peasant. Melon's degree of failure and his abysmal ignorance in impressing ladies of quality can best be understood from reading a selection from the first division of the book. The translation of this passage, and those of all the other passages presented below, are Kane's:

> Still hoping I might number her among my blessed maids,
> I sent her what I could afford, not only beads and braids,
> And finger rings and silly things and clothes of highest grades,
> But sent as well my sweetest songs composed for serenades.

The songs, incidentally, might have won the lady, for love poems were in great vogue and quite acceptable, but the crass and crude offer of clothes and jewelry outrages and insults the ladies Don Melón has hoped to court:

> She would not take a single gift, but scorned them all as trash,
> And held me up to ridicule, and cried, "You men are rash
> To think that women sell their gems for counterfeits of cash;
> Take off your truck and nevermore Love's sacred image smash."

Poor Melon tries again and again to succeed in the game of love, all to no avail. He simply does not know what ladies expect and is unable to satisfy their refined demands and their insistence that lovers have aristocratic manners and a philosophy of love he cannot comprehend. In desperation he resorts to an old Spanish custom and seeks out a go-between, who later solves his problem. But at this early stage of his amatory development he does not even have the gumption to make a proper choice, for he chooses a man as his messenger and, like Miles Standish, loses the lady:

Wanting her within my hand,
I sent Garcian Ferdinand
(Consummator suave and bland)
    To her house at night.

Gladly did he say he'd go;
Secretly he crossed her though—
He ate cake while I ate dough—
    She was his delight.

He gave her, as he was told,
Hares, and grain a full year old.
I was left out in the cold
    By that cunning wight.

This brings us to the second division of the book, as I see it. Obviously instruction is the only solution to poor Melon's problem. The instruction comes in a dream, and the lessons are extremely detailed. They are taught by no less personages than Cupid, called "Don Amor" by Juan Ruiz, and Venus. As soon as these deities of love appear, the *Book of Good Love* begins to unfold its plan. Don Amor says to poor disconsolate Melon:

"You tried to be a master ere you learned the simpler arts,
But if you listen to my lectures, where all wisdom starts,
You'll get from me the sweet degree of Bachelor of Hearts
To gain your soul's desire or learn to traffic in Love's marts."

Now several philosophies of love existed in medieval Spain, as elsewhere in Europe, to which Juan Ruiz could have had Don Melón subscribe. Perhaps courtly love was the most esteemed and at the same time the most complex and difficult to understand and to obey. Less literary, and certainly more easily understood, was Ovidian love, for it was carnal and earthly, whereas courtly love in its purest form was spiritual and lacking in physical contact. Otis Green, in his excellent *Spain and the Western Tradition*, Vol. I (Madison, Wisc., 1963), has written at length on an even more carnal kind of love that was based upon the doctrine of plentitude, about which more will be said subsequently.

In the second division of the *Libro*, Juan Ruiz, it would seem, focused attention upon all three types, but used courtly love as the butt of his wry humor and constant satire. Courtly love was too complex, too unrealistic, and far too unrewarding for a man like the Archpriest of Hita, for an anxious Sir Garden Melon, or for any red-blooded, passionate Spaniard. Courtly love was, one may recall, a philosophy of the troubadours and of the aristocracy. It had three main tenets that stood out above all its myriad intricacies, but only to the first of these—the power of love to improve and ennoble—did the Archpriest, and by extension of his character, Don Melon, subscribe wholly. Unless, as is possible, he was speaking tongue-in-cheek, Juan Ruiz firmly believed in this tenet and therefore could have young Melon accept it enthusiastically:

> Love makes a lout grow elegant, refined and e'en astute;
> It makes a clever talker of a man who erst was mute;
> And love, an arrant coward to a hero can transmute,
> Or make a lazy slug-a-bed pipe nimbly as a flute.

> Love keeps a young man in his prime (a physiologic truth);
> Love helps a senile patriarch retain the sap of youth,
> Love cleanses white and beautiful those sullen hearts uncouth;
> And yet poor tinsel sells for gold when love is at the booth.

But the second and third tenets of courtly love Juan Ruiz could not have Melon accept. How could a dyed-in-the-wool realist believe that the lover should place the beloved high on a pedestal above him and serve her from afar, making her wishes his law? And how could he possibly consider the third tenet, the one that even the devotees of courtly love found difficult, and often impossible, to keep—the tenet which stated that the ideal of all pure love is deepest desire that is never intended or allowed to reach physical fulfilment?

And so Juan Ruiz left courtly love to the aristocrats and to the troubadours who had developed it from Arabic philosophy and from the teachings Avicenna offered in his *Treatise on Love*. For Juan Ruiz, the *De Amore* of Andreas Capellanus, the handbook of courtly love, became a source of parody and satire rather than of true instruction. Most of the instruction of Melon's two great teachers, Cupid and Venus, stresses Ovidian love and the doctrine of plentitude, at times even sinking to the level of a love not far above animal lust. The reader at first is impressed by the fact that the lady is not to be won by anything but a courtly approach and that the usual gifts are of no avail, and he expects to find young Melon succeeding in his quest after the two love gods have taught him this approach. It soon becomes evident, however, that this is not the kind of instruction they wish to provide. Their brand of love can best be secured through seduction, and the goal they strive to gain for Melon is the very one he had himself been striving for—physical possession of the lady.

The alternative to courtly love, Ovidian Love, was to provide all the answers, unless, as is quite possible, Juan Ruiz was also satirizing even this more carnal and pagan philosophy, which is a possibility. After all, it is not difficult to believe that Ovid himself wrote his *Amores* as a kind of caricature of seduction or a mischievously pseudo-didactic treatise on love-making. Latinists now are saying that this is the case. But whether Juan Ruiz treats Ovidian love seriously or facetiously, he treats it thoroughly, enthusiastically, and eloquently. No small part of the instruction provided by Venus and Cupid comes straight from the *Amores*, but it receives a peculiarly Spanish handling, unfolds in a Spanish milieu, and must often be regarded as so far removed from Ovid's model as to be original. Among the first of the lessons Melon receives is that of choosing a lady worthy of being loved—a lesson in keeping with any of the various philosophies of love, for they all stress the importance of physical beauty. In this passage, by the way, Kane, though he strayed from direct translation in order to meet the demands of full rhyme, nevertheless managed to parallel the Archpriest's delightful concupiscence as he described the physical attributes the lover must seek:

"Seek out a woman sensuous and beautiful and gay
Who's neither dwarfish, stumpy, or built the other way;
And if you can, avoid a wench of boorish peasant clay
Because love's subtleties are lost on women such as they.

Her eyes should glow like tinted jewels, lustrous in their hue
With long, outcurving lashes, clean as grasses washed with dew;
Her ears should be like little shells, close set and not askew,
And if her neck is graceful, she's a woman for the few."

Next in importance—perhaps even of greater importance
—is the selection of a go-between. The go-between of the
Archpriest of Hita was the forerunner of all the go-betweens
that later appeared in Spanish literature, and at the same
time the model, and, except for one example, the apogee.
Even Fernando de Rojas' Celestina herself, the go-between
par excellence, with her vivacious personality and amazingly
portrayed character, had her beginnings in the Trotaconventos, or Convent-Trotter of the *Book of Good Love*. Trotaconventos is Juan Ruiz's great literary creation, his one outstanding human character, unless one can consider Don
Melón, who is at least at times Juan Ruiz himself, as a character in the *Libro*. Admittedly, Ovid's Dipsas, the magic-
working, drunken crone of the *Amores*, may have been her
prototype, as may have been some of the *viejas* of the
*exempla* from Eastern literature, but Juan Ruiz went far beyond Ovid in characterization and was able to impart to his
own bawd the glow and sparkle of life, far surpassing all
other models. Convent-Trotter is not a pretty character, but
she is one not soon forgotten. Venus has no illusions about
her virtue when she describes her to Mr. Melon, but then
virtue is of small account in the business at hand. Venus'
advice must have met with Melon's approval, for he most
certainly follows her guidance when the opportunity for
selecting his go-between comes:

"Seek, then from that accursed tribe, some vile black-hearted bawd
Employed by nuns and monks and others sanctified by God,
Such well deserve the shoes they wear in prowling much abroad—
There's not a maid these convent-trotters cannot win by fraud."

*The Book of Good Love* [xxvi]

Ovid, in the *Amores*, had warned young men against the dangers of alcohol, and Cupid, in the *Book of Good Love*, informs Melon that ladies do not care for drunkards for lovers, who, under the influence, indulge in fisticuffs and brawls likely to attract attention, and from attention, scandal.

> "Excessive drinking shortens life and makes the vision faint;
> It takes the vital forces away if drunk without restraint;
> It makes the members tremble and gives the mind a taint;
> Indeed, with every bottle comes another new complaint."

Needless to say, a successful lover must not approach the object of his desire empty-handed. However, although money is indeed important, it must be spent on a lady prudently, and not in such a way as to offend her good taste and her finer sensibilities:

> "Suppose a man's an utter fool, a farmer or a boor,
> With money he becomes a sage, a knight with prestige sure,
> In fact the greater grows his wealth the greater his allure,
> While he not even owns himself who is in money poor.
>
> Now I have heard full many a monk in many a windy sermon
> Inveigh against the power of gold and persons clad in ermine,
> But I have seen those very same ecclesiastic vermin
> Absolve a man if he has wealth and his excuse determine."

Thus thoroughly indoctrinated and instructed, young Melon feels ready to embark upon the sea of romance. Part III of the unity mentioned earlier is hereby initiated. Courtly love is left behind with the married ladies who must be loved madly by young gentlemen who are never to be granted physical contact, let alone sexual fulfillment. With the aid of Convent-Trotter Melon sets out to win the beautiful Doña Endrina, recently widowed, alone, and beset by creditors and would-be wooers. Her name, by the way, like her suitor's, is of the everyday garden variety, and may be translated as Lady Sloeberry or even as Lady Sloe, as Kane prefers. She is a woman endowed with all the practical wisdom of a Spanish housewife, with more than a pinch of passion, and with a very Spanish dread of the taint of scandal. Convent-Trotter, therefore, must work with the greatest diligence to overcome this lady's fears and scruples. For example, Lady Sloe offers the following arguments against a possible alliance with Don Melón:

> At that the lady answered her, "But I can hardly marry
> Because the year has not expired which widows ought to tarry;
> A full long year a modest girl should every suitor parry,
> Since mourning does to marrying this prohibition carry.

Convent-Trotter answers this objection as she does all the rest. She cajoles, pointing out that a widow is in great peril without a man to protect her; she praises the physique and features, the manners, the virtues of Mr. Melon and fans the fires of Lady Sloe's deep-seated need for a lover; and she shows the lady how lonely life already is for her and how grim the future will be without male companionship.

Lady Sloe is impressed. She admits that Melon's charms are all but irresistible, that his good looks, worldly wisdom, and polish strongly attract her. At last she agrees to meet him, with the place of rendezvous to be the house of Convent-Trotter. Young Melon arrives and knocks at the door. The old woman, to allay the fears of Lady Sloe, who at the last minute pretends that she does not want to see Melon after all, tells her that she will not open the door to him. At length, however, she says that she will have to open it, lest the door suffer irreparable damage from the blows that are now being rained upon it. Before the old woman slips the bolt, however, she torments Melon a bit:

> "Is it a man or just the wind? Some one is surely there—
> The swarthy devil must have come to pry in this affair—
> I wonder if it's—surely no—yet stay—how could he dare—
> Yes, by my honor, it's Sir Melon! Well now I declare!"

At last Melon enters and greets Lady Sloe with passionate affection. At this moment Convent-Trotter says that a neighbor is calling her and that she will have to go. She leaves, and the lovers are alone at last. This is obviously the climax of the *Book of Good Love,* or at least of its primary plot. It would be a shame to reveal here the denouement of the affair, for it is unusual and should be read in the full context of the story. Let it suffice to say that Don Melón is rewarded for his efforts, and that he wins the love of Lady Sloe, violating all the elements of courtly love.

There are, then, three over-all divisions of the principal plot of the *Libro*: the first part, which deals with Melon's ignorance in amorous matters and his failure at courtship; the second part, which describes the instruction given him by the gods of love; and the third, in which he continues to follow the guidance offered by his two remarkably apt and experienced instructors and wins the lady's charms.

This may be the only unity of the *Libro de Buen Amor;* certainly, it is a very well-defined unity. Yet the sequences which deal with the courtship and winning of Lady Sloe extend no further than half way through the entire book. Perhaps Juan Ruiz intended to end his work with the final scenes of that sequence. If so, then the unity of that first half of the volume was kept intact. But since the book, as we have it today, goes far beyond the lives and loves of Sloe and Melon, some mention should be made of other unifying elements.

All through the part of the book which describes the romance of Sloe and Melon, and throughout the remainder of the entire book, there are elements which seem designed to hold the disparate parts together.

First, one finds, interpolated into the *Libro de Buen Amor's* long series of disconnected parts, further amours of the protagonist, who is sometimes referred to as Don Melón, sometimes as Hita, and occasionally is made to speak in the first person. This fluctuation between the first and the third person and the variety of names attached to the hero have led to a great deal of confusion and speculation. Does the use of the first person indicate that at least a part of what Juan Ruiz wrote was autobiographical? Or is it a device of the author's to hoodwink his audience or his readers into seeing the autobiographical where it actually does not exist? It should be mentioned here in passing that the entire plot and presentation of the love affair between Sloe and Melon, despite whatever indications of autobiography may seem evident, was a direct borrowing from a well-known and widely read play written in Latin sometime in the twelfth century by an anonymous French poet. Juan Ruiz simply took this play, *Pamphilus et Galatea*, and re-worked it to suit his tastes, filling it with his own zest and with his Spanish background and developing it from a rather unliterary and uninspiring beginning into the wonderful tableau of life and passion it is in his *Libro*. Ruiz's erudite readers would have recognized this borrowing and would have savored the skill of its reworking; but the common man, who knew no Latin, might never have suspected that the entire story of Melon was plagiarized from this twelfth-century drama. Certainly the uninitiated audience might have considered the sequence autobiographical and would have laughed heartily at the ad-mission of the author that he, in the guise of poor Don Melón, had experienced such difficulties in getting his sweet-heart to bed. And the scholarly reader, who knew perfectly well that *Pamphilus et Galatea* had furnished the entire plot and most of the incidents in the Archpriest's rendition of the Melon-Endrina affair, would have laughed at Juan Ruiz's clever manipulation of the Latin work and his ability to give the tale a personal and even an autobiographical touch. A skillful piece of manipulation it is, for even the learned Cejador y Frauca, whose edition in *Clásicos Castellanos* (Madrid, 1913) though not the best from a paleographic point of view, is used today by most people who read the *Libro* in Spanish, thought the sequence autobiographical, never suspecting that Ruiz had leaned so heavily upon the *Pamphilus*. But whether or not the audience or reader recog-nized correctly the autobiographical aspects of the *Libro*, these aspects, false and contrived or true and natural, con-tinue to appear until the denouement. Ruiz has been called the most personal author of the Middle Ages. This personal quality, woven into the fabric of the entire book, serves as a unity, and it was this unity that Kane mentioned and saw as the book's only real unity.

Perhaps Juan Ruiz, if he had pared away many extraneous elements and nonsequiturs, might have produced one of the most unified books in literature; but apparently he could not bring himself to omit bits and portions—incidents, short lyrics, proverbs, and puns—that he had written and come to love. All of it had to be packed into his *magnum opus*, and if the inclusion of such items produced a plethora of unrelated incidents and confused his reader, he apparently did not worry about it. Indeed, perhaps the inclusion of so kaleidoscopic a panorama was not careless at all, but was the result of oral presentation. The *Libro de Buen Amor* is far too long to have been recited by a troubadour at one sitting. A complete reading or recitation would have required many hours. It is all but certain, therefore, that professional troubadours or *juglares* who presented the *Libro* divided their presentations into several sessions. As the reader may recall, the most up-to-date of theories today about the recitation of long narrative poems—the *Iliad* and *Odyssey*, for example—point to multiple sessions and to a variety of different renditions of even the same sequences to fit the moods of a variety of audiences. Quite possibly, then, Juan Ruiz composed many versions, some short, some long, and in his oral presentations maintained unity, whereas when he finally set down the entire production in writing, he patched together what in written form appears to us a potpourri and not a unified work.

### Juan Ruiz's Rapport with Readers

Modern scholars concerned with the medieval period often investigate, insofar as is possible, the matter of author-reader rapport, for such investigations can demonstrate, often quite substantially, the importance of medieval works in their own times, as well as their continued importance in later periods. Juan Ruiz, of all medieval Spanish poets, seems to have had strong rapport with his public. As late as the fifteenth century, more than a hundred years after his death, a troubadour could ask his audience if it would like to hear the "Book of the Archpriest" recited. Apparently audiences were always eager to hear readings or recitations from the *Libro de Buen Amor*.

The several means employed by Juan Ruiz to maintain rapport might possibly be regarded as a kind of unifying element. Rapport seems, then, to have been strong, and something of this rapport should be examined here.

One concept used by Juan Ruiz to establish author-audience rapport is the constant reminder, wryly expressed and subtly humorous, that the protagonist is no Casanova in spite of all the help received from the immortal gods. Ruiz never allows the reader to lose sight of his, or of Don Melón's, failure at the game of love. At the outset Fernán García, the male go-between, snatches for himself the charms of Cruz, the baker-girl. Melon fails again when he seeks the affection of the *dueña encerrada*, so well guarded by her family that no man can trifle with her affections or besmirch her virtue. But what of Lady Sloe, whom he finally wins and possesses? At first glance she might be regarded as a prize successfully won by an adroit lover. But reflection will reveal that Melon gains her charms through the machinations of Trotaconventos, the go-between, who actually traps the young woman in her house where, behind closed doors, Don Melón carries out a seduction perilously close to actual rape. Endrina is not won, then, but taken. Amorous skill is not required at all—only physical strength and a set of circumstances and surroundings arranged in favor of the man's lusty instincts and not of the lady's feminine sensitivities. All of this is a far cry from the skills one expects from a Casanova or a Don Juan, and Juan Ruiz's medieval audience would have noted this and would have savored it. It is in reality the apogee of his failure, for it is love not won but seized.

Other examples of Don Melón's failure at love can be

found periodically dispersed throughout the *Libro*. Hardly has Lady Sloe been deposited in her tomb—her death not clearly explained—when young Melon begins again his fruitless search for love. A noblewoman quickly avoids his approaches, a nun withdraws from all commerce with him, and even a Moorish girl rejects his advances. Not even the skills of Trotaconventos can help him, surely a sad proof of his inadequacy.

As to the wild, coarse, gross, and sometimes grotesquely ugly *serranas* or mountain lasses with whom Melon reaches sexual union, it is always evident that the choice is not his, and that it is the prowess and brute strength of these amazons that leads him, wryly unwilling, to the consummation of their needs, not his own.

This continued failure of the protagonist, his inability to succeed at love, man's most highly prized ability, is a delightful and most clever manner of maintaining rapport with an audience or with readers. It leaves no doubt that the author, like most men, was a poor fellow hungry for love but rarely savoring its delights.

One final means of attaining rapport and sympathy was the author's reiteration that he was a sinner, like all mankind, that he was weak and easily tempted, and that he was tolerant, therefore, of the sins and weaknesses of his fellows.

THE PURPOSE OF THE *Libro* AND OF ITS ENIGMATIC AUTHOR

So much for the book's unity and general content. Far more complex and myriad are the mysteries surrounding the *raison d'être* of the *Libro de Buen Amor*. Probably no book in any language is the subject of so much controversy. Who, indeed was Juan Ruiz? Is the name a pseudonymn? Why did Juan Ruiz write his masterpiece? Did he intend his audience to learn some lesson or lessons from it? Is it an allegory or rather a series of allegories? Was the Archpriest a stern moralist, a cynic, or a human being conscious of the sins and weaknesses of his fellow men and tolerant of their shortcomings? Is the tone of the *Libro* serious or mock-serious? What was Ruiz's background—Jewish, Old Castilian, Mozarab, or something else? For whom did he write—the erudite or the common people? Had he a patron or did he write to please himself rather than to satisfy some obligation?

These questions and a great many others have been asked and answered in several ways, but to this day no one really knows the truth, notwithstanding the fact that scores of the greatest Hispanists have given their opinions in learned articles and even in entire books devoted to the problem. Probably no other book written in Spanish, possibly not even *Don Quixote*, has raised such a harvest of criticism, theory, and study of sources and influences as has this one. And yet, after more than two hundred years of research and publication on the subject of the *Libro de Buen Amor*—research that has, through the years, become more learned and sophisticated in quality—not a single theory has been universally accepted by the scholarly world. It seems appropriate, however, to set before the reader of this introductory study some of the most impressive thoughts of the greatest critics, for each of these writers enjoys a following and each has created something like a "school" on the subject of the *Libro*. These critical opinions, after all, provide important contributions to literary history and have influenced, and will continue to influence, those who write histories of Spanish literature. Names like Américo Castro, Menéndez Pelayo, Menéndez Pidal, Leo Spitzer, Otis Green, María Rosa Lida de Malkiel, and Valbuena Prat, to mention only a very few, cause heads to turn and students to pay heed whenever the various schools of thought on the *Book of Good Love* come up for discussion.

There is little likelihood, of course, that any mingling of minds or of schools will ever be obtained, and perhaps it is just as well. Controversy is desirable because it stimulates investigation and research; such endeavors are healthy and tend to produce, if not scholarly agreement, at least new scholarly ideas that enrich the entire area of Hispanic and medieval studies. Eventually, of course, a comprehensive eclectic theory, or compromise, will probably emerge from the chaotic sea of speculation, and this may be the only successful road to an understanding of the book. Martín de Riquer has demonstrated this in his eclectic theory of the origins of medieval epicry.

## The Early Critics

A substantial part of the copious research that has been published on the *Libro de Buen Amor* seeks to unravel the mystery of its purpose. Theories vary enormously, and although it would be simply unfeasible, if not impossible, to discuss all of them here, some of the most important will be considered below.

Concerning the author himself, there are various theories. As mentioned previously, Kane thought Juan Ruiz was an orphan who was reared in a monastery where he came to scorn religion and the Church in general; that he took to the roads and lived like a goliard; and that in old age, wiser and more cynical than before, he went back to the cloister to escape the hardships of the world. This theory diverges completely from the ideas of the great nineteenth century critic and historian of Spanish literature, J. Amador de los Ríos (1818–1878), whose works may still be read with profit. In his *Historia Crítica de la Literatura Española* (Madrid, 1863), Amador de los Ríos wrote that he considered Juan Ruiz to be an exemplary priest, who, if he was indeed describing his own past sins, did so in an effort to crucify himself before his parishioners in order to expiate his wickedness and to impress them with his repentance and virtue. This belief is still held by many today and cannot be relegated to the ashheap of rejected scholarly theory.

Don Ramón Menéndez Pidal (1869–), whose forte was medieval epicry and the *Poema de Mío Cid*, regarded the Archpriest of Hita as a poet of the *mester de juglaría*, the troubadour's trade, who had decided to write in the erudite meters of the *cuaderna vía* or *mester de clericía*, in vogue in the mid-thirteenth and fourteenth centuries. Whether or not poets who were not writing for cultured audiences used this meter is a question that will not be answered here, save to say that Gonzalo de Berceo, who is the first known to have employed it and who may even have invented it, probably aimed his verses on the lives of Spanish saints and the miracles of the Blessed Virgin at the common man as well as at the clergy and the educated groups. It should be noted, in support of the theory of a possible audience of common people, that Juan Ruiz vulgarized the *mester de clerecía* and may have done so—indeed probably did so—in order to make it more palatable to the man in the street. This is part of the originality of Juan Ruiz, according to Menéndez Pidal, who stated that Ruiz, even writing in a purportedly learned meter, nevertheless spoke to the audiences he addressed in much the same way that troubadours were speaking in the *mester de juglaría*, inviting his listeners to come forward and contribute. He thought the long sequences in *cuaderna vía* were probably recited or read aloud by the performers, while the lyrical passages were sung by them to musical accompaniment. This also would have been characteristic of the troubadours who sang or recited, often with the assistance of an accompanist. P. Henríquez Ureña, in his article, "El Arcipreste de Hita," published in *Sur* in 1943, also noted the Archpriest's ability to bring the *cuaderna vía* into the ken of the Spanish masses.

Menéndez Pidal saw the *Libro* as marking the period when didacticism, which had reached its peak in the thirteenth century, was ending, and as helping to inaugurate the period of rebellion—social, religious, and personal—that was about to sweep through the Western world. In his opinion, Ruiz's pious statements were much in the spirit of those Boccaccio appended to his not-very-pious *Decameron*, in which recreational aims superceded didactic ones. Both A. Valbuena Prat and P. Henríquez Ureña, support those beliefs and strengthen them (see bibliography, pp. 266 and 268).

Menéndez Pidal thought that the three extant manuscripts represented truncated versions of the *Libro*. The manuscripts we know as *Toledo* and *Gayoso* (the names of the libraries in which they were once found) were early versions of the *Libro, circa* 1330, while the *Salamanca* was the author's final redaction, written in prison. The *Salamanca* contains the request to be delivered from prison, the famous and controversial prose prologue, songs in praise of the Blessed Virgin, and the sequence treating Trotaconventos, lines 910–949 and 1318–1331. Menéndez Pidal's lengthy study of the *Libro* in his *Poesía Juglaresca y Juglares* (repeatedly published) must be read in toto, if one is to imbibe his wisdom on the *Libro de Buen Amor*, but it has been possible to give at least some of his most important beliefs here.

Don Marcelino Menéndez Pelayo (*Antología de Poetas Líricos Castellanos*, Madrid, 1882), although not as deeply involved in the earlier epic period as Menéndez Pidal, was able to go into greater depth with the *Libro* of Juan Ruiz. He, too, stressed the age of rebellion, showing how chivalric society was giving way to bourgeois society. To him, the *Libro* contains two sequences that make it excel other works —a *comedie humaine* and a comic epic. Juan Ruiz, then, caught and gave unity to the picturesque spectacle of the waning of the Middle Ages. He had a zest for living, a keen interest in his own affairs and those of his neighbors, and a deep desire for a mutual sharing of feelings with others. And fortunately for us he had a personal style, a thing uncommon in a period when writers used models and tried to fashion their literary efforts in the mold of earlier great writers. Ruiz, in Menéndez Pelayo's eyes, put himself and his personality into his work and thereby made it one of the most personal books ever composed. And, along with himself, he put the times as he, wonderful observer that he was, saw them.

A valuable part of Menéndez Pelayo's work is his history of the editions of the *Libro*, which shows how the first printing under the aegis of the great Tomás Antonio Sánchez was curtailed and censored, with such important sequences as the seduction of Lady Sloe completely removed. Another feature of interest in passing is his comment that the incidents of the book should be illustrated by a contemporary artist. One wonders what he would have thought of Kane's illustrations in his original edition.

The word-picture of the individual Juan Ruiz describes as himself has long been the subject of argument. Menéndez Pelayo believed that the word picture (*coplas* 1459–64) was indeed meant to show how Juan Ruiz looked. Kane believed that these features and physique were chosen by Ruiz simply because they represented in the minds of the fourteenth century man all the characteristics of the sexually potent male, i.e., that the hairiness of the protagonist, his long nose, deep chest, and powerful thighs would have connoted a very definite kind of masculinity in his audience's mind. Today one is inclined to agree with Kane and to add that perhaps Juan Ruiz was really describing himself as he would have liked to be, for if he had actually possessed the physical attributes described, he would have made many more amatory conquests than actually occurred in the *Libro de Buen Amor*.

As to the moralizations in the *Libro*, Menéndez Pelayo believed that Juan Ruiz added them to balance the sinfulness of his life as a tavern priest and a libertine, indeed, as a goliard. He thought Ruiz protested too much about morality, thereby destroying his own moralistic tone, and that what seems to us in the twentieth century to be a facetious comment on morality was indeed humorous and satirical in his day also. The book, then, in Menéndez Pelayo's eyes, was written for sinners as well as for those who pursue good works. Gonzalo Menéndez Pidal, in his article on Juan Ruiz in *Historia General de las Literaturas Hispánicas*, IV (Madrid, 1949), an article much studied and of considerable influence, agreed in nearly every aspect with Menéndez Pelayo. He refuted Puymaigre, who thought that Juan Ruiz hated the Church, and proved this by citing the hymns of praise to the Virgin, which, he said, no hater of religion could have included. Probably in the mind of Menéndez Pelayo, Juan Ruiz was a kind of Spanish François Villon, a mixture of piety and lubricity. To him, the *Libro* was a kind of picaresque novel which expressed no repentence and possessed no moralizing intent. To him, Ruiz was a cultivator of pure literary art whose purpose was to amuse and entertain, not to berate other sinners. Otis Green, of whom more will be said later, shared these feelings; he has given a very up-to-date set of views in close conformity with those of Menéndez Pelayo. Interestingly enough, the well-known American Hispanist George Tyler Northup (*Introduction to Spanish Literature*, Chicago, 1960) has perpetuated most of Menéndez Pelayo's statements, thus making them available to the thousands of students who study his book.

Menéndez Pelayo explained the lack of order of the *Libro* by saying it was autobiographical, insisting that a novelistic work would have been better plotted and that the Archpriest's verses were his own memories exaggerated and embroidered upon. This, I think, may be true of some sequences but not of others, e.g., the Lady Sloe and Don Melón episode or that of the Priests of Talavera, both of which are to be found in almost identical form, insofar as plot is concerned, in earlier and widely disseminated works in medieval Latin.

The meaning of the words *buen amor* as the term appears in the book, still the subject of lively discussions, was clear to Menéndez Pelayo. He saw *buen amor* as love in the general sense, and believed that the term *amor* might mean what *amour* and even *cortesía* meant to the poets of the Provençal school of the troubadours, and that it might even mean something as general as *poesía*. Many scholars violently disagree with this interpretation, however.

Julio Cejador y Frauca, whose view of the *Libro* may be read in the Introduction to his edition (Madrid, 1913), held radically different opinions from those of Menéndez Pelayo. As we have seen earlier in Kane's introductory study, Cejador, a priest himself, considered the *Libro de Buen Amor* to have had no equal in medieval literature. Kane, however, felt that Cejador carried his enthusiasm too far. He believed, as do critics today, that Cejador could not bring himself to see in Juan Ruiz anything but an exemplary priest who did not lead a wicked life and who, when he wrote of wickedness as if he were a participant, did so merely to help his audience to understand its power and danger. Cejador's own religious feelings led him to make statements that cannot be regarded as scholarly, e.g., his statement that no "tavern priest" could have produced great poetry, nor could an irreligious poet be great. But what of the better poets among the goliards? What of Villon, of Rabelais? According to Cejador, Juan Ruiz's use of the first person in the *Libro* was a device to produce rapport and not to show that Ruiz had ever actually sinned. He also thought that the principal theme of the *Libro* is that man, though weak and subject to temptation and wrong-doing, will finally overcome sin, just as the fictitious Don Melón did. In Cejador's mind, the only true unity of the *Libro* is that of a prolonged satire on evil clerics, a satire directed at these men to aid in their moral improvement. Indeed, said Cejador—and not without cause—the entire book is a satire on fourteenth century manners. In his opinion, Juan Ruiz did not hide life's ugly side and did not intend that humor, save a kind of biting satirical humor, should be seen in his work.

Julio Puyol, in his *El Arcipreste de Hita: Estudio Crítico* (Madrid, 1906), said it seemed clear that Juan Ruiz was born and reared in New Castile because he made so many references to places there and because his Spanish is the pure Castilian of the period, save, of course, for the deliberate use of dialogue from other languages for the sake of humor. In Puyol's opinion, Ruiz came from lowly stock and may have spent his childhood in some mountain village, an idea no doubt derived from the author's many references to folklore and country life. Puyol also thought that the times, filled with violence and revolt, when the peasantry were being ground into the earth by the aristocracy, might have produced the pessimism he saw so evident in Juan Ruiz. Indeed, the picture Puyol more or less realistically and authentically painted of those times suggests that life was cruelly hard. Probably, he believed, Juan Ruiz supported himself by selling songs to wandering troubadours and *juglares*, to blind men, and to Jewish and Moorish entertainers of both sexes. Evidence, or at least mention, of such sales can be found in the *Libro*. Puyol considered the imprisonment of the Archpriest by Don Gil de Albornoz authentic but thought that this incarceration could not have lasted beyond 1350. As to the Archbishop, he believed he was a cleric of extreme severity and ferocity toward waywardness and might have indeed imprisoned such a man as Juan Ruiz. Although he felt sure that Ruiz lived a worldly life, at least before he was a priest, and maybe thereafter, he doubted that much of the *Libro* was truly autobiographical. He even blamed the copyists for some of the seemingly autobiographical material, although he suspected that Juan Ruiz did include some of his youthful experiences in the *Libro*.

Puyol's belief, quite modern, incidentally, that Juan Ruiz, in a sad world, thought that mankind must wrest as much joy from life as possible is quite acceptable. Another of his ideas which seems sound is his notion that although Ruiz was wry, cynical, and pessimistic, he was not truly angry at the world, nor was he a rebel, but rather was resigned to life's foibles and to the sadness all mankind must endure on earth. Perhaps, thought Puyol, Juan Ruiz really loved erring humanity, since he was representative of such humanity.

He believed that Ruiz had considerable culture and learning, but was inferior in these areas to Prince Don Juan Manuel, a rather obvious assumption, since Don Juan not only enjoyed the many privileges and opportunities of a prince of the realm but also was the nephew of no less a sage and scholar than Alfonso the Wise. Puyol saw in Juan Ruiz's writing a knowledge of Plato, Ptolemy, and Hippocrates, though not necessarily a deep knowledge of these great men. He also thought Ruiz knew certain other classical authors, much of the wisdom of the Church Fathers, much of chivalric law and custom, and probably a great deal about the world he lived in. But, he pointed out, Ruiz divorced himself from truly erudite subject matter, save to satirize it, and concentrated upon the humorous, the amorous, and the sensual in an effort to entertain his fellows at a time when entertainment was at a nadir. To Puyol, Juan Ruiz's greatest originality lay in his realistic treatment of subject matter and in his satire. He believed, then, that Juan Ruiz had produced a kind of Epic of Everyman.

Puyol's study is detailed and exceptionally profound for the most part. In it he traces literary influences, too numerous to mention here, and stresses the importance of Ovid and the *Pamphilus*, even comparing the lines in the *Libro* with those in the *Pamphilus* from which they stemmed or upon which they were based.

Some of Juan Ruiz's ideas, as seen by Puyol—e.g., his concept of a world of wickedness and crassness in which man must strive to live through his skill, to endure a minimum of suffering, and to gain a maximum of prosperity and happiness—are quite oriental in outlook. Puyol believed that this quality of Ruiz's work, plus his condemnation of the evil deeds of the ignorant and cynical clerics of the time, gained the Archpriest a strong rapport with his audience. His brand of religious parody, a kind of parody rampant in the fourteenth century, was delightful to his readers, according to Puyol. In short, Puyol thought Juan Ruiz made every effort to please and delight his audience and succeeded eminently.

### Contemporary Critics

Américo Castro, in *The Structure of Spanish History* (New York, 1954), said that the *Libro* is not didactic in the true sense of the word, but only seems to be so because its form stems from the autobiographical plan of the Jewish and Arabic *maqamat*. Castro draws interesting parallels between the *Libro de Buen Amor* and the *Dove's Neck Ring* of Ibn

Hazm. The *maqamat*, developed to a high degree in Catalonia, especially by the Jewish poet Joseph Ben Meir Zabara in the *Book of Delights*, presented moralizations or mock-moralizations, interpolated into a pseudo-autobiography, in which surely most of the incidents and events were fictitious. This form of writing enabled authors to spin fine yarns to audiences and readers who no doubt realized that a great deal of the story was fictitious and that the moralizations need not be taken seriously. Juan Ruiz may not have actually read either the *Dove's Neck Ring* or the *Book of Delights*, although he could have, since both were extant in his time. If he had been unable to read the Arabic originals, it is possible that translations into Catalan, or even Spanish, may have been available. Even if he did not know these works through the written word, it is possible also that he could have heard all or parts of them read or discussed.

An outstanding contemporary critic who shares many of the ideas of the critics considered above and whose work is much discussed today is Gerald Brenan, author of *The Literature of the Spanish People* (New York, 1957). Brenan sees autobiographical unity as the strongest unity and regards the autobiographical quality of the book as authentic; e.g., he believes the Archpriest was imprisoned. He thinks Juan Ruiz had a higher purpose than mere entertainment, that he described love as it is, and not as it perhaps should be, and was therefore anti- courtly love. To Brenan, the extent of satire in the book was great but was included primarily to discourage worldly love. He sees much material that is valuable and salutary to saint and sinner alike. In his view, if the *Libro* did not lead more people to God, it could at least have made many of them more cheerful, charitable, and sensible. Juan Ruiz's irony embraces himself, Brenan thinks. In his mind, Ruiz was so sensitive to life's gloomier side that he used irony as an escape from it. But even in this retreat, Brenan says, he could not entirely avoid sadness, and from time to time, therefore, like outcroppings of sharp stone in a verdant meadow, melancholy concepts appeared in even the lighter passages of the *Libro*. He thinks this sadness expresses medieval man's fear of loneliness, old age, and death, which the hope for a heaven—whose existence was under scrutiny in the fourteenth century—could not dispel. These dark thoughts, according to Brenan, seem to have driven the Archpriest to laughter.

Gerald Brenan points out, as a good many critics have failed to do, that in the period in which Juan Ruiz wrote a definite juglaresque genre existed, in which the troubadour spoke to his audience in the first person, describing a wide variety of disgraceful, ignominious, and even scurrilous adventures which he claimed to have indulged in, even though they might not have been a part of his experience at all. Ruiz followed this genre in much of the *Libro*. As Brenan knows and states quite correctly, during the time of Juan Ruiz Spain preserved a number of literary forms, genres, and concepts, out of fashion in other lands and even forgotten, and therefore it was quite natural for the Archpriest to employ such forms—the juglaresque genre mentioned above and the goliardic meters, for example.

To Brenan, the passages in the *Libro* that were seemingly aimed at salving the feelings of the clerical sinners the Archpriest attacked were but an "impish apology which a priest who is in trouble with his superiors has felt obliged to make for a book such as priests, even in a relaxed age, are not supposed to have written." (p. 70) One must say, in connection with this, as Kane so often said, "Perhaps, and perhaps not."

Love, in the Archpriest's eyes, according to Brenan, is a refining thing, even for the lowly, for love—and carnal love is what is meant here—is for all people and is an education for all, since all mankind can share in it. In this Brenan agrees, though only partially, with A. Valbuena Prat (*Historia de la Literatura Española*, Madrid, 1960), although Valbuena believes that a triple ideal of womankind appears in the *Libro*—the ideal of the Blessed Virgin; that of the abstract and metaphysical personified, as in Petrarch's Laura;

and finally the ideal of the lusty, sensual ladies exemplified by Chaucer and Boccaccio.

Brenan sees, as have most critics, that satire runs high throughout the *Libro*, but especially in the sequence known as "The Battle between Flesh and Lent" and in the *serranas* episodes. The latter are to Brenan anti-pastoral sequences, filled with satire; these sequences show how the shepherdesses really were, not how they ought to have been. The book is indeed a full-dress satire of an era and a people—the Spanish in the fourteenth century. Juan Ruiz is a disciple of carnal love and therefore is never truly critical of it, but is critical of "meagre Lent." Compared to Chaucer, Ruiz, in Brenan's opinion, is more compressed, deals more with ideas and modes of conduct, is more vivid, racy, more varied in his versification, dialogue, and dialect. Also, according to Brenan, he used proverbs more freely, relied upon the double entendre, was the product of a more alert and more mature society than Chaucer's, was far more humorous in general tone, but possessed less warmth and charm. And, unlike Chaucer, Brenan says, Ruiz wrote as much for the lower echelons of society as for the upper, for he was of the proletariat class while Chaucer was not.

In Brenan's opinion, Juan Ruiz's most outstanding literary qualities are his dry humor, a real sense of style, and his irony. The boring parts of the *Libro*, he thinks, are its moralizing passages, but one must question whether these passages represent true moralizing or mock-moralizing. If they are the latter, and I think that they are, then they could not have bored Ruiz's anti-clerical audiences; rather, they would have delighted them, and therefore would have been deliberately chosen by the poet for a definite effect.

The irony of the Archpriest, in Brenan's eyes, lies in his ability to view a cruel, unfair, and immoral world, to take it for granted, and to smile at it wryly, leading his audiences to do the same for their emotional benefit. The Archpriest, then, as Brenan sees him, was not a heartless person, laughing at life and his contemporaries in a cruel way, but rather a man who saw sadness and grieved for mankind but used irony and satire as an antidote, a device for producing pleasure rather than indignation.

Brenan also sees the autobiographical juglaresque genre in the same focus as Puyol had seen it. Juan Ruiz used this genre, since it was still a formal literary convention in Spain, in order to reveal himself to his contemporaries to a degree no other medieval writer anywhere ever attained.

One of the greatest and most interested scholars of our times, the late María Rosa Lida de Malkiel, wrote copiously about the enigmas found in the *Libro de Buen Amor*. She saw, of course, the importance of medieval dualism in Juan Ruiz's masterpiece and thought it explained a great deal. She believed that Juan Ruiz portrayed all of nature, life and man, and allowed the reader to choose the part or parts he preferred. She dwelt long upon the Archpriest's sources, she saw him as a goliard of sorts, and believed that he made it possible for us to assess his personality through our understanding of the books he used as sources. At one period of her career she saw the *Libro* as a doctrinal work, thereby agreeing with another of the *Libro*'s great critics, Leo Spitzer. She stressed the influence of a literary genre known as the *maqamat*, used especially in Catalonia by Jewish and sometimes by Moorish writers, and believed that the *Libro* was definitely shaped by this genre. To her, Juan Ruiz's masterpiece was the work of a *mudejar*—a Christian who lived under Moorish domination and was immersed in Moorish and Jewish culture; she thought the book applied Christian motifs to the structure of the Hispano-Hebraic ideals of the *maqamat* and that the result was an artistic composition with a didactic purpose, which above all proposed to inculcate precepts of moral behavior and to that end utilized the autobiography of an author-protagonist and teacher, who repeatedly heaps ridicule upon himself in order to warn the public against its own moral misconduct.

All this, or all but a small part, is probably true, but in

that small part, María Rosa Lida de Malkiel erred consider-
ably. One can level this accusation freely, because this remarkable critic soon detected the fallacy of her position that
the *Libro* was purely didactic in its message and hastened to
correct—indeed to refute—herself, an act which required
considerable courage and integrity. Later she carried this
reversal still further, even to the point of differing, by impli-
cation, if not directly, with Spitzer himself, who never gave
up his belief in a didactic aim for the *Libro*.

In a long study, "Una Interpretación Más de Juan Ruiz
(*Romance Philology*, 1961) she stated that at last she regarded the *Libro*, regardless of all its possibly moralistic
tones, as a work which moralized for humorous effect and
which was, therefore, a book written for recreational reasons,
that is, to amuse. Her *Juan Ruiz, Arcipreste de Hita: Selección* (Buenos Aires, 1941) contains an introductory study
especially valuable for its presentation of the book's influence upon Spanish letters throughout the centuries and particularly the early centuries.

Thomas Hart, like Mrs. Malkiel, was influenced by Leo
Spitzer, especially by the views Spitzer expressed in a sig-
nificant article, "Zur Auffassung des Kunst des Arcipreste
de Hita" (*Zeitschrift für Romanische Philologie*, 1934). It
was primarily Spitzer's belief in the *Libro*'s medieval allegorical intent that led Hart to write his book, *La Alegoría en el
Libro de Buen Amor* (Madrid, 1959). Hart, however, went
far beyond Spitzer's teachings, seeing the *Libro* as largely
allegorical and its author as a poet with a thorough clerical
training, or at least sufficient training to have familiarized
himself with the tenets of Augustinian philosophy as well as
the better-known tracts of the Church Fathers. Like Spitzer,
Hart thinks Juan Ruiz was serious in his invitation to his
readers to look for deeper meanings, to search for the allegorical. His is a study made in the light of medieval theories of
typological interpretation.

Hart believes that Juan Ruiz unintentionally misread Aristotle and therefore used Aristotelian philosophy errone-

ously. It is possible, however, that it is Hart who has failed to understand Juan Ruiz, and that the poet deliberately misinterpreted the great philosopher for the sake of humor. According to Hart, Juan Ruiz even misread St. Paul's teaching that man should verify all things, for he believed that the poet's *provar las cosas* did not mean to try or to prove or verify all things, but rather to experience them or try them out. Again one might suspect that Juan Ruiz deliberately misread or misstated the Saint's words, and did so for humorous purposes. One could go on, but there is no need. Hart may be correct, admittedly, and if he is, then all statements contrary to his opinions are useless. On the other hand, if Hart is in error, then the theory of a humorous and deliberately incorrect handling even of Scripture, can stand.

The latest and most interesting criticism of the *Libro* is that of Otis Green in Volume I of his *Spain and the Western Tradition* (1963), mentioned previously. Green points out that Huizinga, in his *Waning of the Middle Ages*, has shown how important it is to distinguish clearly the serious element from pose and playfulness in connection with nearly all the manifestations of the mentality of the Middle Ages. If this is true, it is no wonder there is so much speculation and controversy regarding the *Libro de Buen Amor* and other medieval works. According to Green, the entire Prologue of the *Libro* is a parody, for it cannot be a serious sermon if it is carefully read and evaluated; the book is not a statement of Juan Ruiz's moral beliefs, for there is too much innuendo and tongue-in-cheek philosophizing and preaching; and it is not a warning against anything. Kane's translation of the prose Prologue is clear and will help the reader to understand exactly what Green means here.

In Green's opinion, for Juan Ruiz, the *Libro* was a book of favorite poetry, a poetic artifact that gave him pleasure. It was a work of literary art, then, not a didactic treatise. In it, according to Green, the poet began and sustained a long and constant parody. The Introduction itself is the very apogee of parody; every word Ruiz uses is a kind of bait or a trail that leads the mind to concepts other than those that actually appear on these pages.

The *maqamat*, a genre mentioned as early as 1894 by Francisco Fernández y Gómez, a noted Spanish Arabist, was not seriously considered by the scholarly world as being the poetic origin of the *Libro* until recently. Today, since there are virtually no other prototypes closely resembling the *Libro*, most scholars believe that the *maqamat* probably was Juan Ruiz's model. This flexible and fictitious variety of autobiography certainly appears to be a close parallel of the *Libro*, and Juan Ruiz, whose contacts with Spanish jewry were many, may well have utilized the *maqamat*, although he included in his own version aspects not necessarily found in the model. For further study, the reader may wish to refer to an article by G. Gibbon-Moneypenny entitled "Autobiography in the *Libro de Buen Amor* in the light of Literary Comparisons" (*Bulletin of Hispanic Studies*, 1957).

As to love itself, Green sees in the *Libro* a recognition and treatment of all its varieties. As mentioned previously, courtly love is certainly included, and some of its vocabulary is even used, but it is not courtly love in reality, nor does the lover successfully follow all the tenets of that type of love. As has also been discussed earlier, Ovidian love, which, though certainly carnal, is above the lust found in the *serranas* episodes, is more strongly stressed. The doctrine of plentitude, the rationale for which was that it was nature's purpose for men and women to make love and populate the earth, is also prominently treated in the *Libro*, according to Green. To support this doctrine, as Green indicates, was to fly in the face of a church which advocated for its priesthood virginity and purity. Such physical, procreative love also violated the tenets of courtly love, in which physical contact and, therefore, parenthood were excluded.

The *Libro*, Green says, is "a merry art of love," and even though the protagonist is a failure, the book is nonetheless an *ars amandi*, or a kind of delightful satire on the art of love. Green emphasizes what Lecoy mentioned some decades ago, that is, that the *Libro* begins with a *sermon joyeux*, a parodied sermon, and insists rightly that this sermon is of great importance to the understanding of the book's very soul. The entire text of this mock sermon, Green says, is an accommodated text of a Biblical quotation which originally meant something entirely different. The "I," which in the Bible referred to God himself, is, in the prose prologue of the *Libro*, no less than Juan Ruiz himself; the "thou," in the Bible, mankind as addressed by Jehovah, is the reader or audience of Juan Ruiz; the knowledge which is to be imparted is a knowledge of what is needed for success in love; and the "way" is the path that will lead the lover to the lady's bedchamber, or at least to a successful interview with the beloved. This is a perfect example of an accommodated text. Little imagination is required to see how it might have affected the reader in the fourteenth century. The Church authorities who may have permitted such a prologue to exist and circulate must have been lax indeed in carrying out their ecclesiastical duties.

From this opening parody the author proceeds to others. He parodies the very Canonical Hours of Our Lady, brutally, frankly, and shockingly, in full accordance, of course, with medieval practices. Green's interpretation of this parody is detailed and tastefully written, and should be read in toto for a good understanding of this important part of the *Libro*.

Still another important parody is that of Lord Flesh and Lady Lent. In this parody, the forces of Lent—that is, abstinence and the foods permitted to be eaten during Lent such as certain fishes and vegetables—do battle with the forces of Flesh—beef, pork, fowl, etc. Green, who studies possible parody at great length, admits that this one might have had a serious and moralizing purpose. But whether such doctrinal and didactic lessons were evident to Ruiz's medieval audiences, the author subordinates them to the overall spirit of fun and joy, to a delight in sensual love, and to feelings of pleasure in living, however fleeting these feelings may be.

Green sees Juan Ruiz as able to solve a serious dilemma that most medieval creative artists encountered: the problem of cleaving to spiritual or earthly ideals. One way Ruiz solves this problem is in claiming that the seemingly worldly part of his work has deep allegorical value; the other is by means of palinode or recantation. In many passages, the Archpriest insists that the book has meanings other than those most apparent. But in *copla* 1043 there is what Green regards as a recantation of the sinful. Here, the author places an invocation to Saint Mary of the Ford immediately after the rough-and-ready bawdiness of the adventures with the wild *serranas*. In Kane's translation, this passage reads as follows:

> Saint James, the blest apostle, says that every perfect gift
> And every good descends from God who ne'er deserts His shift;
> Wherefore, as soon as I got through my amatory rift,
> I turned to pray to God on high to cast me not adrift.

Green may be correct in his assumption that this is recantation and the palinode to the earlier, "sinful" parts of the book. But one can wonder if even here the Archpriest is not sustaining his consistent tongue-in-cheek visualization of all things. If he could *seem* to seek the palinode and yet imply, as to me he does imply, that here he is even mocking a return to virtue, then his art of parody is indeed supreme.

## Some Additional Concepts

The above discussion includes some of the most important theories—though by no means all of them—concerning the art and meaning of the *Libro de Buen Amor* of Juan Ruiz, Archpriest of Hita. To these theories only a few ideas can be added. These additional concepts do not form the eclectic theory, which is certainly now a desideratum, but may be considered a foundation for such a theory. In this foundation the reader will observe a crystallization of some of the ideas set forth by the scholars whose works have treated Juan Ruiz and his unfathomable work—if it is indeed unfathomable;

it is possible that in its plan and presentation it is deceptively simple.

In my opinion, Juan Ruiz was of the common people and probably grew up in some small village far from the centers of politics and power—perhaps on some Castilian farm. Certainly, whether he lived in a rural district or in some city, he managed to pick up a great quantity of country lore. It is possible that any ubiquitous medieval person might have had access to this kind of knowledge, and it appears that the Archpriest, at least in periods of his life, was much-traveled. In any case, Juan Ruiz understood the common people, both rural and urban. He also understood the ways of farm animals, of domestic creatures such as the dog, and of the many birds that inhabited the Castilian landscape. He knew Spain's flora as well, her skies and her plains and mountains, her valleys and her rivers, and all this knowledge repeatedly crops up in his book. The very off-hand way in which he mentions some of these subjects indicates that he knew them so well that they were mere commonplaces to him.

Among the folk he knew so well moved the professional entertainers. Troubadours wrote poems and songs, and *juglares* generally presented them, usually with musical accompaniment. Juan Ruiz was familiar with all the musical instruments of his time, and his descriptions of the many he used or understood is detailed. Indeed, the *Libro de Buen Amor* could serve alone as the basis for a study of medieval musical instruments. He also had a knowledge of other types of entertainers. He knew the Jewish and Moorish dancing girls and their accompanists, the story tellers in the oriental tradition as well as native spinners of folktales, and, though not specifically mentioned in the *Libro*, we can assume that he knew the other varieties of entertainment offered the fourteenth-century Spaniard—dramas, pageants, carnivals, and festivals such as the Feast of Fools, to name a few.

Juan Ruiz knew the Church, its traditional literature, its decretals, its saints, and its sinners. He knew the monasteries and the convents and described some of their more interesting and often pleasantly immoral doings. Perhaps, as Kane suggested, he lived as did Fra Lippo Lippi, brought up in some monastic house, imbibing the strange mingling of piety and practicality prevalent in those days. Perhaps, also as Kane suggested, he deserted the life of religious orders to take to the roads as a *juglar* and a troubadour, for he indicates that he did indeed write for blind beggers and Jewish dancing girls, and as a priest behind cloistered walls, he might not have been able to sell such ditties. But as a wandering goliardic poet and singer he would have learned much more; one suspects that he knew the world quite well and that he may have learned it long before he took orders.

I believe that in these travels and pilgrimages—for he made pilgrimages as did most of the people of his times—he saw all that life presented—the grim and cruel aspects, as well as the bawdy and often hilariously funny ones—and that he must have weighed all he saw. The unfairness, the unreasonableness, the unexplained catastrophes of plague and war, the quiet calm and repose some obtained in the cloister all combined to show him that much of life makes no sense and very little brings satisfaction. He could not accept all that the Church preached, although I do not think that he renounced its fundamental teachings, as some suspect, but rather saw its weaknesses and its inability to explain much of the tragedy of life. At least one suspects that he doubted the truth of the Church's tenet that all earthly life is a vale of tears, but that in the life to come the repentant sinner, or the one who had not sinned, would receive an eternal reward. I feel that he did have doubts, but that at the core of them lay one chamber of refuge. Like so many Europeans of his time, he revered the Blessed Virgin and seems to have taken solace in the traditional concept of her protective interest in even the most insignificant of her children. But apparently Kane thought that even Juan Ruiz's treatment of the Virgin was facetious, as some of his illustrations reveal all too graphically.

Still, not even Our Lady could erase Ruiz's wry and tolerantly pessimistic view of life. Such feelings of doubt and confusion about the plight of his fellows, even as he perhaps felt secure behind monastery walls, seems to have led him to a philosophy that made him identify closely with all that went on around him, with the people of all classes with whom he rubbed shoulders. He saw their weaknesses, their greed, their selfishness, their crass disinterest in others, their cowardice, but he did not hate them for these failings. Rather he sympathized, because he was one of them and considered himself no better than many of them. He wanted to entertain them, and above all he wanted to prove to them in his *Libro* that he was, like them, a soul adrift in an alien world. Acceptance of this world was, after all, a necessity—acceptance and the ability to regard life's perils and tragedies with wry amusement.

Juan Ruiz was one of the first Castilians to recognize that the period piece, the exotic tale, the theme bound by philosophy and erudition were of little interest to the common folk, and that the current scene, the story about people who could be his audience's neighbors had much more appeal. (In this respect he was like the successful contemporary novelist who writes of life in the slums, on farms, or in the military service—about things and people most familiar to his readers and therefore most interesting to them.) Consequently, Ruiz did not write of the affairs of kings and queens in the *Libro*, nor of knights, save occasionally to satirize them. Except for a few personages in the interpolated tales, the people he characterized in his book are all of the middle or lower classes —bakers and farmers, Moors and Jews, peasants and roustabouts, go-betweens, and aged trots whose livelihood stemmed from leading damsels astray. Wild mountain women, middle class widows, nuns, and occasional noblewomen viewed from afar round out his human comedy. His audiences could hear of the deeds and valor of the great warriors when the minstrels recited the *Poem of the Cid* or the other Spanish epics. But the *Libro* made fun of such things; it regaled the reader with stories of familiar men and women, sketched with realism and color.

As for Ruiz's reason for writing the *Libro,* the purpose he himself stated in *copla* 13d may be all we really need to know:

> For I a book on love divine would write for souls that parch
> And I would stiffen up their smocks with love's
>      old-fashioned starch.

In other words, he wrote both to delight the mind and to improve the state of the soul. If he wrote to entertain and to show that although mankind is sinful and doomed to hell, he should derive some happiness on earth before he pays for his sins; if he managed to obtain such strong rapport with his audience that his work lived through many centuries, in oral as well as written presentations; if he succeeded in creating a book of universal appeal, a kind of parodical *Pilgrim's Progress,* or what María Rosa Lida de Malkiel so happily described as a "dance of life," perhaps we need not understand his other motives, his techniques, or his sincerity. His *Book of Good Love* is there for the reading, and each reader, as the Archpriest himself has told us, can choose from it what appeals to him most.

# THE BOOK OF GOOD LOVE

### This Is the Prayer Which the Archpriest Made to God When He Began This Book of His

1    Thou Lord of Hosts who led from Egypt, out of Pharaoh's hands,
The most accursèd race that ever thwarted Thy commands,
As Thou hast succored Daniel from a den in Bible Lands
Wilt Thou not also hear my prayer and fend my prison bands?

2    Thou didst deliver Mordicai, by grace, from Haman's spleen,
And stirred Ahasuerus' heart and thus made Esther queen;
I know Thou art the living God what though Thou art unseen;
Then hear me when I cry to Thee from this my dungeon mean.

3    Thou didst deliver from the pit a prophet of Thy law
And Saint Iago from the mob Thy grace did likewise draw,
Yea, Saint Marina Thou didst rescue from the dragon's maw;
So free me, too, since evermore Thy name I hold in awe.

4    From those who falsely slandered her, didst Thou not vindicate
Thy Saint Susanna, bringing her again to glad estate?
Then succor me, oh God of mine, for I in prison wait;
Have pity when I pray to Thee, Thy wrath to mitigate.

5    Though cast into the open sea by those who feared the gale,
Three days did Jonah lie within the belly of a whale,
And when at last thou broughtst him out, lo he was whole and hale;
Then, God, bring me out scatheless, too, and blameless from this gaol.

6    When three young men in Babylon were in a furnace cast
Thou keptst them from its raging fire while kings looked on aghast;
Thou drewest Peter from the waves when he was sinking fast;
Then save, oh Lord, thine Archpriest, too, from his distress at last.

7    Why should they dread to speak with men who have Thee for a tower?
Yea, though they came to trouble kings, Thy grace would be their dower
For Thou wouldst send Thy Holy Ghost to loose their tongues that hour;
Then strengthen me, for here I stand within a traitor's power.

8    By prophets old the name of Christ was called Immanuel;
The living God His Father is who saveth Israel.
To Mary with a message came the angel Gabriel
And spake to her those blessed words which did her doubts dispel.

[3]

9    Oh Virgin Mother, by those words and by those prophecies,
And by that name, Immanuel, and by Thine ecstasies,
I pray Thee, send Thy blessing—yea, I ask on bended knees
To intercede with Christ for me and ease my miseries.

10    Show me Thy mercy, Sovereign Lady, Queen of womankind,
And turn aside Thy wrath from me, or, if Thou beest inclined,
Dear comforter of sinful man, perhaps Thy grace will blind
The eyes of all that e'er have shown toward me a perverse mind.

"I will instruct thee and teach thee in the way which thou shalt go;
I will guide thee with mine eye." Thus the prophet David, inspired by
the Holy Ghost, speaking, tells us in the tenth verse of the thirty-first
psalm,[1] which is the one that I have first written above. In this verse I
understand three things which some learned doctors say are inherent
in the soul and partake of its nature; they are as follows: understanding, will, and memory. These, I affirm, are so good that they
bring consolation to the soul, and prolong the life of the body, and
bestow upon it honor with worth and good fame. For by means of
a good understanding man perceives good and recognizes both it and
evil. Hence one of the petitions which David made to God in order that
he might understand His word was this, "Give me understanding."
For man, through perceiving good, will have fear of God and such is
the beginning of all wisdom as the aforesaid prophet affirms. "The fear
of God is the beginning of wisdom." And the same David speaks in like
tenor in another passage where he says "A good understanding have all
they that do His commandments." Besides, Solomon says in the Book
of Proverbs, "He who feareth the Lord, let him do good." And since
the soul is aware and is taught that it must preserve itself in a clean
body, man dwells upon and desires the good love of God and His
commandments. Even such the aforesaid prophet means in the verse
"And I will delight myself in Thy commandments which I have loved."
And moreover the soul abhors and rejects the sin of the carnal love of
this world. Therefore the psalmist says: "Ye that love the Lord, hate
evil." And thence comes the second meaning of the verse which says,
"And I will instruct thee." And thus the soul with good understanding,
good will, and good discernment turns to and loves the good love
which is of God, and puts it in the keeping of the memory, because in
being mindful of it the soul leads the body to do good deeds by which
man is saved. And this the apostle Saint John says in the Apocalypse
concerning the good who die while doing good: "Blessed are the dead
which die in the Lord and their works do follow them." And further-

more the prophet says, "Thou renderest to every man according to his work." And this is the third meaning of the first verse which says: "In the way which thou shalt go I will guide thee with mine eye." And therefore we ought to be convinced that works are always well appreciated, for with good understanding and good will the soul seeks and yearns for the love of God in order to save itself by works. And this is the meaning of the verse which first begins with "Brief . . ." as one who sometimes remembers sin and desires it and commits it. This mistake does not come from a good understanding; rather it springs from a feeling of liberty in the human nature of man which cannot escape from sin. For Cato says: "No man liveth without crime"; and Job says thus, "Who can make a clean thing out of an unclean," which is as if he would say, "no one save God." And it comes besides from the lack of good understanding which he does not have then, because man thinks upon the vanities of sin. And with such a meaning the Psalmist says, "The lord knoweth the thoughts of man that they are vanity." And moreover he speaks to those persons of evil and wicked understanding, "Be not as the horse or as the mule which have no understanding." And I say further that this error comes from the poverty of the memory which is not trained by good understanding for it cannot love good nor bring it to mind in order to do it. And this happens besides on account of the fact that human nature is more prepared and inclined to evil than to good and to sin than to good; this the Decretals say. And these are some of the reasons why the Books of the Law have been made, and the statutes and the instructions, and the conventions and the other sciences. Moreover, painting and writing and pictures were first invented because the memory of man is unreliable; this the Decretals say. For to have all things in the memory and not to forget anything is more pertaining to divinity than to humanity; this the Decretals say. And therefore it is more appropriate to the memory of the soul, which is a spirit, created of God, perfect, and which lives in God forever. Furthermore, David says, "My soul lives for that, love ye the Lord and your soul lives," and it is not fitting for the human body which endures but a little time, as Job says, "Seeing his days are determined." And likewise he says, "Man that is born of woman is of few days." And concerning this David says, "We spend our years as a tale that is told." Wherefore, I with my small understanding and much and great rudeness, perceiving how much wealth can cause the soul and the body to be lost, and the many evils that accompany it and bring to pass the foolish love of the sins of the world, choosing and loving with good intentions salvation and the glory of paradise for my soul, I made this little writing for the glorification of the good and I prepared this new book in which are written some of the manners and masteries and deceitful subtleties of the foolish love of the world which some persons follow in order to sin. By reading these and giving heed to them a man or woman with good understanding will amplify them and will follow them, and will say with the Psalmist, "I have chosen the way of truth." On the other hand, those of little understanding will not be lost because by reading and by contemplating the evil that they do or have a desire to do, and those who are stubborn in their sinful ways and in the manifest disclosure of their many deceitful practices which they follow for sinning and deceiving women will remember and will not despise this authority because he is a very obdurate man who would hold its repute in contempt; the Decretals say so. And they shall more esteem themselves than sin, for then the requisite benevolence begins to work of itself; the Decretals say so. And then they shall forsake and abhor the conduct and evil dominion of foolish love which causes souls to be lost and which incurs the wrath of God, shortening life and bringing ill fame and dishonour to men. However, inasmuch as it is a human thing to commit sin, if there be any who desire (albeit I advise it not) to sample this foolish, worldly love, they will here discover certain directions to that end. And thus this book of mine, for every man or woman, wise or unwise, whether he perceives the good and perceives the way to salvation and works through loving God well or otherwise desires worldly love, in whatsoever direction he may go each one may well say, "I shall give thee understanding." And I beseech and advise whomsoever sees and hears it to guard well the three things of the soul; the first that he may well understand and judge of my intentions wherewith I wrote it and of the meaning which is therein contained and not rather to the dirty sound of my words because according to all rights words are subordinate to meaning and not meaning to words. God knows that my intention was not to compose it in order to provide directions for sinning nor to utter wickedness, but it was to convert all persons to the chaste remembrance of doing good and to set a good example of upright conduct together with exhortations to the way of salvation, and also in order that all persons may be warned and may the better ward themselves from such habits as those are prone to who follow after worldly love. For, as Saint Gregory says, those darts which are seen beforehand wound a man least; so we can best protect ourselves from that which we have already witnessed. And finally I composed this book in order to give instructions and examples to others of rhyme and meter for the making of verses, for I made all the poems and songs and rhymes and ditties strictly according to the rules of this science. And now because the beginning and foundation of every good work are God and the

Catholic Faith, as the first Decretal of the Clementines says which begins, "The foundation is the Catholic Faith," and where this is not the cement there cannot be made a firm work or secure edifice as the Apostle says. Therefore I began my book in the name of God and took the first verse of the psalm which speaks of the Holy Trinity and the Catholic Faith which is "Whosoever will." It is the verse which runs "God the father, God the son," and what not.

11    God the Father, God the Son, and God the Holy Ghost,
       May He who was of Virgin born inspire us through His Host
       That we in song and spoken word may praise His being most,
       And may the mantle of His grace become our bravest boast.

12    May He who formed the sweeping heavens, made the land and sea,
       Upon me concentrate His grace and shine His light on me
       'Till I compose a book of songs that will so joyous be
       All men who hear them will forget their present misery.

13    Thou gracious God who first set man upon his earthly march,
       Inspire and aid this priest of Thine whom thou createdst arch
       For I a book on love divine would write for souls that parch
       And I would stiffen up their smocks with love's old-fashioned starch.

14    So, gentlemen, if you would hear a hearty, merry tale,
       Come all who heavy laden are and I'll your ears regale.
       I shall not tell you silly lies nor spin some romance stale
       But sing of things just as they are, of men and women hale.

15    And that I may the best secure the whole of your attention
       I'll trick the story out in rhymes of my supreme invention—
       While in its pretty style you'll find no word unfit to mention.
       No, you will find my broadest jokes conform to strict convention.

16    Don't think this is a foolish book replete with giddy verse,
       Nor hold the jests therein contained as something even worse;
       For oft, as goodly money lies within a filthy purse,
       A messy book may likewise hold much wisdom sound and terse.

17    The fennel seed is kettle-black, as black as poison bane,
       But inside all its meat is white as is the marmot's mane.
       And whitest flour is wont to lie within the darkest grain,
       While sugar sweet and white resides within an ugly cane.

[7]

18    There grows upon the crabbèd thorn the rose's noble bloom,
And parchments writ in strangest script great learning oft entomb.
Full many an honest tippler wears a shoddy cape and plume,
And I to sorry covers cheap this Book of Good Love doom.

19    Yet since the root and principle of every good that is
Lies in the Virgin Mary's grace, I therefore, Juan Ruiz,
Archpriest of Hita, have a song to please the lady. 'Tis
One where in verse I shall rehearse her seven pleasures, viz:

# The Joys of the Virgin Mary

## I

20   Oh blessed ray
Of brightest day,
Dear Mother, pray
Guide me for aye.

21   Oh bless me, Virgin, with Thy grace
And pray Thy Son to send apace
His comfort to a sinner base
        That I may sing alway

22   The joys our Father sent to Thee
That day beside the holy sea
When angels came to Galilee
        From heaven-land to say

23   "All hail, oh Mary, blessed queen
For Thou by God hast chosen been
To bear his Son a Nazarene
        Divine in human clay."

24   And when this message Thou receivedst,
Full straight the words Thou then believedst
And, while a Virgin still, conceivedst
        With joy supreme that day.

25   A second joy of greatest worth
Befell the hour Thou gavest birth
Unto that Sovereign of the earth
        To whom all Christians pray.

26   Another joy the Gospels name
When Magian kings before Thee came
To worship Him without all blame
        Who in a manger lay.

27   There Melchior's gifts of incense were,
There Gaspar brought Him precious myrrh
And Balthasar the gold of Ur
        As bright as morning's ray.

28      The fourth delight next came to Thee
That Sabbath after Calvary
When Magdalen did Jesus see,
     New risen, on her way.

29      Thy fifth great ecstasy took place
When Thou Thyself beheldst His face
Enthroned on high by God's own grace
     In radiant display.

30      The sixth, oh Holy Saint, I name
When on the blest disciples came
God's spirit like a living flame
     With Thee and them to stay.

31      Then came the seventh joy of thine
As Thou, to leave the church a sign,
Wast caught up to that realm divine
     Where angels Thee obey.

32      Thou reignest now, Exalted One,
In heaven with Thy loved Son.
Oh save us when our years have run
     Forever and for aye.

## II

33    Thou Virgin queen of heaven's band,
Thou balm and comfort of this land,
I pray Thee, listen while I stand
And sing to Thee in verses bland
Those joys that came at God's command;
    Thus may I serve.

34    For I shall sing Thy happiness
And with an humble heart confess
    My sinful days,
But, gracious Mary, this I press,
Do Thou from heaven come to bless
    The song I raise.

35    Thou wast with seven pleasures blest;
An angel's greeting was the best—
    A salutation
For Thou at His divine behest
Conceivedst a God within Thy breast
    For our salvation.

36    The second joy beyond compare
Came when Thou didst that angel bear
    From labor free
While radiant angels in the air,
Sweet singing, did the babe declare,
    Our Lord to be.

37    The third befell that time a star
Appeared where God's high pathways are
    To light the way
For Magian kings who from afar
Came searching for those gates ajar
    Where Jesus lay.

38    Then came to Thee the fourth delight
When angel Gabriel, shining white,
    Cried, "Mary, Hail!"
And promised Thee the blessèd sight
Of Jesus in His godly might,
    And without fail.

39   The fifth which was of sweetness great
     Befell as Christ was caught up straight
       In ecstasy
     Unto His Father's glad estate
     Whilst Thou below didst longing wait
       With Him to be.

40   No joy but one can e'er displace
     The sixth, for then on Jesus' face
       There shone a light.
     Thou, too, wast in that sacred place
     And saw the Ghost of Holy Grace
       In radiance bright.

41   None with the seventh can compare
     For then God sent for Thee to share
       His holy throne
     And up in His vast kingdom there,
     Christ's mother, thou shalt ever wear
       A crown alone.

42   Oh lady, hear a sinner's cry
     Because for us Thy son on high
       Came down to earth
     And left his heaven in the sky
     While Thou, white flower to whom we sigh,
       Didst give Him birth.

43   Though we be sinners, hate us not,
     Since for our sakes Christ was begot
       And Thou wast made
     God's mother—pray for our sad lot,
     Ah pray, when in God's balance caught,
       Our souls are weighed.

## Herein Is Related How All Men Should Disport Themselves amid Their Cares, and Also Herein Is Related the Disputation Which the Greeks and the Romans Had with One Another

44    These are the words which Cato spoke—they well become a sage—
He holds that man amid his cares should now and then engage
In such delightful pleasures as may well his woes assuage
Since work and worry unalloyed bring premature old age.

45    Still, since no grave, important wight all by himself will giggle,
Among my sermons, here and there, I've caused a jest to wriggle,
So surely, when you come to them, you'll have no cause to niggle
Save in their style which, I confess, does somewhat jolt and jiggle.

46    But comb the meaning from my words as you would card out fleece.
Take warning from what happened to the learnèd man of Greece
Who with a Roman rounder once debated for a piece
That time the Romans tried to get Greek culture on a lease.

47    It seems that in the Roman land no manners did abound
Wherefore they begged them from the Greeks who were for such renowned.
But mightily their supplication did the Greeks astound
Because they viewed the Roman minds as barren, fallow ground.

48    However, just to be polite and make their stand seem fair,
They said that first of all before they would their wisdom share
They'd have to quiz Rome's wisest men, and from their showing there
The Greeks could see if Roman wits were fit for culture rare.

49    The Romans fell into the trap nor saw the Greek designs
But pledged themselves one day to speak by every oath that binds.
However, since they knew no Greek, nor yet could read Greek minds,
They begged the Greeks to suffer them to argue all in signs.

50    The Greeks agreed. A day was set to hold the disputation.
Then, sudden witting what it meant, a frightful consternation
Took hold upon the Romans for they found in all their nation
No man who even claimed to have a college education.

51    Now in that hour when Roman hopes seemed just about to flounder
A sharp old Roman, who one time had been a pulpit pounder,
Told them to choose as candidate some lewd, ungodly rounder
And let God send him arguments, if he had nothing sounder.

52     Thereat they chose a rounder fit to personate Priapus,
       Loud-mouthed, obscene, and bold. They said, "The Greeks intend to trap us;
       It's up to you to win the bout—beware lest aught mishap us.
       But if you win, man, name your price—there is no sum can strap us."

53     They capped and gowned him like a Doctor of Philosophy
       With all the costly, flowing robes of that grave faculty.
       Then in the lecture hall he strode, as pompous as could be.
       "Bring on your Greeks!" the rounder bawled, "we'll see what we will see!"

54     Forthwith into the lecture hall there crept a learnèd coot,
       A Greek professor, wondrous wise, with ten degrees to boot,
       While both the Greek and Roman nations crowded in to root
       And watch their champions, all by signs, engage in fierce dispute.

55     Full confident the Greek uprose and with unruffled calm
       Showed but a single finger, slim, extended from his palm;
       That done he took his seat again without the slightest qualm.
       The rounder rose like one who would his enemy embalm.

56     He thrust three fingers, tensely stretched, out toward his adversary,
       The thumb, forefinger, and the next, like some rude harpoon, hairy;
       He shook them in an attitude belligerent yet wary
       And then sat down to wait the sign of repartee contrary.

57     At this the Greek uprose and showed his empty open hand
       And once more smiling, bowed to all, and sat down, ever bland.
       The rounder jumped up from his bench—'twas more than he could stand—
       He clenched his fist and shook it like a furious command.

58     Before that vast concourse the Greek exclaimed in accents quiet,
       "The Romans well deserve our culture, friends, I certify it."
       So every one was satisfied and left without a riot.
       The case was won by Rome because they got a boor to try it.

59     They asked the Greek what were the signs he showed the Roman hun,
       And how on either side the case did back and forwards run;
       Quoth he: "I said, 'There is one God,' he answered, 'Three in one,'
       And made a sign to show it thus, and there of course he won.

60     "I signified with open palm 'No power God's purpose blocks';
       He said with earnest doubled fist 'God's will the world unlocks,'
       From which I judge the Romans all in faith are orthodox
       And well we may entail them all our intellectual stocks."

61    They quizzed the rake to see if aught this version might belie,
       Said he, "He held one finger up to mean he'd gouge me eye,
       And, gents, to think a runt like that would have the crust to try
       To dim me lamp made me so mad I showed the little guy

62   "Three fingers, meaning two of them would gouge his goggles out
       While with me thumb I'd bust his teeth, but after that the lout
       Held up his palm to let me know he'd give me ears a clout
       And set me head to buzzin' till I lost this monkey bout.

63   "I showed him then how with me fist I'd sock him such a crack
       The longest day he ever lived he couldn't pay me back
       And you can see he realized his chances was too black
       Because he quit just like a Greek and all that lousy pack."

64    This brings to mind the old bawd's saw—its truth has ne'er been shaken—
       "No word is wicked in itself unless it's wrongly taken."
       Thus anything that's taken right should ne'er a qualm awaken.
       This book will teach success to one whom women have forsaken.

65    Don't hold my mockery as dull or heavy or forlorn
       For if you read between the lines you'll find no cause for scorn;
       Not one among a thousand poets in this world is born
       Who can with merry, subtle words a tragic thing adorn.

66    No eye can fail to see a heron flying through the air
       But where that bird has hid her nest few hunters can declare;
       Don't let the 'prentice tell the tailor how he should repair;
       Don't think my Book of Love holds naught but smut beyond compare.

67    My book lies open to the world, it is both grave and jolly;
       The wise will in their wisdom plumb its grimmest melancholy;
       The fool will only laugh and drink its shallow scum of folly;
       The best in it the good alone will ever fathom wholly.

68    To grasp my book's true, hidden wealth, few persons I allow,
       For men must sharply pan its ore ere they discover how;
       But should you hap on precious gold and wash away the slough,
       No more you'll hold this Book of Love as vain as you do now.

69    Beware, for when my words sound false, there truth the loudest cries,
       And when I paint reality my deepest truths are lies.
       How shall you judge what's good or bad? What standards shall you prize
       When fictions live in art, while truth, if it be actual, dies?

[15]

70  This book is like an instrument, to every tune it's true;
    Your heart it is which makes the song seem merry, sweet, or blue.
    You can't interpret from my book save what resides in you,
    And if you'd guess what tune I'd play, you'd have to learn me too.

## Herein Is Related How Man and the Other Animals Desire to Have Intercourse with Their Females According to Nature

71    Man labors, Aristotle says, upon a dual mission,
His first and most important care concerns his own nutrition,
His second, and the pleasantest, is afterwards coition
With any dame that proffers him the opportune position.

72    If on my own authority about a point so mooted
I made this bold assertion I would surely be disputed,
But what a wise philosopher has said cannot be hooted,
Above all, when his arguments can never be confuted.

73    And that this venerable sage has spoken truth 'tis clear
For men and birds and animals—all critters far and near—
According to the laws of nature find their females dear;
Particularly man to whom the act brings extra cheer.

74    The beasts have all a stated time wherein they join to breed,
But man, superior to the brutes, can couple without need;
Wherefore he consecrates this act and writes it in his creed,
And then, to show his sanctity, he oft repeats the deed.

75    An incandescent coal indeed is passion's fierce desire;
The more you try to blow it out the hotter burns its fire.
What boots it if the soul should see her body in the mire
When nature makes of man a hog and urges him no higher?

76    So I, because I am a man, the same as any sinner,
Have got of woman all she had whenever I could win her.
To learn and sample is no shame for this sincere beginner
Since thus I choose the good from bad and make my errors slimmer.

[17]

## In What Wise the Archpriest Was Enamoured

77    One time it came to pass a lady held my heart in fee,
And in her love I felt such joy I never would be free,
For sweet the smiles and greetings were the angel had for me,
But that was all—no more she did nor more I wished to be.

78    The little world she moved within could see in her no flaws,
Yet ne'er could I enjoy with her an unmolested pause;
They watched the men who called on her (but not without good cause)
And kept her stricter than the Jews keep their religious laws.

79    Full skilled she was in needlework with thread of silk and gold,
And yet despite such luxury as makes most women bold
She had a sweet and gracious mien and would not nag or scold
Nor was she one to let herself for costly gifts be sold.

80    Wherefore a pretty song of love unto the dame I sent
By one, a crafty messenger, who guessed at my intent.
I found when bold proposals come to girls on pleasure bent
If they like not the messenger they never give consent.

81    Wherefore unto my messenger this gentle lady cried,
"I've seen too many girls deceived, when such like tricks are tried,
To swallow all you say, to find out afterwards you lied.
So listen to this fable, for my meaning lies inside."

## A Fable Relating How a Lion Was Suffering and How
## the Other Animals Came to See Him

82 "A lion lay—the story goes—in agony of pain;
   Whereat to bring him condolence, all critters to him came.
   This greatly cheered the king of beasts and helped him health regain
   And hence his loving subject beasts could scarce their joy restrain.

83 "To render him some signal homage he might always treasure
   They planned a monstrous banquet, asking only beasts of leisure,
   And begged the king to order killed whate'er might give him pleasure
   To feed the guests—he said the bull would furnish greatest measure.

84 "He told the wolf to carve the bull and give each guest a bit.
   The wolf, however, gave the lion naught but horns and grit
   While for himself the carcass whole upon his plate he split,
   Then begged the kin to render thanks to God as he saw fit.

85 " 'My Lord,' the wolf explained, 'you see your body is so thin
   These horns will act as props to keep your sides from falling in,
   While I shall eat the ruddy meat and spare you carnal sin!'
   At this the king was wroth for he was famished to begin.

86 "The lion raised his paw as if to ask God's grace at table
   But smote the wolf upon the head as hard as he was able;
   It tore the skin from off his head and cracked his spinal cable.
   'Here, see if you can carve this meat!' he told the fox of sable.

87 'With fear and trembling in her eyes the crafty little fox
   Gave to her lord the greatest part—while wishing him the pox—
   But for herself she kept no more than hooves and horns and hocks;
   And that divine partitioning the king deemed orthodox.

88 "The lion smiled and said to her, 'My pretty child, I must
   Inquire who taught you how to carve so equally and just.'
   Quoth she, 'I learned my lesson from the skull I saw you bust
   And hence it was the wolf who showed me how to curb my lust.'

89 "Now therefore hark, old brothel trot with innuendoes base,
   If ever with such messages again you show your face,
   I'll bless you as the wolf was blessed when the lion offered grace;
   Go! Act the fox and learn your lesson from another's case!"

90    As Jesus Christ himself once said, "There is no hidden thing
That time will not eventually to the surface bring."
Wherefore as luck (or Providence) must e'er some kill-joy fling,
My secret was discovered and my love went on the wing.

91    And never have I seen her face since we were torn apart,
Yet once she sent for me to write with my profoundest art
Some little song of love, full sad, which might old shadows start,
And she would dream of me at dusk and sing it in her heart.

92    To please the lady and evoke those memories of yore
I made a song as mournful as the mournful love I bore.
And well I knew her voice would thrill and give it feeling more
Than I could put in words alone with my poetic lore.

93    "Whoe'er would kill his dog by stealth," declares an ancient preacher,
"Pretends he's sick, and by that trick he starves to death the creature."
So those who sent my dame away where I could never reach her
Told her such lies I vow she had the devil for her teacher.

94    They swore they'd heard me boast to friends I'd fondled her and pawed
Her holy parts as easily as if she'd been a bawd.
At that my lady cried in wrath, "Now by the living God,
I see all garments have their seams and every friend his fraud."

95    A proverb well describes the way they warp a woman's mind,
"According as the twig is bent so is the tree inclined."
That dame was goaded so with taunts, she cried, in anger blind,
"False lovers, are there then no vows your blackguard lips will bind?"

96    Because the lady much had delved in books of wit and science,
And subtle was and sensible and full of self reliance,
When next my emissary called, she told her, with defiance
This one of Aesop's fables, trusting me for its appliance.

97    When o'er the matrimonial plunge a timid dame has tarried,
Her lover starts to promising, but once let her be married,
Before he'll carry out his vows he must be sorely harried
And even then he bellows like the earth when it miscarried.

98    "It came to pass the earth began to lose her figure flat
       And groaned and swelled and swelled and groaned
          and seemed to burst with fat.
       The timid people all around suggested this and that
       Because she acted like a wench delivering a brat.

99    "The dullest man perceived that she was in the family way
       Since she had spasms bearing down and would so loudly bray.
       All thought she'd bring at least a dragon to the light of day,
       Or else some monster such as might the population slay.

100   "So while she bellowed, young and old began to take to flight,
       But when the fearful hour arrived for her confinement night,
       Instead of that the earth engendered, much to their delight,
       A tiny mouse, whereat the people laughed with all their might.

101   "Go to your master, messenger, and tell the silly calf
       That often men have promised wheat but given only chaff;
       Perhaps I might believe him if he said he'd poison quaff,
       But when the yokel says he loves me—messenger, I laugh!"

102   Who boasts of his unflinching stand is quickest in evasion;
       He little does although he makes a deaf'ning detonation.
       The dearest things men sometimes hold in smallest estimation
       While those which mean and worthless are, grow precious on occasion.

103   From such a little trifle did great hate and loathing get her,
       That, full of rage, she set a trap to punish me the better.
       But traps mayhap will snap and slap the fingers of the setter,
       And so, to prove this true I wrote to her, in verse, a letter.

104   Indeed, 'twas she they trapped with lies, as I told her in rhyme
       Which, having writ, I sent to her to read at any time.
       But she refused, whereat I cried, "Hark, passion flower, sublime,
       The day shall come when you must wilt and go back into grime."

[21]

## How All Things in the World Are Vanity
### Save the Love of the Lord God

105    As Solomon himself has said (this once he preaches true),
"All things of earth are vanities; all things are dour and blue;
All things behind the march of time fade like a distant view;
All things except to worship God are frivolous to do."

106    Since I have seen a woman change and alter with her age,
I say to love, when love has fled, does not become a sage.
To answer when I am not called, that too is folly's rage,
Wherefore about such ladies' thrones, no more I'll play the page.

107    Yet God, my maker, knows this dame, and all that I have seen,
I've always worshipped in my heart as heaven's very queen.
E'en though they will not have my love, I cannot hold them mean.
Should I who long for constancy change my love, too, for spleen?

108    A very boor that man would be, a pagan to true bliss,
Who 'gainst the name of woman-kind says anything amiss,
For women, jaunty, spirited, and exquisite to kiss,
Are things most precious in this world—in them all pleasure is.

109    If God, when He had fashioned man, at any time had thought
That woman was an evil thing He never would have brought
Her out of man's constricted breast to comfort him when fraught;
He must have destined her for good, so perfect she is wrought.

110    If man did woman not adore with such divine despair,
The God of Love would ne'er have caught so many in his snare.
The purest monk, the chastest nuns that saintly vestments wear
All burn in secret torment for communion without prayer.

111    A saying runs to this effect, "A lonely nightingale
Will through the aching hours of night her absent mate bewail."
All things must have their complements—the mast, his flimsy sail—
Why even cabbages will die without their water pail.

112    So I, because I was alone, and must my passions slake,
Bethought me how I might with art my neighbor's woman take.
His wife I knew, not good but fair, yet for her body's sake
I crucified myself although she chose another rake.

113    Then since I could not find a chance for intimate converse
        I sent a messenger to her my passion to rehearse.
        But him I sent shut me out—I couldn't find a worse—
        He gulped my morsel, leaving me to ruminate in verse.

114    To drown my grief I wrote a song—this mocking little ditty—
        And if that lady hears it—well, I ask of her no pity;
        Let only fools bewail their fate—misfortunes make me witty,
        And even when the jest's on me I think a story pretty.

## What Befell the Archpriest through His Messenger Fernando Garcia

115    Yes, you'll ne'er behold the light
       Since I've lost my Cross tonight.

116    Cross, my Double-Hot-Cross-Bun,
       Trails I took for you to run
       Every place beneath the sun
         Like an errant knight.

117    Wanting her within my hand,
       I sent Garcian Ferdinand
       (Consummator suave and bland)
         To her house at night.

118    Gladly did he say he'd go;
       Secretly he crossed her though—
       He ate cake while I ate dough—
         She was his delight.

119    He gave her, as he was told,
       Hares, and grain a full year old.
       I was left out in the cold
         By that cunning wight.

120    Damn that subtle emissary!
       Smooth he was, and fast, and wary.
       May God send him luck contrary
         For my sorry plight!

121 But still whene'er I see my Cross, I bow my reverend head
    And bless myself when unawares I chance near her to tread,
    What though my pious messenger still takes my Cross to bed
    I see no evil in my Cross but worship her instead.

122 But on that bachelor of hearts, that fornicationing goat
    Who'd live on milk and honey but would never pay a groat,
    I made a verse I'd like to ram clear down his greedy throat
    For ne'er a lad so innocent could sing so bass a note.

# Here the Archpriest Tells of the Constellations and of the Planets under Which Men Are Born, and Also of the Prophecies of the Five Sages Uttered at the Birth of the Son of King Alcarez

123     Those ancient wights who read the stars and secret meanings saw,
Maintain in their astrologies this universal law
That planets o'er the lives of men some occult influence draw
Which from the cradle sweeps them on as currents sweep a straw.

124     So Plato thought, and Ptolemy in other times afar
While many learnèd masters now of this opinion are;
In truth, it seems when one is born beneath some rising star
That planet rules his life and will his fortunes make or mar.

125     Hence many study all their lives ecclesiastic learning
And spend great sums while through the hours their midnight
          oil is burning;
But in the end they nothing gain, however great their yearning,
Because the stars to other ends their destinies are turning.

126     Some dig their graves in monasteries to save their precious souls,
Some hack their fellow men and hope through arms to reach their goals,
Some merely drudge like stupid beasts in humbler, witless roles,
But most go down unfamed, unknown, to their eternal holes.

127     Few reach an order's highest rank, few wax as famous knights,
Few toilers from their masters wrest their monetary rights;
And who can doubt the reason held by those illustrious wights
Who one and all ascribe the cause to God's celestial lights?

128     Once five star-gazers read the signs upon the Zodiac girt
(This story shows what awful power the heartless stars exert)
And from them learned an infant's fate no mortal might divert,
And each when he forecast his fate predicted grievous hurt.

129     To Alcarez, a Moorish king, a handsome son was born,
But beauty was not all the monarch wished, and so next morn
He summoned his astrologers and told them to forewarn
Him of his fate, and if his star were happy or forlorn.

130     Among that learnèd faculty who stood before the king
Just five had graduate degrees and hence knew everything,
So when these five had theorized on what the stars would bring,
One said, "Down some deep precipice the stars this prince will fling."

[25]

131    The second quoth, "Nay, burned alive this youth is going to be."
Up spoke the third, "A storm of hail will kill him, that I see."
The fourth man held he knew the lad would hang upon a tree;
The last proclaimed that drowning would the prince's spirit free.

132    The king was vexed that learnèd men with such diverse convictions
Should each so bitterly maintain his partisan addictions;
Wherefore he clapt them all in jail, imposing harsh restrictions,
Pretending that the common weal was threatened by their fictions.

133    Now years rolled by, the little prince grew up a sprightly wag,
But being restless, oft he would the aged monarch nag
To let him in the mountains go to hunt the wily stag,
Until at last the king gave way and cried, "Well, fill your bag!"

134    They waited till the weather cleared, then started on their chase
But when they reached the mountain lands, a sudden storm apace
Swept down and it began to hail in that deserted place
While from the sky fell stones of ice as large as is your face.

135    At that the prince's guardian chanced to recollect the fate
Which those astrologers forecast his master would await;
"Your highness, may it please you, haste before it is too late,"
The poor man cried, "lest that betide which those five men did state!"

136    Full fast they ran, and anxious hoped some shelter might appear,
But all in vain—what's fated stands as changeless as the year,
For even God, should He desire man's slightest fate to veer,
Would first of all be forced to shift the heavens out of gear.

137    The prince was fleeing o'er a bridge when on a sudden, lo,
A lightning bolt and stone of hail struck him a mortal blow;
The flaming bridge was cleft in twain and dashed him far below,
But falling in a tree he caught and hanged in dying woe.

138    Then while he hanged the tree bent down and drowned him in the stream
As helpless looked his guardian on and loud for aid did scream.
So thus all five contrary fates, like some fantastic dream,
Were all fulfilled, and hence the king those seers did truthful deem.

139    As soon as that same monarch had attended to the mourning
He freed those wise astrologers he had so long been scorning,
And with his medals, ribbons, orders, made a grand adorning,
Decreeing, too, the planets true by parliamentary warning.

140    Those mystic, starry characters, illegible and dim,
         I do believe the secrets hold of God, but since by Him
         The world was made, He, too, can wreck it, should He take the whim;
         All this is Catholic doctrine which I hold with zealous vim.

141    What wrong attends a man's belief in naturalistic things
         Provided that his faith in God takes not therewith to wings?
         I'll illustrate my meaning with a parallel which brings
         My points to light and you will see what truth unto it clings.

142    'Tis certain that a ruler in his kingdom has the might
         To issue laws and open courts and set offenses right.
         For this he organizes bands of men to bring to light
         All criminals, that they may feel his speedy justice smite.

143    Perhaps it comes to pass a man commits some wicked treason
         For which the law finds he deserves to die by every reason,
         Yet if he have some friends at court, he still may save his weasand,
         For they will beg the king 'till he releases him in due season.

144    Or if, perchance, the malefactor any time has been
         A soldier in the army, that will also save his skin
         Since loyal service always moves a monarch to step in
         And thrust the law aside to let a higher justice win.

145    What boots it that a court decrees a man shall die with cause
         When he who authorized the court can give its sentence pause?
         Or, turning tables, set the judge inside the culprit's claws,
         For he can break who once did make those flimsy things called laws.

146    The Pope with his Decretals, too, can penalize our slips,
         Or by a word damn saints to Hell with his benignant lips,
         But likewise he can dispensate, and by his pious quips
         Can save from everlasting fire the most ungodly rips.

147    Each day, indeed, we see such things occur before our faces
         And yet, withal, the laws and codes and precedented cases
         Come not to naught—but rather, when some power their course displaces,
         Man's justice seems to be endowed with God's sublimer graces.

148    So when our busy Lord engaged in stellar occupations
         He figured out the movements of the separate constellations
         And made each planet play its part in anthropoid relations,
         But made it clear He'd interfere with unjust operations.

149    Wherefore, by prayers and continence or passing up a meal
       Or doling beggars pennies with a shrewd, ostensive zeal,
       A man can somehow dislocate stupendous heaven's wheel—
       For what's a star or two to God when man begins to squeal?

150    When things like that befall, of course, you cannot hold as fools
       Those poor astrologers who scanned according to the rules—
       Their methods stand approved by all the best prophetic schools
       Although they cannot counter God by their archaic tools.

151    In astrologic lore I am no master nor astute,
       I cannot read an astrolabe much better than a brute,
       But I have known the stars to tell what no man could confute,
       And stand convinced from instances of singular repute.

152    Some men are born in Venus' sign and all their days aspire
       To making love to females, doing all that girls require;
       For them they fret and shame themselves and set their souls afire
       Though few there be who gain the goal they secretly desire.

153    'Twas under such a sign I think I must have seen the light
       Because I long for girls by day and lust for them at night,
       Yet though I ne'er ungrateful was for favors how so slight,
       And served a host of ladies, ne'er I seemed to come out right.

154    Still, since planet Venus is and she will be obeyed,
       I must adore no other star and never be dismayed;
       What though my lemon trees won't yield their fragrant lemonade
       'Tis sweet to loiter near their limbs and bask beneath their shade.

155    Who consecrates his heart to love, his talents oft quadruples,
       His wit, his verve, his luck, his nerve, with amatory pupils;
       Although he toils for honest dames and shows that he has scruples
       If he should look for pleasure, there's a stick for little hooples.

156    Love makes a lout grow elegant, refined, and e'en astute;
       It makes a clever talker of a man who erst was mute,
       And love, an arrant coward to a hero can transmute,
       Or make a lazy slug-a-bed pipe nimbly as a flute.

157    Love keeps a young man in his prime (a physiologic truth);
       Love helps a senile patriarch retain the sap of youth,
       Love cleanses white and beautiful those sullen hearts uncouth;
       And yet poor tinsel sells for gold when Love is at the booth.

158    It matters not if one should be both crippled and ill-favoured
       Or have for wife an ugly shrew with Hell's own acid flavoured,
       Poor fools—once love has unto them his old-new message quavered,
       Their foulest traits to either seem divine and heaven-savoured.

159    The lecherous, the scatter-brained, the nincompoop, the poor,
       Seem chaste or wise or fine or rich, with powerful allure;
       Wherefore let every man take heart—as long as girls endure,
       Should any woman turn him down, of substitutes he's sure.

160    However, if a man be born as I 'neath Venus' sign,
       And should his luck in love be poor, behold these words divine:
       "Dame Fortune is not wooed but raped." Still, women, I opine,
       Like melons dure, time will mature and mellow on the vine.

161    I find that most consuming loves all share this blemish vicious
       Which, ladies, I should ne'er divulge from deference to your wishes,
       But any-way, as I'll be thought a prattler and malicious,
       I might as well confess—'tis this, "Love's truest troth's fictitious."

162    For just as I have said before, a woman dull and mean
       With love becomes transformed and wears an iridescent sheen,
       For lovers' eyes alone can prize things worthless as a bean
       Although such blest illusions but for little on us lean.

163    If apples were as good inside as promises their skin,
       If those who look so pink and blonde were half as sweet within,
       No fruit in summer's garden could more estimation win;
       But they get full of rot inside ere other fruits begin.

164    Such stuff are lovers' promises; magnificent with words,
       Undying as perpetual time, inspired as singing birds,
       But every noise is not a song nor gold each chain that girds.
       So, ladies, be advised and learn that milk must turn to curds.

165    A dose of truth will kill a friend—withheld he dies of hate
       For mortal though his sickness be such cures will aggravate,
       But let wise persons ancient truths in proverbs tolerate
       And rather fear those gilded lies which their false friends relate.

## How the Archpriest Was Enamoured, and of the
## Fable of the Thief and the Mastiff

166    The dour, ascetic sage desires a monstrous thing indeed;
'Tis that we leave our habits and the pleasures which they breed.
But habit is man's inner life, his nature, pattern, creed,
And he must e'er its rigor bear until Death intercede.

167    Now since the custom is with youths whom nature has not botched
To yearn always for women that might possibly be notched
In order to obtain from them the bliss of love unscotched,
I took, myself, a sweetheart new—a lass most strictly watched.

168    The maid this time was noble born and nobler still in heart,
And every grace of manners knew, and every subtle art.
Both shrewd and innocent was she, nor would from virtue part,
But kept such poise no circumstance could e'er her passion start.

169    A comely, sportive maid she was and amorous of mien,
And when she walked her body swayed like rushes near a stream,
Full beautiful, impetuous, cajoling, sly, serene,
While in her eyes there slumbered love as in a fleeting dream.

170    For love of her I vow I uttered many a passioned lay,
But like wild oats sown near a creek whose floods sweep all away,
They brought me naught—thus true it is what proverb mongers say;
"The man who sows in river sand will ne'er his barn array."

171    Still, hoping I might number her among my blessèd maids,
I sent her what I could afford, not only beads and braids,
And finger rings and silly things and clothes of highest grades,
But sent as well my sweetest songs composed for serenades.

172    She would not take a single gift but scorned them all as trash,
And held me up to ridicule, and cried, "You men are rash
To think that women sell their gems for counterfeits of cash;
Take off your truck and nevermore Love's sacred image smash.

173    "I will not forfeit paradise nor lose my soul to Jesus
For any sin the world may have, however much it pleases,
Nor am I such a senseless fool but that I know who seizes
Must pay in full for what he took 'till he the law appeases."

174    It came to pass my love affair reached just the same conclusion
As happened to the thief who made a forcible intrusion
But stumbled on a mastiff fierce which started such confusion
The rogue, to rob in peace and safety, hit on this delusion.

175    He coaxed, and whistled to the dog, and tossed the brute a bun
Inside of which were pins and glass. Of such, the dog would none,
But quoth, "I'd be a fool indeed after that food to run,
And just to satisfy my hunger find myself undone.

176    "For this suspicious little bit you offer me tonight
I will not lose the victuals that are daily mine by right;
I well perceive I'd choke and die if such a bun I'd bite,
While you would rob the house I guard—I'd be a traitor quite.

177    "Betraying through my falsity the master I adore;
What, think you, I'll forsake my trust while you ransack his store?
If I permitted that I'd be a Judas ten times o'er.
Be off, you thief! Away! Away! I'll talk with you no more!"

178    The savage beast began to growl and clamor wondrous hard,
And chased the robber 'till he fled beyond his master's yard.
Well, now you see the parallel 'twixt thief and me, the bard
Who tried to filch that precious thing which modest maidens guard.

179    My gifts went fallow, I was shamed, and felt much like the ass
Who one thing thought while his master brought a different thing to pass.
Therefore I did what wisest was—forgot my winsome lass
Nor cried for milk which I had spilt, but turned to greener grass.

180    I know my star has fated me to love with wretched luck,
Because I never get the posies that I fain would pluck;
On that account I sought the god of Love and ran amuck
As mickle did we two debate on amatory truck.

## How Sir Love Came to the Archpriest and of the Contention Which He Had with the Aforesaid Archpriest

181   I'll tell you all about the strife I had one evening, late.
While I was steeped in moody thoughts and brooding o'er my fate,
There suddenly appeared a man, seraphic-faced and great.
I asked him who he was; said he, "I'm Love, your constant mate."

182   At that I felt a mighty rage surge upwards from my soul,
And with a curse I said, "Then, Love, go back to Hell's hot hole,
You lying sneak, whose sweet illusions human hearts cajole,
You torture thousands in your toils to one you give parole;

183   "With trickeries, and flatteries, and cunning, sly deceits,
You venom all your shafts to canker every heart that beats;
The man who serves you faithfully is wounded by your cheats,
And when you hate you raise such strife as every love defeats.

184   "Your magic arts have maddened men until they've lost their wits
And cannot eat or drink or sleep, yet will not cry for quits,
While others you infatuate with amatory fits
So that their souls and bodies go to Hell's unholy pits!

185   "No method have you when you fight, no laws, no self-restraint;
At times you swoop with roaring wings and strike without a feint,
At others you are gentle, sweet, and prayerful as a saint;
You know full well it's truth I tell, oh Love, in this complaint.

186   "You will not help your wretched souls after the fools are caught,
But drag them on from day to day in agonies distraught.
All those who did believe in you are to Gehenna brought
And for their momentary bliss have endless torments wrought.

187   "So brutal and ill-willed you are that when you smite a man
You will not medicine his wounds with herb of ortolan;
E'en though he were a reckless knight, a fighter in the van,
You'll always slay and conquer him as only Amour can.

188   "Full many learnèd books relate how artfully love picks
Away the hearts and souls of men 'till they are lunatics,
Yet though your snares are oft disclosed few guard against your tricks
For men in love are rarely wont to kick against their pricks."

## The Fable of the Young Man Who Wanted to Marry Three Women

189    A dunce there was whom nature had with vigor so invested
       He could not tolerate the thought of being wed and nested
       With just a single woman; three at least he loud requested,
       And that despite the way in which the neighborhood protested.

190    His father, mother, brother, all, with a tremendous hue
       Besought him urgently to take a smaller retinue,
       Conceding if he limited himself to one or two
       Or bore one marriage for a month then others might ensue.

191    To that condition he agreed and brought one wife to bed
       But when the merry month slipped by, his parents to him said
       'Twould please them if his brother took the other girl to wed
       As then no blame of church or state need either couple dread.

192    "Nay God," he cried, "this girl I've got can never get enough,
       So if my brother's wind is good for one perpetual puff,
       Come let him share the wife I have and help me do my stuff—
       To make him sate one wench alone would use him pretty tough."

193    Now it befell the good old man, the father of that drone,
       Possessed a grinding mill which had a monstrous upper stone.
       The married son, ere he was wed, could stop this whirling cone,
       It mattered not how fast it spun, with just one foot alone.

194    So strong he was and muscular, albeit addle-pated,
       He stopped the stone with greatest ease—but then he wasn't mated—
       Now since a month of joy had passed and he was wondrous sated,
       He thought he'd try his strength again to see if it had 'bated.

195    The stone was spinning round so fast it whistled like a fife
       When he with all his might stamped down—still thinking he was rife—
       But like a shot he catapulted, losing near his life,
       "Ah lusty, lusty stone," cried he, "I wish you had my wife!"

196    This lad ne'er took a second wife, so much he owed the first,
       But wore his manly strength away to slake her quenchless thirst,
       And as for stopping stones again not e'en his own he durst,
       And thus you see how lechery a youngster's vigor burst.

[33]

197     Oh Love, your kin are living coals, your father is the fire,
        And most he burns in agony whom most you do inspire.
        Both heart and soul he feels consumed who loves with fierce desire,
        And writhes in passion's Hell devoured like faggots in a fire.

198     Oh blessed, blessed are those men who never were in love,
        For free of care they live their lives and bless their God above,
        But let them once encounter you, black sorrow like a glove
        Constricts their lives as with those frogs who for a ruler strove.

## The Fable of the Frogs and How They Besought Jupiter
## for a King

199    Some frogs there were who in a pond were amorously jumping
Yet had no cares, like married men, to set their hearts to thumping,
Until the devil counselled them to give their luck a trumping
And go campaigning for a king—which they did with much stumping.

200    Then soon they cried to Jupiter to send that very thing,
So Jupiter picked up a beam of wood and with a fling
Sent it careening down to earth—the noise made heaven ring
And scared the frogs until they saw the log was not a king.

201    Forthwith a senate of grave frogs assembled on the log
And blinked and puffed and croaked and bluffed like every demagogue;
But knowing their constituents for rulers were agog
They sent again to Jupiter their King Bill from the bog.

202    Great Jupiter was vexed and cursed those stupid aldermen,
Yet ne'ertheless he sent a stork to rule their noisy fen—
A bird most ravenous—who loved a fat, frog-citizen
And with a king's magnificence devoured them ten by ten.

203    The frogs at this were panicky and screamed out loud in fright,
"Oh Jupiter, who banes and blesses, set our state aright,
Because this king we vainly wished, has such an appetite
He spoils our afternoons for us and kills our joys at night!

204    "His belly sepulchures our friends, his beak impales our kin,
By tens and twelves our senators are silenced 'neath his skin;
Yea, soon our ministers will see the next world in his bin,
Forgive, and save us, Jupiter, from our presumptuous sin!"

205    But them the godly Jupiter with grisly humor taunted:
"Dear frogs, recall when you were free and were not tyrant haunted.
You scorned your sweet security and said a king you wanted;
Well now, come show yourselves with woe, as erst with peace, undaunted!"

206    "The man who finds his fortune meet, let him not want a vaster,
And he who calls his hide his own, let him not seek a master,
Nor let a free and skeptic soul be hoodooed by a pastor;
E'en though for gold you freedom sell, the trade must bring disaster.

[35]

207 "And so it comes to pass with those who hold their hearts in fief
      To love, for though they once were free, when that tyrannic chief
      Is suzerain, the body wastes in torments past belief
      While all the substance of the soul is sacked and seared with grief.

208 "Your vassals, Love, would fain rebel but what can it avail
      When double chained you keep them bound within your noisome jail?
      Why e'en the wretched life you force on them they can't curtail.
      Is that not true? Come, answer, Love! Or leave, lest more I rail.

209 "Why stay you here to haunt me, Love? Be off! I love you not!
      For you bring travail to the soul beyond its wonted lot,
      As day and night, you subtle thief, you lay your plans and plot
      To steal from unsuspecting man the wretched heart he's got.

210 "That done his plundered, kidnapped heart is into exile sent
      And left unransomed with some dame in vile imprisonment
      Who tortures it on passion's wrack and does new hurts invent
      Until the disembodied heart through agony is rent.

211 "Like as the swift erratic flights of swallows through the air,
      So veers the heart on wings of love, from heaven to deep despair;
      A sudden madness sweeps it up, exulting, strong, and fair
      And flings it in a moment down to the dark fens of care.

212 "Like to a homeless vagabond the heart with love is made
      So that it journeys here and there on a purposeless parade,
      Alone and sad, in storm and rain, unsheltered and afraid,
      Rebuffed and threatened, scorned and hurt, where'er it turns for aid.

213 "Sir Love, what would you have of me, what debt have I contracted
      That you should hound me where I go 'till every claim's exacted?
      So quietly you stalked me down, I wonder what attracted
      That you unseen could pierce my heart and leave my life distracted?

214 "I cannot put you in arrest, so sly a rogue you are,
      And if I did, my heart would plead for you before the bar;
      But you, you boast how easily you can my fortunes mar
      And day and night set pitiless on me full many a scar.

215 "Reply! What have I done to you that you withhold your grace?
      Whene'er I've loved a damoiselle with heaven in her face
      The promises you made to me—'twas they brought me disgrace;
      O damn the hour I set these eyes on such a traitor base!

216 "The more you linger, Love, the more my heart with anger beats,
But now, at last, I have my say for long I've borne the cheats
Which you have foisted onto me with subtle, mean deceits;
I know you go disguised to plot, in tattered, evil sheets."

217 "The seven ugly mortal sins your retinue discloses
But through cupidity you lead us mortals by our noses
And make us greedy with desire, for others' beds of roses
Until we wreck the ten commands God handed down to Moses.

218 "Cupidity the root of evil is, and in addition
She is your eldest daughter, while your steward is ambition;
She is your standard bearer, symbolizing your position,
Who works destruction on the world and brings ill to fruition.

219 "The vices, arrogance and wrath, which burst the largest craw,
And avarice and lechery that blaze like tinder straw,
And envy, gluttony, and sloth, like hopeless chancres raw,
Are children of cupidity who live in Satan's maw.

220 "They live, you traitor, housed with you like greedy, treacherous swine,
And call to men with honeyed words and many a shameless sign,
Or lure them in with promises of amorous entwine
'Til they, poor men, do anything the courtesans design.

221 "When greed holds out its promises, men hasten to her mill
And set their hearts on others' gold, and rape and rob and kill
To get the price their sin demands, or for brief solace will,
If need be, sell the soul to free the flesh from passion's grill.

222 "Men die fantastic deaths for love—the sudden end of thieves,
Bear rope and rack or quartering, or don the red hot greaves,
While you, sly rogue, become a god—the one God man believes,
Though your religion smacks of greed, and your paradise deceives.

223 "Through greed you brought down towered Troy to ocean's level rim,
And grew for Troy within your garden Discord's apple grim
Which Paris unto Venus gave because she promised him
The woman Helen, radiant and beautiful of limb.

224 "And through your sin cupidity, great Pharaoh's hosts were slain
For the God of Mercy drowned them all in the deep and ruddy main;
So every one who has that vice, God's mercy must sustain—
Besides, the ones who covet most, on earth, get smallest gain.

225  "Man loses by cupidity what good he now possesses.
     By craving more than God intends; by uncontrolled excesses
     He never sates his greed, nor proffers generous caresses—
     My meaning, well this story of the hungry dog expresses.

## The Story of the Dog Who Was Carrying
## a Piece of Meat in His Mouth

226    Along a stream a hungry hound was carrying some liver
When suddenly he spied his own reflection in the river,
But, thinking it another dog, with jealous rage did quiver
And, snatching at that mirrored meat, he lost his luscious sliver.

227    Thus for a fair, illusive shadow, coupled with his greed,
That critter forfeited the meat intended for his feed,
Because his wild cupidity his judgment did exceed
And, wanting much, he lost the little that was his indeed.

228    Thus every day, with coveters, such accidents befall
For through their rash presumptive greed they sacrifice their all.
From coveting, those ills take root which human kind enthrall,
Wherefore a mortal vice, this sin the Holy Scriptures call.

229    Whate'er is valuable and good, and high esteem commands,
Which man has wrested from the world and holds in both his hands,
Let him not set that down to quest through far, illusive lands,
For certain 'tis he wastes his gold and delves but barren sands.

## Here He Speaks of the Sin of Arrogance

230 "You, Love, bring with you arrogance, and unrestrained by fear,
Your lack of dread has no extreme to which you will not veer.
How can you buy your paramours their gems and golden gear
But from the robberies for which you soon must pay, and dear?

231 "Your arrogance must goad you on to many a brutal crime—
You plunder jewels from travellers, rape virgins, and begrime
Alike young wives and widows shrunk, and maidens past their prime,
While as for nuns, those brides of Christ—you ravish the sublime.

232 "For felonies as vile as that the law says you must die
And that by tortures horrible from which you cannot fly,
While after death you'll burn in Hell beneath a flaming sky
As Satan thinks new tortures up your own to magnify.

233 "For arrogance a multitude forever, Love, you damn—
There's Lucifer and all his host who once did heaven cram
Who showed outrageous insolence to God, the Ghost and Lamb
Till God in his grace, right in their face, the gates of heaven did slam.

234 "Although their natures reek of sin, God did create them good,
But ne'ertheless through arrogance they warped themselves like wood,
And now the number of that host—Hell-damned as right they should—
A thousand documents to date, can't list, and never could.

235 "How many grim ordeals, Love, and raids and night alarms,
Bushwhacking feuds, and ugly broils, and brutal feats of arms,
Your arrogance has wrought on men! I vow the grisly harms
That wrack this earth can all be laid to your deceptive charms!

236 "The arrogant, presumptive man, with spirit bold and strong
Who never stands in dread of God or halts at doing wrong,
Dies long before the weak and sick and joins a sombre throng
For his reward is like the steed's who jibed the ass so long."

# The Fable of the Horse and the Ass

237    A gallant knight who forced a dame and had to fight her lord
        Rode down the lists on horse to back his outrage with his sword.
        And proudly did his charger sweep with armour plate aboard
        While farther down the field there crept a timid ass, abhorred.

238    With ringing hoofs and jingling reins and flaming pennants set
        The noble steed his master bore with lance-long bayonet
        And like a thunder peal his charge struck fear to all he met,
        Particularly to the ass who cowered at the threat.

239    With terror then, beneath his load the ass began to balk
        And right before the coursing steed stood rooted like a stalk
        While swiftly toward him dashed the horse as at a dove the hawk,
        "Sir Paralytic," screamed the steed, "take up your bed and walk!"

240    The ass stirred not. The courser made one frantic leap to clear him
        Just as his master's adversary couched his lance to spear him,
        But missing rider hit the horse and let his weapon shear him
        So that his blood ran gushing out and fearfully did smear him.

241    And after that the lordly steed was left forever lame,
        Wherefore they made him drag the plough and plod in ways of shame,
        Tread mills, and turn the bucket-wheel—'twas he who paid the claim
        Against the time his master took his pleasure with a dame.

242    Forevermore a galling yoke set on his withers bare,
        While men, to force him down, would oft his muzzle twist and tear,
        And kneeling thus he seemed like one who dumbly says a prayer
        Yet rolls his sunken, blood-shot eyes in bitterest despair.

243    One day, beholding how his ribs stuck like a wash-board out,
        And how his sharp protruding bones seemed just prepared to sprout,
        The ass who caused the accident, let go this heartless shout,
        "Now gossip, where's that panoply with which you swanked about?

244    "Where have you hung your broidered reins and put your gilded saddle?
        Where is that overbearing mien which made us all skedaddle;
        Your high aristocratic pride, that erst your pate would addle,
        How can it now endure the yoke and bear the rustic's paddle?"

245    Let each presumptive person take a warning from this tale,
        And let its chastening moral tone his arrogance curtail,
        For vigor, valor, honor, wealth, and hearty age and hale
        Though for a space are full of joy, with time grow quickly stale.

## Here He Speaks of the Sin of Avarice

246    You, Love, are also Avarice, and you are parsimonious,
       You love to take but find the name of giving not euphoneous;
       The stream bed of the Duero couldn't sate you greed felonious;
       Whene'er I've hearkened to your voice I've found your words erroneous.

247    The wealthy, avaricious Dives in flaming Hell was thrust
       Because to saintly Lazarus he wouldn't give a crust.
       Thus, miserly, you hate mankind; your heart is dry as dust;
       You would not from your hoard lend out a copper groat on trust!

248    Although it is commanded by the holy word of Jesus
       To feed the hungry, clothe the naked, shelter from the breezes
       All homeless, poor incompetents—in you all pity freezes
       So that you never render aid when grim misfortune seizes.

249    Oh heartless wretch, what will you do when Judgment Day rolls round
       And God demands close reckoning in pence for every pound
       Of all the vast accumulated wealth you have around?
       The treasures then of fifty realms will not avail you—hound!

250    When you were erst of poor estate and lived in wretched want,
       Ah how you sighed and took religion, clasped your fingers gaunt,
       And cried to God for health and food, and made the pious vaunt
       That if He blessed you, 'mid the poor you'd ever make your haunt.

251    Well, evidently you were heard, for God rained down His blessing
       Of health and wealth together with much shrewdness in possessing,
       But now, whene'er you see the poor, instead of great caressing
       You act toward them just like the wolf whose thanks were most distressing.

## The Fable of the Wolf, the Goat, and the Crane

252  While lunching out one afternoon, a wolf devoured a goat,
But as he gulped its pelvis down the bone stuck in his throat
And choked him, 'till in great alarm he sent for men of note—
Great surgeons, doctors, barbers, all, to fetch an antidote.

253  He promised treasure to the one who could extract the bone,
Wherefore a crane from heaven came to work the cure alone,
And with his long and narrow bill he drew it from its zone
But left the wolf with such a hunger he could eat a stone.

254  That done, the crane recalled the wolf's remunerative clause;
The brute replied, "Say, when you thrust your head inside my jaws
I could have bit your neck right off—you're therefore paid, because
I let you live your life instead of giving it a pause."

255  "You, miser Love, have done as bad, for now you have your fill
Of bread and money which you've wrung from neighbors weak and ill,
You will not give the starving poor a single wretched mill
For lo, your pity dries like dew upon the sunny hill.

256  "It never pays to render good unto an evil shrew
For wicked ones who recompense good Christians number few,
As gratitude's a thing unknown to men of sinful brew
And when you work them good they merely take it as their due."

## Here He Speaks of the Sin of Lewdness

257   "Wherever you are, Love, there lewdness burns like raging fire;
     Adultery and fornication always you require;
     Whenever you see any one, to sin your thoughts aspire;
     You wink and leer at women to fulfill your foul desire.

258   "You made the prophet David lust, and for his lewdness slay
     Uriah, since, to get his wife, King David sent one day
     An order to his Captain, Joab, cunningly to say,
     'Let stout Uriah fight in front and fling him in the fray.'

259   "Thereby through lust for Bathsheba, this man of God's own heart
     Dispatched Uriah and became the Devil's counterpart.
     But God severely punished him and would not let him start
     The temple, and this penitence made David sorely smart.

260   "Five noble towns the Lord destroyed with His consuming flame
     Though only three were lewd and vile, but angry God o'ercame
     The rest for their proximity, although they weren't to blame.
     Thus they who dwell near evil men are punished just the same.

261   "Begone, Sir Love, I will not win through lewdness, ridicule,
     Like Virgil, when his dame let down a basket reticule
     And coaxed him in—she said she'd hoist him to her vestibule
     But stopped half way, so all night long he hung there like a fool.

262   "At such a dirty trick as that the poet and enchanter
     Devised a lamp which he bewitched by occult art and canter
     In such a wise that every light in Rome went out instanter
     Except his, which he told the dame he was prepared to grant her.

263   "Accommodating Virgil placed this lamp between her thighs,
     Then up and down the streets of Rome by posters and by cries
     He made announcement none might get a light in any wise
     Except from hers which was, it seems, sufficient in its size.

264   "There was no other way to get a light, for if one lit
     His neighbor's wick, a sudden darkness both their candles smit.
     The lady had a vogue immense, in fact she made a hit
     And thus the prophet Virgil gained his vengeance through a skit.

265 "Now after he had done this shameful thing and eased his spite,
This poet lecherous grew tired and quenched his lady's light,
But just to keep the world at large reminded of his might
He wroght another miracle ne'er seen by mortal sight.

266 "The bed and channel he transformed where Tiber's waters flow
Into a solid sheet of copper with an amber glow
(E'en so lust's necromancy turns a maiden chaste as snow
Into a brazen huzzy whom the lewd and unchaste know).

267 "Soon after Virgil's dame was humbled she began erecting
A winding stairway in her house, set round with knives projecting
So that if Virgil called again on amorous prospecting
He'd spike himself and find a death from which there's no protecting.

268 "But Virgil learned her purpose through his necromantic arts
And never came nor wished to come, but left for foreign parts;
'Tis oftener though, where lechery and love have cast their darts,
The world of men are hurt and shamed, or die of broken hearts.[2]

269 "To all the men by lewdness maimed, I know not one it cured;
E'en those who staunchest are in love 'gainst lust are not insured,
While lechery destroys a fool as soon as it's endured;
'Tis like the story of the eagle whom the hunters lured."

## The Story of the Eagle and the Hunter

270   "The lordly eagle screams above the jagged mountain peaks
     And watches all the lesser birds dart off with frightened shrieks,
     But when, perchance, a feather downward from his pinions streaks
     The archer for it all day long upon the upland seeks.

271   "For with its plumes are feathered arrows, bolts, and quarrel hafts,
     And all the divers missiles of the fletchers' handcrafts.
     Then, in the air these wingèd darts the cunning hunter wafts
     And shoots the lordly eagle with his cruel barbèd shafts.

272   "The plumèd monarch bows his head, and like a dying king
     Looks mournfully upon the dart that does his finish bring.
     'Alas!' he cries, with futile rage, 'this unkind, feathered thing
     Which flies away with mine own life, has issued from my wing!'

273   "The fool, the wretch, who does not care for his immortal soul
     But lets the heat and lust of love his better sense control
     Brings death alike to soul and flesh, nor will it him console
     To know he nurtured in his breast that which his spirit stole.

274   "There is no man or bird or beast consumed by passion's heat
     Who does not, when he has performed Love's noble, unsung feat,
     React most suddenly from that intoxicating treat
     And growing sad and weak and stale, abhor what once was sweet.[3]

275   "No tongue can tell how many men has lechery laid low
     After its enervating bouts have set their coals aglow.
     But all who burn in lechery or to Love's market go
     Will burn in Hell when Satan comes to take them down below."

276 "You, Love, are envy unalloyed—there's not in all the land
A searing like your jealousy that can so deeply brand.
If your own wife talked with a man you would not understand
Because suspicions sad would take your jealous heart in hand.

277 "Such jealousy is always born where envy rules supreme;
It makes you think your dame is up to some unfaithful scheme;
It makes you mad to brood upon that one engrossing theme
Until your mind grows warped and wracked with love's distorted dream.

278 "As soon as jealousy takes root, the turmoil in your breast
Chokes you with agony and sighs, and yearnings unrepressed
So that you bear towards self and friends a miserable unrest
While all the time your heart, aflutter, thumps its pained protest.

279 "Through jealousy and false suspicions, all mankind you hate,
And thus you play a losing game with passion as your mate,
A wretched, rash, one-sided flight, from which, intemperate,
Like a fish caught in a net, you meet at last your fate.

280 "A bitter insurrection then flares up throughout your being,
Your harried soul takes to its keep from which there is no freeing,
Too faint to sally out and fight, too weak to think of fleeing,
It waits the final overthrow of passion, death decreeing.

281 "Through envy Cain his brother slew, and now he lies in Hell
Burnt with the hot, volcanic heat of Mountain Mongibel.
Through envy Jacob stole a blessing, treachery so fell
That Esau swore he'd kill his brother—so the Scriptures tell.

282 "Through envy Jesus was betrayed, our God's belovèd son,
A veritable God himself, Incarnate Three-in-One.
Through envy He was caught and killed, and utterly undone—
No good has sprung from envy since this planet was begun.

283 "By coveting, men cause each day dissentions without end,
As jealousy and envy make both beast and man contend.
Where'er you set your altar up, there jealous fools ascend,
And though with envy they are torn, to envy's god they bend.

284 "Because you may have only chaff when all your friends have wheat,
Your mighty envy drives you on to break with them complete,
Until at last they bring on you a shameful, sharp defeat
Just as the peacock trounced the crow from envious conceit."

## The Story of the Peacock and the Crow

285   "An envious crow beheld a peacock spread its pretty fan
      Wherefore she muttered to herself as only women can,
      'I'll be as beautiful as that!' And with this foolish plan,
      The sooty bird to change herself to lily-white began.

286   "She stripped her suit of feathers off from body, brow and face
      And dressed herself by sticking peacock feathers in their place.
      That done, she went to church bedecked in others' borrowed grace,
      (And there be many like the crow who use disguises base.)

287   "This crow, be-peacocked like a peacock, gorgeously was clad,
      And being changed through beauty treatments, she was very glad,
      So out in high society where leisured peacocks gad,
      The vulgar crow, incognito, went swanking like a cad.

288   "But ah, it chanced a gallant cock espied the naughty crow
      And catching at her tail he twitched those plumes she tried to grow.
      Then where the grass was high but dry he stretched her—apropos.
      Well, after he was through she wasn't quite as white as snow.

289   "Thus Love, your envy tempts us all to dress with false pretenses,
      But when we bluff a better man we get the consequences.
      We sacrifice for envy's sake our very hearts and senses
      Wherefore I find in envy, Love, the vilest of offenses.

290   "Whoever wants what's not his own or seeks to change his state
      By putting on what is another's, finds, though oft too late,
      That what was his as well as others', luck will confiscate,
      For when a nothing thinks he's something, he must abdicate."

291 "You, Love, bring gluttony with you, for you are so voracious
You are the first to snatch and eat with appetite edacious;
In stomach entertainment you are clever and salacious
And store up vim and vigor through your wolfish greed rapacious.

292 "Since I have known you, never once have I beheld you fast
Because you breakfast in the morning, take a big repast,
And then at noon you hog it down, but ere the day has past
You dine, and after that you make another meal your last.

293 "From bibbing wine and wolfing meat the humors so increase
That when you grow familiar with a girl your lungs release
Sufficient phlegm to strangle you. May Hell consume your grease
For you advise our younger men to eat and be in peace.

294 "Our father Adam did from greed and gluttony partake
Of fruit forbidden just to please his wife, and a wily snake,
But for his appetite God made the patriarch forsake
His paradise, and dying go in Hell fore'er to bake.

295 "When Moses through the wilderness conducted greedy Jews,
Their gluttony brought death to them and all their retinues,
And thus the prophet bears me out when I declare this news
That always you go open mouthed your belly to abuse.

296 "Through greed the estimable Lot, a noble citizen,
Got drunk and lay with both his daughters (though without his ken),
So now your formula for lust is, 'women, wine and men,'
And from their conjunctivities you breed new ills again.

297 "The sin of gluttony brings on a sudden death with chill
Both to the flesh intemperate and to the spirit ill,
A fact which many fables tell and histories instill
And one of these I'll mention just to let you see my will."

# The Story of the Lion and the Horse

298  "A very fat, expansive horse was grazing in the field
When up to him a lion came with his intent concealed,
Although 'twas plain unto his palate how this horse appealed,
'Come vassal,' said he 'kiss my hand and royal homage yield.'

299  "Then to the greedy lion straight the cautious nag replied,
' 'Tis true I am your vassal, lord, and you're my king beside,
And that I should bend down to kiss your hand can't be denied,
But I can hardly come to you because—I must confide—

300  " 'While shoeing me a clumsy smith but yesterday drove in
A cruel nail clean through my hoof and half way up my shin;
It left me lame, so may your highness bend your blessèd chin
And draw it with your royal teeth from my unworthy skin.'

301  "Down bent the lion graciously to lend his vassal aid
When heinously the tricky steed his monarch's love repaid
By dealing him with iron hoofs a heartfelt accolade
Which struck him right between the eyes and killed him—I'm afraid.

302  "Then like a mountain torrent swift the frightened horse took flight
Albeit from the stubble grass he'd crammed his belly tight
So that he got the retching heaves and died that very night,
Exemplifying thus how death will greedy fools requite.

303  "Devouring food without restraint and tragalistic snacking
(Like glutting wine until it brings spasmodic retch and wracking)
According to Hippocrates, kill more than weapon-hacking
And sousing brings to man and maid the urge for belly-smacking."

304 "There's no such boastfulness as yours throughout the world's domain
Since, Love, you have more pride and pomp than all the land of Spain;
But he who does not do your will, drives you with wrath insane,
As in your company walk ire and evil will profane.

305 "The regal Nebuchadnezzar who was king of Babylon
While filled with pride and arrogance beyond comparison,
Showed disesteem and disrespect to the mighty Three-in-One,
So God took all his power away and left the king undone.

306 "God made of him a being dumb, as dumb as cows and asses,
Then turned him out where he could graze upon the mountain grasses,
And all that time his hair grew long in beastly shaggy masses
While he had nails like eagle claws as green as ancient brasses.

307 "Your servants, Love, are homicides, and spiteful brawlers such
As cry, 'Do you know who I am? Well, see if you can touch
The chip I've on my shoulder set!' with other boastings much,
For where you are, you blackguard, Love, there Death and idiots clutch.

308 "Through anger Samson was undone in spite of all his force:
Remember how Delilah's shears brought scalp and hair divorce,
And how he lost his strength with hair—'till once he had recourse
To might again and slew himself with many from remorse.

309 "With wrath intense and madness Saul, who was the first real king
To rule the Jews, upon his sword himself in rage did fling.
Therefore let all be warned by this, nor trust the lightest thing
To wrath, for by my faith, I vow, it shall misfortune bring.

310 "Whoe'er has come to know you well will never trust your toils
Because a man who sees your works forthwith from you recoils.
And those who deal the best with you the least esteem your spoils,
While he who frequents you the most, himself the most embroils."

## The Story of the Lion Who Killed Himself with Anger

311   "Vainglory caused a lion who was boastful and malicious
      (And who on every lesser beast committed actions vicious)
      To kill himself from very wrath. His story's so delicious
      I'll tell you how it happened—may the moral be propitious.

312   "It seems when he was in his youth this lion oft would chase
      The other critters round the lot with motives low and base
      And some he'd kill and mutilate or forcibly embrace,
      But ah, when old age came he could no longer stand the pace.

313   "Then when the hunted beasts found out the lion had grown weak
      They all rejoiced to know that they no more would have to sneak
      Away in fear, so they resolved on him to take their wreak,
      And foremost came the ass to kick his tyrant on the cheek.

314   "They all charged in and bravely struck, for he was down and out;
      The boar, indignant, gored the lion with his tuskered snout,
      The bull and steer both used their horns and tossed him all about;
      But, as I say, the valiant ass rushed on him with a shout.

315   "He set his seal of wrath upon the feeble lion's nose,
      Yet more from shame the lion suffered than from all his blows.
      Wherefore, at last, the senile beast with outraged pride arose
      And tore his heart out with his claws before his abject foes.

316   "Now any man of high estate and mighty power and pelf
      Should never do to others what he would not like himself,
      Because he may, at Fortune's turn, be put upon the shelf
      And if he's dug another's grave it may become his delf."

317 "Besides, Love, you're the residence and dwelling place of sloth;
To work on man the slightest good you are exceeding loth.
When you have found an idle lout, I swear upon my oath
You bring him weariness and sin, while sorrow follows both.

318 "Yet you yourself are never idle when you seize a man
Because you make him work deceits and do what ills he can
(Such as the sinful dallying with every courtesan)
Until at last he dies a victim to your evil plan.

319 "With sloth you likewise bring with you hypocrisy and cant
And while you feign the innocent you play the miscreant;
You plot and spy how you can get the girls for whom you pant
For though you bow your pious head you wink at them aslant.

320 "It matters not how well you preach, if you break your injunctions,
Albeit you deceive the world with counterfeit compunctions,
You want just what the wolf desired. Full well I know your functions;
So, saintly shyster, hearken while I lash you without unctions."

## Here He Speaks of the Suit Which the Wolf and the Fox Had before Sir Monkey, High Constable of the Province of Chicane

321   "A neighbor kept a rooster 'till a fox once chanced to thieve it,
     But, witnessing her theft, a wolf commanded her to leave it,
     (Although in secret he himself was planning to retrieve it),
     He cried, 'My dear, to think you'd steal! I hardly can believe it!'

322   "You see the sin he often wrought, in others he accused,
     And though he oft forgave himself when piously infused
     All those who shared his secret vice he damnably abused
     Since none, he thought, should dare to take the liberties he used.

323   "Therefore the Wolf swore out a warrant on his quondam friend
     And summoned her before a judge, most grave and reverend,
     Sir Monkey he was called, an ape whom heaven and earth defend
     As he was shrewd and learned and wise in cases without end.

324   "The Wolf prepared a formal suit and reinforced his brief
     With countless precedents and laws against the foxy thief,
     And hired the greyhound for his lawyer, famed abroad as chief
     Of prosecutors who had brought sly foxes to their grief.

325   "In formal style the wolf began, 'Before this court supreme
     At which, Sir Monkey, you preside with honor and esteem,
     I, plaintiff Wolf, bring suit on Fox, and pray the court to deem
     The evidence and render judgment 'gainst her guilt extreme.

326   " 'I do affirm on February, such and such a date,
     This year of grace in thirteen hundred one and thirty-eight,
     The first year of King Lion's reign, that bloody magistrate
     Who to our noble city came in search of moneys great.

327   " 'This Fox broke in Lord Buck's estate, the man who keeps my flock,
     And creeping down his chimney robbed our precious crowing cock
     Who gave his regular alarm each morning like a clock—
     Fox bore him off and ate him up and thus despoiled our stock.

328   " 'Wherefore I do accuse said Fox and pray Your Grace to give
     Her judgment irrevocable that she may no more live
     But on the gallows die the death of thief and fugitive;
     But if she's guiltless, then give me like sentence punitive.'

329   "Now when this charge was read before that grave assembled court,
       The cunning Fox bethought her how to tricks she might resort.
       'Your Honor,' quoth she, 'since in law my learning's somewhat short,
       Give me a lawyer, for my life to make a fair retort.'

330   "The judge replied, 'Though I am new to this especial circuit,
       And do not know your district well, I still think I can work it
       To give you grace of twenty days; get counsel and don't shirk it
       For if you are not ready then the gallows tree must jerk it.'

331   "At that the case was docketed and posted everywhere.
       Defendant Fox and Plaintiff Wolf 'gan scurry here and there;
       This one got money, that one bribes for witnesses to swear,
       But Fox secured a lawyer who could well her plea prepare.

332   "The day arriving for the trial, when the court convened
       The sly Defendant Fox brought in the lawyer she had gleaned;
       A Shepherd Dog he was with collar, spiked and filed and cleaned;
       At that Wolf grew so terrified he wot not where he leaned.

333   "Thereat this advocate of hers proposed before the judge
       To quash the case and throw it out where it would no more budge,
       'Because,' said he, 'This Wolf's complaint is just an artful smudge,
       Since he himself the robber is and sues Fox from a grudge.

334   " 'Wherefore,' said he, 'I make exception to the plaintiff's brief,
       And hold as most legitimate and of my reasons chief
       This one, which I do here proclaim—that to my best belief
       Yon Wolf should be debarred from court because he is a thief.

335   " 'While guarding day and night my flocks it often came about
       That this same Wolf would rush at them and throw them in a rout,
       When, seizing on some straggling lamb, he'd tear its vitals out,
       Ere I could snatch it, bloody, dead, from his rapacious snout.

336   " 'For stealing he has many times been given sentence short,
       Wherefore, by legal estimate, he bears such ill report
       That none should be accused by him for any act of tort,
       Or by his instance be constrained to plead before your court.

337   " 'And furthermore I do object, he's excommunicated:
       By church as well as civil court he oft has been berated
       Because he keeps a public whore and shamefully is sated
       Albeit he with Lady Loup has legally been mated.

338 " 'His concubine's a mastiff bitch who prowls about my sheep,
And hence I claim his oath must be contemptible and cheap,
And none should have to make defense against this villain deep;
I pray Your Honor, my poor client from his clutches keep.'

339 "Now Wolf and Dog stood face to face, each anything but cheerful,
For either one had had his say and now stood waiting, fearful,
The judge's doom, when suddenly, the Fox spoke up an earfull
And said, 'Condemn them both unheard to mortal sentence tearful.'

340 "Then when the essence of the suit had been by each compressed,
The plaintiff and defendant made His Honor this request,
That he should name a certain day to set the case at rest,
Wherefore till past Epiphany the action was recessed.

341 "Sir Monkey set off towards his house and with him quite a crowd
Of milk and honey, easy money politicians loud.
Some shysters too were there who use the statutes to enshroud
Their treacheries, 'twas they who tried his Honor to becloud.

342 "These lawyers put their clients up to give the judge a bribe;
One brought him trout, another salmon, one more did provide
In secret some refreshments which his Honor might imbibe,
While both contestants covertly to falseness did subscribe.

343 "But when the fatal day arrived for judgment to be read,
And either party stood before the Judge, Sir Monkey, dread;
Quoth he, 'Why must you fight it out? Come, compromise instead,
And if you will, I'll make delay ere I have judgment said!'

344 "The lawyers strove as best they could and used up all their tricks
To find what was the judge's mind, what sentence he'd affix,
And in its execution what dread punishments he'd mix;
But lo, his lips were like a lock for which there are no picks.

345 "By jests they sought to draw him out and get what they were after,
And mightily they tried to fool the old judicial grafter,
But though they made him show his teeth it never was in laughter;
They thought his snarls were fooling, but 'twas they who were the dafter.

346 "Both parties then informed the judge through either's advocate
That they could never be agreed and would not arbitrate,
And wished no overtures of peace to reconcile their hate,
But prayed they might no longer be for sentence made to wait.

[57]

347  "At that the learnèd judge prepared his legalized deductions
        (But kept his conscience well in hand lest it might cause obstructions)
        And thus, while seated in the court, he read out his instructions
        That all might hear, both far and near, his sapient eructions.

348  " 'Here in the name of Jesus Christ and God His legal father,
        I, Judge Sir Monkey, do proclaim with full juridic pother,
        That having read the plaintiff's charge—which cost infinite bother—
        And all its pleas concomitant—pursuant to it rather—

349  " 'And having noted the defense with each of its excuses
        And shrewd disclaimers which the Fox sets up for her abuses,
        And having seen the refutations which the Wolf, as ruses,
        Against the Fox's explanation, in this action uses,

350  " 'And having heard how Fox makes claim in her asservation
        By way of equity against the plaintiff's accusation,
        And having well perused and weighed both sides' expostulation,
        Besides considering the prayers for legal condemnation;

351  " 'And having weighed the evidence that's relevant and pesant
        (With wits that have been sharpened by full many golden besant)
        Through intercourse with men at law, both rational and pleasant,
        And holding God before mine eyes—ignoring prayer and present—

352  " 'I find the claim that Wolf has made is well substantiated,
        Is pertinent, and in procedure clearly formulated;
        Yet, on the other hand, the Fox has likewise actuated
        A clear defense, which in some parts, is ably vindicated.

353  " 'The first demurrer, in its essence, stands at law peremptory
        But excommunion here is held by civil courts exemptory—
        On this I shall expostulate for 'tis a point redemptory
        In equity, though shallow lawyers hold it as contemptory.

354  " 'Well, as I said, the first demurrer's surely absolute,
        But excommunion as a charge you cannot prosecute,
        Because Archbishops only such proceedings institute,
        While men so charged have nine full days its onus to refute.

355  " 'Now this delay is justified, and by the court is borne
        So that the many witnesses, and affidavits sworn,
        Can all be got together ere the ninth and final morn,
        For were the case dispatched in haste the law would be forlorn.

356 " 'So when an excommunication suffers this delay,
       Remember that its term is fixed and none can it gainsay,
       Until the limit has expired after its latest day,
       Though often many lawyers this injunction disobey.

357 " 'This charge of excommunication only is employed
       In courts ecclesiastical, for if it be convoyed
       In civil, its validity at law is null and void,
       And such as sue despite this fact should have their pleas destroyed.

358 " 'I therefore find the Fox cannot this counter charge here press,
       And having guilt, in equity she's shorn of more redress—
       On what's exempt in law, of course, I cannot bring duress;
       The Fox must in this ruling with her counsel acquiesce.

359 " 'Although against the plaintiff or his evidence adverse
       Such counter charges could be proved, I would inflict no worse
       A punishment, but rather would both sides at once disperse
       And throw the case right out of court with reasons strong and terse.

360 " 'And if the court should e'er suspect a witness of repression
       The judge can have him tortured 'till he make a full confession,
       Not just because its relevant but rather to keep session
       All times with truth; in this the judge is given wide discretion.

361 " 'When there has been a counter charge, one must the plea withdraw
       And have the witnesses debarred or grilled to find some flaw;
       Upon such charge I can't condemn or execute a straw
       Since never can a judge exceed the limit set by law.

362 " 'But now this Wolf has just confessed, and from the facts extorted,
       And them alone, by tortures wrung to which I have resorted,
       I find there's truth in every charge that Fox has here reported
       And hence I do declare said Wolf to have his action thwarted.

363 " 'Since from his own confession and his use by habit bred
       'Tis manifest and evident just what the Fox has said,
       I do pronounce against the suit which he has made and plead,
       And do direct that it be quashed for reasons I'll have read.

364 " 'Whereas the Wolf confesses to the crime the Fox accuses
       'Tis clear the very tort he blames, himself in covert uses,
       Wherefore the Fox need guard in law no more his wrong abuses
       And I receive her full defence and all her good excuses.

365 " 'What Wolf has said will help him not, for loud he did complain
        While making his confession stretched upon the rack of pain,
        Not much he said was rational, as terror made it vain,
        Though men experienced can tell what truth such shifts contain.

366 " 'I may concede the Fox the right to range the woods for game
        But never will I pardon her for stealing creatures tame;
        I charge her, hence, to rob no roosters from her neighbor dame.'
        Said Fox, 'I'll then leave cock for hen although the sin's the same.'

367 "So neither side appealed the case for neither party lost,
        As none got sentenced by the judge, and no one paid the cost,
        The reason being not a soul conceived his honor lost;
        The case was not contested then nor into limbo tossed.

368 "Their lawyers, on the other hand, with wrath condemned the case
        And claimed the judge's precedent was new and out of place,
        And said the way His Honor judged was lately a disgrace,
        But all their talk Sir Monkey thought was hardly worth his ace.

369 "He told them he could very well, in settling such rows,
        Fulfill the ends of justice with what power the law endows;
        Then he reminded them that some had made unlawful vows,
        Which covert warning silenced them and smoothed their angry brows.

370 "They therefore said his every count was brilliant, clear, and just
        But still it seemed to them that when the case had been discussed,
        'Twas not in order for the court a compromise to trust,
        For when the guilt had been confessed the sentence should be thrust.

371 "At that His Honor made reply that touching this position
        The King had specially provided in his own commission
        Complete discretionary powers for every such omission,
        Which power the lawyers must consider covered each addition."

## Here Again He Speaks of the Quarrel Which the Archpriest Had with Sir Love[4]

372   "You, Love, behave just like that wolf, the sins which you commit
     In others you condemn as foul, the while in filth you sit.
     You are an enemy to those you seem to benefit,
     And though you have a pleasant tongue, 'tis only to outwit.

373   "You never spend a moment's time in godly works of piety
     Nor ever visit prisoners nor dole the sick a moiety,
     But mix instead with brawling blades, unfamed for their sobriety,
     While ladies lewd you whisper with who aren't in good society.

374   "You have a rascal's breviary to pray with vagabonds,
     *With those who hate the ways of peace* your psaltry corresponds;
     *Behold how good* you signify with clack-dishes of bronze;
     Your rout *All night lift up their hands* to crime ere it absconds.

375   "You rise up from your leman's bed; *'Thou shalt unseal my lips'*—
     You sing aloud to waken her, and utter wicked quips;
     *'Hear thou our prayers,'* while o'er a viol you thrum with finger tips
     Or chant *'In the beginning God* made women loose for slips.'

376   "All through the limp and chilly dawn when austere friars chant
     Sad matins for their sinful dreams, and hopelessly recant,
     You feel the warmth a woman gives, and for her body pant
     Until the sun with morning songs steals in your cell aslant.

377   "Then you begin the prayer of primes, *God, in Thy holy name*—
     Which you address your pander with that she may take your dame
     And, on pretense of getting water or excuse as lame,
     Convey the trollop from your cell where she has stayed in shame.

378   "But if your wench is not the kind who slinks through streets and alleys,
     Perhaps she is the sort who may be coaxed down flowery valleys;
     At any rate, if she is charmed by your deceptive sallies,
     She'll eat of bitter fruit, like Eve, where'er she dilly-dallys.

379   "Yet even then if she's too nice to gather random flowers
     You still can bend her to your will by using all your powers,
     Your tongue, your mind, your very soul, until at last she cowers
     And takes all comers you invite to your indecent bowers.

380   "You next to God's cathedral go, but not to hear His mass,
     Nor gain a pardon for your sin, but just to see your lass—
     You like a mass that smacks of ass—at such you're bold as brass;
     When to those sacraments you go, fleet runners you surpass.

381 "When finished is your assey mass, you then lift up a prayer
      To some old bawdy go-between to bring your mistress there.
      *'My soul for thy salvation pants,'* you oft unto her swear;
      *'I'm like a bottle in the smoke* from passionate despair!'

382 " *'I meditate on thee all day and love to do thy will!*
      Take pity on my shaven pate, *that I may live my fill!*
      *Thou art a lamp unto my feet,* your body love I still!'
      *'Thy words are honey,'* she replies, 'come let us clasp and thrill!'

383 "That done you pray at nones unto your jaunty whore,
      *'Thy testimonies wondrous are, my soul doth them adore;*
      *Direct my goings in and out,'* you ardently implore.
      *'Upright art thou, oh Lord,'* says she, 'let's ring the bell some more!'"

384 "I never saw a sacristan who better vespers jingled,
      Or who could win so easily the women he had singled;
      *The rod of thy virility* which oft has sweetly tingled,
      You prod her with until you two in Zion have commingled.

385 " *'Sit thou at my right hand,'* you say as soon as she has come,
      *'I am exceeding glad!'* But then, if some rude censor glum
      Looks on, you cry, *'Go up thou bald-head* join Jehovah's scum,
      When every cake's a birthday cake why rob me of this crumb!'

386 "I never saw a curate who for souls said such complines
      For blonde or dark or fair or foul envisaged concubines.
      They cry *'Convert us!'*—You invert them for your lewd designs
      And *hide them underneath thy wings* in passionate entwines.

387 "*Thou dost prepare* the woman whom for laying-on you're girt;
      *Before the face of all* you take away the wanton pert
      And just before the consummation when you raise her skirt
      You cry, *'Hail, Virgin! Heaven's Queen'* if she complains of hurt."[5]

## Here He Speaks Further of the Quarrel Which the Archpriest
## Had with Sir Love

388 "Sir Love, you bring with idleness these other kindred taints;
Distresses, worries, discontents, and sinful unrestraints.
You are not pleased with virgin men or chaste and worthy saints
But rather strive to set your serfs aflame with fierce complaints.

389 "The creature who obeys your will is filled with pure deceit
And will not stop at heresy to do your works complete.
Such even put more confidence in your illusions sweet
Than in the faith of God Himself—away, impious cheat!

390 "No more of you, Sir Love, no more! nor of your son, Desire!
You rouse me out with false alarms by screaming, 'Fire! Oh Fire!'
You goad and shout at me to haste when most I do perspire—
I vow your glory is not worth a millet grain entire.

391 "You show not dread nor due respect for mighty king or queen
But pitch your tent where'er you list in court or common green
Where, gipsy-wise, you steal men's hearts behind your transient screen
And as one coal lights many hearts, you fire the whole demesne.

392 "You drug men's hearts with promises as with narcotic wine
But few indeed you lead into their ladies' inner shrine.
You find more ways for tricking men than leaves upon a vine;
You harvest in more silly fools than nut-cones on a pine.

393 "You prowl about for women like some stealthy, poaching churl;
You swoop down like a sparrow hawk on some unwary girl,
Or brigand-wise in ambush hide where suddenly you hurl
Yourself upon a maiden whom you brutally unfurl.

394 "Suppose a man should keep his daughter ever in his thought,
If she be jaunty, joyous, fair, and by young gallants sought,
Though she be watched with tender care and be in wealth upbrought,
Let him not think he rules her heart—Alas, he governs naught!

395 "Should such a father try to marry her to one of wealth
Whereby his own household might grow to more financial health
He'll find his daughter balkier than Satan is himself,
For like a wanton ass she'll seek wild asses out by stealth.

396 " 'Tis you who whisper in her ear and give her bad advice
By telling her the road to love's the road to paradise.
She'll preen herself with glass and comb to make her coiffure nice
But no one save the lout she loves can ever her suffice.

397 "You make her heart a weathercock which easily you shake,
And though she marry one today, she'll love tomorrow's rake.
Be she in skirt or flimsy-shirt, she's ready to partake
Of every fickle folly be it only for your sake.

398 "The one who most believes in you is ever most misled;
O'er youth, o'er maid, o'er all in fact, insidiously you spread
The shadow of your mortal sin—let every being dread
The transient sweet and lasting gall with which one's heart is fed.

399 "An ever, everlasting death you bring those souls you smite
Besides inflicting torments on their bodies through your might;
You take good name and honor from the men whom you delight
And then with loss of heaven you your devotees requite.

400 "Their persons you destroy and their possessions you consume—
Like Death, you bear off soul and body to the dismal tomb;
You bring the noblest vassal to the state of scottish groom;
Your promises bear never fruit but wither in their bloom.

401 "Though like a very giant in the promises you give,
In executing them you seem a dwarf diminutive;
Though you are quick to offer much, 'tis water in a sieve
Albeit when you ask of us you're clear and positive.

402 "A woman that is spirited you knead with passion's yeast
'Till she becomes with wolfish lust a wild and maddened beast,
The most ill-starrèd loup-garu who scurries to love's feast
Unsought, unmasked, in noisome dens, until her rage has ceased.

403 "Thus many women learn your arts and once they drink your potion
Grow so insane they take men on whene'er they get the notion,
It matters not how foul the man, they make the frenzied motion,
For always they worst bargains make who show Love most devotion.

404 "You ruin men of eloquence through love for quean and jade,
And dames of high repute bring low for clown and brawling blade;
You joyously blight all men's lives where'er your eyes are laid,
So let whoever has the will, your felonies upbraid.

405 "Your nature like the Devil's is, wherever dwells your wraith
There men are seized with palsy-shakes, and pale and sweat like death,
Grow dizzy, suffer endless pains, and fainting lose their breath
While they who heed your baseless creed grow sightless in its faith.

406 "You capture like the fowler when he sounds his call for game
And charms with art and sleight of voice wild creatures as if tame
Until they step inside his noose, when lo, it's kill and maim;
You slay the beings you cajole—Away, Away, for shame!"

407   "It happens every day to those who put their trust in you
      As once it happened to the mole when he desired to woo
      A painted frog who bore him off (a most ill-natured shrew);
      Reflect upon the story, for it has a teaching true.

408   "An observant mole possessed a hole down by the river bank
      But one fine day the water rose and made his dwelling dank,
      And when, at last, it reached his door—the mole in terror shrank
      When lo, Miss Frog accosted him (with some designing prank).

409   "'Sir Bright-eyed Lover,' thus the frog addressed the lonely mole,
      'Come, let me be your mistress, wife, or what will most console,
      And let me bear you on my back from this dark flooded hole,
      We'll live our lives and find our love on some dry, inland knoll.

410   "'Come, let us tie our legs together, lashing stump to stump—
      Good, now you're ready, spread your knees and clamber on my rump,
      For well you know that I can swim—I'll take a little jump
      And set you, in a moment, dry, within some weedy clump.'

411   "So well the mole was thus cajoled the beastie grew enchanted,
      Albeit in her heart Miss Frog had dark designs implanted,
      This mole let both his limbs be bound as they had covenanted:
      Her legs he caught, but not her thought (he took too much for granted).

412   "Miss Frog then turned her belly upmost, diving downwards yonder,
      But there the upper 'neath her crupper soon began to ponder
      How in all thunder, being under, he'd outlive his blunder
      Because his tether kept him nether where he soon must founder.

413   "Meanwhile it chanced a hungry kite was flying up the river
      In search of something récherché to stimulate his liver.
      He spied at once the loving pair, so, blessing God the Giver,
      He swooped and bore them to his nest, and ate them without quiver.

414   "'Tis even so with those, Sir Love, who taste your poison bane,
      Although your hunger is not cloyed by those whom you have slain.
      The yarn of love, the thread of life, when woven are the twain
      You twist their strands until they snap—but oh, with what sweet pain.

415 "When silly men and wanton women baste their skins together
     With such a wild incontinence you wet and welt their leather
     They care not for Jehovah's thunder bolts nor raging weather
     'Till Satan bears them in his claws to flaming regions nether.

416 "Both male and female you destroy in sinful acts perverse,
     Seducer and the one seduced alike endure your curse
     And perish like the frog and mole or find a fate still worse;
     You are the Fiend, but one disguised as mankind's loving nurse!

417 "For every evil in the world, and pestilence, and sin,
     With love's deceitful utterance and semblance false begin,
     Besides the speech of honeyed words which men unwary win,
     And covetings and wantonness and evil deeds akin.

418 "What though a man be good and true, when Love o'er him presides
     His heart grows false, his lying tongue his fellow men misguides.
     May God Almighty damn the breast where such a heart resides;
     May God Almighty tear his tongue out by its roots besides!

419 "No man of sense believes at once what other men declare
     Until he weighs the words he hears with grave and seemly care;
     It is not fitting for the good to flatter anywhere,
     But rather should their speech be true, and unafraid, and fair.

420 "You have a wolf's projecting fangs beneath your lamb's disguise,
     And once you fasten on a man you bear away the prize.
     You kill the things you love the most, you hide the truth with lies,
     Pretending weight and circumstances rest on your lanky thighs.

421 "But I am glad with all my heart I do not owe you aught
     Because you compound interest on every loan that's sought;
     With little bait unwary whales upon your lines are caught—
     Oh, I could tell more tales on you were I not so distraught.

422 "Yet if I did full many dames would show themselves my foes,
     While many giddy boys my words would boorishly oppose,
     Wherefore I will not tell the tenth of what I could disclose.
     Come, Love, be silent; let us cease; away, be on your toes!"

## Here He Speaks of the Reply Which Sir Love
## Gave to the Archpriest

423 Thereat Sir Love replied to me like some grave tempered squire,
"Archpriest, I beg of you, restrain this ill-occasioned ire,
And ne'er in jest or earnest rail against the heart's desire
Because a dash of water often damps a glowing fire.

424 "And through a spiteful word or two the greatest loves are lost—
Look how a little quarrel breeds a frightful holocaust,
How vassals lose their lord's support ere scarce a word is crossed,
But kind words blazon noble deeds like arms with gold embossed.

425 "Be moderate in all you do and never play the scoffer
Because the one whom you insult may never pardon proffer,
So make your mouth, with words of love, a never-emptied coffer.
Then, if you act as I advise, no girl can keep you off her.

426 "If up to now you haven't got the thing which made you ache
When women high and low you sought, your burning lust to slake,
Go blame nobody but yourself—'tis all your own mistake
Because you neither came to me nor sued them in my sake.

427 "You tried to be a master ere you learned the simplest arts,
But if you listen to my lectures, where all wisdom starts,
You'll get from me the sweet degree of Bachelor of Hearts
To gain your soul's desire or learn to traffic in love's marts.

428 "Howe'er it is not meet to waste on every girl your passion
Unless she corresponds to you in temperament and fashion;
That love is dangerous and vain which goads a man to dash on
Each chance amour with wanton hand—such injures purse and ration.

429 "If ever you should Ovid read, my poet and apostle,
You'll find he gives directions how to render women docile,
But I it was revealed to him the way to make them jostle
For I taught Pamphilus and Naso all their arts colossal.

430 "Now if you would a lady woo or trull of lower sort
You'll have to master all those tricks to which young swains resort
So that the dame herself will long to have you pay her court,
But first and foremost learn to choose the girl with whom you'd sport.

[68]

431 "Seek out a woman sensuous and beautiful and gay
      Who's neither dwarfish, stumpy, short, or built the other way,
      And if you can, avoid a wench of boorish, peasant clay
      Because love's subtleties are lost on women such as they.

432 "Be sure she's medium figured, then, and rather small of head,
      With hair a gleaming, yellow gold, not fiery henna red,
      With arched and parted eyebrows like a long and narrow thread,
      And wide across the cantles—that's the kind to bless a bed.

433 "Her eyes should glow like tinted jewels, lustrous in their hue
      With long, outcurving lashes, clean as grasses washed in dew;
      Her ears should be like little shells, close-set and not askew,
      And if her neck is graceful, she's a woman for the few.

434 "Her nostrils must be delicate, her teeth be small and white,
      Well-spaced and even, spotless, clean, and each with each unite.
      The lips that close her little mouth of scarlet must excite
      The stormy-tender kiss of love, for that is love's delight.

435 "Her little mouth should ever curve with love's voluptuous line;
      Her skin should not be hairy but so soft and white and fine
      You'll lust to have her when you see her naked and supine,
      For well I know her form will show her amorous design.

436 "Now when you send a go-between to take your lady's measure
      Be sure she's your relation or indebted to your treasure
      And not the lady's servant, kin, or confidant in leisure,
      Nor yet ill-mated lest her own soured nature spoil your pleasure.

437 "So strive to find as messenger some foul, abandoned fright,
      Accomplished in the trade of pimp, well-versed in love's delight,
      Then put her on your lady's trail and work her day and night—
      A kettle boils the hottest when the lid is kept on tight.

438 "If you're not blessed with such relations, hunt some bawdy trot
      Like those who haunt the churches yet who know each filthy spot.
      Their rosaries have beads like eggs, they're up to every plot,
      And for enchanting women's ears, old magics they have got.

439 "Those shrill sea-mews are scavengers who at a fishy smell
      Come clattering from garbage dumps where they are forced to dwell.
      What though they raise their heads to God, o'er carrion they yell—
      Oh how much sombre evil know these harlots, none can tell.

440   "Get one of those old trollops who are skilled at making drugs,
      Who act as midwives, patch up maids or charm a nurse's dugs,
      Or mix up dyes and strange cosmetics out of toads and slugs,
      Or blind young girls with evil eyes, or cheat with odd humbugs.

441   "Select, then, from that tribe accursed, some vile, black-hearted bawd
      Employed by nuns and monks and others sanctified by God.
      Such well deserve the shoes they wear in prowlings much abroad—
      There's not a maid these convent-trotters cannot win by fraud.

442   "And where these blessèd women are, there joy is unconfined;
      Few virgins need bewail their state with such promoters kind.
      'Tis well to win their loyalty with words and gifts combined
      Because the women they enchant become with passion blind.

443   "So when from all these saintly trulls you've picked your proper hag,
      Secure her loyalty with gifts, nor in your giving lag.
      Remember that a trader shrewd can sell a worthless nag
      While clothes repulsive oft are hid within a dainty bag.

444   "Suppose this bawd describes your lady a posteriori
      And mentions graceful members in her detailed inventory,
      Do ask her if her breasts are small, and if they are, why glory
      To hear the rest—such revelations make a gripping story.

445   "If she affirms her arm-pits sweat a lusty, wholesome smell,
      And says her legs are slender while her thighs and hips out-swell,
      With supple waist and saddle wide, with insteps high as well—
      Believe me, such a perfect woman has no parallel!

446   "Then if she's passionate in bed but modest while she's out,
      Don't miss the chance that God may send to try a little bout.
      This I advise, and Ovid, too, concurs, I have no doubt:
      First send your trot to clear her decks, then board her with a shout.

447   "Three things there are I do not dare to mention at this time
      Since they, like Holy Trinity, partake of the sublime;
      'Twere blasphemous to speak in vain, yet this I'll say in rhyme,
      'All women have a place where men can into heaven climb.'

448   "Take care your lady has no whiskers on her lip or chin,
      To Hell with such! for that is one unpardonable sin,
      But if your dame is small of hand and delicately thin,
      Inflame her passions all you can—then gallantly begin.

449   "Now when the bawd is through describing, ask her, heart to heart,
      If love will liven up your girl and make her nature tart,
      And if her saddle tree is cold enquire about that part,
      For though she's willing, you must ride her with the greatest art.

450   "Yet such a one is to be loved, for if you once caress her
      In love's forbidden pleasures, she's the pleasantest transgressor,
      So if you have a taste for her and hanker to possess her,
      Do all you can in word and deed that offers to impress her.

451   "Give her some pretty gem that will her sentiment enthrall,
      Or, if you do not want to give, or lack the wherewithal,
      Just promise things in princely state, but in the giving stall,
      And when she trusts you with her jewel—rob, and make a haul.

452   "Be never tired in serving her—love thrives on sacrifice,
      And in a noble cause like this the end is worth the price.
      Do not despair when she delays, love will for all suffice;
      The faithful through such penances at last win paradise.

453   "But thank her most profusely every time she's kind to you,
      And if she says that black is white, esteem her words as true
      And never argue though forthwith she swears that both are blue,
      Nor stubbornly prohibit anything she wants to do.

454   "Go press her for the thing you want until your prayers prevail,
      And then if God sends luck to you, by all the saints, don't fail!
      Nor let your modesty or shame unmake what should be male;
      Behold the day of threshing, man, be valiant with your flail!

455   "For when a woman finds her mate is something less than man
      She hisses through her teeth, 'Get out, I want some one who can!'
      Rip off your cassock then, bare skin will often ardor fan—
      A woman loathes a lot of clothes—put bundling under ban.

456   "In natures impotent reside timidity and fear,
      The lack of manly vigor, filth, and heart-sick failures drear.
      I tell you from this vice I've lost young men that had no peer
      Besides a lot of dames who move in fashion's lofty sphere.

## A Parable of Two Lazy Men Who
## Would Marry One Woman

457 "My meaning here will be more clear if I a tale relate
About two lazy gentlemen who with one dame would mate
And in their eagerness to have her could not bear to wait
Although their handsome persons might have warned them of their fate.

458 "For one had lately from the socket lost his better eye
Whereas the other, maimed and hoarse, could neither walk nor cry,
Yet each was jealous of the other—much did either try
To win the lady so that she with him alone might lie.

459 "The lady, on her side, proclaimed she was prepared to wed,
But only with the laziest (for him she'd hold her bed);
In this she spoke not from her heart but out of jest instead,
Whereat the cripple straightway quoth—these are the words he said—

460 " 'My lady, look no farther then, where laziness is sung
You'll hear my name, for once while I upon a ladder clung
I felt so tired I could not keep my feet upon the rung
And so I maimed this leg you see, as I was downward flung.

461 " 'Then furthermore, one summer's day while swimming down a stream
I got so hot and thirsty that my lips began to steam
But out of utter laziness I would not wet a seam
And thus I spoilt my voice—right now I cannot sing or scream.'

462 "No sooner had he ranted than the one-eyed swain upspoke,
'Why lady, as for being lazy, this man's just a joke,
But when it comes to first-class sloth—I'll say this if I choke,
Great God himself, compared to me, ain't such a lazy bloke!

463 " 'One sleety day I happened on a girl with passions hot
But just when luck was breaking fine for kissing or what not
There sweetly trickled from my nose a rivulet of snot—
Because I would not wipe for sloth I lost her on the spot.

464 " 'Another time I lay in bed while it was raining torrents
With one big roof-leak over me, and by the good Saint Laurence,
A stinging jet of water fell to my immense abhorrence
Straight in my eye the whole night long (to prove this I have warrants).

465 " 'Yet here again for laziness I would not budge an inch,
And though the water hurt like Hell, I lay and did not flinch
Until it washed my eyeball out—now lady, it's a cinch
That I'm the laziest of all, wherefore you're mine to clinch.'

466 " 'Between two such distinguished sluggards,' spoke the lady then,
'I can't decide; I think you've tied, but I can't wed two men.
So this I say to you, be off, and don't return again;
Who wants a sluggish mate? Not I, nor any dame I ken!'

467 "The moral to this tale, Messire, I beg you to remember
Because it shows how hateful sloth is to the female gender,
Since sloth can never passion fan into a glowing ember,
Hence, be not slothful anywhere—above all in your member.

468 "Once drag a woman into shame, she'll ne'er regain her state;
The only road for her is down, her only time 'too late!'
Whatever man would have her do, she does, his lust to sate,
For never was a man so vile but found a viler mate.

469 "Lo, who can read a woman's heart or prophesy her mind,
Or pierce the blackness of her wiles to see what's there designed;
Once fan a woman's lust to flame, to everything she's blind;
Her soul, her body, her good name, all will she leave behind.

470 "Just as a gambler who has lost in gaming all his riches
Will cast his modesty aside to stake his very breeches,
So when a woman hears the tune that's danced by bawdy bitches
She tingles like a tambourine and for love's movement itches.

471 "A weaver and a dancing girl, their toes are always wiggling
Since stepping on the loom and dancing keep their pedals jiggling;
A hot wench gives herself away by her perpetual giggling
And straightway shows she's in the throes of love's erotic niggling.

472 "A girl is like a garden which does constant ploughing need;
A maid's a mill that's built inside for stones to grind her meed;
And maid, and mill, and garden, all require of man his seed
So much that when a rest day comes the three are sad indeed.

473 "A garden spaded every night will yield a bumper crop;
A heaping hopper never caused a busy mill to stop;
A woman tightened where she's loose will never leak a drop;
And if you tend the three with care you'll likely be on top."

### A Very Edifying Tale Wherein Is Related All That Which Befell Sir Peter Pious, a Painter of Brittany

474 "I'll tell you what befell a man who would not watch his dame;
'Twill pay you well to give close heed lest you be served the same;
A famous Breton painter once, Sir Peter Pious, came
To wed a young and lusty girl whose passion was aflame.

475 "Yet hardly was he wed a month before the artist quoth,
'I must away to Flanders, love, but this upon my oath
I swear, I'll bring you back some gift.' His wife replied, 'I'm loath
To see you leave my bed and board; pray, sir, remember both.'

476 "Thereat Sir Peter Pious said, 'But first, my lady fair,
Do let me paint upon your skin a picture quaint and rare,
A picture that will keep you chaste when you behold it there.'
Said she, 'Go work your will on me, forsooth you see me bare.'

477 "Below her belly-button, then, he drew with famous skill
The image of the Lamb of God, and sketched it with a will,
But when he left he stayed two years his business to fulfill—
Now how could any girl be true with all that time to kill!

478 "Her loneliness was hardly equalled, nor was the longing feigned,
But paradise though lost was sequelled by paradise regained
Because she found a sprightly lad who rubbed her where she pained,
Yet rubbed the Lamb of God so hard that not a trace remained.

479 "Then came the news her painter man was coming home at last,
So straight the damsel called the lad who'd been her sole repast
And ordered him to paint on her another lamb full fast
Right on that very self-same spot the Lamb of God was cast.

480 "He wrought upon her mightily but drew a ram with horns,
Great prongs they were that sprouted out like sharp and piercing thorns
(One other detail, too, he made which every ram adorns);
'Twas scarcely done ere Pious entered, limping on his corns.

481 "Now when this poor long-truant husband stepped inside the house
A torrent of abusive words descended from his spouse,
But through this matrimonial welcome Pious smelt a mouse
Whereat he charged his faithful wife to doff her skirt and blouse.

482 " 'You wretch,' she cried, as she undressed, 'perhaps you think I'm tainted!
Well, look! here stand I naked, pure as any woman sainted.'
Alack-a-day he raised his eyes to see the lamb he'd painted
But when he saw that monstrous ram—Sir Peter Pious fainted.

483 "As he came to, that fearful view once more bemazed his eyes,
No lamb, thought he, could thus assume a grown up ram's disguise.
'Look here,' he said, 'my faithful wife, come tell, but without lies,
How came my little Lamb of God to grow to such a size?'

484 "Since women in such situations never lose their wits
She said, 'My lord, this mighty ram your two years' stay befits
For during all that time your lamb was grown by little bits;
Had you not stayed so long you'd find him still beneath my teats.'

485 "The moral lesson to this tale you'll find is clear as day—
Don't be a Peter Pious for some understudy gay;
Go entertain the girl you've got in love's peculiar way
But watch out lest another man comes hankering for play.

486 "Sir Peter Pious flushed the game, but after was unwilling
To hold the chase; perhaps he thought the exercise too grilling.
Another sportsman caught the scent and rode without a spilling
Until he clipped his quarry's tail and made a pleasant killing.

487 "The lady doubtless reasoned thus, 'This man I wed at first,
Beside my second gallant is a very babe, ill-nursed;
Since first is worst, then first be cursed, I'll take the better versed,
And while I durst, I'll slake his thirst and live in love immersed.'

488 "Now should you ever see a man conversing with a beauty,
No matter if the girl is his or not, make it your duty
To scrape acquaintance with him, don't adopt a manner snooty
But do him favors for her sake—'twill help you win your booty.

489 "A little money often helps to make a wondrous spree
For ne'er was woman born who would not jiggle for a fee.
If every man has got his price, each girl has two or three,
So be it much or be it little, give with gesture free."[6]

## Certain Examples of the Power Which Sir Money Possesses

490 "Much power, indeed, Sir Money has and much for him we dabble,
   He makes the dolt a man of worth and sets him o'er the rabble,
   He makes the lame leap up and run, he makes the deaf-mute babble;
   Why those who have no hands at all will after money scrabble!

491 "Suppose a man's an utter fool, a farmer or a boor,
   With money he becomes a sage, a knight with prestige sure,
   In fact the greater grows his wealth the greater his allure,
   While he not even owns himself who is in money poor.

492 "If you have money you can get the blessèd consolation
   Of worldly bliss, or from the Pope can gain a lofty station,
   Or purchase seats in Paradise and buy yourself salvation—
   Where wealth is great, there lies the state of beatification.

493 "I noticed over there in Rome where sanctities abound
   That every one to Money bowed and humbly kissed the ground,
   And paid him many honors with solemnities profound,
   Yes, homaged him upon their knees, as slaves a king surround.

494 "Sir Money makes Archbishops sleek, and Abbots fat, and Priors,
   With Bishops, Doctors, Patriarchs, and other saintly liars,
   Conferring highest dignities on superstitious Friars—
   His falsehoods sing with truth, his truths sing out in falsehood's choirs.

495 "He constitutes no end of clerks and causes ordinations,
   Lets monks with sisters celebrate religious fornications.
   By Money even dolts are passed in their examinations
   While learnèd men, if they are poor, are kicked out with impatience.

496 "Sir Money causes sentences and unjust dooms at court,
   He urges shysters for his sake to sue on false report
   With all the sundry other frauds to which they will resort,
   In short, for money, one condemned can cut his penance short.

497 "Sir Money breaks those mortal bonds that chain a man for life,
   He empties stocks and prisons grim with noisome vermin rife,
   But one who has no gold to give must wear the iron wife;
   All up and down throughout the world Sir Money causes strife.

498 "Myself have seen real miracles occur through Money's power
   As when a man condemned to die is freed within an hour
   Or when those innocent the gallows presently devour
   Or when a soul is prayed to heaven or damned in Hell to cower.

499 "Sir Money often confiscates a poor man's goods and lands,
His vines, his furniture, and all the things his toil commands.
The world has got the itch and scab of money on its hands;
When Money winks his golden eye, there justice stock-still stands.

500 "Sir Money makes a knight presumptuous from a village clown,
And out of peasant farmers chooses coronet and crown;
With Money anyone can strut in gilt and broidered gown
While all his neighbors kiss his hands and bow their bodies down.

501 "I've seen Sir Money's lordship in the growth of vast estates
With costly mansions high and fair, enclosed with painted gates,
With grounds wherein a towered house or castle dominates,
And there a horde before that lord of gold itself prostrates.

502 "Sir Money has a table set with rich exotic food
And he puts on the noblest clothes where threads of gold protrude;
He wears expensive jewels when he goes to parties lewd,
His steeds are noble and his trappings strange and many-hued.

503 "Now I have heard full many a monk in many a windy sermon
Inveigh against the power of gold and persons clad in ermine,
But I have seen those very same ecclesiastic vermin
Absolve a man if he has wealth, and his excuse determine.

504 "In public monks at Money bray as loud as rutting asses
But in their monasteries, ah, 'tis hid in cups and glasses,
For should there come a rainy day 'twill help them till it passes;
They have more hiding places than the daws in meadow grasses.

505 "Whenever pastors, clerks and monks who love to serve the Lord
Perceive a wealthy man is ready for the Jordan's ford,
They swoop upon his bed of death to snatch his jingling hoard
And he who grabs it throws the rest in monstrous disaccord.

506 "Although these godly ministers have vowed to take no cash,
They make themselves executors and after funerals dash
To cheat the heirs legitimate by tricks as vile as rash;
No matter what their treasures are, they act like beggar trash.

507 "Like crows about a rotting beast, these stinking vultures draw
Round dying men, and scarce the prayers have left the parson's craw
Before they pounce on what is left, and quarreling they caw,
'Withdraw your claw, he's mine to chaw, because, because it's law!'

508   "Well, every woman in the world and every dame of worth
     In riches finds her heart's delight, in money finds her mirth;
     I never yet a beauty saw rejoice in money's dearth—
     Where'er the greatest riches are dwell dames of highest birth.

509   "Sir Money is a famous judge and governor besides;
     He pleads as does a lawyer sharp, as councillor he guides,
     As sergeant bold and bailiff stout the province he bestrides,
     Indeed in every walk of life he powerfully presides.

510   "Above all, let me tell you this, do with it what you can,
     Throughout the world Sir Money is a most seditious man
     Who makes a courtesan a slave, a slave a courtesan,
     And for his love all crimes are done since this old earth began.

511   "All worldly ways and customs for Sir Money's humor change,
     His women, covetous of wealth, grow honey-mouthed and strange
     And in their greed for jewels from the path of honor range;
     I swear that money sickness is contagious as the mange.

512   "Sir Money breaks the strongest walls and topples wondrous towers,
     Yet in pursuit of misery both far and wide he scours
     For e'en the most abject of slaves he liberates and dowers
     But if that slave has naught to give, Sir Money him devours.

513   "Sir Money starts great enterprises both with ease and glee,
     So therefore towards your pander bawd be generous and free
     Since neither boxes big nor small withstand a golden key
     And I myself hate love affairs where stingy lovers be.

514   "Still, if you've naught to give your girl, not e'en the smallest toy,
     At least be generous with words and say what won't annoy;
     If you've no honey in your crock it must your speech alloy
     E'en merchants who observe this rule make profits to their joy.

515   "Perhaps your fingers have been trained at playing instruments,
     If so, when she comes near to you with sweetest voice commence
     Some old romantic roundelay of love's sweet innocence
     Or other talent exercise which will not cause offence.

516   "Yet if a single thing will not upon your dame prevail,
     Then many things together must her stubbornness assail.
     If she but once give ear to you your suit will never fail
     For soon her love will correspond to yours in equal scale.

517 "You cannot, with a feeble rope, expect to raise a ton
　　　Nor with the single shout 'giddap' get spavined plugs to run,
　　　Nor with a handspike budge a crag—great weights will yield to none
　　　Unless by wedges, inch by inch, the moving's slowly done.

518 "Show feats of strength or sleights of skill or deeds of derring-do,
　　　It makes no difference if she sees, she soon will hear the hue,
　　　Then be her breast an icy flint, 'twill surely melt for you,
　　　So weary not in your campaign 'till victories ensue.

519 "The man who hangs about a maid and thus his moments uses
　　　In spite of her will steal her heart 'till him at last she chooses
　　　E'en though the whole wide world for that the woman much accuses,
　　　She cannot help but long for him as over him she muses.

520 "The more a girl is sermonized, the more she is berated,
　　　The more she's flogged and bruised and whipped to get her lust abated,
　　　Just so much more she yearns for man, grows wild and aggravated
　　　And thinks she ne'er will see the day when all her passion's sated.

521 "Her mother dear most likely hopes by yammering the child,
　　　By proving oft how men are vile and maidens are defiled,
　　　To make her modest, decent, chaste, and tractable, and mild—
　　　But such are only spurs and goads which make a woman wild.

522 "Her mother ought to realize when she herself was young
　　　How her own mother likewise laid about her with her tongue,
　　　And how such harpings did no good but only roused and stung—
　　　She ought to learn from past experience daughters can't be wrung.

523 "There's not a woman born but has the mulish disposition
　　　To mutiny with vehemence at every prohibition;
　　　The very things that curb a man incite them to sedition,
　　　But just remove those same restrains—they're filled with inanition.

524 "All creatures, fiery spirited, with time are rendered tame;
　　　The mountain stag when hunted down is brought to such a frame
　　　The hunter finds that his fatigue has made him gentle game—
　　　A frisky lass that's ridden much will for that sport grow lame.

525 "For every single time by day love's bounty is exacted,
　　　A hundred times or more by night the drama is enacted,
　　　And in such functions Lady Venus' help can be extracted
　　　So that the passion of a man is pleasantly protracted.

[79]

526   "Now water's soft, but if it falls upon the hardest stone
      Its constant dripping wears away in it a spacious zone;
      A dolt by constant studying can learn to read alone;
      A woman fiddled day and night will sound a lower tone.

527   "Take care when you're in love with one you also don't devote
      Odd moments and attentions to some passing petticoat
      As sordid gallivantings vex a noble dame of note;
      One bitch is always ready for another bitch's throat."

*How Sir Love Instructed the Archpriest to Be Temperate, and*
*Above All to Refrain from Drinking Much Wine,*
*Both White and Red*[7]

528 "Be temperate and never taste intoxicating waters,
   Recall how God for drunkenness on Sodom sent His slaughters,
   And how for thirst Lot's wife turned back, and how to salt God wrought her
   And how her husband, being drunk, lay with his naughty daughters.[8]

529 "Through drinking wine a hermit lost his body and his soul
   Though never he had drunk before. The Devil filled his bowl
   And tempted him to drink, thereby exacting heavy toll.
   The story is so edifying you must hear the whole.

530 "There was a hermit, forty years or thereabout of age,
   Who served the Lord while dwelling in his desert hermitage
   And never did in all his life his thirst with wine assuage,
   But circumspectly lived in prayer and fasting like a sage.

531 "This put the Devil out because such sanctities annoy him
   And so he figured out a way whereby he might destroy him;
   He came to him with honeyed words which he bethought would cloy him,
   'God Save you, blessed monk,' he cried, in order to decoy him.

532 "The monk, astonished, answered him, 'Now by the Savior, just
   What sort of being are you, sir? Come, tell me quick, you must,
   For all the time I've worshipped God by kneeling in the dust
   I've never seen your likes about—hence in this cross I trust.'

533 "Beholding that, the fiend drew back, because the cross of Christ
   Such magic has, it smote him in the place where he was spliced,
   In spite of that the fiend returned and thus the monk enticed,
   I'll help you get that flesh and blood which Jesus sacrificed.'

534 " 'You see there's not the slightest doubt but that good wine will turn
   To genuine deific blood—in this I oft discern
   A sacrament miraculous since God doth there sojourn,
   So all you need's a little wine if you for Jesus yearn.'

535 " 'But,' quoth the hermit, 'I don't know what sort of thing is wine.'
   For that the Devil was prepared and handed him this line,
   'Look! See those merchants winding down the road from that incline?
   Ask them, they'll give you all you want, but hurry, for it's fine!'

536 "With that he made him run for it and when he brought it back
   He said, 'Come now, set down the jar and take a little smack,
   It really isn't hard to swallow once you get the knack—
   And then you'll bless my kind advice that put you on its track.'

537 "Forthwith the hermit seized the jar and took a mighty swig,
But since 'twas strong his head spun round just like a whirligig.
No sooner did the Devil see his wits were out of rig
Than on the monk he cast his spell and muttered his mumbledyjig.

538 " 'Now friend,' said he, 'you cannot tell the brightest day from night,
What time it is, nor if the world is spinning round all right,
So buy a rooster for he'll crow when day begins to white,
And also get a hen or two ('twill add to his delight).'

539 "Upon the Devil's bad advice he drank a daily booster,
Then once, when drunk, he saw his hens disporting with their rooster,
He watched the cock waylay a chick and saw how he seduced her,
And thought were he that lucky bird he likewise would have used her.

540 "While looking on he grew inflamed with concupiscent dreams
And since obscenity's a root which with all vileness teems
He soon was filled with pride and lust and homicidal schemes.
(This, bibbing wine will do to those who push it to extremes.)[9]

541 "He left his holy hermitage and raped a little girl,
Though vainly she while squirming did her screams to heaven hurl,
Then, fearing lest some accusations might about him whirl,
He strangled her and damned himself as Satan's proper churl.

542 "But there's a wise old proverb with a truth no man can doubt,
'Whatever's hid will come to light, and murder soon must out,'
So men suspected, here and there, that clergyman devout
And called upon him to explain his sacramental bout.

543 "Upon the rack they neatly stretched that eminent divine
'Till he confessed what happened 'neath the influence of wine,
That done, they next exalted him upon a gallows shrine
And let him hang, a warning for the evils of the vine.

544 "Excessive drinking shortens life and makes the vision faint;
It takes the vital force away if drunk without restraint;
It makes the members tremble and it gives the mind a taint;
Indeed, with every bottle comes another new complaint.

545 "But worst of all it fouls the breath by causing halitosis,[10]
And science yet has found no cure for such a diagnosis,
Besides, it burns the gut and wastes the liver with cirrhosis,
So, if you will succeed in love, take wine in smaller doses.

546 "Wine bibbers, sots, and drunken men grow quickly old and sterile
Resorting, then, to vileness base since they're no longer virile;
Such men get wasted, pale, and dry, and slender as a ferule;
They lose not only earthly joys but put their souls in peril.

547   "Strong wine is only harmless when it's sealed in kegs and crocks,
      For where it's cheap, there drinkers crowd in rough, unruly flocks
      To make more noise than grackle-clack or crowing fighting cocks
      While murders, brawls and bloody feuds are kindled by their shocks.

548   "Yet wine is quite well suited for its own peculiar uses,
      There's virtue in the moderate consumption of its juices,
      But when a person takes too much, the drink his judgment looses
      And all the evils in the world and follies it induces.

549   "So, therefore, flee this naughty wine—adopt a manner sprightly,
      And when you speak to ladies fair, talk pretty nonsense, lightly,
      As clever words and compliments for love are fitted rightly
      If, while you talk to girls, you sigh, and gaze at them contritely.

550   "Take care you do not speak too fast, yet by all means don't drawl;
      Be not with words incontinent nor let your gossip pall;
      Do not be stingy with a girl in anything at all
      But give her what you've promised, quick, before she starts to squall.

551   "No girl can comprehend a man if he should talk too fast
      But listening to a drawler speak, she's even worse harassed;
      All rapid chatterboxes should with maniacs wild be classed
      While windy droolers, worse than fools, deserve to be outcast.

552   "A stingy man can never hope to have a maid in haste
      For when she sees he's slow to give she will pretend she's chaste;
      The man who only promises is in her eyes disgraced,
      But if he keeps his word he'll find her geared to be embraced.

553   "In every single thing you do, in word as well as deed,
      Choose moderation; never from conventions old recede,
      But use in all things common sense—observe it like a creed,
      For without moderation, life would painful be indeed.

554   "Don't play with dice or find yourself in gambling games contending;
      As wealth by winning, worse is sinning than by money lending;
      A Jew lends three for four a year, but, given luck transcending,
      A man can double in a day by just a finger's bending.

555   "When gambling gets into the blood it utterly bewitches
      A man until upon the dice he hazards all his riches;
      Then sharpers get his shirt, his cash, and like as not his breeches;
      Or, if he does not lose, they scratch him next time when he itches.

556   "One Messer Roland notes in his exhaustive 'Book of Craps'[11]
      With scholarly precision, countless clever sharping traps,
      Since dice, although they eat no corn, to crops cause more mishaps
      Than all the sheep at Easter time which make in fields such gaps.

557   "Be not familiar with a tough, and from all fighting fly;
      Be not a mocker, saying things with double meaning sly,
      And do not boast about yourself because I prophesy
      Your nature will to what you say most loudly give the lie.

558   "Don't envy people; do not be a slanderous forswearer,
      And if a woman is discreet don't be a jealous terror;
      Don't nag and weary her to death unless she is in error
      Or covetously yearn to be of her estate a sharer.

559   "Above all, never, never praise a pretty girl before her
      As such laudations never fail to irritate and bore her;
      Of course she'll think you love that girl and hanker to explore her
      Which thought will put her in such rage you'll lose forevermore her.

560   "Praise her alone and she will grow more soft the more you give her
      And never will suspect your *flèche* was in another's quiver.
      Tell her she's fair although her form would make your body quiver
      For if you don't observe this rule there's naught can you deliver.

561   "Yet tell the truth when truth will pass, avoid too much deceit,
      And when you sport about with her, in talking be discreet;
      But should she speak of love, then be particularly sweet:
      The man who learns and holds his tongue will have her at his feet.

562   "Don't ogle her with others near, resort to mawkish cooing;
      Or ever make her secret signs, don't be your own undoing;
      As men who've done those things before will know there's
          something brewing—
      Ransack her all you want alone, but, publicly—no wooing!

563   "Be cleanly, neat, and temperate, be gentle as a dove,
      Yet like the peacock, gay and poised, as one from ranks above;
      Be sensible, not sullen, stern, nor rudely full of shove—
      Such cautions e'er should be observed by one who is in love.

564   "But let me tell you once again, beware while you are courting
      Your lady doesn't learn that you with others are consorting,
      For if she does, you'll be eclipsed, and all your plans for sporting,
      Like verses writ in water, ne'er will suffer twice reporting.

565   "Don't think because you have a horse accustomed to the bit,
      Your jade won't take it in her head to shy or buck or skit;
      If you dismount, her saddle may another rider fit
      And then you'll find some buckaroo where you intend to sit.

566 "Above all flatter her by swearing she's your one ideal,
But never speak about yourself as that's a danger real
Since many men have lost their dames through what they did reveal,
So, if she has been kind to you, tell no man how you feel.

567 "Then, if you keep her secret well, she'll grow surpassing kind.
(I too, when I spy close-mouthed men, show pleasure in my find,
But those who give their dames away, their prayers I never mind,
Indeed, I part them from the hearts with which they are entwined.)

568 "Just as your stomach and your paunch in private hold your meat
So should you keep a secret down, a much more ticklish feat.
Is it not Cato, Rome's old sage, who in his book does treat
Of secrecy as that one trait of every friend discreet?

569 "The bramble gives itself away by scratching with its thorn;
And hence, from garden, plot, and bed, it's flung away in scorn.
The toad-stool shows its button large most plainly every morn,
But silence, all times, everywhere, by noble hearts is borne.

570 "A spiteful tattler brings distress upon a countless host,
But though he injures other folks he hurts himself the most
Since women from his contact fly because they know he'll boast—
When people bury stiffs at night they do not want a ghost!

571 "Because a squeaky little mouse did with the larder tease
They say, 'A host of blackguard rats have eaten all the cheese!'
Or when a little secret's out, they cry, 'May Satan seize
Such filthy, spiteful, vicious, scoundrel slanderers as these!'

572 "Of those three things which you might ask a sportive girl to give,
You'll get the second if the first won't make you talkative,
And then if you are close with both, upon the third you'll live,
So do not make her give you up because your mouth's a sieve.

573 "Then if you conquer all those faults which I so oft attack
You'll find her front door open where she wouldn't show a crack;
Although she curses you today, she soon will call you back;
Trust me—your friend—but others watch, their words of malice smack.

574 "A great deal more on this I'd speak if I could here remain
But there are other lovers in the world I must sustain
Who fret as much at my delay as I fret for their pain;
If now, you're wise as I advise, go help some other swain."

[85]

575    I, Juan Ruiz, 'foresaid Archpriest of Hita, do object
That though for love both verse and song I never did neglect,
I still have found no paragon as you, Sir Love, expect,
Nor do I think such girls exist for all our sorry sect.

## How Sir Love Took Leave of the Archpriest and
## How Lady Venus Instructed Him

576    At last Sir Love bade me farewell and I went off to sleep
But when the morning came again I pondered how to keep
His full instructions, for in truth, I found his counsel deep,
So I decided, with his words, I should my being steep.

577    Yet I was puzzled, recollecting how my whole life long
Untiringly I courted dames, but though I wooed a throng,
And never gave a maid away and never bragged of wrong,
For some cursed reason my address and conquest ne'er were strong.

578    At that I did with bitter sighs upon my own heart turn
And angrily cried out to it, "Once more you shall sojourn
With one who seems in love with love, but it she wants to spurn
My heart, I know I'll never get the thing for which I burn."

579    My heart replied, "Do what you will, yet be not sad nor vexed
For if you don't succeed today, return and try the next;
It matters not although for years with love you've been perplexed,
Since girls surrender suddenly, and on the least pretext."

580    A fact approved this proverb states, and one with wisdom teeming,
"A day of toil avails a man more than a year of dreaming;"
I said goodbye to gloomy thoughts and morbid fruitless scheming,
And sought, and found, and loved a lady, beautiful and beaming.

581    Her wanton form was eloquent, her glances were inflaming
For she was jaunty, graceful, gay, and lief for lovers gaming,
Yet coy besides, with modesty her ardent nature taming,
Although her eyes were passionate—love's one desire proclaiming.

582    The noblest figure she possessed that ever I have known;
A widow rich she was yet scarce beyond her girlhood grown.[12]
Above the dames of Calatud she stood as on a throne;
My neighbor too, my life and death, for whom I lived alone.

583    The daughter of a wealthy don of high, distinguished birth,
She seldom left her father's house as 'fits a dame of worth,
So Venus' help I sought in sending messages of mirth,
Since Venus guides, from start to end, all amours on this earth.

584    She is our life, she is our death, this goddess we revere
Who wounds and slays or deeply lays love's stoutest pioneer;
In truth, she governs absolute this whole terrestrial sphere
And all men at her bidding act when she deigns to appear.

585  Thou holy Venus, bride of Love, our Savior-lord divine,
     Oh blessed lady to thy power thy slave doth here incline,
     For thou and Love, of all that live, the rulers are benign,
     Whence all men worship thee like God, and bend to thee and thine.

586  Kings, barons, counts, and churchly lords, with every creature less,
     Obey and fear thee as they do the Maker whom they bless,
     So grant thou then my heart's desire and spend me happiness,
     And be not obdurate nor yet thy charity repress.

587  No monstrous or stupendous thing it is of thee I ask,
     Albeit for my hands alone it is a mighty task;
     I can nowise begin nor end, if thou thy grace dost mask,
     But if thou wilt support my suit I shall in pleasure bask.

588  I'm hurt and wounded unto death, the shaft of love has hit me,
     And in my heart it's deeply hid, but custom won't permit me
     To show it, yet if it's ignored, the pain will never quit me,
     But, as I say, I dare not breathe the woman's name who smit me.

589  I suffer so my wound prevents all seeing and perceiving,
     While from it evils worse I fear my heart will be aggrieving,
     Yes, greater dangers still may come from which there's no reprieving,
     Nor is there chance of medicine my agony relieving.

590  In what direction shall I go so that I may not die?
     Unlucky me! What shall I do? I see no rescue nigh;
     I know my plaint is just, but still I cannot help but sigh
     As there is none that I can find on whom I might rely.

591  Yet inasmuch as many ills my guerison prevent
     I fain must seek as many cures, it seems, to my intent;
     Full often arts assuage a hurt or, sometimes worse, augment.
     As many live by art while others by those arts are spent—

592  Now if I should reveal my wound and tell how it arose
     Or should I say who wounded me, I could so much disclose
     That in my zeal for being healed I would my cure oppose—
     Through seeking comfort, often one his dearest hope o'erthrows.

593  But if I utterly conceal this wound and all its pain,
     And if I never ask for aid to get my health again,
     Perhaps some mortal sickness, then, will seize on me amain
     And I shall die the saddest death that mortal can sustain.

594 Perhaps 'twere better for a man to show his pain and grief
To some good friend or doctor who might give him some relief
By offering a medicine or word of counsel brief,
Else death and woe will surely hold his wretched heart in fief.

595 A hidden fire more hotly burns, its coals more fiercely glow
Than one whose brands upon the ground are scattered where they show;
I, therefore, think the wisest course would be to let men know—
Hence, Lady Venus, in thine hands I do my heart bestow.

596 There dwells a certain Lady Sloe within our neighborhood,
Surpassing all in wit and grace, yet tantalizing good,
She overcomes the stoutest hearts that e'er before her stood;
I tell the truth—a lover's truth—for mine's no breast of wood.

597 This lady took a poisoned dart and drove it through my breast;
It pierced my heart and now its barbs still there imbedded rest;
In vain I plucked with all my might at that unwelcome guest,
It stuck, and there it festers still, a painful, constant pest.

598 So far, in all the world there's none I have informed about it
Because her station is so high I know that all would flout it;
Indeed, her birth compared to mine, would give them grounds to scout it,
But though I dare not breathe my love, I cannot live without it.

599 With gifts and dowries wealthy men have sought to win her hand
But less respect she gives to them than to a grapevine strand.
Aristocrats may show disdain to all who 'neath them stand
While riches great and high estate ne'er speak with accents bland.

600 A girl may be a swineherd's daughter, yet if she grow rich
She'll have her pick of noblemen who for her money itch—
Well, if I cannot fairly get my lady without hitch
I'll work my will by villainy and into scheming pitch.

601 Because she's inaccessible, I hanker to possess her;
Because my love is steeped with fear I dare not now address her—
Oh, Lady Venus, thou alone canst amorously press her,
In thee I trust, without thine aid I never shall caress her.

602 One time, distraught by love, to her I some proposal mumbled
But in my hot-haste eagerness I got my prayer so jumbled
She only laughed at me to hear how bashfully I fumbled.
(Were we not dwelling neighbors close, I would not feel so humbled.)

[89]

603　Just as a man when he is stripped and stretched before a fire
　　　Can feel its torture hotter grow each step they thrust him nigher,
　　　So I, since she lives close to me, am burnt with worse desire—
　　　Oh, Lady Venus, snatch me from Love's incandescent pyre.

604　Oh, blessed goddess, thou dost see the gyves which lovers gird,
　　　Thou knowest all those yearnings great with which their hearts are stirred.
　　　Oh wilt thou give me no reply? Oh wilt thine ears be surd?
　　　Nay! gentle and indulgent lady, let my prayers be heard.

605　Dost thou not see my countenance with passion pale and sad?
　　　Pluck then this arrow from my heart, and let its anguish mad
　　　By woman's fondling hands be soothed until my soul is glad;
　　　Show me such comfort that I'd wish my wound were twice as bad.

606　What goddess of mankind could be so stubborn and austere,
　　　As, from her wounded worshipper, to hold her aid and cheer?
　　　With grief and sorrow I beseech thy help, my lady dear,
　　　Because long agony has made my sickness more severe.

607　My face is pale, my senses fail, my shrunken haunches creak;
　　　My strength is gone, mine eyes are wan, and sunken is my cheek;
　　　If thy help cometh not at once my members will grow weak!
　　　Quoth Lady Venus, "Courage, priest, in love let service speak.

608　"Sir Love, my lord and husband, offered good advice to you—
　　　For amorous emergencies he gave you counsel true,
　　　But since you were enraged with him he bade you brusque adieu,
　　　Yet if you heark I will myself instruct you what to do.[13]

609　"And if it chance that what I say's substantially the same
　　　As what my consort did to you short time ago proclaim,
　　　You may be doubly sure of it and from it dread no blame
　　　Since good advice when given twice deserves much greater fame.

610　"Now every girl that ogles much, or has a riggish smirk[14]
　　　You can accost and without shame get straightway down to work,
　　　Not one out of a thousand will your navel battles shirk
　　　Because their thoughts, engrossed on love's delights forever lurk.

611　"Go after such and never tire—love thrives on sacrifice,
　　　And in a noble cause like this the end is worth the price;
　　　Do not despair when she delays, 'tis love's way to entice—
　　　The faithful through such penances attain their paradise.

612 "This gospel Love taught Ovid from his academic bench,
        'No girl there is in all the world, proud dame or skittish wench,
        When into her you drive your spur that will not long to clench,
        For late or soon they'll offer you their burning breasts to quench.'

613 "Don't be abashed at any dame who gives an answer rude
        Because she soon will change her tune with steadfast servitude;
        What though her virtue's obdurate 'twill yield to homage shrewd—
        As water wears a cliff away, love undermines a prude.

614 "Bethink you if the first wild waves from off the roily deep
        Had terrified the mariner when storms to landward sweep
        He never would have launched his tub upon the billows steep;
        Well, never let a woman's tempest make you lose your sleep.

615 "An avaricious trade oft will obstinately feign
        That he'll not sell his merchandise except at monstrous gain,
        But let a persevering buyer haggle him amain
        With some third party's cheapening, he'll soon the goods obtain.

616 "By serving sweep your girl away on love's impetuous flood
        (A dog that licks repeatedly is doubtless lapping blood)
        For art and virile mastery lift weakness from the mud;
        With skill a hare might serve a mare as nobly as a stud.

617 "When men have cut the nether stone for some huge grinding mill
        With art the jack and tackle lift it from its quarry sill;
        A clever bawd with art and tact bends wantons to her will
        And women move all kinds of ways for one who has the skill.

618 "With art men break the hardest hearts or overthrow a city,
        Tear walls to pieces, topple towers and raze them without pity;
        With art men lift the gravest weights, iron bars and stone blocks gritty,
        With art men swear and give a flair to perjurations witty.

619 "With art the fishes of the sea are lifted out of nets,
        And men skim o'er the sea dry shod in rakish, swift cuvetts;
        With art and persevering much, a man great riches gets,
        Indeed, with art there is no thing that can withstand your sets.

620 "With art a poor man 'scapes his work and ne'er his fingers soils;
        With art a felon doomed to die the grisly hangman foils,
        And one who erstwhile wept as poor sings rich 'mid money's spoils;
        A walker diligent to serve more than a horseman toils.

[91]

621 "Those wrathful lords that have been roused into a passion fuming,
　　　Grow tractable when meekly rendered service unassuming;
　　　With homage mercenary knights forget their blustrous booming;
　　　Why should it then be hard to give a frisky lass a grooming?

622 "A parent fond can ne'er bequeath unto his son and heir
　　　His trade, profession, wisdom, skill, or learning quaint and rare
　　　Nor can a girl be handed down a full-fledged love affair;
　　　All such by labor are acquired—by yearning, tact, and care.

623 "Although your woman answers, 'No!' and has some mulish notion,
　　　Don't stop at that in serving her or cease to show devotion,
　　　But bathe your heart in love of her as if she were your ocean—
　　　A bell that's often jingled cannot help but get in motion.

624 "Thus service will at last o'ercome her spitefulest rebuff,
　　　Till she who hated you at first at last can't love enough.
　　　First, find the places she frequents, and though the roads be rough
　　　Particularly much and oft there let your buskins scuff.

625 "Then if you should espy the chance, say to her something funny
　　　With clever words and gestures smart, and glances sweet and sunny;
　　　I tell you jestings amorous and words that smack of honey
　　　Make love increase at faster rates than interest on money.

626 "Your mistress then will yearn for you in love's delicious sport
　　　Because a woman always likes an amiable consort,
　　　Whereas she holds a surly dolt as some unsightly wart,
　　　Since natures sad and rancorous, love's consummation thwart.

627 "Delight and pleasure give a man a wondrous sense of poise
　　　And make him steadfast in his quest for love's enchanted joys,
　　　But don't forget a languid sigh a woman oft decoys
　　　And let her not see through your talk—a flagrant lie annoys.

628 "By trifles insignificant a woman's love is turned;
　　　Perhaps some blemish in your make-up which she has discerned
　　　May cause her to detest you so you'll find your homage spurned—
　　　Such things ere now have injured you, and will, until you've learned.

629 "Now should, when you converse with her, the blessèd chance arise
　　　To nuzzle, rub, and fondle her—go to it careful-wise
　　　And pantingly entreat her for the thing which she denies,
　　　Then, if you're slack, she'll give you what will be a rude surprise.

630　"All women love bold, forward men who know just how it's done,
　　　Indeed, they'd rather have those men than money by the ton;
　　　Before such lads their arms grow lax, their legs too weak to run,
　　　Though while they yield themselves they feign they don't enjoy the fun.

631　" 'Tis therefore best to force your will a little on your dame
　　　Than have her say, 'Go to it!' like a woman versed in shame,
　　　Because with force, she'll feel, of course, she's not so much to blame.
　　　Why even with the animals the process is the same.

632　"All women act like horses when they're on the field of battle,
　　　They first begin to balk and shy at every little rattle,
　　　Then rear and plunge and snort about like wild unbroken cattle,
　　　But though they buck they never throw their riders from the saddle.

633　"No matter how a woman squeals when once she feels her master,
　　　Pay no attention—pity then would only bring disaster—
　　　The wound that is the sorest is the one that needs the plaster,
　　　And rough and ready poultices will heal her hurt the faster.

634　"Not modesty, but fear and shame, restrain her when she must,
　　　Hence, even while her passion rages, she pretends disgust.
　　　Why then hold off when both of you are burning up with lust?
　　　Go, live your little hour of life before you join the dust.

635　"But keep your secret with your lips as tight-shut as a clam
　　　And let none guess what sweet delights your moments with her cram;
　　　Don't let even your lady know what blows against you slam
　　　And if you're poor, hide your distress 'neath some convincing sham.

636　"A man who out of self respect, with smiling manner lifts
　　　A veil across his poverty and miserable shifts,
　　　Who grits his teeth, gulps down his fears, and ne'er a sigh uprifts,
　　　Does better than to show his want to men who give no gifts.

637　"By grace of God a clever lie will often better pay
　　　Than all the honest statements which a truthful man can say—
　　　To climb a mountain never take a straight, steep road, but stray
　　　Along some crooked, narrow path that doubles on its way.

638　"Whenever you encounter others whom your lady treats,
　　　Be courteous, and greet them well with sychophant deceits;
　　　The lady's heart will melt toward you when she perceives such feats;
　　　A servitor through flatteries with ease his mistress cheats.

[93]

639 "Where many firebrands make a fire and many stokers blow,
  Right there it hottest burns and there its coals most fiercely glow;
  So, likewise, where a multitude your talents to her show,
  Your suit will brightest shine and there her love will hottest grow.

640 "Now all the time your lady's friends proclaim your worth and merit,
  She'll be debating whether she should keep her heart or share it,
  Then, when you see her virtue falter, quickly snatch and snare it;
  Go, make a hot assault on her—she's yours if you will dare it.

641 "Unless one drives one's rowels in a sluggish lagging plug,
  He will not lose his laziness or e'er be worth a slug;
  The lamest ass will fleetly run when goads are in him dug,
  And so a man must prick a dame who hesitates to hug.

642 "Whenever men have any doubt what course they ought to choose,
  A little argument will quickly crystallize their views;
  When once a tower begins to rock, a mighty crash ensues,
  And when a woman hesitates, she's yours to win or lose.

643 "If by mischance she has some mother death is slowly eating,
  The hoary crone will see you get no chance at secret meeting,
  For age is envious of youth, and dotage e'er is bleating
  This counsel sad to maidens mad—'Love's hopes are sorry cheating.'

644 "Those surly and decrepit sluts know every crooked trick
  And often are the wary hens who guard a pretty chick
  Because they see instinctively a coming danger quick—
  Full well know they the fowler's blinds who've felt his arrows prick.

645 "Therefore avail yourself at once of some old go-between
  Who knows the crooked alley-ways of vice and love obscene,
  She understands what both you need, she knows just what you mean—
  Get such a trot Sir Love described and much upon her lean.

646 "But do not leap upon your lady at the first occasion,
  Nor frighten her away by some uproarious invasion;
  Without her will you'll never bring the child to your persuasion.
  First, therefore, sate the girl with bait, and then make your abrasion.

647 "And now I've said enough to you, I cannot longer stay,
  But when you see your girl begin to parley right away,
  You'll find a thousand methods then to lead the lass astray
  Since time and chance will set the scenes for love's improper play.

648   "What more in this connection, friend, is there for me to tell?
      Just persevere and be astute and you shall have your belle,
      But, as I say, I cannot stay—I've other hearts to quell."
      At that my Lady Venus went, and left me neath her spell.

649   A jongleur's music cannot cure, though it may soothe the ailing,
      Still, dolour oft increases at the sound of music's wailing;
      My Lady Venus gave advice but did not cure my failing—
      I've no help left but my own tongue, for amorous assailing.

650   My friends, I go in pain like one who must through oceans sweep,
      That is, I go to see my dame—May God my spirit keep!
      My mariner has flung me out upon the stormy deep
      Where, lonely, on its muddy waves, and without oars, I weep.

651   Ah wretched me! Shall I escape? I fear that I shall die!
      I see no port though everywhere I scan the sea-met sky.
      Now all my comfort, all my hope, must in that goddess lie
      Who forced me, lifeless, battered, dazed, to sail through passions high.

652   Right now I'll go to Lady Sloe to bare my heart complete
      Because she may on hearing me become surpassing sweet,
      At least I'll ease my breast and she will realize my heat,
      And then, perhaps a little word will fetch a wondrous treat.

## Here He Tells How the Archpriest Went to Speak to Lady Sloe

653     Ah God, how lovely Lady Sloe looked walking through the square!
      What swanlike neck and girlish waist, what grace beyond compare,
      What little mouth, what color fresh, and what outshining hair,
      Though mortally her beaming eyes shot missiles everywhere.[15]

654     But that was not the sort of place to hold a lover's talk,
      And, worst of all, a trembling fear did then my pleasure balk
      'Till I could neither raise my hands nor use my feet to walk
      But lost my strength, my senses, vim, and grew as pale as chalk.

655     I had composed a little speech I thought to say to her,
      But bashful fear of passers-by made all my memory blur
      So that I scarcely knew myself nor wot which way to stir,
      And then, alas, I found my will and words would not concur.

656     To talk to maids in public squares is clearly indiscreet;
      Once let the cat out of the bag, it's over all the street;
      A lover's parley should be screened as is a dark deceit,
      And where the place sequestered is, there intercourse is sweet.

657     However, this I said to her, "Dear Lady Sloe, my niece
      Sends from Toledo, where she lives, her greetings without cease,
      And begs, should time and place agree, that you would give her lease
      To come to see your grace and thus good fellowship increase.

658     "There is a wealthy maid, the daughter of a rich upstart,
      Whom all my kin would have me wed to be their money mart,
      But I declared I hated her, both part and counterpart,
      And I would only give myself to one who holds my heart."

659     I lowered then my voice and said, "I spoke only in jest
      Because so many in the square about us closely pressed."
      But when I saw that all were gone and not a soul did rest,
      I straight began to talk of love, and this the dame addressed:

660     "There's something I must say to you which I've held back," I quoth,
      "Because I feared the world might learn and much of that I'm loath;
      Let no one else share any word—on this let's take an oath—
      When lovers keep their secrets, then is faith assured to both.

661     "There's nothing else in all the world I love so much as you;
      Two years I've suffered since you came in my unhappy view;
      I love you more than I love God, yes, God, and all His crew!
      But none there is whom I dare trust to go between us two.

662 "With one sharp, passionate desire I come to speak my pain;
This love and need I have for you which torture me amain,
Give me no rest, no moment's peace, nor quit my breast nor brain;
Ah me! the longer you put off, the sooner I am slain.

663 "Yet much I fear you will not hear this frenzy I declare,
(And sooth it is a very fool who would to deaf mutes swear)
Believe me, oh! I love you so, I have no other care,
My love surpasses everything and throws me in despair!

664 "My lady, I am sore afraid to tell you more about
My love until I hear your answer to my prayer devout.
Come, let me know your will in this, and may our hearts speak out!"
Said she, "I hold your words as less than lees and dregs and grout!

665 "Why many Lady Sloes that way have been seduced by men,
For men are tricky and deceive the women of their ken.
Don't think that I am such a fool as to believe you when
You patter thus—seek some one else to lure into your den!"

666 I answered, "Now my pretty one, how angrily you sport;
As if all fingers were the same—lo, some are long, some short,
As if all men in word and deed were of the same report,
Or if a rabbit's changing fur made him another sort.

667 "Sometimes an upright man (as I) is rated as a wretch
Since oft the wicked on the just their reputations sketch,
'Till men impeccant and devout, their punishments must fetch,
Although the guilty knaves alone upon the rack should stretch.

668 "Let not another's naughtiness my innocence mis-mark,
But come, and let me more explain beneath yon archway dark
As I would not have all behold us in this open park;
There I may speak in private; here, the world's wide ears will hark."

669 Then, step by step, she softly came beneath the dim, arched hall,
Surpassing beautiful and proud, yet wondrous sweet withal;
Upon a little stone she sat and let her lashes fall,
While I once more began what I had hoped her heart would thrall.

670 "Oh blessed lady, hear me out, and have on me compassion
This little space, while I reveal a lover's pain and passion;
You think I only speak in some deceitful, foolish fashion
And fancy that I trouble you and argue out of ration.

671  "No, lady, by the living God, and by this earth, I swear
      That everything I said was true and open as the air—
      But you are colder than the snow upon the mountains bare,
      And young besides—scarce grown a girl—and much on this I 'ware.

672  "For had I spoke as youth to youth I know that you would think
      That all my words were foolishness or did of lewdness stink.
      Alas, what hope have silver years to purchase cheeks so pink;
      You'd rather romp at shuttle-cock than here in secret slink.

673  "And truly, 'tis a wondrous thing, when hearts are young and airy
      In life's enchanted summer time, for then the world is merry.
      But years bring wisdom, and our minds with later seasons vary,
      'Till what was wise in youth becomes for age a thing contrary.

674  "Much usage brings all things to light, howe'er obscure they lie.
      For art and usage make us wise to understand and try;
      But for this use, with skill allied, would human wisdom die;
      Men know their hearts and others' when with other men they vie.

675  "Farewell, but let us speak again, I ask, some other day
      Since now you will not take my word, or fate is in the way;
      Farewell, but let us speak again: those doubts that so affray
      I'll conquer, and you'll understand my grief from what I say.

676  "My lady, will you not concede this gracious little boon,
      And come alone to speak with me some other afternoon?
      I'll tell you what you want to know—I'll sing another tune;
      No more I dare, come without fear, but, blessed lady—soon!

677  "By talking, people penetrate each other's hidden hearts;
      By talking, you and I'll discover all our inmost parts.
      Farewell, but let us come again, for man with woman starts
      Through speech an understanding close which ends with lovers' arts.

678  "Although a man may never sink his teeth into a fruit,
      Its fragrance and its color still give pleasure to the brute;
      So, too, the sight and chatter of pert women constitute
      A wholesome pleasure, bringing men an ecstasy acute."

679  Thereat my Lady Sloe replied, that gentle, noble dame,
      "When speech is decent, surely 'tis an honor void of blame
      For women of whate'er degree an answer kind to frame
      To any one who speaks to them in honesty's good name.

680 "Wherefore I'll gladly talk with you or any other crank,
      And you may say whate'er you will, provided it's not rank;
      I, too, will answer as it suits with wit and humor frank,
      But, be advised, I'll tolerate no underhanded prank.

681 "But as to seeing you alone—I certainly will not!
      No woman ought to be alone with persons of your lot,
      As slander from such meetings comes—such would my honor blot;
      Talk if you must, before my friends—I'll bring a little knot."

682 "My lady, for this kindness great which you herewith concede
      I cannot give you thanks enough, nor are there thanks, indeed,
      In all the world for such a boon; great charities impede
      Due gratitude and cannot hence exact their wonted meed.

683 "Yet, ne'ertheless I trust to God that still a time will come
      When friendship true may prove itself by deeds that won't be dumb;
      I would say more, but fear to speak lest I grow burdensome."
      Said she, "Well, let's hear what it is, and do not look so glum."

684 "My lady, will you promise out of friendship's gentle grace,
      Since you and I alone are in this solitary place,
      That you will grant my heart's desire and yield me one embrace,
      Then, when that precious boon is granted, we shall part apace."

685 Said Lady Sloe, "It is a fact, and proven true, I wis
      That women give themselves away with nothing but a kiss
      Because there lies in lovers' lips such fierce consuming bliss;
      A girl is conquered once she yields a jewel such as this.

686 "So all I'll give you is my hand, and that's encased in leather,
      But quick! for mother comes from mass and I must hasten thether
      Lest she should guess my little wits are fickle as a feather,
      But time will come when you and I can softly talk together."

687 With that my lady went away and cut our conversations;
      Not since my birth have I e'er had such lucky constellations,
      Nor felt such bliss and happiness, nor made such jubilations;
      Indeed, I think great God Himself did prosper my flirtations.

688 Yet I was greatly worried since I could not ascertain
      If she were much inclined to prattle indiscretions vain,
      Because I feared our love affair might come to ears profane,
      And if I lost my love 'twould be a most surpassing pain.

[99]

689     She'll think that I've forgot unless I constantly pursue her,
And then she'll love another man and I'll be nothing to her.
Love dies at truce but thrives with use—no fact was ever truer;
No girl respects one who neglects, nor will she let him woo her.

690     Where you add wood, there grows the fire, of this there is no doubt,
But if you take the wood away, the fire as sure goes out;
So, likewise, love and sweet desire, with intercoursings sprout;
If you neglect a woman, she will your petition flout.

691     Upon me then from every side I saw new cares increase
Until my heart's contrary thoughts left me no moment's peace,
And yet I knew no art nor plan to make my worries cease.
But love, if one be constant, will from terrors bring release.

692     How often chance and circumstance with mighty force and power
Prevent a man from finishing the purpose of the hour
So that the world, now on the make, may soon abjectly cower,
But God (with man's intelligence) can any fate devour.

693     Good fortune helps only that man whom she intends to guide;
She thwarts the rest or does her best to turn their hopes aside,
Still, often she accompanies work, and will with toil abide
Though without God's consent, e'en that can no success betide.

694     Since naught can come to pass without the great Omnipotent,
I bade Him consummate my love as 'twere His sacrament.
You see, my conscience clearly showed 'twas His divine intent;
To all He did I said "amen" and gave my full consent.

695     Save God's, no other person's help did I desire for aid,
Since where the fire of love consumes all hearts are so unmade
That none keeps faith or loyalty or is at all afraid;
For woman's love is friendship lost, and blood by blood's betrayed.

696     A man of sense should make his choice when he has much reflected,
Then he, of course, should choose the best—let dangers be rejected;
Above all, she who pimps for him should never be suspected
As men of high repute through such have their ideals infected.

697     I found a convent-trotter, such as Love described before;
Among a choir of rotten sluts, I chose the smartest whore;
With luck—and God, my personal, divine solicitor—
I happened in a bedlam den of bitches by the score.

698    'Twas there I found this bawdy crone I needed for my pleasure,
       And she was wily, wise, and vile—a veritable treasure;
       For Pamphilus my lady Venus never heaped such measure
       As this old trull piled up for me to give me merry leisure.

699    A higgler was she, one of those who hawk and peddle gauds,
       And lure young wenches to their stews by baiting them with frauds;
       There are no peers in all the world to these old Trojan bawds,
       They give a maid the *coup de grâce* which every man applauds.

700    Now since these mongering old trollops go from house to house
       To tout and haggle off their trash, to gossip and to chouse,
       They're closer to a maiden than an unsuspected louse,
       And they can talk her out of what she hides beneath her blouse.

701    As soon as this most reverend slut stepped in my house I cried,
       "Oh welcome, Lady Mother mine! May good your call betide!
       Because in those sweet hands of yours my health and life abide,
       But if you do not haste to heal, my soul is crucified.

702    "Much praise sincere I've heard about the miracles you've wrought
       For those who come to seek you out with hearts by love distraught,
       And inasmuch as bliss divine arises when you're sought,
       I sent for you, my adoration by your virtues caught.

703    "As persons in confessional, let us in secret speak,
       And may you hear all that I say with kindly patience meek,
       But let none learn besides yourself what sufferings blench my cheek."
       The trot replied, "Come, tell me all—no word shall from me leak,

704    "So bare your heart in confidence, and freely talk with verve
       And I will do the best I can but ne'er from honor swerve—
       The worshipful career of pimp requires extreme reserve,
       And we conceal more love affairs than bawdy stews conserve.

705    "For when we hawk our trash about we learn what ladies tingle
       For gentlemen of your persuasion, and we help you mingle;
       We hook up many cheated wives who wish that they were single;
       I sell them off like tambourines, yet no one hears them jingle."

706    I said, "I love a woman more than e'er I loved a maid,
       And she, unless I greatly err, has equal love displayed,
       But up to now I kept it hid because I was afraid;
       Yes, even now, all things I fear, and greatly am dismayed.

707 "Because from very little things much gossip can arise,
      And, whether it is true or not, with stubbornness it dies;
      Some people out of envy start a tale that stupefies
      As almost nothing can prevent a wretch from telling lies.

708 "My sweetheart lives hard by my house, and I beseech you, go
      And talk awhile with her alone as shrewdly as you know;
      But keep our plot completely dark, let nothing overflow,
      And probe her thoroughly to find just how much love she'll show."

709 "I'll go right to your mistress' house," thereat exclaimed the trull,
      "And addle and bewitch her 'till I've dazed her silly skull,
      Then, all this suffering of yours I quickly can annul.
      But tell me who she is." Said I, " 'Tis Lady Sloe I'd cull."

710 "Well, wax is very stiff and hard," said she, "when it is cold,
      But knead it in your fingers and 'twill fit in any mould,
      Or with a little heat 'twill yield to every kind of fold;
      A woman can be softened, too, if she is well cajoled."[16]

711 She told me then that Lady Sloe was her most precious friend
      And so I said, "For God's sweet sake, may no mischance forfend!"
      "Ha, ha!" she cried, "She's had a man, I know that she will bend,
      There never was a riding mare such saddles would offend.

712 "Recall, Sir Friend, a saying with an old, familiar sound;
      'The grain that first goes to the mill is first to come out ground,'
      A message that is long delayed is likely to confound
      But never men of character succumb when griefs abound.

713 "Awake, my friend, don't fall asleep and lose the girl you're wooing—
      Another wants to marry her and sues for what you're suing,
      A man he is of noble blood, with wealth to him accruing,
      Unless you press your suit at once, he'll be your sure undoing.

714 "So far I've hurt him unbeknownst, and will his chances spoil
      Because, though rich, he's close, and I from misers e'er recoil—
      'Tis true he gave me furs and cloaks inwrought with golden foil,
      But while those gifts were fair enough they are not worth my toil.

715 "A present given on the spot, provided it is fine,
      Is lord of justice since it can court judgments undermine;
      It makes some men grow into power, it makes some men decline;
      At times it helps, at times it hurts, as chance may so design.

716  "This lady whom you're speaking of, is right beneath my thumb
      So if she will not budge for me she will for no man come;
      I know just how to handle her, I can her nature plumb;
      To please me, rather than herself, she will grow frolicsome.

717  "I shall not tell you any more, I've spoken all I should,
      But hark! this is my only trade, my only livelihood;
      There have been times I've come to grief and been misunderstood
      By gallants mean who didn't pay me well for doing good!

718  "Now if you help me out a bit and I am richly pleased,
      Not only this but other lasses ripe for being squeezed
      I'll use my magic arts upon, and when I have them seized,
      I'll crush their juice out through my sieve until your thirst's appeased."

719  "Dear Lady Mother," I replied, "I'll pay you large and grand;
      This house and all my property is yours at your command;
      Here is a handsome cloak of fur—come take it out of hand,
      And don't delay, but ere you go, this must you understand:

720  "Bend all your care and diligence upon this love affair,
      And labor so that some result you can at last declare,
      Then I'll requite you for your work with payment large and square,
      So lay your plans with cunning sure, and weigh your words with care.

721  "From first to last consider well the speeches you invent,
      And talk in such and such a way that you will not repent;
      Let honor, not dishonor, crown your efforts fraudulent,
      And if you are successful, I shall be munificent.

722  "A man of sense and understanding strongly I advise
      To hold his tongue when it won't hurt, and be reputed wise,
      Than gabble when it will not help, and have the world despise;
      Hence let sage words and silence shrewd mark all your enterprise."

723  My peddler left, and filled a sieve with silly knicks and knacks,
      Then down the street she rang her bell and hawked her trashy quacks,
      "Come buy my cloths and fancy stuffs, my needles, gems, and sacks!"
      At that cried Lady Sloe, "Come in, and open up your packs."

724  The trollop slipped into her house and said, "My Lady Daughter,
      Upon your blessed finger wear this gem of finest water,
      And, if you will not breathe a word (all curious she caught her),
      I'll tell you something." Thus she led her, step by step, to slaughter.

725 "My child, why do they coop you here?" again began the crone,
"You will grow old and ugly living by yourself alone,
Go where your beauty, so acclaimed, will set you on a throne;
'Twill not avail you here, within these sullen walls of stone.

726 "Now in this very town of ours there dwells a pleasant crowd
Of handsome and attractive youths, most gallant, gay, and proud,
So virtuous in manners that they seem by God endowed;
Nobody ever saw such men—a fact by all avowed.

727 "They all have been so kind to me and on my want took pity,
But best of all in noble birth, and most exceeding pretty,
Sir Melon of the Garden is, and furthermore most witty,
Indeed, in beauty, virtue, grace, he leads our little city.

728 "Of all the matchless youths this world has brought before my sight,
None is his peer in wealth and breeding, none is so upright;
Yet he can folly with the fools and give the wise delight,
And he is gentle as a lamb and ne'er has had a fight.

729 " 'Tis no small thing to argue down one minded like a mule,
Talk wisdom with the wise and yet make jestings with a fool
And still not show one's self a clown with all one's ridicule—
My tambourine has silly bells, yet 'tis my earning tool.

730 "There's no one like him in this town, of youths he is the cream;
He would not foul a sweetheart's name! he'd hold her in esteem.
Sure such a son as this must like his Heavenly Father seem,
Indeed, he is as like our Lord as bullocks in a team.

731 " 'Tis proved that many, many times the son is like the father,
But this resemblance 'twixt the two is no new thing but rather
An ancient fact, since men are known by what their hearts most bother,
And love and hate if they be great can't help but show their pother.

732 "This very upright mannered man who's lived a decent life,
I know would gladly marry you and have you for his wife;
Now if you want a paragon with every virtue rife,
You'll take this man I tell you of, without much wordy strife.

733 "Sometimes a long drawn-out harangue will little profit draw;
'A sermon long is always wrong,' with justice says the saw.
From small beginnings wondrous pleasures spring without a flaw;
From tiny wrongs can likewise come great griefs that overawe.

734 "Sometimes a clever, wee request, when most discreetly read,
 Works wonders in the way of deeds and pleasures of the bed.
 A tiny spark will often to a conflagration spread,
 While dangers great sometimes arise from phrases lightly said.

735 "I make a point with my ideals, like all unselfish dames
 Who sacrifice themselves in matching girls to higher frames,
 To broach, as though it were in jest, my upward, onward, aims,
 Until I learn their aspirations, dreams, and nobler claims.

736 "Wherefore, my lady, tell me now exactly how you feel
 And whether what I've said to you has made its due appeal;
 I'll keep in secret what you say, your choice I will conceal,
 So speak whate'er your will, nor fear that I shall aught reveal."

737 The lady answered with restraint, and cleverly as well,
 "My dear good woman, what on earth is all this tale you tell?
 Who is this man you praise so much? What does his coffers swell?
 I might consider what you say if it be nothing fell."

738 To that the convent-trotter cried, "My Lady Daughter, who?
 Why who else could it be but one whom God has brought to you;
 A most accomplished man that lives on your same avenue,
 Sir Melon of the Garden, girl—be glad to have him woo.

739 "Believe me, Lady Daughter, all your suitors, good and bad,
 Amount to nothing when compared to this surpassing lad.
 I vow when you were born that God some lucky shuffle had,
 And won for you this very man, to make your bodies glad."

740 Then Lady Sloe replied to her, "Oh stop your silly preaching,
 I know your gibble-gabble tongue has some deceitful teaching,
 For many times in days gone by your man has come beseeching.
 But neither he nor you will get the thing for which you're reaching.

741 "The woman who believes the lies you whisper in her ears,
 Or takes in all the shamming vows of lovers that she hears,
 Will wring her hands and beat her breast in grief and rage and fears;
 Oh bitter water has the girl who bathes her face in tears.

742 "Stop your solicitations for I've other cares to face;
 Some men have robbed my property and trespassed on my place.
 This is no time to worry me with your seductions base;
 This is no time to lay the plans to bring down my disgrace."

743 "Now by my faith!" the crone rejoined, "no wonder you are harried
Worse than a cow, it's all because men see you are not married,
And therefore take advantages a husband might have parried;
You'd better get this man before you find too long you've tarried.

744 "Because he will preserve you with his stalwart arm courageous
From lawsuits, insults, robberies, and violence outrageous—
Why I recall a doughty knave who even now engages
In plans to drive you from your home and all your heritages.

745 "Beware these plots, my Lady Sloe! Oh greatly do beware,
Lest there befall you speedily a similar affair
As happened to the bustard when a swallow tried to share
With her just such inspired advice as I right now declare."

# The Fable of the Bustard and the Swallow

746   "A very clever fowler once went to a fertile field
      To sow the hemp with which he made, when he had reaped his yield,
      The bustard traps and ropes and nets he could so nimbly wield;
      Right at that time a bustard plump upon his hemp grounds kneeled.

747   "Some turtle doves and sparrows too were there but most of all
      The bustard was in danger, so a swallow loud did call,
      'Eat all the hempseed that you see—it's deadly though it's small,
      Because from it they make the snares which bring about your fall.'

748   "The bird, however, laughed at her and held her words in scorn,
      And bade her go because her counsel seemed of wisdom shorn.
      She thought the hemp was merely sowed as farmers sow their corn,
      Nor realized how nets and cords would of the hemp be born.

749   "Again unto the bustard bird the kindly swallow shouted
      To eat the hemp no matter even though the shoots had sprouted
      Because whoever spread the hemp, it ought not to be doubted,
      Had planted it for her undoing, though the fact was flouted.

750   "The bustard said to her adviser, 'Crazy, senseless fool!
      Your constant chitter-chattering brings only ridicule,
      And I won't have a bit of it—Go, driveller, with your drool!
      Leave me in peace, here in this meadow, beautiful and cool.'

751   "At that the swallow flew away to where she had her nest
      Hard by the clever fowler's house, well-built on a crest,
      And since she was a singer sweet and warbler of the best,
      She pleased that early-rising man by rousing him from rest.

752   "The hemp was cut, the snares were made; with his equipment bound,
      The fowler went to hunt for birds on his accustomed round;
      He caught the bustard soon and brought her back to his compound,
      Whereat the swallow cried, 'Ah ha, not hemp but hurt you've found!'

753   "The arbalasters plucked the plumes that grew upon her wings
      And never left a single one except some hairy things.
      She would not follow good advice—for such the kettle sings—
      Beware of your harassers, lady, trouble to them clings.

754 "I tell you many rascals now are hatching up a plot
       Whereby they hope to rob and ruin everything you've got,
       While others say they'll prosecute and sue you on the spot,
       Thus, like the bustard, you'll be stripped and left uncared to rot.

755 "Sir Melon would protect you from their countless suits and cheats,
       Because he has been educated in the law's deceits;
       He will defend, and run to help whoever him entreats;
       No man can guard you as he can or work such mighty feats."

756 To other shrewd, enticing lures my aged bitch gave birth;
       "When 'neath this portal sat the man who late was of this earth,
       He brought you prestige, and your home was bright and gay with mirth,
       But where there is no master there the house has little worth.

757 "Yet here while young you mope and linger in your widowed state,
       A lonely little turtle-dove, without a happy mate,
       You'll shrivel and you'll yellow and you'll wither if you wait;
       Wherever women live alone, there worries breed, and hate.

758 "God's blessing lies upon the house that's governed by a man;
       There happiness forever lives with all her joyous clan,
       So take a gallant lover who will pleasures for you plan—
       You'll find a wondrous change in you within a little span."

759 At that the lady answered her, "But I can hardly marry
       Because the year has not expired which widows ought to tarry;
       A full long year a modest girl should every suitor parry,
       Since mourning does to marrying this prohibition carry.

760 "So if I married him before my year, I'd be disgraced;
       Besides I'd break the old established custom on us placed,
       And I'd not have my second husband's honor on me based,
       Which knowing, I could never bear by him to be embraced."

761 "Why daughter, dear," exclaimed the slut, "that's practically passed,
       So take this man for your new spouse; don't think about the last.
       Let's go to him and talk to him, let's make this wedding fast—
       Believe me, kindly were the fates that have your luck amassed!

762 "What profit is it now to wear those ugly weeds of black?
       Why slink about like one ashamed with woe upon your back?
       My lady, cast your grief away; let mourning go to wrack!
       The swallow's counsel never did of better wisdom smack.

763 "To put on sack-cloth for the dead and frieze for those who sleep
May show that persons due respect for their departed keep.
But men should little mourning wear and dames should little weep,
Since all would have their sorrows scarce and joys both vast and deep."

764 But Lady Sloe made answer then, "Be silent! I'd not dare
To do what you and he would have—you really must forbear.
Don't press me any more today with your cajoling prayer,
Nor ask so much and all at once in this unlooked affair.

765 " 'Till now I never thought I'd care to take another mate
Although a hundred men or more, you know, upon me wait;
But now, your arguments, I swear, my judgment alienate
And almost make me want to change this quiet, blessed state.

[Here six quatrains are missing from the manuscript, the sub-
stance of which is as follows: The lady hesitating to change her
widowed condition for fear of worse, illustrates her sentiments
by a fable. A wolf, provided with bacon to eat, was advised by
altruistic friends to change his happy state for that of missionary
to other animals. Dressed as a priest the wolf sets out but hears
someone sneeze. As sneezing is an evil omen, the wolf hesitates.
Here Juan Ruiz takes up the story.]

766 "The wolf sat down to ponder over what should best be done
When suddenly some valiant rams came charging on the run.
They smote him down, they gored his breast, and round and round he spun.
Then all took to their heels as if they were a single one.

767 "Much time had passed, when stunned and dazed, the wounded wolf arose
And cried, 'The Devil sent me warning through another's nose;
It was the best of auguries and did God's will disclose.
Well, no more appetite have I for bacon or for blows.'

768 "Therefore he left that grassy plain and ran as fast he could,
Until within a small ravine, secluded in a wood,
He saw some kids a gambolling, while goats all round them stood.
'Now by my faith!' said he, 'this sneeze may augur something good!'

769 "But when that flock beheld the wolf, although they all were scared,
A solemn, bearded goat came forth, with welcome speech prepared,
'Our lord and guardian most esteemed,' the tactful wight declared,
'This joy as seeing you again is by your servants shared.

770 " 'These four of us the honor have most happy to invite you
To grace this festival of ours which surely will delight you;
Come, say a mass for us and we with viands shall requite you;
Yea, sing it, lord, for surely God did hither expedite you.

771 " 'Here you can change your cloak six times with solemn noise of bells,
(And without any fear of dogs or shepherd sentinels)
So if you'll sing with mighty voice, we'll answer you with yells,
And sacrifice our kids to you, well cooked savoury smells.'

772 "The foolish wolf believed their words and raised a hullabaloo,
Whereat the herd of bleating goats their hub-bub added too
Until some shepherds heard afar that most melodious hue
And came with staves and mastiff dogs to hold an interview.

773 "The wolf did not his going stay, but scarce had he departed
Than all those shepherds and their dogs surrounded him, and darted
Both sticks and stones against his pate until it throbbed and smarted.
Cried he, 'It looks as if in Hell I'll end that mass I started!'

774 "Yet finally he got away, and by a water mill
He found a sow with many piglets wallowing in swill.
'Aha!' said he, 'a bit of luck is sticking to me still;
My splendid augury today has something to fulfill!'

775 "The wolf with courteous words addressed that sweet, maternal sow,
'God send you, lady mother, peace! I've come to you just now
To ask how you and all your darlings fare beneath this bough;
I'm at your service, madam, if you do as I avow.'

776 "The sow that all the while had lain beneath a willow tree,
Upspoke as follows to the wolf, 'Sir Abbot, 'tis my plea
That you with your own hands baptize my precious piglets, wee,
So that they may true Christians be, and die in sanctity.

777 " 'Then after you have consummated that religious rite
In thanks and gratitude to you I promise to invite
Your Grace to have your heart's desire upon each proselyte,
And eat them all beneath this shade, to your divine delight.'

778 "The wolf stooped down beneath those willow trees to snatch a pig
Which underneath the sow was taking his diurnal swig,
When suddenly the sow gave him a thumping buffet big
That sent him in the mill race flying like a whirligig.

779   "The wolf was carried down the race and sucked beneath the wheel,
      Whence he emerged as bruised and hurt as you might think he'd feel;
      A wondrous foolish thing it was for him to try to steal,
      Because it brought him dangers great and made him lose his meal.

780   "A prudent man should never wish to try a risky task,
      Nor underestimate the thing which his ambitions ask,
      Nor look at what belongs to him with some disdainful mask,
      But rather take what God provides and in His favor bask.

781   "Some men content themselves at home with one or two sardines,
      But when they eat with others, then their appetite o'erweens,
      And they at mutton sniff and ask for fish of varied sheens,
      Or say they'll eat no bacon save it's cooked with squab and greens.

      [Here again there is a hiatus in which thirty-two quatrains are
      missing. In order to make Sir Melon more sensitive to Trota's
      services, and thereby receive a greater reward for her successful
      pandering at the end, the old bawd tells Sir Melon that Lady
      Sloe's parents have decided to marry her off to some one else.]

782   "So now, my son, I think the wisest course you should pursue
      Is to forget this love affair which thus has gone askew;
      'Tis unwise anyway to yearn for one you cannot woo,
      So strive instead to bring to pass those things which you can do."

783   "Alas with what ill-starred reverse is this you come to me?
      What evil and outrageous news is this you make so free?
      Oh damned love-butcher! Bawdy hag! Why bring you this decree?
      You have not done your promised good, you've wrought but injury!

784   "You old toot-whistler, broken whore, may bad luck curse your days!
      Because you cozen every one with clumsy, botched essays.
      By lyings, flattering deceits faked blames and fawning ways,
      You make a fool believe your frauds are truths that none gainsays.

785   "Ah how my members all begin to tremble and to quake,
      My force and strength now melt away, my thoughts their brain forsake,
      My health and life are failing fast, my mind begins to break,
      And all is lost since all I did upon a vain hope stake.

786   "Ah frustrate, anguished heart of mine, what blows are these you give?
      Why do you batter so against the house in which you live?
      Why must you pour your love in one who holds it like a sieve?
      Ah heart, for such a crime you'll be a harried fugitive.

[111]

787   "Yea, heart, why did you let yourself be captured by a dame
Who has forgotten you ere now, who knows no more your name?
Yourself you put in prison, for your sighs you are to blame,
Well now, oh heart, you'll suffer scorn, oblivion and shame.

788   "Oh eyes, unhappy eyes of mine, why did you cast your glances
Upon a girl who would not deign to smile on your advances?
Oh eyes that would on beauty look, to lose yourselves in trances,
Unhappy eyes, now grieve and die with pain from love's mischances!

789   "Oh hapless and unlucky tongue, why did you wish to speak?
Why did you talk, why did you utter clever things that pique
To entertain a woman who would hardly turn her cheek?
Oh wretched little member, now in agony you'll squeak!

790   "Oh faithless and abandoned woman, traitorous at heart!
No fear, no shame, no self-restraint, nor modest counterpart
Can make your false loves constant when your fickle whimseys start;
Oh may you scream and rage with pain when down in Hell you smart!

791   "Well, since the woman that I love some other man has married,
I hold this world's existence naught; with life too long I've tarried.
This news is worse than death to me, and since my hope's miscarried,
And I can't have her, give me death, as I to death am harried!"

792   My bawd replied, "Poor fool, how now? Why do you so complain
Since by this vain, vehement grief you'll surely nothing gain?
Come, mix your sorrows up with sense, and all these sighs restrain;
Dry up your tears and let us plot upon a new campaign.

793   "Necessity the mother is of every great invention,
And one can set an ill aside by foresight and attention;
Perhaps great diligence will here be worthy of its mention,
As God and good sense sometimes calm a preordained dissention."

794   Said I, "What art, what industry, what sense or cunning slight
Will heal so grievous a wound which sorrow did excite?
Why, since they give a husband to the girl tomorrow night,
All hope is lost and I'm undone! I am abandoned quite!

795   "Until her husband populates the city of the dead
She never will lie down with me in love's adulterous bed.
Now all my grief has come to naught, my plans have all missped;
All that I see is injury and misery widespread."

796   The dear old bitch then answered me, "In but a moment's space
      Great pains are cured and discontents to care-free hearts give place,
      As when the heavy rains are gone and winds spring up apace,
      And clouds begin to break and show the sun's irradiant face.

797   "Why, after grievous sickness comes new lease of health and life,
      And many peaceful pleasures follow hours of storm and strife;
      Believe me, friend, good comfort take, for though she's not your wife,
      Almost within your reach is love, and all its pleasure rife.

798   "This Lady Sloe is surely yours—she'll do my least command;
      By no means does she want to marry any in this land
      For all her passionate desires in your possession stand;
      You think you love her most, but lo, her love does more expand."

799   "My venerable Lady Mother, what is this you say?
      In truth you act like mothers, when their brats begin to bray,
      Who tell them sweet, cajoling things to get them back to play;
      Come now, you swear this lady's mine exactly the same way?

800   "Yea, even so you do to me, good mother, that by chance
      I may forsake my discontent, my grief and sufferance,
      And comfort take, and find delight in pleasure's wide expanse;
      Is it not so? Do you speak true, or spin some sham romance?"

801   "What happens to the hunted bird," said she, "befalls the lover,
      For let the fowl escape the hawk that fiercely swoops above her,
      And she will fear each place conceals a hunter under cover;
      She'll live in dread that enemies about her ever hover.

802   "Believe that I am speaking truth, and you will find it so.
      If you yourself spoke truth in saying you loved Lady Sloe,
      Rejoice, for truly she confessed she loved you long ago;
      Now then, abandon all this grief and outward sign of woe.

803   "The start is oft unlike the end, and your beginning grim
      May end so that the cup you drink will yet with pleasures brim;
      No man can paint the destiny the fates reserve for him;
      No other one but God can peer into the future dim.

804   "A tiny, little accident upsets great enterprises,
      And one by growing faint of heart his valor jeopardizes;
      But earnest work can consummate the ends which hope devises,
      And often riches mountain high by toil one realizes.

[113]

805   "All that we long and labor for, our travail and our hope,
      Rest in the balance fortune holds and lie beyond our scope.
      Men think that lucky starts must e'er to good conclusions slope,
      But many times a goal is won though pauses with it cope."

806   "But surely, mother, can't you guess or somehow ascertain
      If she has sincere love for me, or is for loving fain?
      You know, whoever is in love can't help but make it plain
      Through actions, blushings, speeches, looks, or langorous sighs of pain."

807   "My friend," then quoth the crone, "I see in all the lady's actions
      That she's infatuate and yearns for love's sharp satisfactions,
      Because I've looked at her whene'er I spoke of your attractions,
      And saw her pale and trembling sink in love's profound distractions.

808   "I oft pretend a weariness to talk of you, but then
      She will not let me rest but pecks me like a wren,
      And when I feign I have forgot, she starts me o'er again
      And hangs upon my every word—ay, man, she's yours, I ken.

809   "She throws her arms about my neck, and hours long we two
      Abide, and out of lovers' nonsense make a much ado;
      We talk of nothing all day long but you and you and you,
      Unless somebody comes, and then we prate about the view.

810   "Why every time she calls your name it trembles on her lips
      And suddenly her countenance from rose to ashen slips,
      While in her breast her little heart with frantic tumult skips,
      And her cold fingers squeeze my hand and dew from off them drips.

811   "As often as I mention you she gazes with such wonder
      You'd think my words were oracles all fraught with awesome thunder;
      The poor dear sighs with brimming eyes and stares as if I'd stunned her,
      So when I tell you she's in love, I know I make no blunder.[17]

812   "In many, many other things her love is plain to see,
      Besides she does conceal it not but lets it open be.
      If she won't drop into your lap, I'll shake her parent tree;
      I'll bend her mother, Lady Branch, 'till she comes down to me."

813   I cried, "Angelic Lady Mother, blest and merry saint!
      I feel much better at your words, my love is no more faint,
      Since by your hand divine I'll get from her love's pleasures quaint;
      In God's name, go! Seduce her soon, and stand for no constraint!

814   "Recall how often tardiness has scotched a noble cause
     Whereas a bold and clever stroke has given angels pause.
     Continue with this splendid work, and finish with applause,
     'Twere infamous to fail with her almost within our claws!"

815   "Ah yes, my friend, she's yours; but think, 'twas I who made her ripe;
     Remember 'tis on my account she dances when I pipe—
     Now, save this little cloak, you've been as stingy as a snipe,
     Why surely one who wants a feast would not at paying gripe.

816   "We humans sometimes do not do the things we say we will,
     And possibly our promises we dally to fulfill;
     We're oft immense at ordering but dwarfish with the bill—
     Right now myself, for empty words, am toiling for you still."

817   "Good mother, never fear that I could have a heart so base
     As to deceive the meanest member of the human race!
     Why that would be a mortal sin! I'd fall from heaven's grace,
     And God Himself on judgment day in shame would hide His face!

818   "It seems when two established friends in honor have concurred,
     There is no better guarantee than just their spoken word.
     Had you or I in this compact from upright dealing stirred,
     Then only some suspicion of dishonor might be heard."

819   "Your sentiments are noble but—kind words no biscuits butter,
     And I," said she, "share that same fear my kindred in the gutter
     Have had for men of noble birth, or for a rich, proud strutter,
     Since poor folk scatheless are despoiled, if scarce a word they utter.

820   "Tell me what right a poor old woman has that can't be wrested?
     What chance have the unfortunate, what plea that can't be bested?
     The rich can break them, and the proud have e'er the weak molested,
     And held the wretched in contempt, like rotten fish detested.

821   "On every hand go faithlessness, stupidity and hate;
     Mean trickeries conceal them all, both infamous and great,
     Nor can one's luck avail against calamities of fate
     Which roil the sea of life with storms or make its winds abate.

822   "I set the things you promise me to the account of chance,
     But look, what I have promised you already pleasure grants;
     Right now, besides, I have a plan which will your cause advance—
     I'll wheedle her into my house—there you can hold séance.

823 "If by a streak of luck I bring you two alone together,
    I pray you, show yourself a bird of gallant noble feather;
    Don't rush upon her like a bull that strains against his tether
    But win her heart with gentleness, and you shall lay her nether."

824 Forthwith unto my lady's house this priceless strumpet hied
    And called, "Is anybody home?" "Who's there?" the mother cried.
    "Oh Lady Branch, it's poor old me," the cunning slut replied,
    "Yes poor, afflicted, suffering me, the fates have sorely tried."

825 "Why my good woman!" Lady Branch exclaimed, "what's all this chatter?"
    "What is it, lady? Can it be you haven't heard the matter?
    Some evil tongue, some lumbering oaf, has raised a hue and clatter
    And lied so vilely it did near my reputation shatter.

826 "I'm hunted down and harried worse than any mountain stag,
    Yes, as the Devil seeks the rich, they hunt this poor old hag.
    A ring is stole I meant to give your daughter, and a bag
    Of doubloons—help me, lady, go and seek the guilty wag!"

827 No sooner Lady Branch had heard her sounding off her trumpet,
    Than straight she left her house and child, and off she set to stump it,
    Whereat my trotter changed her tune and thus began to mump it,
    (But first she told my lady this, as well became the strumpet).

828 "I hope to God the Devil rides your hallion of a mother,
    For on account of her no man can see you as a lover;
    Well now, sweet girl and daughter dear, how goes one thing and another?
    You look as plump and pretty as a partridge under cover."

829 My sweetheart asked her, "Tell me, mother, tell me news of him!"
    The crone replied, "What news know I except that he is trim,
    And pretty too, a gallant knave, so graceful, tall and slim,
    And cocky as a rooster which has passed a winter grim.[18]

830 "Just as the bright flames give away a hot and raging fire,
    No lover passionate can hide his inmost heart's desire.
    I know how much you love this gallant whom you so admire,
    Therefore my heart with sympathy is ready to expire.

831 "Because in him a love for you I long have been discerning,
    I know how madly passionate his soul for you is burning—
    Poor man! His wretched countenance to gallows grey is turning
    While all his actions manifest a fierce, consuming yearning.

832    "And yet you have no mercy though there's not a single hitch
       That could or should prevent you two from solacing your itch.
       How can you be so stingy when he's generous and rich?
       How can you put such tortures on the lover you bewitch?

833    "Asleep, awake, abroad, at home, his thoughts to you are bound.
       Look how he sighs and casts his eyes forever on the ground,
       Look how he wrings his hands and does on love's mischance expound—
       Oh unkind woman! Must you long this wretched boy confound?

834    "Poor down-cast, miserable man! He mopes from place to place,
       And labors day and night to find in your cramped heart a place.
       By God! Unhappy was the day he saw your cruel face!
       Since all his trouble is in vain and nothing wins your grace.

835    "Who could expect good fruit to grow in harsh and barren land,
       And who, except a fool, would waste his seed in sterile sand?
       The only harvest he could reap would weary out his hand;
       A minnow might as well expect a great whale to withstand.

836    "Your figure first of all attracted his delighted eyes,
       And then your voice and conversation took him by surprise;
       Through those two things he fell in love, and for your mercy cries,
       Yet you withhold that promised boon which he would idolize.

837    "Why ever since you spoke with him, you've got him worse than dead,
       And you, although you won't admit it, yearn to be abed.
       Don't hide your wound or you will die, but open it instead,
       For smothered fires consume and burn with much more torture dread.

838    "Come, take me in your confidence, reveal your heart complete
       And tell me just what is your will without the least deceit,
       Then we shall either see this through, or drop it while it's meet
       Because your frequent comings yonder hardly are discreet."

839    "This fire in me," cried Lady Sloe, "does ever more increase,
       Though I perceive that in love's game he's moving for a piece
       Which fear and shame should well defend against a man's caprice,
       But I can't save myself—my passions give me no surcease."

840    "Then, daughter, drop your silly, vain, unreasonable fears
       And join yourselves together like two clever, happy dears.
       You burn for him, he burns for you, in that no sin appears;
       The church can bind you afterwards and pardon your arrears.

841   "A thousand things and more disclose this man's distress to me;
     He's told me words with tearful eyes most pitiful to see,
     'My Lady Sloe has pierced my heart, 'twas not her friends,' quoth he,
     'And she can cure my heart without another's witchery.'

842   "Well, since I saw his tearful face, and heard how well he spoke,
     I own that out of sympathy my heart with pity broke;
     Yet glad I was, in part at least, to learn it was no joke,
     And see how guileless was the love which did his grief provoke.

843   "Ah more than you might ever guess, all things to me proclaim
     The love you two for either have is equal and the same.
     Then since you die and languish from this all-consuming flame,
     Why don't you join yourselves together in a lover's game?"

844   Said Lady Sloe, "The very thing you ask of me I want,
     But mother never would consent to let me take this jaunt;
     Still I would try it, but one hindrance does my purpose daunt—
     We have no pleasant rendezvous which lovers need to haunt.

845   "To quench this love I have for Hita much there is I'd do—
     But mother stays with me and gives me her protection true."
     My convent-trotter answered, "Ah your mother! Curse the shrew!
     May she be coffined soon with cross and holy-water too!

846   "Yet love, if love be vehement, can burst through doorways stout,
     Pierce cloistered houses, while their guards it can as dead men rout;
     Come, leave this silly fear of yours—forsake each baseless doubt,
     And every massive hindrance then will seem a flimsy clout."

847   Said Lady Sloe at that to my old pleased solicitor,
     "Now I've revealed my heart to you—you know whom I adore,
     So since you know my soul's desire, advise me, I implore,
     For surely shame won't constipate the counsel of a whore."

848   "Oh dear," said Trota, "I could never misadvise a lass;
     The very thought of such a sin would my pure heart harass.
     Why hiding just this love of yours and trifles of that class
     Make me blush red; they do, you see, my reputation pass.

849   "I'm honest; let who will come forth—accuse me if he durst,
     But let him take me word for word, and though he take the worst
     He will not find the slightest evils in them interspersed,
     But, beaten, he will hold his tongue or go to Hell accursed.

850   "Let anybody come, I say, and badger me with threats,
      Or heap upon my poor grey hairs the foulest epithets,
      That gallant man whose sweet, true love for you no slight forgets,
      Will rescue us and make such eat their insults with regrets.

851   "Believe me, I keep secrets well; from me no tongue shall clatter,
      Yet if, indeed, some knave should murmur, well, what does it matter?
      There's nothing shameful in your act, and since love's highways scatter
      In all directions, much I marvel why you pause at chatter!"

852   At that my lady cried, "Ah God! Who knows a lover's heart,
      How utterly with doubts and fears it's lashed and torn apart;
      How here and there it is constrained while passions through it dart,
      Until one cannot tell which anguish does most fiercely smart.

853   "Two constant, sharp, conflicting pains torment me night and day;
      One is the thing that love exacts, to which I can't say nay;
      The other is the dread that I'll be found out and must pay—
      What heart I ask can long endure such turbulent affray?

854   "I do not know what way to turn, I find my pathways crossed,
      I feel love's pains at his entreaties waxing to my cost;
      Until this hour I conquered love—now from this hour I've lost;
      Love is more powerful than I—love does my will exhaust.

855   "My soul is shattered with this woe, and cares my heart oppress;
      I tell you I am weary of this struggle to possess,
      Yet I am glad with all my heart, though love with pain caress,
      For I would rather die love's death than suffer long distress."

856   The more one talks and listens to the biddings of desire,
      The more one works the passions up and fans them into fire.
      When love's wild, vehement demands a woman's flesh require,
      Then Venus stirs her body 'till it burns as on a pyre.

857   Said Trota then, "Now since you cannot quench your raging flame,
      'Twere best to heed the prayers of one who asks in passion's name
      Because your anguish, daughter dear, will kill your soul and maim
      The pleasures of your life, while still this love you cannot tame.

858   "I tell you night and day you look into your heart and find
      The image there of him you love, your lives are so entwined,
      And you are likewise in his heart most sacredly enshrined;
      Then slay your needs as if they were your enemies unkind.

859 "This yearning harrows you as much as it lays waste his breast;
      I see your eyes and countenance with earth's dull color dressed;
      If you delay or hesitate, Death will you both arrest.
      Whoever doubts my words errs much, for this is manifest.

860 "But surely, Lady Daughter, I believe that you are trying
      To shun and to forget the man for whom you're slowly dying.
      If this be so, that end is vain for which your thoughts are sighing,
      For Death can scarcely conquer love, since love is death-defying.

861 "Still it is true that pleasures oft will drive dull care away,
      Wherefore, my lady daughter, come into my house and play
      A merry bout or two with balls, and other pastimes gay,
      There I will give you nuts to crack—we'll frolic all the day.

862 "My house is never empty when it comes to fruits delicious;
      What apples, peaches, citrons, pears and apricots nutritious!
      What chestnuts, pine and hazel nuts for parties surreptitious!
      Come eat—what most you hanker for you'll find is most propitious.

863 "My house is but a step away, in fact you safely can
      Slip over in your shift and not be seen by any man;
      Besides we all are neighbors here, as loyal as a clan
      And we can softly flit away ere they divine our plan.

864 "Come to my house in confidence, and come without restraint
      As if it were your very own, to feast on dainties quaint.
      God will not suffer scandal there, my daughter, nor complaint,
      So come and you will be secure as if you were a saint!"

865 It sometimes happens that by prayers and importunings strong
      Some people change their minds and do what they well know is wrong,
      But only when the evil's done, repentance comes along—
      So maidens lose their heads when men upon them press and throng.

866 A woman and a hare when hunted down by much harassing,
      Seem shorn of wits and grow so blind they know not what is passing;
      They see no snares but act as if their eyes had opaque glassing.
      Thus women think they're loved when men deceits for them are massing.

867 At last my Lady Sloe agreed to frolic with my trot,
      To play with balls and eat whatever fruits that she had got.
      "My lady," said the crone, "tomorrow's feast day, is it not?
      Well, when I find a chance I'll come to fetch you to my spot."

868    Thereat the joyful convent trot came running with the news
    And cried to me, "Dear friend, rejoice! Come bid your cares adieus
    For this poor charmer now has coaxed your love-bird from her mews—
    Tomorrow Lady Sloe will come wherever I may choose.

869    "Now well I know your little proverb does the truth instil
    Which says, 'Much patter fills the platter when sly beggars grill.'
    In all things be a man, tomorrow lack not strength nor skill.
    Come to my house and when I leave, wrest from her what you will.

870    "But watch yourself and be not backward, recollect the fable,
    'When someone offers you a goat, come running with a cable.'
    Go after her, get what you want, show not yourself unable—
    'Twere better in your face than heart the smutch of weakness sable."

## How Lady Sloe Went to the House of the Old Woman
## and How the Archpriest Got What He Was After

871    So after on Saint James's day which they had set for meeting,
About the middle of the day, when every one was eating,
My trot brought Lady Sloe with her, down alleys furtive, fleeting
Back to her house and got her in with no more vexed entreating.

872    Then as my hoary little whore had fixed it up for me,
Without delay I scurried off, all ready for a spree.
I found her door shut fast, I knocked, the bawd feigned cleverly,
"Dear God!" she called, "who knocks so loud? Dear God, who can it be?

873    "Is it a man or just the wind? Some one is surely there—
The swarthy devil must have come to pry in this affair—
I wonder if it's—surely no—yet stay—how could he dare—
Yes, by my honor, it's Sir Melon! Well now, I declare!

874    "I know his face and eyes—he has the features of an ox—
Let him beware how he comes spying 'round us like a fox—
We'll let him storm and rage outside—I won't unbolt my locks—
But heavens! He'll smash in my door—it can't withstand such shocks.

875    "He seems determined to get in—we'll talk to him at least.
Be off, Sir Melon! Did the Devil bid you to our feast?
Don't break my door in—recollect how for Saint Paul's Archpriest
They have done favors. Fear not, girl, I'll not let in that beast.

876    "Stop! Stop! Hold on! Don't break my door! I'll open it a crack,
Then, if you've anything to say, talk fast and get on back—
Don't be scared, daughter, possibly he has a heart attack—
Come in, Sir Melon, come right in—has something gone to wrack?"

877    "Oh blessed Lady Sloe!" I cried, "My love, can it be you?—
See here, was it for this sweet girl you locked me out, old shrew?
Oh lucky is the day I chanced upon this rendezvous;
God and good fortune smile on me as they have smiled on few."

[*Right at this dramatic juncture thirty-two quatrains are missing. Some ancient vandal, whose motive is still an intriguing
mystery, has slashed from all manuscripts of the* Book of Good
Love *containing this episode the passage describing just how
Sir Melon got what he wanted from Lady Sloe. However, inas-*

*much as this episode is a fairly close gloss of the* Pamphilus de Amore, *a popular Latin play of the twelfth century, some idea as to what the lacuna contained may be derived from the corresponding passages of that play. The lover having arrived, the old bawd invents an excuse for leaving them alone.*]

(a) Old Woman [Trota]:

    My neighbor calls, I'll talk but soon return
      For I'm afraid she's coming here right now—
      I hurry, neighbor, don't make such a row—
    I'll lock my doors lest any you discern—
    Come, tell me, neighbor, since I cannot stay,
      What business makes you call me in this way? [exit]


(b) Pamphilus [Sir Melon]:

    Now love and youth are here conjoined by fate;
      Come, let us feed our hearts on love's delights
      For wanton Venus whets our appetites
    And bids us set about her business straight.
      But why delay with words? I'll cease my prayer,
      For will you not be kind in this affair?


(c) Galatea [Lady Sloe]:

    No, take away your hands, you pant in vain
      For what you want can never, never be—
      Oh take away your hands, you insult me
    Although you once did such affection feign.
      Quick! Take away your hands, lest that old shrew
      Should come and catch me in this act with you!


(d)

    Alas! How quick you overcome my strength!
      It hurts me—Oh my dear Pamphilus! Oh
      You crush my breast by lying on it so!
    Why, cruel, do you force me to this length?
      Stop! Stop! Or I shall scream! I am afraid.
      Oh wicked man, it hurts! I am betrayed!


(e)

    Yes, how it hurts, and yet I scarcely reck,
      For surely, sweetheart, this is not a sin.
      I wonder when that woman will come in;
    I hope she falls and breaks her evil neck!
      Well, it is done—get up, get up, I say—
      The neighbors must have heard our noisy fray.

(f)       But it was all your fault I was betrayed.
          A curse upon the hag who sold me thus!
          Well, you have won, but not without a fuss,
       Because, you know, I struggled 'till you made
          Me do this thing you did against my will.
          Come now, get off! Why lie upon me still?

(g) Pamphilus [Sir Melon]:
       No, blessed darling, let us rest awhile
          And pant and catch our breaths as does a horse
          That blows when he has nobly won his course,
       For, lying with you, I would hours beguile.
          Why is it anger on your face appears?
          Why do you, weeping, wet your face with tears?

(h)       I know that I am guilty, do not halt,
          But punish me beyond my just deserts,
          Yet, still, for mercy let me touch your skirts
       Because, I swear, it was not all my fault.
          Be just to me, and in a lover's court
          Condemn or free me by a judgment short.

(i)       It was your burning eyes and soft, white flesh,
          Sweet-smelling body, and voluptuous face,
          Your words, embraces, kisses, time and place,
       Which drove me headlong in this fatal mesh;
          'Twas love for you which did this deed inspire,
          And goaded me upon you, soul on fire.

(j)       I could not help but throw myself on you
          As fatal passion overcame my will
          And did restraint and chaste affection kill,
       So for this act some blame hangs on you too
          Because you roused the passions you condemn
          And furnished the material for them.

(k) Old Woman [Trota]: (Enters)
       'Twas for a trifle that my neighbor called,
          But for her chatter I'd have come ere now.
          Ah, why the crimson on your cheek and brow,
       Whence, Galatea, come these tears which scald?
          What, in my absence did Pamphilus do?
          'Twas surely not immodest? Tell me true.

(l) Galatea [Lady Sloe]:

> How insolent the question is you ask,
>> As if you did not know, when you yourself
>> Had planned to bring him here—Oh wicked elf!
> To leave us here, and then your deed to mask,
>> You feigned a neighbor called, and stayed so long
>> This Pamphilus has done me grievous wrong.

(m) Old Woman [Trota]:

> I am accused unjustly, if you blame
>> Me for your wrongs, I'll find excuse enough,
>> Since what you lay upon me ne'er can ruff
> My venerable hairs, if any shame
>> Was done while I was absent, your vile spawn
>> Cannot be charged to me, for I was gone.

878   "You claim you knew it was a trick, why then, when I went out
    Did you stay with him here alone? Could you not run or shout?
    Don't cast the blame for this on me; you did it, there's no doubt,
    And now the thing to do is not to noise your guilt about.

879   "The lesser of two evils is to hide your little shame
    For once you give yourself away you'll get an ugly name,
    Then if you want to marry soon you'll lose out for this game;
    My plan is surely better than receiving evil fame.

880   "Since now you must admit the damage all is done and past,
    Maintain your standing right or wrong and hold it to the last;
    Don't ever run when evil's done, but stand against it fast;
    Be silent lest your reputation make you lose your caste.

881   "The parrot talks, but if she kept her counsel like the quail
    They wouldn't hang her in a cage and laugh to hear her rail—
    Just be advised, my little chick, your chirp's of no avail,
    For what Sir Melon did to you is ethics to a male."

882   Then Lady Sloe replied to her, "You old, abandoned slut,
    You trick, betray, and sell a girl, and then her throat you cut,
    But yesterday you had a thousand reasons for your smut,
    Now all of my resources fail and I am made your butt.

883   "If all the joyous, carefree birds would take a little thought
    Upon the snares spread out for them they never would be caught,
    But when, alas, they see the trap, they are so hunger-fraught
    They pounce upon the bait, and, dying, are to market brought.

[125]

884 "The fishes of the waters though they see the baited hook
    Are yanked out by the fisherman and taken to the cook,
    And women ne'er discern a barb until they feel its crook
    But then when most they stand in need they are by kin forsook.

885 "A man when he dishonors one, spurns her without support,
    And she has nothing left to do but sell herself for sport
    Until her flesh and soul are cursed—a crowd are of this sort—
    Well, since I have no other course, I must to that resort."

886 The ancients were with wit endowed and infinite discerning,
    And in the minds of hoary age great wisdom is sojourning,
    Wherefore my venerable sage set all her brains a-turning
    And on this grave emergency she brought to bear her learning.

887 Said she, "A clever girl should ne'er give way to grief profound
    Unless by her laments she can make her afflictions sound.
    What can't be cured must be endured, and thus when cares abound,
    A lass should resolutely bear whatever woes come round.

888 "For griefs supreme, for sharp distress, for misadventures great,
    For accidents and rash mistakes and bludgeonings of fate,
    One ought to seek advice and cures, and antidotes await;
    The wise reveal themselves in woe and circumstances strait.

889 "Discord and anger bring distress 'twixt friend and dearest friend,
    And plant suspicions evil in their bosoms which offend.
    Let there be peace between you two; let this dissension end,
    And let a pleasant love and peace your rage and grief amend.

890 "Now inasmuch as you maintain I brought about your hurt,
    Through my kind offices I would all further grief avert.
    Go take this man and be his wife, then, truly, I assert
    That everything which you desire I'll do with skill expert!"

891 Sir Melon then with Lady Sloe was joined with nuptial glory
    And merrily the twain indulged in joustings amatory,
    Wherefore, my friends, please pardon me if I've said aught that's whorey
    Since Pamphilus and Naso wrote the worst part of this story.

## Concerning the Advice Which the Archpriest Gives to Ladies, and Also the Names of a Procuress

892    Have ears, my ladies, hearken now, and hear some good advice;
       Beware of men, alas, beware, and let my words suffice
       Ere like the earless, heartless ass you pay at length the price
       He paid, that time the lion did him to his death entice.

893    A lion had a headache once and all his pains increased
       But when thereafter he got well and his afflictions ceased,
       One Sunday, during his siesta, every loyal beast
       Appeared before him with a plan for getting up a feast.

894    They made the ass their mountebank because that beast was daft
       And although fat still tried to dance, but most the critters laughed
       To hear him tune his trumpet up and sound off, fore and aft,
       But sad to tell both noise and smell the breeze to them did waft.

895    The lion grew enangered at such vulgar assininity
       And tried to rip him open, but the beast had no affinity
       For rippings rude, so, breaking wind, he fled from that vicinity
       And left the lion growling at that snub to his divinity.

896    To get him back the lion made a special kind concession;
       He said the ass might make request for any rich possession
       If he would grace the feast once more with feats of his profession—
       A mumping vixen said she'd cause the ass's prompt regression.

897    So mistress fox went thither where the silly beast was grazing
       And greeted him most cleverly with flattery and praising;
       "Dear Sir," said she, "the festive glee you made was so amazing
       Our party without you is now a bean not worth the raising.

898    "Your rich and mellow baritone, your entertaining sprite,
       Your talent on the trombone with the sonnets you indite
       Are better than our other stunts—they did our king delight,
       So he commands you to return and not to dread his might!"

899    The ass believed her flatteries but got it in the neck,
       For he returned to sing and dance, but little did he reck
       Of what the lion had in mind in bringing him to beck,
       And thus the scot of trumpeting was laid against the geck.

900 The lion had a troop of cossacks for his mounted guard
Who, as he ordered, seized the ass and haled him in the yard
Whereat the lion ripped him open with his scratchings hard,
Amazing all that he could thus his word and truce discard.

901 The lion ordered next the wolf to guard with drawn out claws
The ass's carcass better than he guarded sheep because
The lion wished to take a turn and limber up his jaws,
But wolf devoured the ass's heart and ears within that pause.

902 Now when the lion had his walk and back all hungry came
He told the wolf to hand him o'er the defunct ass's frame,
But when he saw the butchered carcass which the wolf did maim
A towering rage against the wolf did straightway him inflame.

903 The wolf affirmed the silly ass was born in such a state
And ne'er had heart within his breast nor ears upon his pate
For if he had he would have known the lion's falseness great
And hence the proof of being thus was furnished by his fate.

904 So ladies dear, do understand the moral of my tale
And guard your hearts 'gainst lechery nor let its lures assail,
But open wide your ears, and more, your heart of hearts regale
With God's pure love, and never let your fury mad prevail.

905 A girl who through misfortune either is or was deceived
Must watch herself lest she again by evil be aggrieved.
Let her not be, as was the ass, of ears and heart relieved
But profit through experience which others have achieved.

906 Be warned, and draw instruction from full many a ruined lass,
Nor smile a foolish smile upon the worldly loves that pass,
For many be the wolves that wait to pounce upon an ass—
I say this though I know the truth will wolfish men harass.

907 Let sportive women guard against the wicked whisper brief;
A grape with hard but little seed can bring a tooth to grief,
An acorn makes a lofty oak which towers like a chief,
And from a single grain of wheat grow many in a sheaf.

908 The gossip on a girl seduced spreads over all the town;
Her shame becomes the butt of jests she never can live down.
Now ladies, when I tell you this, don't rail at me or frown,
But rather ponder o'er my words and works of high renown.

909     And realize full well I spin my tale of Lady Sloe
        To teach a moral, not because it happened to me so.
        Wherefore bewail of false old crones and smirking preachers low,
        Nor be alone with men for fear their thorns should cause you woe.

910     Now being after this myself all loveless and forlorn,
        I saw a woman beautiful sit in her hall one morn,
        And from the glory of that sight my heart was overborne
        Since I had never seen such beauty any girl adorn.

911     Her form and gait were fairer too than any I had seen,
        A little girl, still innocent, and wealthy but serene,
        And young and noble born besides, and with a charming mien;
        I ne'er set eyes on such a one—God keep my body clean.

912     Still she was pert and had the look of girls that are beguiled
        Although at home they kept her closer than a beastie wild.
        I told my trot I would not rest, 'till I through love exiled,
        Like pilgrims in a holy place, lay prostrate on that child.

913     But be it advised it was no man I chose to be my trot.
        No messenger like that who once my Cross belovèd got;
        A man with evil company can ne'er succeed a jot
        So from deceitful pimps, sweet Virgin, guard me on the spot.

914     But this, my pander, was a loyal, pious, Christian bawd
        Who went about unmaking virgins in the fear of God,
        And in this love affair of mine things went so well abroad
        The trot sped to my lady with a tried and proven fraud.

915     I then, for love's beginning, wrote an amatory ode
        Which my dear crone brought to the dame with charms which lovers goad.
        "My lady," said she, "buy my wares, they're all of latest mode."
        To which the girl replied, "I'm willing when I see your load."

916     Right then the trot enchanted her and thus began to sing,
        "Look what I brought you, Lady Daughter, 'tis a precious ring.
        Give me your finger (step by step she got her on the wing)
        And if you won't give me away, I'll tell a wondrous thing—

917     "I know a man who daily yearns to see you more and more,
        And who would lay this city at your feet with all its store.
        Dear lady, do not hide yourself behind this dismal door,
        But go and see the merry world which God has borne you for."

918    In such a manner, with my trot's snake-tonguing she was bitten;
       The crone inflamed her 'neath the belt, then showed her what I'd written,
       And giving her the ring she winked which so inflamed the kitten
       She led her where and how she wished like one that has been smitten.

919    But as the proverb says which truly came from some old sage,
       "A strainer new is hung up well, but three days give it age."
       My trot, whose name, Urraca, means "a magpie out of cage,"
       Grew tired and said she would no more in panderings engage.

920    Then just in fun I said to her, "Old Magpie Chatterbox,
       Don't leave your wonted, beaten road to ramble like a fox,
       But serve where you can earn your hire by pimpings orthodox,
       But any one who has the grain can always find an ox."

921    I did not then recall a saying which has this report,
       "A careless word is like a weapon, dangerous for sport,"
       At that my trot flew in a rage and as a last resort
       Told everything, and like a woman, did the truth distort.

922    Thereat my lady's mother watched her closer than she did
       And I could never get my girl—her sight was e'en forbid—
       A man can quickly make mistakes unless he's often chid,
       So let him either weigh his words or keep his tongue well hid.

923    In my Urraca this was proved, so of my plight take stock
       And don't in secret or in public cast a slight or mock;
       Nor wear your heart upon your sleeve but hide it 'neath your smock,
       For nothing hurts as doth the truth, nor carries such a shock.

924    To such a go-between as mine don't say a thing that cuts—
       However well or ill she sings, don't call her "parrot-guts,"
       "Decoy," or "blind," or "rutting-shield," or "mace for cracking nuts,"
       "Door-knocker," "punk," or "crazy-comb," or "halter rope for sluts,"

925    Nor "bridle," "bird lime," "aunt," nor "screen," nor "hook for lady's
            meat,"
       Nor "money-scaler," "scraper-off," nor "scouter of the street,"
       Nor "stall," nor "whetstone," "leading-rein," nor "broker for the sheet,"
       Nor "hot-tongs," "lover's-shovel," no, nor "fish hook of the seat,"

926    "Mill-clapper," "mouth-piece," "bawdy music for a man's gong-beater,"
       Nor "runner," "hitching post for whorses," never "maiden-cheater,"
       Nor call her "godless-whore" because she prays to staunch Saint Peter,
       But if you honor her I know you'll ne'er have to entreat her.

927    Not "blow-fly," "lover's ladder," "cell for purple headed hermits,"
         Not "bitches-leash," nor "virgin-mender," "register of permits,"[19]
         Indeed to tell you all her names, our time the list pretermits—
         She has more tricks than has a fox, more names than all our varmints.

928    "Necessity will own no law," and since that's oft averred,
         My king, my lord, my saviour Love such longing in me stirred
         To take a wench and have it out whatever risk's incurred;
         I felt just like a sheep without the comfort of the herd.

929    Indeed I had such poignant yearning that I found my crone
         And begged her to forgive the slights and insults I had thrown.
         Then, weasel-like, I pulled my rabbit from her burrow lone
         And as a beast can change its coat, I showed a softer tone.

930    "Now by my faith, Archpriest," said she, "your trot has pimped and pined
         But you speak softly just because you can't another find.
         If you would have a loyal trot, be amiable and kind—
         Men kiss the hands they would lop off and smile at eyes they'd blind.

931    "Yet if you spite me ne'er again, the things I said of you
         I'll contradict and all this talk of gossip I'll subdue
         As easily as mud is squeezed beneath one's foot askew,
         And I'll o'ercome all obstacles, for what I want I do.

932    "So never call me evil names nor speak of me amiss
         But christen me, 'Good Love,' and I'll be good for loves like this,
         Because a good repute among my neighbors brings me bliss
         And courtesy will cost no more than names which people hiss."

933    Because I loved that hag and then because it is devout
         I named this godly book, "Good Love"; 'tis what it tells about.
         She helped me when I kindness showed, and did no longer pout,
         Thus virtue reaped its rich reward and meanness went without.

934    The bawd devised a wondrous hoax that did our friends bewitch;
         She feigned a madness, running here and there without a stitch,
         Whereat immediately all cried out, "By God, the bitch
         Must have some sickness in her head to bring her to that pitch."

935    On every hand the people muttered, "One would be a fool
         To pay attention to the talk of that old trollop's drool."
         They thought no ill of me but judged me by another rule;
         Said I, "No bawd I've ever kissed could ply so shrewd a tool."

936    It wasn't long before my scandal crawled into its hole
       And o'er my lady neither nurse nor mother kept control.
       Then fastened I upon my crone as leaf upon its bole,
       For he who has a trot like mine should guard her as his soul.

937    Straightway my old procuress started out to peddle gauds
       And rope my dame by lying snares while baiting her with frauds—
       There are no peers in all the world to these old Trojan bawds,
       They give a maid the *coup de grâce* which every man applauds.

938    Besides, I say, these trollops go unwatched from house to house
       To tout and haggle off their trash, to gossip and to chouse;
       They're closer to a maiden than an unsuspected louse
       And they can talk her out of what she hoards beneath her blouse.

939    Said I, "Urraca, loyal whore, God keep you in His grace!
       For you're determined in your task and few can hold your pace!"
       She answered, "I shall take the chance, whatever be the case,
       To keep the ball a-rolling to a pleasant, cherished place.

940    "Nobody guards your lady now, the time is ripe to notch,
       And since no one suspects a tout, my business cannot botch,
       And what small scandal clings to you I easily can scotch—
       A man can tell the carrion's gone when buzzards cease to watch."

941    Perhaps she gave my dame a philter, aphrodisiac drug,
       A brew of herbs or lover's potion from a magic jug,
       Or else, perhaps, some Spanish-fly extracted from a bug;
       I know not, but at least she made her quite insane to hug.

942    Just as the falcon at the lure sweeps off on pinions free
       So rushed my lady, soul and flesh, to give herself to me.
       Dear friends, I found Urraca with the proverb to agree
       Which says, "No cunning, aged bitch barks up an empty tree."

943    But since it's common to be born and natural to die,
       As luck would have it, soon my lady was obliged to fly
       And in a day or two she started off to heaven's sky—
       God pardon her and lodge her soul in mansions up on high.

944    'Twas then from sudden, sad bereavement, coupled with true grief,
       That I fell dangerously ill, nor was my sickness brief;
       (Indeed I languished two full days before I found relief);
       Ah well, save for the cost, she was a dainty meal of beef.

## Concerning the Old Woman Who Came to See the Archpriest and What Befell Him With Her

945   The month was March when early Summer came upon the land,[20]
     An aged woman came to see me, speaking first off hand;
     "Bad boy, bad boy, now that you're sick it's safe near you to stand."
     At that I clasped her tight and bantered her with jestings bland.

946   But soon with disappointed rage she said a thing that cuts,
     "Archpriest," she cried, "I do believe there is more noise than nuts!"
     Said I, "Did you come here to preach? The devil's in you sluts,
     You drink the wine and curse the lees remaining in the butts!"

947   Wherefore to voice my discontent and pour out my vexation,
     I made some spiteful, witty songs about her conversation,
     But do not shun them, ladies, thinking they are mere stupration
     Because no lady ever heard them without jubilation.

948   So now, my ladies, that I may your courtesy obtest,
     I sue for pardon; please remember I would ne'er molest
     Your scruples, for I'd die of grief. But don't you think it best
     For me, sometimes, between the legs of truth to slip a jest?

949   If you permit me I shall write some story all complete,
     Both word and deed—with all my heart I will narrate the feat.
     Then, if one cannot help at times one's being indiscreet,
     A kindly listener one need not for pardon long entreat.

## How the Archpriest Set Out to Try the Mountains
## and What Happened to Him with a Mountain Girl

950   "Try all things once," this the apostle tells his Christian brood—
      That's why I went to try the hills one day in sportive mood.
      But there I lost my mule and could not find a bit of food—
      He who wants better bread than wheat is both a fool and rude.

951   It was Saint Emiterius' day in March I left this spot,
      And through Lozoya's pass I took the journey at a trot.
      But of protection from the snow and hail—I found no jot;
      Who looks for what he hasn't lost should lose what he has got.

952   Right in the middle of the pass I suddenly beheld
      A cow-girl, standing near a thicket that about us swelled.
      I asked the lady who she was. "My name's Flat-nose," she yelled,
      "I am Flat-nose, the strong armed girl, and men like you I've felled.

953   "I am the keeper of this pass and I collect its toll;
      All those who gentlemanly pay, I leave with carcass whole.
      But he who won't, it doesn't take me long to strip and roll—
      Pay up! Or I will show you how they thresh wheat on this knoll!"

954   She blocked my way which narrow was through that high, mountain glade,
      Indeed, it was a footpath close which herdsmen must have made;
      So when I saw myself close pressed, cold, stiff, and lacking aid,
      I cried, "You can't get blood from turnips, can you, pretty maid?

955   "Come, let me pass, my pretty friend, I'll give a mountain gift
      If I'm informed what you expect of men in such a shrift.
      For, as the proverb says, 'To bargain is the best of thrift.'
      But for God's mercy, shelter me, I'm freezing in this drift!"

956   "Well, beggars can't be choosers," here replied my fair coquette,
      But promise you will give me aught or I'll upon you set,
      Then if you do, you needn't fear this snow will make you wet,
      And I advise you to agree, or I will hurt you yet."

957   Then as the aged spinners say while sucking at the thread,
      "He who can do no more with life perforce must serve the dead,"
      I promised her, since I was seized with suffering, cold, and dread,
      A pouch of rabbit's fur, a brooch, and trinket made of lead.

958    She tossed me up upon her neck because I pleased her so,
And I was not averse that way across the hills to go,
Because she would not let me tramp the glades and crests through snow;
I therefore made a song of what befell; 'tis here below.

# The Song of the Mountain Girl

## I

959    One morning as I crossed the pass
      That over Malangosta lay,
    There rushed at me a lumpish lass;
      The minute that I came her way
        She cried, "Poor fool, where go you now,
        What do you seek, and where, and how,
    Along this narrow, deep crevasse?"

960    Then to her question I replied,
      "I would to Sotos Albos go."
    Said she, "The devil must abide
      In you to make you swagger so,
        Because I keep this country here
        And where I guard, I tell you clear,
    No man can pass with unscathed hide!"

961    She blocked my passage through the trail,
      That ugly, vile, mis-shapen hag,
    And cried, "Now, youngster, by my tail,
      I'll stay right here upon this crag
        Until you promise something nice.
        But if you fight about the price
    Your hopes to cross this path will fail."

962    "By God, cow-girl," I told the toad,
      "Don't block my way this country through
    But stand aside and give me road
      For I have got no gift for you."
        She said, "Well, then, turn right around
        Or go through Somsierra's ground;
    You'll not cross here in any mode."

963    So that bedevilled, flat-nosed slut
      (May Santillano damn the bitch)
    Hit me with staff behind the nut
      And knocked me whirling in the ditch,
        And cried, as I lay on the sod,
        "Now, by the upright, living God,
    You'll pay for drinks or back you strut!"

964    The hail and rain were churning mire
      When Flat-nose muttered to me quick,
  But with a sudden, threatening ire,
    "Pay up or I'll show you a trick!"
      I said, "By God, my pretty girl,
      I'll promise much if I may curl
  My frozen body near a fire."

965    She cried, "I'll take you to my cot
      And after, guide you on your way,
  I'll make you fire and fan it hot,
    And give you bread and wine today.
      Then, by my faith, if we accord,
      I'll hold you as a noble lord
  And dawn may bring you better lot."

966    And cold and stiff and much afraid,
      I promised her a handsome coat,
  And more than that, the offer made
    Of brooches to close up her throat,
      Yet she kept saying, "Give me more!
      Then come, and we'll play such a score
  No fear of cold will you pervade."

967    She took me firmly by the hand
      And set my legs astride her neck
  As if I were a sack of sand,
    And trod the crags as o'er a deck.
      "Don't be afraid," said she, "poor lad,
      I'll give you what will make you glad
  As is the custom of our land."

968    She quickly bore me to her hut
      Where all was snug and quite secure;
  She made a fire of oak she'd cut
    To broil a rabbit, young but poor.
      On roasted partridges we fed,
      Big loaves of badly kneaded bread,
  And sucking kid, which filled the gut.

969    Of wine we drank about a keg,
      No end of butter, cheese so ripe
  It stank worse than a rotten egg,
    Then milk, rich cream, a trout, some tripe,

And then she said, "Make haste, my son,
  Eat this hard bread and when you've done
I'll let you wrestle with my leg."

970    When I had stayed a little while
  And got my stiffness all thawed out,
As I grew warm I saw her smile
  For of my heat she had no doubt.
    She gazed at me and did not blink
    But said, "Companion, now I think
We understand each other's guile."

971    That cow-girl lewd began to peep,
  "Let's knead our guts upon this trough—
Get up, my lad, don't fall asleep,
  But frisk your clothes completely off."
    She caught me by the wrist and head,
    What could I do but go to bed—
Believe me, but I got off cheap![21]

# What Happened to the Archpriest with the Mountain Girl

## II

972    When this adventure over was, I towards Segovia hied
But not, indeed, to purchase trinkets for my flat-nosed bride.
I went to see a rib that once was in a dragon's side.
The dragon which old Rando killed where Moya's folk reside.[22]

973    I tarried in that city till I spent what wealth I had,
Then, since I found no silver source that could unto it add,
But saw my wasted pocket-book was shrunken, flat, and sad,
I said, "At least I have a home—for that I should be glad."

974    So on the third day I arose and took the homeward shift,
But did not through Lozoya go because I had no gift.
I thought I'd try the pass that lies along Fonfria's rift,
Yet there I lost my way again like one who is adrift.

975    Below a grove of pines I met a cow-girl fair who lay
Beside a stream and watched her cows to see that none should stray.
I bowed to her and humbly said, "Fair shepherdess, today
I'll either spend the night with you or you'll show me my way."

976    "Well, you who thus invite yourself, have got an ass's look,"
The wench replied, "Stand where you are, such offers I'll not brook.
If you advance, your back I'll measure with my shepherd's crook,
And once it catches you, you'll find it's not so gently shook!"

977    Let him who can't keep out of trouble well this proverb heed,
"The hen that scratches long enough is sure to find a seed."
I proved its truth by walking up to her, for then, indeed,
She smote me right behind the ear so hard she made it bleed.

978    Not only that, she knocked me flying down a hill so dazed
I found those wallops are the worst which off the ear have grazed.
"God damn the brutal mother stork," I muttered all amazed,
"Who welcomes thus into her nest the fledgelings she has raised!"

979    As soon as she with angry hands had given me that scratch
She cried, "Get up, but don't you walk upon my garden patch,
And don't be angry at my fun, for now you've found your match,
But let us stick together like good money in a batch.

980 "Let's come into my cabin while my errant husband's gone;
I'll set you on your way and give you lunch before next dawn.
Come, haste, put horns upon my man, and do not fear my brawn."
I got up quickly when I saw she had begun to fawn.

981 She led me by the hand to where we twain were joined as one,
But when the evening time had come and food I'd eaten none,
While we were in the hut alone, she once more longed for fun
And cried, "Let's trick my man again!"—'twas hardly said than done.

982 Then I spoke up, "By God, my lady, I must eat a bit
For one that's stiff and hungry cannot well himself acquit,
And if I cannot have a bite, I cannot wrestle it."
But that enangered her and she began to fume and spit.

983 Still she gave food to me; I said, " 'Tis proved, my fair consort,
That bread and wine and not new clothes give man the strength for sport."
I paid her by the act in kind, then left the girl's resort
Beseeching her to show the way which was both near and short.

984 She begged me to remain with her that night, since her desire
Was harder to put out than straw when once it catches fire.
I said, "I'm in a fearful rush, so help me God, my Sire!"
At that she grew so cross, in fear I started to retire.

985 Yet she agreed to take me out; she led me where two tracks
Both passable and beaten well, led over gully cracks.
There quick as possible I crossed, foot-sore, without my packs,
And with the early morning sun I saw Herreros' shacks.

986 About this misadventure passed, I wrote a song which should
Compare, although not very pretty, with the best I could,
But, 'till you understand my book, don't slander what is good;
You'd think one thing, the book another, in all likelihood.

# The Song of the Mountain Girl

## II

987
There always comes into my mind
A valiant, female, mountain hind,
          Gadea, Río Frío's girl.

988
Upon the outskirts of the town which I above have named,
I met Gadea guarding cows upon a field unclaimed,
Said I, "Oh lucky was the hour your matchless body framed."
"Now I perceive you've lost your way, because," the wench exclaimed,
          "You act like some bewildered churl."

989
"Bewildered, yes indeed, I act, my lady, in this thicket,
Yet sometimes people win or lose as fortune marks their ticket,
But since I've seen you I don't care for pathway, hedge or wicket,
Because I've got you in this meadow, sister, where we'll nick it,
          And listen to the river purl."

990
"I, too, with laughter purled to hear the angry lass reply,
As boldly she ran down the hill with all her clothes awry.
Said she, "I'll show you how we drive a hog into his sty;
The devil must have trimmed that tongue which you so pertly ply—
          Well, let this crook upon your curl."

991
She curled her crook and let it fly—it caught me on the ear,
Whereat, knocked backwards down the gulch, I catapulted clear.
The little wretch cried, "That's the way we skin the cat up here—
I'll beat you 'till you learn to keep your saddle next your rear—
          Be up and off, you ass's ear!"

992
Yet still this ass she fed and bedded but demanded pay
And when I did not do her bidding she began to bray,
"Why did I leave my man, your cold and wretched prong won't play,
If you don't acquiesce I'll peel your fur off right away
          For cheating such a trusting girl."

# What Happened to the Archpriest with the Mountain Girl

## III

993   On Monday, ere the day had dawned, my journey I began,
      And near Cornejo, chopping pines, into a girl I ran,
      A stupid wench, who I must say, conceived the silly plan
      Of wedding me as if I were a member of her clan.

994   She thought I was a shepherd when she'd asked me many a thing,
      And stopped her work to hear the jokes which I so well can spring.
      I guess she thought she had my heart already on her string,
      But there she overlooked a saying with an honest ring.

995   A man was trying to advise his friend, and said to him,
      "Don't lose what you have gained for something, when the chance is slim,
      For if you leave what you have got for some illusion dim
      You'll surely fail because your brains are cozened by a whim."

996   I made a little song, the kind they call a pastourelle
      Which you have in your hand below, describing what befell.
      The summer's weather then was harsh on upland hill and dell
      Wherefore I crossed the pass at dawn to rest that evening well.

# The Song of the Mountain Girl

## III

997 Once, near Cornejo's little village,
  Upon the first day of the week,
Amid a valley's verdant tillage,
  I met a little mountain freak
Who wore a smock with scarlet frillage
  And woolen sash of mode antique,
"May God preserve you safe from pillage,
  My sister dear," I said with cheek.

998 She said, "What do you where it's hilly?
  If you have lost your way it's queer."
I said, "I'm looking for a filly
  To wed, my pretty mountaineer."
Then she, "Indeed the man's not silly
  Who would obtain a girl up here—
If you look close, you'll see a dear.

999 "But, kinsman, look your talents over
  To see if you know mountain lore."
Said I, "Well can I guard wild clover
  Or ride a mare 'till I am sore.
And I can kill that mountain rover,
  The wolf, for when I wage him war
I get him while the greyhounds snore.

1000 "Then I can bed and fodder cattle,
  And tame a young and frisky bull,
And give the butter churn a battle,
  Or blow the bagpipes loud and full,
Or make the thread and needle rattle,
  Or sweetly on the whistle pull,
And ride a mustang, wonderful.

1001 "My feet I well can set a-flying
  To skip and dance in any mode,
None have I found could do such plying,
  Though he were tall or squat as toad,
And when at wrestling I am vying,
  I catch a man up like a load
And fling him headlong in the road."

1002     "Well here," she said, "you can't miscarry,
       For you can find what you require—
    Why, I myself, will gladly marry
       If you give me what I desire,
    And surely you're too wise to tarry."
       Said I, "For what do you aspire?
       Speak up, I'll sate your wants entire."

1003     "Give me," she cried, "a pretty fillet,
       And let it be of scarlet thin.
    Besides, I want a handsome skillet
       And six or seven rings of tin.
    I want a gown and coat, and will it
       To be of fine angora skin,
       But don't, with ruses, take me in.

1004     "I want earrings with great big bangles
       Of brass, shined 'till they fairly glow;
    A yellow hood I'll have with spangles
       Striped in the front where they will show,
    And knee boots cut at fancy angles
       So folks will say, where'er I go,
       'Well married is poor so-and-so!' "

1005     I answered, "I'll provide each treasure,
       And more, if after more you sing,
    And they'll be fine beyond all measure—
       Now go, and all your kinsmen bring.
    Then let's arrange our nuptial pleasure;
       Do not forget this little fling
       For I shall get you everything."

# What Happened to the Archpriest with the Mountain Girl and What She Looked Like[23]

## IV

1006    The weather in high altitudes and mountain lands is rough
        Because it either snows or hails, and ne'er is hot enough.
        Above the pass I found, alas, the growling breezes gruff,
        But spite of wind, a freezing mist lay numbly on the bluff.

1007    Then, since men do not feel the cold so keenly when they run,
        I ran down hill just like a stone flung at a tower by one
        Who tries to scare the hawks away, but finds the stone he spun
        Flies back before the birds—I cried, "God's help, or I'm undone!"

1008    Ne'er since the day that I was born was I in such a plight,
        For, coming down the pass, I saw a most horrific sight,
        A worse phantasm than one sees in troubled dreams at night—
        It was a mare-girl, stark and stout, and featured like a fright.

1009    But, worn by cold and suffering in that high, frozen hill,
        I begged her then and there to give me shelter from the chill;
        To which she answered that she would if I could pay the bill,
        Whereat she took me by Tablada while I blessed God's will.

1010    Her members and her figure were the sort one cannot hide
        Because she seemed a prancing mare no herdsman could bestride—
        Indeed, the man who'd wrestle her would comfortless abide
        Because without that jade's consent he could not get topside.

1011    Not even in Saint John's divine apocalyptic book
        Has there been seen a figure with so horrible a look.
        And quickly she would fight because offense she quickly took,
        Although I hardly know what fiend could that phantasm brook.

1012    Her head, inordinately large, was huger than a keg;
        Her crow black hair was shiny, slick, and shorter than a peg;
        Her eyes were sunken, crooked, red, lop-sided as an egg;
        And bigger than a bear track was the imprint from her leg.

1013    Her ears were greater than the ones that from a donkey sprout;
        Her neck was black, thick-set, and short, and hairy all about;
        Her nose was beaked and longer than the great flamingo's snout;
        And with the thirst she had she'd clean a merchant's money out.

[145]

1014    Her mouth was fashioned like a hound's, with muzzle thick and short;
        With long and narrow horse's teeth of every crooked sort;
        Her beetle brows were dirty grey and bulged out like a wart—
        Let not the man who'd marry her be deaf to my report.

1015    And blacker than the beard I have was that upon her lip;
        I noticed nothing else, but if you'd scratch about her hip,
        I'm sure you'd find some funny things to pay you for your trip—
        But it were best to mind your flail than thus about her skip.

1016    However, if you'd scrutinize her well above the knee,
        You'd find her shanks enormous and her bones a very tree;
        While on her legs a hen house full of chicken pox there'd be,
        And like a yearling heifer's, great big ankles you would see.

1017    Much broader than my palm extended was the lady's wrist,
        All fuzzy too, with crinkly hairs, more sweaty than a mist;
        Her hawking, snorky mouth you'd find revolting to be kissed,
        Besides her raucous voice would drown a damned evangelist.

1018    The little finger of her hand was larger than my thumb
        (Conceive the biggest you have seen and then add to it some).
        If ever she should pick the lice that o'er your body come,
        Her fingers, like a wine-press beam, about your skull would drum.

1019    Beneath her bodice, plain to see, there dangled boobies brown—
        Indeed, they reached her belly since she wore a loosened gown—
        And hence they freely flopped about and thwacked her navel's crown—
        If set to music they'd keep time by bobbing up and down.

1020    Her ribs protruded large and long above her filthy flanks;
        I've counted them far off because they stuck out worse than planks.
        Now nothing else I noticed that is worthy of your thanks,
        Besides I hold a prying man the worst of mountebanks.

1021    On what she said, on how she looked, on every circumstance,
        I wrote three songs, yet can't do justice to her countenance;
        Now two of these are chansonettes, the other is a dance!
        Should you not like them, see her first, then laugh at my romance.

V

1022      Tablada I was near
When, passing mountains sheer,
I met Aldea, dear,
As dawn was breaking dear.

1023      Upon that pass I thought
I'd die, for I was caught
In snow and bitter cold
Since numbing mist uprolled
     That season of the year.

1024      Yet on my long descent
I ran like one Hell-bent
And met a mountain girl
With whom a god would curl,
     She was so pink and clear.

1025      Said I unto the jade,
"I doff my hat, fair maid."
Said she, "Since you can hop,
Don't think with me to stop,
     But take yourself from here."

1026      I answered, "I've a chill,
And for that reason will
Entreat you, pretty one,
So that God's will be done,
     To lodge and give me cheer."

1027      Thereat the buxom slut
Said, "Kinsman, I've a hut
That's empty, since my man
Away but lately ran.
     But pay me from your gear.

1028      I countered, "I'd be glad
But I'm a married lad
Just from Herreros come.
But I will give you some
     Fair payment, never fear."

1029     Said she, "All right, come on."
So quickly we were gone
And she prepared the fire
Which customs there require
    Of every mountaineer.

1030     She gave me bread of rye,
All grimy, dark, and dry;
She gave me watered wine
And meat besoaked in brine
    So that it tasted queer.

1031     She gave me cheese of goat
And said, "Sir, let your throat
In this brown bread delight
And in this crust of white
    Which I have hoarded here.

1032     "Eat well," said she, "my guest,
And drink and take your rest;
Get warm and then be gay,
No harm can come your way
    'Till your return career.

1033     "The man who isn't daunted
In giving what I've wanted,
May share my bed with me
And have a wondrous spree
    Which will not cost him dear."

1034     I answered, "While you talk,
Do not in begging balk
To ask a certain thing."
"What," quoth she, "will you bring
    The goods in faith sincere?

1035     "Well, give me then a belt
Of full-dyed scarlet pelt
And after that a waist
Exactly to my taste
    With pendant collar sheer.

1036     "Give me a string of beads
Of tin, and more than needs
Give me some precious gems
As good as diadems
And furs without a peer.

1037     "Give me besides a hood
With ample ribbons good,
And give me next some shoes,
High topped, in scarlet hues,
And carved like checked veneer.

1038     "With all those presents then,
I tell you once again,
That you shall welcome be
To live as spouse with me
While I as bride adhere."

1039     Said I, "My lady peasant,
So many a costly present
I do not bring with me,
But I'll leave surety
Until I can appear."

1040     At that replied the wench,
"No bargain can we clench
Unless some money shows—
Without it nothing goes
And faces look severe.

1041     "No good was e'er the trade
That moneyless was made.
I do, myself, detest
An empty handed pest
And will not lodge him here.

1042     "Politeness never will
Get credit on a bill
But one with money can
Have all that's loved by man,
A truth which all revere."

## The Hymn Which the Archpriest Offered
## to Saint Mary of the Ford

1043    Saint James, the blest apostle, says that every perfect gift
And every good descends from God who ne'er deserts His shift;
Wherefore, as soon as I got through my amatory rift,
I turned to pray to God on high to cast me not adrift.

1044    Nearby this mountain land there lies a place that's much adored,
A very holy spot men call Saint Mary of the Ford;
'Twas there I went, as I was used, to fast and serve the Lord,
And there I wrote a hymn to Mary, and Her grace implored.

1045    Ah noble Lady, Mother Thou, who are compassionate,
Thou shining lantern of the world and light of heaven's gate,
My body and my soul I give to Thy majestic state,
Together with some hymns I wrote with humbleness innate.

1046           Thou Mother of our Lord, our queen,
               I bow before Thy shrine;
           Most holy Virgin, pure, serene,
               Unto my prayer incline.

1047           My soul I do in Thee confide
               And to Thy glory pray,
           Nor shall my hope e'er turn aside
               From Thee in any way.
          Oh help me, Virgin, and abide
               With me without delay
And intercede for me with Christ, Thy blessed son divine.

1048           Although in glory great Thou hast
               Thine happiness complete,
           Yet would I still in verses cast,
               As for Thy memory meet,
           The story of that tragic past
               Of Christ, our Saviour sweet,
Who, suffering with grief and pain, in prison vile did pine.

## The Passion of Our Lord Jesus Christ

### I

1049
The third hour had begun
Upon a Wednesday when
Christ's body glory won
From all Judea's men;
Yet Thy belovèd son
Was little honored then
By Judas, that disciple false, who sold his lord benign.

1050
For thirty coins was had
The ointment sweet, which rolled
Upon our Saviour sad,
And for that sum of gold
The Jewish lords were glad
To buy, and have Him sold,
Wherefore to Christ's betrayer false, they counted silver fine.

1051
And thus at matin's hour,
As Judas had agreed,
The council in full power
(All dogs of Jewish breed)
As if they would devour
A thief for very greed,
Beset Lord Jesus round about with villainous design.

1052
Then didst Thou near him stand
About the hour of prime,
And saw on every hand
Men smite Thy son sublime
At Pilate's dour command,
And spew their filthy slime
Upon His clear and radiant face that did with glory shine.

1053
And when the third hour came,
They judged the Christ, our Lord,
But in the Torah's name,
(The law of race abhorred),
Now for that single blame
That captive Jewish horde
Shall never taste of liberty but must oppressèd pine.

1054
    Then with a retinue
      They brought Him to His death;
    And for His vesture threw—
      Just as the Scripture saith—
    Their lots. And Thou didst view
      Thy son's last, dying breath,
And who could say which grief was worst of all those griefs of Thine?

1055
    The sixth hour coming, lo,
      They crucified Thy son,
    And grievous was Thy woe
      Endured for that sweet one.
    Yet from it grace did flow
      And light was here begun—
That everlasting light of heaven which never shall decline.

1056
    But at the hour of nine
      He died, and with a crack
    Great heaven left its throne
      And all the sun grew black.
    And when the lance was thrown
      Earth trembled at the wrack—
Then blood and water issued forth, the world's sweet holy sign.

1057
    At last at eventide
      They took Him from the tree,
    All wounded, limbs and side.
      With spice embalmed was He,
    And in a rock-vault wide
      Was laid, and by decree
Centurions were ordered there to guard that holy shrine.

1058
    Since He those wounds endured
      And passion for me bore,
    May all my woes be cured
      By Thy sweet comfort's store,
    And thou, by God secured
      Bless me forever more,
That I may always be Thy servant, loyal though indign.

## II

1059
    All we who are in thrall
       To Christ, and to Him cleave,
    Should evermore recall
       His death, and for Him grieve.

1060
    The prophets did relate
       What things should come of worth;
    First Jeremiah great
       Said Christ would come on earth,
    Isaiah next did state
       That He should have His birth
          Of Virgin, whom we all
          As Mary pure receive.

1061
    Another seer averred,
       As the Old Bible saith,
    That just to save the herd
       The Lamb would die the death.
    And Daniel then was stirred
       With his prophetic breath,
          Our king the Christ to call—
          At least so I believe.

1062
    Then as the prophecy
       Foretold, it was fulfilled.
    He, Virgin, grew in Thee
       And issued as 'twas willed.
    Oh blest by all is He
       Who for us all was killed
          For now on altars tall
          That Man-God we perceive.

1063
    Because our Lord descended
       To save the human race,
    By Judas He was vended
       So cheap, 'twas a disgrace.
    With blows He was offended
       By Jews, a nation base.
          And then in Pilate's hall
          Was flogged without reprieve.

1064        They spat on Him with scorn
           Whose face was heaven-clear;
        They did His brow adorn
           With thorny crown severe;
        He was on cross upborne
           By heartless men austere;
           Oh may His wounds appall
           And sorrow in us leave!

1065        They pierced His hands and feet
           With nails, and for His thirst
        Gave vinegar unmeet.
           The wounds that from Him burst
        Are more than honey sweet
           To us who from the first
           Our hopes in Him install
           Which none can ever thieve.

1066        He suffered for our sin,
           Was bruised and crucified,
        And with a javelin
           Men opened up His side.
        The world and all therein
           Are by Him sanctified.
           Let us before Him fall,
           Salvation to achieve.

## The Fight Which Sir Carnal Had with Lady Lent

1067   A season consecrate to God was now approaching near,
      And hence, to rest awhile, I went into my homeland dear.
      Dour Lent was just a week away, and its duration drear
      Inspired throughout the whole wide world misgivings, dread, and fear.

1068   While I was dining at my table with Sir Thursday fat,
      A nimble messenger brought me two letters where I sat
      Which I shall tell you all about if you can wait for that,
      For written in those letters was disclosed this caveat.

1069   "From me, your holy Lady Lent, the liege of your Creator,
      Sent down to sinners here from God as His administrator—
      To each archpriest and clerical who is no fornicator,
      Be greetings in the name of Jesus Christ 'till Easter Greater.

1070   "Know ye that I have been advised that for a year at least
      Sir Carnal has been strangely wroth, and like a very beast
      Has wasted my domains, and damage more he has increased
      By shedding blood in quantities—this has my rage released.

1071   "Now therefore, for this reason, and in virtue of my power,
      I do command you strictly under pain of sentence dour,
      That for me and my penitence, and for my fastings sour,
      You do defy him with my writ of Christian faith this hour.

1072   "So tell him clearly, out and out, that ere a week shall amble,
      That I in person with my host will make his belly wamble,
      For I shall fight the brute and all the routs that with him ramble;
      I trust no one will strike at us in butcher shop or shamble.

1073   "Once read, return this letter to the messenger with care,
      Nor let its summons be concealed—broadcast it everywhere
      So that no folk can make excuse that they were unaware;
      At Castro de Urdiales issued—in Burgos noted there."

1074   An open letter, too, there was which had a seal attached,
      A conch-shell, fine and very large, and well for such like matched,
      It was the seal of Lady Lent who had the writ dispatched
      And this is what there was inside—'twas all for Carnal scratched.

1075   "From Lady Lent, Chief Magistrate and Justice of the Sea,
      High Constable of Pious Souls who shrived and saved would be,
      To you, hog-bellied guzzler, Carnal, to stop your gorging spree,
      I send this summons of my fast—come, fight it out with me!

1076   "Be present just one week from date with all your arms and host
      Upon the camp and field of war assembled at this post,
      For on the holy Sabbath day I'll fight you, and I boast
      You either shall surrender arms or else give up the ghost."

1077   I read both letters, understanding all therein contained,
      And I perceived that I was through a dread command constrained,
      Though I, that time, was not in love, nor had a leman gained:
      Both I myself, and guest as well, were by the missal pained.

1078   My guest the good Sir Thursday was who then sat at my board
      Yet he got up so cheerfully it did much joy afford,
      Said he, "I am the adjutant against this dame abhorred
      And I'll as champion battle her—each year she tests my sword."

1079   Thereat he did with many thanks my kindness well requite
      And went away. I drew a brief, and said to Friday's knight,
      "Go find Sir Carnal on the morrow. Tell him this forthright,
      That he must come prepared on Tuesday for a bloody fight."

1080   Then insolent Sir Carnal, having read the letters, made
      A show of summoning his strength, although he was afraid.
      He did not deign to make reply but speedily arrayed,
      Since he was very powerful, a mighty cavalcade.

1081   No sooner had the time arrived upon the day agreed,
      Than to the field Sir Carnal came with all that he could lead
      Of troopers, well and heavy armed, with all the men they'd need—
      King Alexander would have loved to have such pomp indeed.

1082   As soldiery on foot to hold his foremost battle line,
      He set his pullets, partridges, his hares and capons fine,
      And wild and tame ducks so they might with his fat geese combine;
      Then in review he passed them all where roasting fires could shine.

1083   The lances which they carried, as the outpost fighting men,
      Were mighty spits of iron and wood, sharp pointed as a pen,
      While every one was shielded with a platter for, I ken,
      The first course in a feast is oft a dish of hare or hen.

1084    Behind these bearers of the shield, the arbalasters were,
That is, the geese, dried beef, and sides of mutton stript of fur,
Next hams entire and legs of pork, unsalted I aver,
And then behind these stood the knights, each with his golden spur.

1085    They were the luscious cuts of beef, of goat and suckling pig,
That reared and snorted here and there with cries and squealings big;
Just after them I saw their squires, the smart fried cheeses sprig
Which goad a man to ruddy wine 'till he takes many a swig.

1086    He also had a goodly troop of lords of royal birth,
Full many pheasants it contained and proud peacocks of worth,
All bearing crests and gorgeous plumes—of pomp there was no dearth,
And they were clad in armor strong, the strangest on the earth.

1087    For it was armor wondrous wrought, adorned and tempered fine;
The helmets all were copper pots which did their pates enshrine,
The shields were kettles, frying pans, and plates of odd design—
Indeed, Dame Lent's sardines could ne'er in such equipment shine.

1088    Then came some buck deer, and besides a mighty mountain boar;
Who cried, "Sir, I'll not be exempt from serving in this corps,
For many times against the Jews my pigs have served in war
And therefore, being used to battle, conquer evermore."

1089    Yet scarcely had they said their say and mustered in their clan,
When lo, behold a nimble stag up to Sir Carnal ran,
"I bow before you, lord," said he, "I am your loyal man,
For was I not a vassal made to be your partisan?"

1090    Then swift and prompt to that assemblage dashed the willing hare,
Quoth he, "I'll give to Lady Lent a strange disease to bear,
A fever dread with boils and itch for which she will not care,
But when the chills take hold of her she'll want my fur to wear."

1091    Thereafter came the mountain goat, roe deer and ring-dove, too,
With bleatings bellicose with threats and warlike hullabaloo.
The goat said, "Lord, if I top Lent the way I'd like to do
Not she nor all her fishy things will ever trouble you."

1092    With slow and plodding steps arrived an old ox, sleek and stout,
Who bawled, "I'm given only fodder by the stable lout,
And be not nourished for the fray on battlefield or route,
But I can do you service with my meat and hide throughout."

1093    Sir Bacon stood there 'mid a crowd, with Sausage, Salted Beef,
        Fine Loins, and Choicest Cuttings, from his culinary fief,
        All garnished for the fight marine. Yet from her ocean reef
        Not quickly Lady Lent arrived, of all her fishes chief.

1094    Now inasmuch as Carnal was an emperor of note,
        Who exercised the power of lord o'er regions most remote,
        The varied animals and birds who did upon him dote,
        Came humbly, and with fear, because of rumors wild afloat.

1095    Sir Carnal, full of majesty, sat down in rich array
        To loaded tables in his hall 'mid sumptuous display;
        In front of him some minstrels were that for a king might play,
        And there were lavish viands stocked against a distant day.

1096    Before him was his standard bearer with a humble mien
        On bended knee, while in his hand he held a huge canteen
        And often blew the Moorish flute which made a shrilling keen,
        But wine, the bailiff of them all, talked loud, and so obscene.

1097    At last, when dead of night arrived, long after they had dined,
        And every man had filled his paunch nor left a scrap behind,
        Their bedtime past, each fell asleep, but with determined mind
        To battle Lady Lent, and give her many cuts unkind.

1098    That night the rooster sentries walked their posts with wild surmise
        Or fearfully they stood their guard and never shut their eyes,
        For since the day their wives were slain to make up chicken pies,
        The smallest noises made them start and crow with dread surprise.

1099    About the middle of the night, down through the banquet halls
        Charged Lady Lent—the roosters crowed, "God save us from
            these brawls"
        And beat their wings and cock-a-doodle-dooed their battle calls,
        Until Sir Carnal heard the racket from their hellish squalls.

1100    But since that good old toper knight had eaten over much,
        And with the salted meats had taken wine in measures such
        As fiddle-faddled all his wits and left him in their clutch,
        Quite unexpected burst the call to battle through his hutch.

1101    Yet dazed and boozy-groggy out they started for the clash
        But when their battle line was ready, none felt battle rash.
        Then with their shining armor swept Lent's sea men with a splash,
        And shouting, "Die!" they struck at them with many a grievous gash.

1102    The foremost of them all who smote Sir Carnal was the leek,
        A hoary headed wight, forsooth, who did so dourly pique
        Sir Carnal that he coughed up phlegm which seemed a lucky streak.
        So Lady Lent concluded all the loot was hers to seek.

1103    Thereat a salted sardine came and rendered her his aid
        By dealing to Sir Rooster such a hearty accolade
        Upon the bill, he choked to death by swallowing the blade;
        Then, afterwards, he smote Sir Carnal, splitting his cockade.

1104    Some monstrous dogfish at that instant charged the foremost rank,
        While both their allies, grey and green, were guarding either flank,
        And thus the tide of war was turned by Lent's grim foemen lank
        Who left, from bashed out skulls, a mess of bloody brains that stank.

1105    Some eels from near Valencia's coast came wriggling to the fray
        In squirming masses, dried and salted, blocking Carnal's way;
        They flayed his rib bones mightily and made him lose the day
        As fine Alberche trout upon his flanks brought disarray.

1106    The gamy Tunny fish fought like a veritable lion,
        For he transfixed Sir Lard and smote Sir Bacon, Carnal's scion,
        So hard, that had not Lady Beef preserved that sorry cion
        By warding off the blows he took, he'd now be up in Zion.

1107    More dogfish from Bayona came, with war lust agitated;
        They killed Sir Carnal's partridges; the capons they castrated,
        While from the brook Henares, where the crayfish best are rated,
        To far up clear Guadalquivir, the shrimps in camp awaited.

1108    Right there against the ducks some barbels made a bloody row;
        A hake cried out unto a hog, "Where hide you, Lady Sow?
        Come stand against me for I swear I'll stick it to you now,
        Or lock you up inside a mosque, since prayers you disavow."

1109    A bulldog shark, to join the carnage, swam up streams and brooks,
        Completely armed in hide of mail, embossed with grappling hooks,
        So that his foemen's ribs and legs were writ to Satan's books,
        For like a cat he all impaled upon his barbèd crooks.

1110    From everywhere—from salty ocean, puddle, sea, and pool—
        Came, helter-skelter, companies of many a garish school,
        All armed with bows and arbalasts and every battle tool—
        'Twas worse than at Alarcos when the Moors made Christians pule.

1111    From off the coast of Santander squirmed choice vermillion eels
Who carried countless darts and arrows in their quiver creels;
They made Sir Carnal pay the scot for all his gorging meals,
Until what part of him was fat grew slim as his ideals.

1112    A proclamation ordered then a year of jubilee
Whereby all fish might save their souls through Christian recipe
By killing Carnal—hence a host forsook their native see
To join the herrings in a holy, hot crusading spree.

1113    A certain doughty fish kept fighting there with many knights,
A-laying right and left and killing most of Carnal's wights.
The valiant shad slew flocks of thrush, but greatest of all sights
Was when Sir Dolphin broke old Ox's teeth in little mites.

1114    Some shad and dace conducted by a lamprey of birth,
From Seville and Alcántara came hunting loot of worth,
And each drove in Sir Carnal's guts their weapons without mirth,
Nor did it help to loose his belt and void a little earth.

1115    A spotted dogfish bravely strode like some stout hearted boor,
And brandished in his brawny hands a mace-like truncheon dure
With which he based a suckling pig and stunned a sow mature,
Then straight in strong Valencian brine he soaked the twain to cure.

1116    An octopus no time the peacocks gave to strut around,
Nor let the pheasants take to wing and soar above the ground,
But strangled goats, and kids, and hams where'er they could be found,
For since he had so many arms he could a lot surround.

1117    The oysters, too, for battle with the timid cronies thrilled,
Meanwhile the armored crayfish jousted with some rabbits skilled,
And here and there, with mighty blows, Sir Carnal's troops were killed,
While fish scale armor and red blood the valley bottoms filled.

1118    There grimly battled those who hailed Laredo suzerain,
The fresh and sun dried conger eels—they wrought such grievous pain
Upon Sir Carnal, pressing him and hacking him amain,
That he was saddened unto death, nor comfort could attain.

1119    Yet ne'ertheless he rallied strength and raised his battle flag,
All rash and fierce from desperation, spurring on his nag.
He charged upon Sir Salmon who from Urdiales' crag
Had just arrived. That noble fish did not for combat lag.

1120   But hard and hot and long and oft some cruel buffets struck.
       Yet had not others come, Sir Carnal might have changed his luck,
       For lo, a most gigantic whale came lumbering like a truck
       And closing in upon him bore him down into the muck.

1121   The greater part of Carnal's band already had been hurt;
       A goodly number wounded were and many bit the dirt,
       Still Carnal, though unhorsed, afoot, did desperately exert
       Himself upon his own defense, with hands almost inert.

1122   Then since few troops supported him, for worse his fortunes changed;
       The stag and boar deserted him and o'er the mountains ranged,
       While every head of cattle in his army grew estranged,
       And those who did remain with him were measly and bemanged.

1123   Indeed if it were not for damsels Beef and Bacon Fat
       Who deathly yellow pale, were much too fleshy for the spat,
       Because they could not fight without wine-bibbing by the vat,
       He would have been alone, harassed, and wretched as a rat.

1124   Thereat the sea food company assembled in a troop,
       And driving spurs into their mounts, rushed on him with a swoop.
       They did not try to kill him, pitying the nincompoop,
       Wherefore they bound Sir Carnal and the members of his group.

1125   Then keeping watch lest they escape, those wights with fetters fraught
       Were handed o'er to Lady Lent as soon as they were caught.
       That dame commanded straight that Carnal be to prison brought
       While damsels Beef and Bacon Fat should have a gallows wrought.

1126   Upon a scaffold, watch tower high, she said they should be strung,
       Forbidding all to cut them down as loftily they swung.
       Thus from a beechwood wine press beam, with gibblets they were flung;
       The hangman cried, "Who does the like, will also here be slung!"

1127   Sir Carnal was commanded then to keep the lenten fast,
       And where no one could come to him he was in prison cast.
       None saw him but the priests and sick who meatless could not last
       And Carnal there each whole long day got only one repast.

### Concerning the Penitence Which the Friar Imposed upon Sir Carnal, and in What Wise a Sinner Should Confess Himself, and Furthermore, Who Has the Power to Absolve Him

1128    Now then a pious friar came Sir Carnal to confess;
        He puled and preached to him about Jehovah's holiness
        And ranted 'till Sir Carnal grieved he'd got in such a mess,
        And begged the priest for mercy under dour religious stress.

1129    Sir Carnal signed a writing covering each and every sin,
        And sealed and folded up the writ with all his secrets in.
        The priest protested in such wise he could not pardon win
        And quoted scriptural passages anent this point, *sans fin*.

1130    It seems that penitence is never made through writ or letter
        But by the very word of mouth of every contrite debtor;
        No one can be by brief absolved from one's transgression's fetter,
        Since what is needed is the word of some divine abettor.

1131    Now while on this absorbing theme of penitence I touch,
        I would reiterate to you one churchly tenet much—
        You must devoutly swallow this, with faith and hope and such,
        That penitence gains paradise; else we'd not use that crutch.

1132    Since penitence is thus esteemed ecclesiastic leaven,
        Forget it not, kind friends of mine, a single day in seven,
        But talk about it much to God, let it be e'er your steven—
        The more you prate of penitence, the more you'll get in heaven.

1133    To me it seems a matter grave in such to be a teacher
        Because this subject like the sea's too deep for any creature,
        Wherefore, since I'm unlettered, dull (in other words, a preacher)
        I dare not venture on it save to treat a casual feature.

1134    Yet for this business which I've set my heart upon to write,
        I am afraid I can't express my meaning to you quite,
        Since with my scant, untutored wits, of failing I have fright,
        So please, dear readers, with your learning set my faults to right.

1135    In scholarship I'm very rude—no doctor I, nor master
        (I've had too little academic lore for that disaster),
        But take my words as best you can, esteemed grammaticaster,
        And I will subject my mistakes to your corrective plaster.

1136    The sanctified Decretals touch a point that's strongly mooted,
        On giving pardon solely when admission's constituted;
        It first defines confession, then it says it's executed
        Upon a sinner only when contrition's firmly rooted.

1137    However, though such talk is true, it should not quite suffice
        When time and life are long enough to wean one's ways from vice,
        But only when one's days are brief can one gain paradise
        By words devoid of works, since then one can't pay other price.

1138    One can be quits with God, as He's almighty and all-snooping,
        But since the church can't read the secrets which the heart is cooping,
        One must show outward signs of grief by blubbering and whooping,
        That all may know one has sunk down to Christian nincompooping.

1139    By abject thwacking of the paunch one shows that one has sinned;
        By caterwauling, grunts, and sighs as loud as breaking wind,
        By snuffling, bawling, all the while Christ Jesus' name is dinned,
        And then, when one can do no more, by postures spittle-chinned.

1140    Through such divine hypocrisy one cheats the fires of Hell,
        But still to Purgatory goes—that Catholic hotel
        Where God in His supreme compassion, fries His creatures well,
        'Till, being men no more, He deems them safe with Him to dwell.

1141    And that contrition of this nature God Almighty pleases,
        Is one of our better known ecclesiastic wheezes.
        By prayers and penitence and like emotional diseases,
        God pardoned Mary Magdalene her love affair with Jesus.

1142    Our lord Saint Peter who was such a pious, holy critter,
        Through cowardice denied the Christ and proved himself a quitter.
        Then like the man he was, he wept, both copious and bitter;
        (For edifying tales I know of no example fitter).

1143    The king, Sir Hezekiah, when Jehovah said he'd die,
        Rolled over to the wall and much from penitence did cry
        'Till God in pity changed His mind, gave him another try,
        And added fifteen years of life to that old actor sly.

1144    Now there are many clergymen, unhampered by much learning,
        Who hear the pleas of penitence of all who are sojourning
        In ways of sin, be they their flock or strangers to them turning,
        And they absolve them all alike without the least discerning.

1145    But much they err in doing this, for that should not be done,
And what should not be done, it seems, is logical to shun,
For if the blind will lead the blind the twain must surely run
The risk of falling in the pit whence there shall issue none.

1146    Can Cartagena's judge exert in Rome a legal power?
Or can Riquena's mayor in France give doom a single hour?
No man should stick his sickle in another's planted bower—
Let him who does such trespass suffer retribution dour.

1147    All problems of significance which need attention drastic,
To Bishops and Archbishops or some high ecclesiastic
Are given over to receive their curing antipastic
Save those the Pope preserves for his enlightenment monastic.

1148    And those especial problems which engross the papal ear
Are numerous in churchly law. Indeed to make them clear
Would spin a tale that well might fill two volumes (somewhat drear);
But who would know them let him go and the Decretals hear.

1149    Yet since Archbishops have been blessed and duly consecrated
With pallium and staff and mitre as it's regulated,
And ornaments pontifical and rights denominated,
Shall matters for their wisdom by a simple monk be prated?

1150    Moreover both the Bishops and the Elders of the kirks
Can audit God's accounts and play ecclesiastic quirks;
They can absolve and dispensate and juggle mighty works
Which strictly are prohibited to humble, lowly clerks.

1151    The first of these are numerous, the next, as much, I'm sure;
But anyone can learn of them if study he'll endure
By thumbing glosses, books, and texts, and manuscripts obscure,
Which study furthermore will make a scholar of a boor.

1152    Let him begin the *Speculum* to read, and *Repertory*,
The Cardinal of Ostia's books (a prolix category),
The works of Innocent the Fourth which point the way to glory,
Guy's *Rosary*, and one that's called *Novela* (not a story).

1153    Some hundred doctors erudite in book and legal suit,
With reasons subtle, arguments, and with no end of bruit,
Have opposite conclusions drawn which utterly confute;
Wherefore, my friends, don't censure me because I won't dispute.

1154    You, Mister Simple Clergyman, be careful lest you break
        Your bounds on my parishioners, and their confessions make.
        And further, don't presume to judge of powers you don't partake,
        Nor lacerate your spirit for some other sinner's sake.

1155    Without the Prelate's power supreme, or without license given
        By his own curate, let not strangers of their sins be shriven;
        Take care! Absolve them not, nor be to giving sentence driven
        In cases certainly from your own jurisdiction riven.

1156    This is, at least in common right, the practice tried and true,
        But in the hour of death or when necessities ensue
        Wherein the sinner cannot tread another avenue,
        Absolve not only those of yours but all that cling to you.

1157    In times of peril, as I say, when Death prepares to snatch,
        You are Archbishop, Pope, indeed, the whole religious batch,
        Whose power is vested then in you a sinner to dispatch,
        Since great necessities all things from rigid rules detach.

1158    Yet in such cases even then you should instruct the sinner,
        If there be time before he die, to wait his ghostly dinner,
        If possible, 'till his own priest may probe his person inner,
        For with one's own religious coach one's sure to be a winner.

1159    And furthermore you should unto the sick man give injunction,
        If, through some oversight of God's his dying shouldn't function,
        When he gets strong he must (because you gave extremest unction)
        Go rinse his body in some river with supreme compunction.

1160    There is no doubt but that the Pope is our perennial source,
        Since he's the Vicar General of things in this world coarse,
        But others are the tributary streams of papal force;
        Archbishops, Bishops, Cardinals, and those the Sees endorse.

1161    Now this especial preacher who, I said, to Carnal came,
        Was by the pudgy, paunchy Pope and others held in fame,
        And since Sir Carnal's case was one necessity might claim,
        That preacher straight absolved him from all vestiges of blame.

1162    As soon as this most saintly Parson, Carnal had confessed,
        He ordered him a penitence which well he might detest,
        For 'twas to limit him to one sole viand, daily dressed;
        Then, if he ate no more than that, he might as pardoned rest.

[165]

1163    That preacher said, "When Sunday comes, since you did mortal sin,
        You must some chick-peas eat with oil—but let the oil be thin;
        That done, devoutly go to church—don't loaf about the inn,
        So that you'll not desire lewd things, nor long for worldly kin.

1164    "On Monday, since you burdened were with overweening pride,
        You may eat naught but bastard-peas—no trout or salmon fried;
        Then kneel in humbleness at prayers—don't wrestling matches bide,
        Nor go to quarrelling again, for now you're sanctified.

1165    "Because you had great avarice, I say, when Tuesday comes
        Eat only of asparagus, as much as both your thumbs;
        Let but two-thirds or half a loaf of bread suffice your gums,
        And I command the poor be given all remaining crumbs.

1166    "The spinach for your Wednesday meal should not be thick nor rich
        Because I would not have your lusts, through banqueting, to twitch;
        You never did restrain yourself from nun, nor wife, nor bitch,
        But made them promises to soothe your fornicating itch.

1167    "On Thursday you shall dine, as punishment for mortal ire,
        (And also for the perjuries in which you played the liar)
        On melancholy salted beans—then oft to God aspire,
        And when such practice cools you off, you will naught else require.

1168    "To show repentance for excessive gluttony and greed,
        On Friday, eat just bread and water without other feed;
        Distress your body with the rigors of our holy creed,
        And God will show you mercy and restore you in your need.

1169    "Eat stale horse-beans the Sabbath day without a bit of flesh,
        And as a punishment for envy, eat no fishes fresh;
        Then if this tribulation does your spirit somewhat thresh,
        You may be sure your sinful soul will 'scape the Devil's mesh.

1170    "Meanwhile I order you to ramble through each cemetery,
        To visit every church, and pray, and read your breviary,
        And when you see priests juggle bread and wine, be humbly chary—
        Then God will help you to derive some gain from fate contrary."

1171    When penitence was given and confession made direct,
        Sir Carnal struck an attitude devoutly circumspect,
        Exclaiming, "Mea culpa," or some words to that effect,
        Whereat the friar blessed and left him with the Lord's elect.

1172    Sir Carnal then remained locked up, distressed beyond belief,
       All weak and sorry from the war and macilent in beef,
       Worn out and smitten grievously, consumed by bitter grief,
       While ne'er a pious Christian man dealt with that fallen chief.

## Concerning What Was Done Ash Wednesday and During Lent

1173     As soon as Lady Lent had brought her victory about,
      She gave the word to strike her tents and set upon the route;
      Then through the whole wide world she marched and made
          all men devout,
      'Till none remained that time who had desire to fight it out.

1174     So the first day, upon Ash Wednesday, in those houses where
      She entered, neither pannister nor tray of basket ware
      She overlooked, nor yet a platter, pot, or juglet rare
      That was not in a dishpan scrubbed of grease and fat with care.

1175     The many cups and frying pans, large earthen jugs and pails,
      With barrels, kegs, carafes, and casks, and kitchen-like details,
      She ordered washed full cleanly by her scullery females,
      Together with some crocks and lids, some dishes, spits, and grails.[24]

1176     She did the dwellings over, had the side walls renovated,
      While some she put new plaster on and some she calcinated.
      Indeed, where'er she cast her eye, the rubbish abdicated,
      'Till, save Sir Carnal, none I knew that had not jubilated.

1177     Since for the body's benefit comes this day of the year,
      And for the spirit's sake one shelves, this day, one's worldly gear,
      Dame Lent, with pleasant countenance, called Christians far and near
      To mend their ways with Mother Church, and come with conscience clear.

1178     And such who of their own accord for abject doings yearn,
      She crossed on the brow with ashes where men might discern,
      And told them all to know themselves and ne'er the knowledge spurn
      That they are ashes, too, and soon to ashes must return.

1179     She gave each Catholic Christian then that sacrosainted sign,
      That through Lent's term they might lead lives both worthy and benign.
      She put a gentle penitence upon the most indign
      As they with tear-wet handkerchiefs, their natures would refine.

1180     Yet all the while she went about on works of such like style,
      Sir Carnal, sick and sorrowful, grew better in his bile,
      Until at last by slow degrees, he left his bed awhile
      And wondered how he might find something that would help him smile.

1181    So when Palm Sunday came, he told Sir Fast, a meagre wight,
        "Let you and me together go to hear the mass, Sir Knight,
        For if you'll listen to the mass I shall my psalms recite,
        And we shall hear about the passion—since we're idle quite."

1182    Sir Fast was pleased and said the plan did piety bespeak.
        Now Carnal by that time was stout, yet feigned that he was weak,
        And though he went to church 'twas not the one that Christians seek,
        For while he pious was indoors, outside he played the sneak.

1183    Hence, fleeing from the church of Jesus toward the Jewish one,
        He entered their religious slaughter pen upon the run,
        And since they held Passover then he was gainsayed by none—
        In truth they made him welcome for he pleased them with his fun.

1184    When early Monday morning dawned, a rabbi called Ben Ham
        Lent him his nag that he might flee the Christian hue and jam.
        He went to Medellín and there the Guadiana swam,
        Whence came a cry, "Now comes the end!" from many a bleating lamb.

1185    For there a bedlam herd of kids and lambs, and sheep and goats
        Cried this advice to him the while from bleating, frightened throats,
        "If you take us from here, Oh Carnal, by the roads and moats,
        From you as well as lots of us they'll tear the woolly coats!"

1186    From meadow lands near Medellín, from Cárceres, Trujillo,
        La Bera de Palencia, down as far as Valdemorillo,
        In fact from all the mountain lands, young Carnal with punctilio
        Corralled the brutes, albeit thus he did a peccadillo.

1187    Through fields about Alcudia, past all Calatrava's scope,
        The champs of Hazalvaro, and beyond Valsaín's far slope,
        He flew, and made it in three days by going at a lope,
        And terror made the Rabbi's nag afraid to poke or mope.

1188    Now when the bulls beheld him come, they bristled at the spine,
        While cows and oxen rang their neck bells up and down the line,
        And yearling calves and heifers bawled with all the other kine:
        "Help! Help! Good shepherds, succor us, and bring your mastiffs fine!"

1189    Sir Carnal sent his letters out—himself he would not go
        But 'mid the high sierras stayed and mountains clad with snow,
        For he was wroth with Lady Lent whom he would overthrow,
        But all alone he did not dare to march against the foe.

1190    This was the burthen of his summons, both the gloss and text,
         "From us, Sir Carnal, matador, who's coming for you next,
         To you, weak Lent, vile scabby slut, and scrawny bitch, weak-sexed,
         Not health but bleedings, as to one by rheumy sickness vexed.

1191    "Your enemy full well you know we are in mortal war—
         We therefore send Sir Breakfast out, who is our friend of yore,
         To challenge you in our behalf and say we'll lead our corps
         Against your host next Sunday, which from now is days just four.

1192    "Since you came like a thief at night while all the world was black,
         And we were lying fast asleep, secure upon our back,
         You shan't in castle or by wall be saved from our attack
         And we shall ne'er on your account have bodies thin and slack."

1193    Again, in quite a different tenor, came this other brief,
         "From us, Sir Carnal, by the grace of God your mighty chief,
         To every Christian, Moor and Jew who dwells within our fief,
         Be health between us evermore—the health of brawny beef.

1194    "My friends, I think you well know how (thanks to the evil sinner)
         Just seven weeks ago we were disgraced and barred from dinner
         By false old Lent, and all the fishy things that are within her,
         And as she caught us unprepared, she came away the winner.

1195    "Now therefore, I command you all, that having seen this writ,
         You challenge Lent before she is of any district quit,
         And seize and guard her well because she can the world outwit.
         Send Lady Lunch to tell the news, as she is fat and fit.

1196    "Then, inasmuch as Messer Breakfast is the first to rise,
         Let him inform her Sunday ere the sunlight greets her eyes,
         That we shall make attack on her with deafening battle cries—
         I think, unless she's very deaf, she'll hear our lullabies.

1197    Our mandate having been perused, a copy of it make
         Which you will give Sir Breakfast that he may the order take;
         Let him not tarry with it but be speedy for our sake;
         We issue this from Valdevacas, famed for veal and steak."

1198    The letters all were writ in red with living blood for ink,
         And gaily all sought out the place to which they thought she's slink
         And cried to her, "Ha, catiff! Tell us whither do you shrink?"
         That such rude talk bode pleasure for her, Lent could hardly think.

1199    Although she had not yet received the warsome letters dread,
As soon as they were given her and she their contents read,
With hollow, pale, and flaccid cheeks, in accents weak she said,
"God save me from this news of war which rumors now have sped."

1200    Be sure that everybody here this proverb understands,
"Whoever slights his enemy will perish at his hands."
However, he who spares his foe, when he is 'neath his brands,
Will by that enemy be slain, as policy commands.

1201    The natives have a saying that not only are the cows,
But all the female sex as well of beasts that hunt or browse,
As weak as stakes affixed in bran, for fighting or carouse,
Unless they're very hairy, as for instance, are wild sows.

1202    So therefore Lady Lent who was of very weak complexion
Shrank back from battle, prison, death, and things of like connection,
Besides she vowed she'd travel in Jerusalem's direction
And e'en engaged a passage for her maritime trajection.

1203    This lady in her former challenge set a certain date
In which she promised she would fight, as you have heard relate;
That passed, she was not bound upon her vanquished foe to wait
But might proceed where'er she would without dishonor great.

1204    Moreover summer now had come, and no more from the ocean
Were fishes coming to her cause with all their erst devotion;
Besides, alone, a woman can't endure a war's commotion,
And hence, for reasons such as these, to fight she had no notion.

1205    Thus Friday of Indulgences she donned a palmer's pall,
And with it wore a wide, round hat, bedecked with conch shells small,
A pilgrim's staff with figures carved and palm leaves top it all,
A basket fit for alms, and beads when prayers she'd drawl.

1206    A pair of round toed shoes she wore with extra heavy soles,
And on her shoulders bore a pack, as big as bedding rolls,
To carry safe her crusts of bread and other beggar doles,
For such accouterments all roamers need for distant goals.

1207    Slung 'neath her arm the thing which was of greatest worth she bore;
A bottle gourd with rind more red than jay-bill covered o'er
Which might contain a half gallon plus a little more—
No roamer for emergencies forgets to bring this store.[25]

1208   So Lady Lent was, as you see, disguised from foot to head,
         When on the Sabbath night she leaped the ramps and walls, and fled,
         "You who keep watch for me, I think, won't get me yet!" she said,
         "Because not every bird is caught for whom the nest is spread."

1209   With muckle haste she left and fled through all the streets and cried,
         "I vow you will not catch me, Carnal, in your 'weening pride!"
         That night she reached Roncevalley's pass, steep cliffed on either side.[26]
         (God speed and guide you, Lady Lent, o'er hills and valleys wide!)

## How Sir Love and Sir Carnal Came, and How People Went Out to Receive Them

1210    'Twas vigil tide on Easter morn, with April scarce begun,
        When, glorious, on earth there came the bright new-risen sun,
        And joyous bells throughout the land all clamouring did run
        To say two emperors had come to rule o'er everyone.

1211    Those emperors were Love and Carnal, birds of kindred feather,
        Hence all who longed for them went out to greet them both together,
        While budding trees and mating birds gave signs of fairest weather,
        But those whose hearts were high with love, ran fastest o'er the heather.

1212    The butchers first received Sir Carnal with a welcome howl,
        Next, with their many implements, rushed out the Rabbis foul,
        Then timbrel banging tripers came who dealt in gut and bowel,
        And full the hills with hunters grew who on the mountains prowl.

1213    A shepherd waiting for Sir Carnal just outside the road
        Now blew the pan pipes, now a horn, as eager he abode.
        His boy shrilled on a slender flute of cane with hollowed node,
        While on a zither played their chief and sang a merry ode.

1214    Then blood red through the pass appeared Sir Carnal's carmine flag
        Which bore a lamb upon its field as white as bleachèd rag;
        About this standard danced some sheep, each merry as a wag,
        Besides some kids whose downy wool had not begun to shag.

1215    Some valiant goats and many cows and bulls of great virility
        Came round in denser crowds than make Granada's Moor nobility,
        With chestnut, dark, and yellow oxen (prized for great utility)—
        Be-treasured Darius could ne'er have bought them with facility.

1216    Sir Carnal was arriving in a very precious wain,
        Completely covered o'er with hides and pelts of beasts he'd slain,
        And he tucked up his royal smock such wise as butchers feign,
        With skirts at girdle fastened, while he carried arms for twain.

1217    A mighty cleaver in his hand he brandished with a will,
        With which, all kinds of quadrupeds his habit 'twas to kill.
        Besides to stick his heads of beeves he had a keen-edged bill,
        And this he used to cut their throats and skin their hides with skill.

[173]

1218 Begirt up round about his waist, and tied fast with a string,
  He wore an apron, one time white, now red as anything;
  'Twas dyed that color by the goats whose blood did to it cling
  And who did in the throes of death the scales with "ba, ba" sing.

1219 He wore a puffed cap on his head to keep his hairs from straying,
  And with a tunic white was clad, and kept some greyhounds baying.
  Nobody rode abreast of him within his chariot swaying,
  But when a rabbit crossed his path, he loosed a hound for slaying.

1220 Around about himself he kept a pack of mastiffs great,
  With shepherd dogs, and many more from mountains desolate,
  Some bloodhounds, too, and other curs which eat a heaping plate,
  And watch dogs who lie wake at night to guard from thieves the gate.

1221 Moreover he had cattle halters, different weights and scales,
  Sawbucks for joints, and cutting blocks, meat tables, meat hooks, nails,
  And for the trulls who made his tripe, all sorts of kneading pails,
  Besides some new-whelped bitches which he chained against the rails.

1222 The shepherds out of Soria with the flocks from Old Castile,
  Received him in their hamlets where they gave him welcome real,
  By singing him the *Gloria*, and making belfries peal
  Until the world could not recall the like in joy and zeal.

1223 This emperor lodged fittingly inside the butcher shops,
  While villagers from farm estates came tendering their crops.
  Then he, in arrogance, let fall much boasting from his chops,
  And aped a lordly manner as the fashion is with fops.

1224 For killing, skinning, and beheading subject heads of stock
  Which he gave the Castilians and the English by the flock,
  They all paid him in reals or in coins with Gallic cock,
  'Till he recovered what he lost within the past month's shock.

## How Clerics, Lay Brothers, Friars, Nuns, Ladies, and Mountebanks
### Sallied Out to Receive Sir Love

1225 It was the holy Easter time of Jesus' resurrection,
When, noble hued, the sun uprose with clear and fair complexion,
And men and birds and noble blooms, light hearted with affection,
Came out to greet the Lord of Love and sing for his delection.

1226 To welcome him, the birds outsallied—jays and nightingales,
Some buntings gay and parrots too, with long and little tails;
They sang their pleasant songs of love in sweet and tuneful scales,
But those that were the smallest with most music filled the dales.

1227 The trees received them with their branches green and with their flowers
In many divers manners with fair colors in their bowers—
And man and maid their homage paid by loving at all hours,
And drums with many instruments came forth to noise their powers.

1228 There issued, screaming weird and loud, an Arabic guitar,
With shrilly voice and tempo wild as all things Moorish are;
A bulky flute which gave a sound full merry from afar,
'Till Spain's guitar, like sheep in sheepfold, added throb to jar.

1229 A squeaky Persian fiddle came to wail its highest note,
And play the piece, "My Arab Heart," as well as could a rote;
A psaltry with its many strings o'ertopped them like a boat,
But with its pick the merry viol danced with them like a goat.

1230 The harp and half-harp with a Moorish rebeck played a dance,
As merry as the ones they play within the realm of France,
While with its burden mountain high the flute did all enhance,
Helped by the timbrel, without which no music can advance.

1231 A viol such as they play with bow, now purled a dulcet tune,
Now turned to soft and dreamy airs, now shrilled, and now did croon,
But always with enchanting sweetness, singing like the moon,
'Till everyone in ecstasy from very joy did swoon.

1232 A sweet full-harp then sallied out accompanied by a tabor
And tambourine with brassy jingles, clinking like a sabre;
Some organs, too, with hand worked bellows played the scores with labor,
And found a meddling mountebank who made himself their neighbor.

1233    The dulcimer and Moorish flute played with a swollen horn,
A music box and mandolin their sweetness helped adorn,
But bagpipes from the land of Provence added wails forlorn
Until the small, three-stringed guitar was by them overborne.

1234    Then clarinets and Moorish tubas marched with many a drum;
I vow not e'en in times agone had such rejoicings come,
Or celebrations on such scale, or did crowds make such hum—
The hills and fallow dales were full of jongleurs frolicksome.

1235    The streets and roads were flowing full which that parade contained
For there one saw now hallowed men who pardoned sinners pained,
Now brothers lay, now some who wore the cloth but weren't ordained,
Besides an abbot marching there who for Saint Bernard reigned.

1236    I saw some Blessed Saints and some which I Cistercians guessed,
With monks of Cluny, sable-crossed, who brought their abbot blest—
Indeed, the orders that I saw can't be in verse expressed,
But each sang, "Come, let us rejoice!" with loud cries from the breast.

1237    I saw some Hospitaler knights, and monks of Saint James' guise,
Alcántara's good men and some that Bonaval comprise,
And Calatrava—abbots who that feast would solemnize;
"We praise thee, Love!" they sang to him and did naught otherwise.

1238    There went Saint Paul's Dominicans, the famous preaching friars,
But not Saint Francis' tribe except some lesser monkish squires,
With many Augustinians. All sang in loud voiced choirs,
"We will rejoice and gladsome be"—both ministers and priors.

1239    The Order of the Trinity, the Carmelites, and then
The Band of Saint Eulalia came, all loving friends again,
Commanding each to sing and shout to those within their ken,
"Oh blest be He who cometh!"—while the rest replied "Amen!"

1240    The brothers of Saint Anthony rode likewise with this gang;
Their horses were the best, their saddles caused them many a pang.
Young squires were there whose tunics short were smart in cut and hang,
In sooth the whole town sallied out and "Hallelujahs" sang.

1241    Dear Sisters Black and Sisters White and every order went,
Cistercians, querulous Dominics, Francis' nuns love-bent,
All singing as they marched this song which showed their hearts' intent,
"Abide with us, oh Lord, 'tis eve, and far the day is spent."[27]

1242    Thereat out toward the rising sun I saw a flag unfurl,
Resplendent, white, o'ertopping all the hills that did upcurl;
It bore emblazoned on its field the image of a girl,
Not made of serge but costly wrought of thread of gold and pearl.

1243    Upon her head the figure wore a rich and queenly crown,
With love bedizened round about with gems of great renown,
And full of many noble gifts her hands were weighted down;
Not Paris' gold could buy that flag nor Barcelona town.

1244    I saw the man who bore it, after I had long abode,
In splendid garments clad while he a smile on all bestowed—
The realm of France its revenues to clothe him would have owed,
And much it would have cost to buy the Spanish steed he rode.

1245    Attendant on that emperor came many a goodly band,
Archpriests and ladies, each preceding him on either hand,
Then after that such crowds as I give you to understand—
The tumult of their pandemonium sounding through the land.

1246    As soon as that engaging lord, Sir Love, arrived in town,
All rushed to kiss his hands and low they knelt in homage down,
But any one who kissed him not was held a spiteful clown,
Yet suddenly arose great strife which everything did drown.

1247    The tumult was concerning who should lodge that honored guest,
Because the clergy generously would take him from the rest,
But such a move the honest friars did rightfully contest,
Each Christian order piously contending for the best.

1248    Right then the monkery cried out with those who were ordained,
"We'll give thee hallowed monasteries where thou e'er hast reigned;
Our tables, our refectories, with ceilings multi-stained,
And dormitories full of beds where lovers oft have strained.

1249    "Seek not, oh lord, among the clerks to find a worthy host
For they possess no hall where thou mayst dine on festive roast;
Besides, their cramped-up quarters are not fit for thine high post;
They're glad to take but when they're asked they'd rather give the ghost.

1250    "They starve the earth to get their harvest, grabbing where they can,
But still they lack the wherewithal to entertain a man;
A noble lord should have a palace great with lawns to scan,
And not be lodged in cellars dank nor stowed inside a can."

1251 "Nay Lord," replied the clerks, "wouldst thou for woolen monk-garbs
        search?
    Why, monks defile their convent's goods and leave guests in the lurch,
    And their unwholesome, noisy cells would thy well-being smirch—
    Their biggest thing is their canteen, their smallest thing their church.

1252 "They will not do you service in those things of which they said;
    They'll bed you without coverlets and dine you without bread,
    While in their kitchens great you'll find they'll give few viands red;
    No wine they give but water dyed with saffron flower instead."

1253 "Lord, be our guest," the cavaliers thereat did Love enjoin.
    "Don't do it, Sir," the squires cried out, "they'll all your goods purloin;
    Besides they play with loaded dice and you will lose your coin—
    They're quick at grabbing though they're slow at combating to join.

1254 "Great tapestries they have and set their boards for fortune's charms
    All painted yellow, deep as gold, with their emblazoned arms.
    When payment's made they are the first to come in eager swarms,
    But slow to the frontier they go to taste of battle's harms."

1255 "Leave all those men, and let us give you service with our skirts!"
    The nuns exclaimed. "To lodge with men Love's sweetest pleasure hurts,
    For they are poor grimacers all and spleenish-tempered squirts—
    Come, dally with us, Sir, awhile, and try our hairy shirts."[28]

1256 There every one replied he'd not advise such course because
    All nuns love falsely whomsoe'er they catch within their claws
    Since nuns are kith and kin of crows who cry, "Ah pause! Ah pause!"
    And late or never yield that thing which trusting lovers draws.

1257 Their greatest feat is foisting off some wretched scurvy trick
    With painted words and blandishments, and pretty rouge laid thick;
    With gestures amorous and smiles that catch one in the quick,
    While they, with bursts of laughter false, a host of lovers pick.

1258 If Love, this suzerain of mine, were formed to my intent,
    To what the nuns invited he would speedily consent,
    Since every pleasure in the world and appetite he'd hent,
    For once he found their sleeping quarters ne'er would he repent.

1259 But as a mighty lord should never show a predilection,
    He would not take an invitation causing disaffection;
    Wherefore he bade them many thanks with pleasant circumspection,
    And promised grace to all—but most to me, in this connection.

1260    When I perceived my lord had not a place to bed and board,
        And saw the turmoil had already yielded to accord,
        I bent my knees before his grace and bowed to all his horde
        And forthright asked this signal favor from my liege and lord.

1261    "My lord, you had me with you since I was a little knave;
        What good I have, if aught I know, your kind instruction gave;
        My cleverness is due to you and to your precepts grave,
        Wherefore, let me be host while lasts this sacrosanct conclave."

1262    His kindliness was such he gave consent to my request
        And went with this procession to my house to take his rest
        Where every one attended him with solace in his breast—
        'Twas long, I think, since I the like felicity possessed.

1263    Then most of his attendants to his lodgings went away
        Though in my house those instruments remained that make one gay.
        Yet Love, my lord, took care to see that all were housed that day,
        Albeit he perceived small room for many wights to stay.

1264    Said he, "I order that my tent be set up in this mead
        So that whoever is in love may seek me at his need,
        For night or day right here the way shall to my quarters lead,
        Because I will at any time give help to all, indeed."

1265    As soon as he had dined, the tent was pitched without amiss,
        And never could a man behold a thing so fine, I wis;
        It must have been by angels made and sent down here from bliss,
        For not by any man on earth was aught prepared like this.

1266    I would describe the workmanship to you about this tent
        Although you may be late for lunch if so much time is spent,
        Because it is a great account and should not close be pent:
        Full many men put food aside for tales of pleasing bent.

1267    The pole which held the tent aloft was all of color white,
        An ivory tusk, octagonal, you ne'er saw better sight,
        Beset with precious stones about the whole space of its height;
        The tent illuminated was by its resplendent light.

1268    Upon the tip-top of the pole there was a precious stone,
        I think it was a ruby since like fire the jewel shone,
        There was no need for sun to shine so bright it blazed alone—
        And made of silk the cordage was from which the sheets were flown.

1269    In short, I give you warning, lest I bore you to the brink,
        Describing all would use Toledo's paper, pens and ink;
        There is so much to tell about the work within, I think,
        That if I could relate the whole I should deserve my drink.

1270    Beside the entrance, over on the right, a table stood
        Of wondrous noble quality enwrought of rarest wood.
        In front of it a mighty fire blazed hotly as it could,
        While three men eating there each other watched with hardihood.[29]

1271    Three knights they were and every one devoured his proper hoard,
        For each beside the fire sat down, a solitary lord,
        Yet could not reach the others with a lengthy wooden board
        Although the space between them not a coin's edge could afford.

1272    The first one ate the foremost parsnips which his season yielded,
        And one on carrots 'gan to feed his stock in stables shielded;
        He first of all gave grain unto the oxen that he fielded,
        And he it was who mornings cold and shorter daylight wielded.

1273    He ate of early nuts and roasted chestnuts over brands,
        He ordered sowing winter wheat and clearing wooded lands,
        He slaughtered herds of fatted swine and butchered sheep in bands:
        'Tis then old wives tell tales before the fire and warm their hands.

1274    Of every kind of salted meat the second champion ate,
        Yet ne'er did turbid wintry mists upon his board abate;
        He made new olive oil nor did those days a brazier hate,
        For many times he sucked his hands because the chill was great.

1275    The knight was eating bacon with some cabbage boiled in brine,
        And he, with each hand full of chalk, was wont to clear his wine.
        Both gentlemen wore sheepskin coats and liked warm tunics fine,
        While he who next beside them sat had two heads on one spine.

1276    This double headed monster looked in opposite directions,
        And often ate a stew of hens or similar confections;
        He closed his kegs and through his funnels made his wine injections,
        And covered them on top with ice to keep their dry complexions.

1277    He caused his servants to repair stockades with many a rail,
        Clean out the sewers and fix up his mangers without fail,
        And batten silos, straighten ricks, and drive in many a nail—
        That knight would rather go in furs than clothe his flanks with mail.

1278    Three other nobles sat and dined in that pavilion tall,
But although close to each they were, none did his neighbor call,
For they were far apart as were the vineyards off in Gaul,
And yet so close a maiden's hair could split them not at all.

1279    The first one was a tiny dwarf, a wight of little girth—
Now gloomy, stormy, full of ire, now pleasant, full of mirth.
He put new grasses green upon the old and worn out earth,
And he it was dead Winter left to give the summer birth.

1280    The most that he went out to do was just to prune the vines,
To tie the shoots together and to graft the sharpened spines.
He ordered vineyards planted for the yield of wondrous wines
Because he was not satisfied with jugs of dwarfish lines.

1281    The second one sent diggers to his vines to delve their roots,
While pruners followed after, setting slips for later fruits,
And with good grafting knives tight set the whitened, whittled shoots—
Besides this knight enkindled love in men and birds and brutes.

1282    He kept three devils captive bound with sundry gyves and chains,
The first of which he sent to give the girls delicious pains,
And make them feel uneasy in the place that entertains—
From that time on the grass begins to grow upon the plains.

1283    The second devil stirred up nuns and abbesses discreet,
Archpriests, and dames, to parley in Love's hugger-mugger sweet;
With that fiend for their go-between to free them for the feat
They lost their taste for funeral bread and spoke of things not meet.

1284    Ere they'd leave frolics assinine a crow would turn snow white;
Because those men and women there made folly all the night,
And when the devils found them coupled there with much delight,
Both wickedness and naughty pranks they played with all their might.

1285    He sent the final devil into asses fond of playing,
So in their heads he went without a thought of elsewhere staying,
And not 'till August passed would they forsake their assey braying,
But all that time quite lost their wits—this fact has no gainsaying.

1286    The third fair noble was with flowers covered o'er complete
While with the winds he caused he grew the barley and the wheat.
He made men set out olive shoots to yield an oil full sweet,
In seasons when fierce thunderstorms on frightened youngsters beat.

1287    Next, three rich men were weaving here and there a pretty dance,
        So close that 'tween them could not fit the wedge point of a lance,
        Yet 'twixt the first and second stretched a mighty tilled expanse;
        The third and second could not join their hands by any chance.

1288    The first one seeded fruit and grain and often made his lunch
        On goat's delicious liver with a sort of rhubarb punch;
        From him the chickens scampered since their breasts he liked to munch,
        As well as trout and barbels which he also fain would crunch.

1289    And he was wont to flee the heat by seeking some cool house,
        Because his head in summer ached as from a long carouse—
        He walked as slowly as a peacock spreading 'fore his spouse,
        Yet sought out shade and breezy spots, as hills where chamois browse.

1290    The second held a sickle in his hand for cutting well
        The barley which was ready for the reapers in the dell;
        He gathered rice and ate new figs, that time sans parallel
        But oftener he would choke on grapes of unripe muscatel.

1291    The trunks of trees with grafted shoots from other kinds he fretted;
        Ate honey from new honey combs, and though not lazy, sweated,
        And out of native springs his throat with water cool he wetted,
        And if by chance the cherries stained his hands, 'twas ne'er regretted.

1292    The third man to the harvest went and carried in the sheaves,
        Or threshed away the wheaten grain that to their racimes cleaves,
        Or from a tree shook down the fruit that hung amid the leaves—
        That is, he ruled that season when the gadfly asses grieves.

1293    He also soon began to eat some tender little quail,
        And hoist from wells with spiral screws full many a cooling pail.
        Then biting flies the nostrils of the cattle so assail,
        The critters press their snouts to earth but not with much avail.

1294    Next went three workers, following a single road and aim,
        The foremost waiting 'till the second up abreast him came,
        The while a third one in the frontier likewise did the same,
        Yet he who hurried ne'er could reach the one whom he would claim.

1295    The first of these was eating grapes by now completely ripe,
        Besides some mellow figs he plucked from trees as firm as pipe;
        That done he winnowed out the chaff from wheat of finest type,
        And then he brought the autumn in with ills that mankind gripe.

1296    The second calked and set in order sundry casks and butts,
        Manured all the fallow fields and harvested the nuts,
        And then began to press out grapes from off his arbor struts,
        Or clear the stubble off and wall his barnyards and his huts.

1297    The third one treaded out the better vintages of wine
        And like a careful butler filled all kegs with drink divine;
        Besides, he caused seed to be sown upon each ploughed confine,
        Since winter soon would come again and show its bleak design.

1298    I was bemazed as soon as I beheld that wondrous vision—
        I thought that I was dreaming, but in truth, 'twas no misprision,
        However I besought my lord to tell me with precision,
        Because I was not sure what phantoms held me in derision.

1299    My lord, Sir Love, who was besides a learnèd man of letters,
        Within a single quatrain stript the marvel of its fetters.
        Wherein who runs may read and learn as much as do his betters;
        And here is his reply all stript of figurative tetters.

1300    "That table which you saw, the board, the dance, and eke the road,
        All four the seasons are of this terrestrial abode,
        And furthermore the men are months which run in such a mode
        None with the other catches up, but keeps a mensal code."

1301    I also witnessed other things, whose strangeness passed belief,
        Within that tent, but since I would not hold you I'll be brief
        Because from weary wordiness I would not cause you grief,
        And hence I'll prate no more about the tent things of my chief.

1302    Sir Love, as soon as everything was ready in his tent,
        Prepared to sleep, but little was the sojourn there he spent,
        And when he rose, no man he saw, for as by one consent
        His followers that very night all to Sir Carnal went.

1303    So when I saw my lord had leisure, since I was his man,
        I dared to ask him all about those times which past us ran;
        Why he neglected me, and where he'd lived, and what his plan.
        Then sighing deep like one in grief, this answer he began.

1304    "When winter came I travelled south and visited Seville
        And all the Andalusian towns which I with love could fill;
        There every person joyfully bowed down to work my will;
        There riotously did I live, and got a wondrous thrill.

1305   "But just about the time of Lent I set out for Toledo
       Intending there to wanton it and give no pleasure veto,
       But lo, I found such sanctity and worship for the credo
       That when I asked, 'Who's putting out?' few persons answered, 'We do.'

1306   "Why, even in a house of joy where things were painted red,
       A lot of girls came up to me, lean faced from lack of bread,
       And with sour prayers and paternosters banned me from a bed
       'Till through Visagra's gate at length they cast me on my head.

1307   "Although I felt like fighting back, I sought a monastery,
       Where crowded in the cloisters and the stinking ossuary,
       I found a flock of holy buzzards screeching, 'Ave Mary.'
       I saw it was no place for one who was of penance chary.

1308   "I thought that in some other order for a little space
       I might find remedy for grief, but there was no such place;
       The people all with prayer and fasting showed me such ill face,
       You'd think I was a werewolf come to steal their souls from grace.

1309   "They prated about charity but toward me practiced none;
       I saw their outward faces, yes, but not the tricks they'd done—
       Wise men would gain and profit draw if they such tricks would shun
       For 'twere a thing unspeakable into their toils to run.

1310   "I wandered up and down the city, worried and perplexed;
       The girls and matrons often spoke but seeing what came next
       They answered me with 'Jesus saves' and showed themselves unsexed;
       Wherefore, beholding how things were, I fled the city vexed.

1311   "I left this misery before I witnessed its finales,
       And came to Lent's own capital at Castro Urdiales,
       Where, being full of fish, the people hailed me and my allies,
       And there I e'en god-fathered some in their salacious sallies.

1312   "But now as Carnal has arrived I shall no more lament,
       Besides Saint Kitts has brought us quits from all this Catholic Lent,
       And hence at Alcalá my time will at the fair be spent,
       Which done, I shall harass the land with love's sweet discontent."

1313   Upon the morrow, in the morning, long before 'twas day,
       Sir Love took all his retinue and went upon his way.
       He left me full of cares enough though still my heart was gay,
       But that is e'er the fashion with a heart where Love holds sway.

1314     Because wherever Love may go he wrecks the heart with care,
        Yet withal in the lover puts a bliss beyond compare.
        Love always likes a happy heart, a pleased and pleasant air,
        But ne'er with sad nor wrathful spirits will his pleasures share.

### How the Archpriest Called His Old Woman
### to Look for Some Game for Him

1315 Upon the day of Quasimodo, Churches—yes, and shrines—
   Were full of weddings, joy, and songs, and there I saw the signs
   Of banquetings and sumptuous feasts, and tippling it with wines,
   While both the minstrels and the clergy sought their concubines.

1316 All those who erst were single soon were housed and bedded double—
   I saw them in the company of girls who loved to bubble.
   Then I, to have like entertainment, scoured the female rubble,
   Since men who live in loneliness are always much in trouble.

1317 I had my convent-trotter called, my wise and crafty crone
   Whose prompt and pleasant kindliness would not my prayer postpone.
   I begged her for some pretty girl to make my very own—
   For nights are long and painful living continent alone.

1318 She said she knew a widow both voluptuous and sprightly,
   Not only rich and passing young but one who held love lightly.
   "Archpriest," said she, "if you take her you cannot do but rightly—
   No toil or pain we bear is vain if she receive you nightly."

1319 I therefore, by the ancient trollop, sent the girl some treasure,
   Accompanied by a song or two, subjoined here for your pleasure.
   Though my affair came not to pass, the blame was in some measure
   My own, for while I nothing gained, I did naught with my leisure.

1320 In everything my ancient strumpet did her very best
   But could not slip the noose nor catch the quarry in her quest,
   Wherefore she came to me and said with sorrow in her breast,
   "Where people do not want you much, be not a frequent guest."

## How the Archpriest Fell in Love with a Lady
## Whom He Saw Praying

1321    It was the birthday of Saint Mark, a time of jubilation,
When Holy Church processions formed in his commemoration—
The biggest of the year made by the Christian congregation—
That fortune smiled on me before the fête's full termination.

1322    I saw a woman wondrous fair, so fair her beauty awed,
Kneel down in great devotion to the majesty of God.
I therefore cried gramercy to my blessed, upright bawd
And begged her in sweet charity to get this maid by fraud.

1323    She did as I requested, in a fashion roundabout,
Yet said, "I do not want to pay, if ever this gets out,
As dearly as the Mooress made me when I felt her knout;
However, neither good nor bad should scare off friendship stout."

1324    She set about her trickery, and for me bore its toil,
Adopting as such strumpets do, a peddlar's guise for foil,
And thus she gained the lady's house without a fuss or broil,
Indeed, not e'en a cat nor dog did at her steps recoil.

1325    She told my dame wherefore she came and gave my verses crude,
But thinking of her gain besides, said, "Won't you buy this snood?"
To which the pious damsel cried, "I know the many lewd
Designs and tricks, Urraca, which conceal your turpitude."

1326    "Dear daughter," quoth the slut, "do I not even dare to talk?"
The Lady answered, "No, Urraca, at such sin I balk!"
"Oh, you mistake me," cried the trot, "a decent splice I hawk—
'Twere best a widow never wed than in wrong pathways walk!"

1327    "But still 'tis well to have some trusty refuge for your head,
And good, live lovers count for more than any husband dead;
The man I want for you can always by your will be led—
You'll find him sprightly, diligent, and very kind in bed."

1328    Now whether "Yes" or "No" my priceless messenger was told,
She came to me with signs of glee, and said, "Archpriest, behold,
A man who sends a wolf for lambs expects meat from the fold!"
That said, these verses strange from her my convent-trot unrolled.

[187]

1329   "A little turtle dove once sang within the realm of Rhodes,
        Where lovers' pathways cross, and said, 'Beware, for danger bodes
        All women who, in quest of love, seek out love's antipodes.' "
        Soon after that my lady wed a knight of higher modes.

1330   So when the day arrived that he and she were made a pair,
        The lady broke all bonds with me, and I with her, for e'er.
        Perhaps she did not want to sin, perhaps she did not dare—
        But not all women with their husbands want to play so fair.

1331   Well, when I saw myself alone, without a friend at all,
        I sought my crone, who coming cried, "Hail, Archpriest of Saint Paul!"
        Then, laughing at me, said again, "How now, what shall befall?
        Here comes Sir Good Love, looking for a sweetheart to enthrall."

## How the Convent-Trotter Advised the Archpriest That He Should Love a Nun, and Concerning What Happened with Her

1332    Said she, "Friend, pay attention to a mother's admonition:
Go, love a nun; believe me, son, make that your one ambition,
For they can't marry afterward, nor dare breathe their condition—
With them you're safe to taste for years the pleasures of coition.

1333    "I once was servant to a nun, God knows how many a year,
And I learned how they kept their sweethearts pampered without fear;
Why who could tell what wondrous presents, condiments and cheer
They make them with elixirs potent and prescriptions queer.

1334    "They minister a lot of compounds to their lovers oft;
Sharp, pungent citrons, guince, and sometimes pastes of kernels soft,
Of carrots vile, at which perhaps the ignorant have scoffed;
And these they alternate with brews to be at all times quaffed.

1335    "Of camphor and of cumin seed they mix a recipe,
Of compound ginger, lemon, honey, equal parts in three;
Or brew with cinnamon and pink, rose-honey tinctured tea,
Or with sharp spice and honey prime their gallants for love's spree.

1336    "Sometimes they feed  them dragon weed with sugar for a coat,
Or mash of cloves and marigold which burns the tongue and throat,
Or saffron and satyrion which sexual lust promote
And goad a man to go for women like a very goat.

1337    "All kinds of sugars with these nuns are plentiful as dirt,
The powdered, lump, and crystallized, and syrups for dessert.
They've perfumed sweetmeats, heaps of candy—some with
        spice of wort—
With other kinds which I forget and cannot here insert.

1338    "Not Alexander, Montpellier, nor yet Valencia famed,
Possess the quantities of spice and stimulants I've named.
The ones most potent are bestowed by women most acclaimed
And such their virtues are that passion is by them inflamed.

1339    "And furthermore, I'll tell you this on information proper,
That when these nuns have Toro wine, they never rest the stopper.
Ah woe is me, since them I left! I've never filled my hopper—
Wherefore a man who loves no nun has wits not worth a copper.

1340 "Besides a nun is so well trained that in her sleep the straddles,
Is secretive, yet tutors men just how to dip their paddles.
Why when it comes to worldly love and merry fiddle-faddles,
The servant of a nun knows more than dames with leather saddles.

1341 "E'en like the Virgin's image painted every wondrous hue
Which men may worship with a kiss that thrills them through
    and through,
The figure of a nun inflames a man to have her too,
And since she knows the art of love, to learn from her to woo.

1342 "For every pleasure in the world, the latest styles in whoring—
The peace of sated ecstasy (a bliss you've been ignoring);
All this you'll find in nuns, and thus they'll merit your adoring—
Just try the solace of their charms, and I shall cease imploring."

1343 Said I, "One question, Trotter—just a moment while I ask it;
How can one enter who knows not the gate nor what may mask it?"
Said she, "Just let me look this business over ere I task it,
For she who made the hamper has the skill to weave a basket."

1344 Thereat she went off to a nun whom she had served some time,
And this is what took place as well as it will fit in rhyme—
"How goes it, dear old Trotter? Is your health still in its prime?"
"Nay, only so-so—every day into the grave I climb.

1345 "But harken, since I left you I have served a fine archpriest,
Both young and quite successful, on whose charity I feast,
But since I study always how your joy may be increased,
I've conjured him to wait on you—you'll welcome him at least?"

1346 This lady, named Garoza, cried, "Ah ha, he sent you then!"
To which my trot, "Oh no, indeed, full often and again
I begged him, thinking just of you, since ever in my ken
I keep your welfare—and, my dear, this lad's the pick of men!"

1347 But this good woman certainly was sensible and wise,
And all her life was virtuous and ne'er did sin devise.
Said she, "Just such a thing would happen to me through your lies
As happened to a gardener from a viper he did prize."

## The Fable of the Gardener and the Viper

1348   "There was a silly gardener once, who being kind and fair,
        One January while a storm was shattering the air,
        As he was passing through his garden, spied beneath a pear,
        A little viper, almost dead, coiled up and trembling there.

1349   "What with the snow and with the wind and with the freezing cold,
        A mortal drowsiness upon the little snake took hold.
        But being pious and a fool, the gardener made so bold
        As to take pity on the snake whose fortunes he controlled.

1350   "He kindly wrapped him in his blouse and to his cottage took him,
        Then o'er a brazier's glowing coals he vigorously shook him.
        The viper came to life before the imbecile could cook him
        And slipping through the kitchen floor, most speedily forsook him.

1351   "Yet still that pious man each day would minister him food;
        Some bread and milk or something from his small subsistence rude,
        Until from pampering he grew to such a magnitude
        He seemed the largest specimen of any serpent's brood.

1352   "However, soon the summer came, and with it weather hot,
        So that the snake no longer feared the wind nor cold a jot,
        But full of rage and anger left his cramped-up hiding spot,
        And started out to poison all the creatures on the lot.

1353   "Thereat the gardener cried aloud, 'Be off, and leave this place!
        Don't work your damage here!' Then lo, the viper came apace
        And with his coils began to choke the man in his embrace,
        And while he crushed him cruelly he hissed into his face.

1354   "This paying honey back with poison makes ill natures glad
        For they requite the fruits of love by making others sad,
        For piety they give deceit—look what the gardener had!
        Your gratitude a serpent's is, for you are just as bad.

1355   "You once were in distress and poor, a woman of ill fame;
        You had no livelihood nor e'en a penny to your name;
        I gave you money then and long your mistress I became,
        Yet now you counsel me to lose my soul and sink in shame."

1356  "My Lady," said the crone to her, "why is it I'm reviled?
     When formerly I brought you what you wished, on me you smiled,
     But now you see my empty hands, on me are insults piled—
     Indeed I'm like the hunting hound that age made weak and mild."

## The Story of the Hound and His Master

1357   "There was a splendid rabbit hound, both swift and stout of heart,
       Who was when young so light of limb he shot out like a dart;
       He had a muzzle wondrous toothed, with fangs in every part,
       So when he saw a hare he brought it down with greatest art.

1358   "Unto his master every day some kind of game he brought,
       Returning never from the hunt without the prey he caught,
       From which his master, of his merits very highly thought,
       Besides the neighbors, far and near, who praised him as they ought.

1359   "However, hardship and fatigue soon made the beagle old,
       And then his wondrous teeth fell out, and stiffness sore took hold;
       So when a hare popped out among the carrots he patrolled,
       He either couldn't hold the beast or lost him in the wold.

1360   "His master, therefore, full of rage, belabored him and clubbed him,
       And while the beagle whined for pity, with a cudgel rubbed him.
       'Oh heartless world!' the hound exclaimed whene'er his master
           drubbed him.
       'Old worthless, worn-out, good-for-nothing cur!' the latter dubbed him.

1361   "The dog bewailed his fate and sighed, 'In youth I fairly flew
       And brought my quarry, dead and living, to my master's view—
       Those were the days! Alas, I'm old and treated like a Jew;
       I catch no game and get no praise as I was wont to do.'"

1362   The trot resumed, "The qualities and prestige given youth
       Condemn the weaknesses of age and scorn it without ruth.
       Why should a body lose esteem when wrinkled and uncouth?
       I say, the wisdom of grey hairs is fickle ne'er, forsooth!

1363   "To love a person being young, full-spirited and gay,
       To scorn her afterwards in age, debasing her each way,
       Is folly, villainy, and lack of character, I say,
       But charm and grace are shown when youth is reverent to the grey.

1364   "This selfish, avaricious world is tempered in such wise
       That just as long as one can give, the world will idolize;
       But should one's service end, the world's affection quickly dies—
       Nobody wants a friend upon whose back he cannot rise.

1365 "In just such measure as a man can give is he esteemed,
     And thus when I could give you much, how kind to me you seemed.
     But now when I can render naught, my God! How I'm blasphemed,
     And all the services I've done, are past and thankless deemed.

1366 "Is there no gratitude that may past sacrifice commend?
     Must one who serves a thankless master as a beggar end?
     Will evil persons ne'er esteem the ones whose blood they spend?
     And shall a poor, old woman never hope to find a friend?

1367 "Now lady, has my punishment for serving you arrived,
     The penalty for faithful toil 'gainst all that fate contrived;
     Now since I stand with empty hand am I to be deprived
     Of mercy in this rage and scorn your memory has revived?"

1368 "Dear mother, no!" the lady cried, "this pricks me like a thorn.
     I feel sincere compassion for the miseries you've borne,
     And I repent of everything I said to you in scorn—
     In you I recognize ideals that might a saint adorn.

1369 "Yet still I fear and much distrust some hidden conspiration;
     I would not, like the village rat, be forced to lamentation,
     That time the city rat got him to help in his spoliation—
     I'll tell you what befell them, then let's cease this conversation."

## The Fable of the Mouse from Monferrado
## and the Mouse from Guadalajara

1370   "A mouse from Guadalajara rose before the sun was seen
     To go to Monferrado to the market on the green.
     While there he met a bearded mouse of bluff, outspoken mien
     Who bade him to his cave and there dined him on faba bean.

1371   "The fare was rude and scanty but the comradeship was fine;
     Indeed, it seemed the less they ate the more they fell in line;
     Short rations always find a way with pleasures to combine,
     Hence Guadalajara's city mouse esteemed his host divine.

1372   "Now when the meal was eaten and the scraps had disappeared,
     The Guadalajara and Monferrado mice grew so endeared,
     The city one besought his host that ere the next day cleared,
     He'd see their city fair and be this time his guest revered.

1373   "The country mouse then came to town; the other fed him cheese
     With bacon fat unsalted (such as with a mouse agrees),
     And grease and crispy biscuits all in quantities that please—
     The country mouse considered that the luckiest of sprees.

1374   "Good linen table cloths there were besides a snow-white sack
     Crammed full of flour on which, forthwith, the mice both made attack.
     Much honor thus the city mouse unto his guest paid back,
     And, need I say, of joy and bliss their faces showed no lack.

1375   "Full many famous viands lay upon their lavish board;
     The best of morsels went the rounds and cups were often poured
     Which set the country mouse to gorging as his host implored,
     Since pleasure from good dining always puts men in accord.

1376   "But lo, amidst their banquetings as they made gay with cheek,
     The door into the banquet hall gave out a sudden squeak,
     And straight the lady of the house rushed on them in a pique,
     And hither thither fled the mice with terrifying shriek.

1377   "The city mouse from Guadalajara scurried to his hole
     And left his guest to roam unguided there as on a stroll,
     At which the other, nowhere finding any sheltered goal,
     Was forced to crouch against the wall to save his fearful soul.

[195]

1378   "Once more, when all subsided and the door shut with a click,
The humble village mouse was still from fear and trembling sick;
The other reassured him saying, 'Come now, take your pick,
Sir Friend, and eat whate'er you like but be about it quick!

1379   " 'Just try this bit, it has a taste as sweet as honey ball!'
To which the village mouse replied, 'Such things I poison call—
To one who lives in dread of death, a honey-comb is gall—
To you alone the taste is sweet—well, go and eat it all!

1380   " 'To one beset with terror nothing ever savors sweet;
No being fearful for his life has any lust to eat;
No taste of honey on the tongue the fear of death can cheat,
For everything seems bitter to one perilled, I repeat.

1381   " 'I'd rather gnaw, secure in peace, my lentils on the ground,
Than eat a thousand tidbits while disturbed and chased around;
Fear makes your viands exquisite turn sharp and sour, I've found,
And everything is bitterness where mortal fears abound.

1382   " 'I can no more enjoy my time as long as here I spin it,
Because I look for trouble or some cause that may begin it—
Suppose while I was in this room a pussy should come in it?
God help me, when he found me out! I'd pass a dreadful minute!

1383   " 'You have a palace here, but ah, how many pull your latch-string?
You eat fine victuals, but beware, they'll cause your prompt dispatching.
How sweet is peaceful poverty beneath my humble thatching,
For men may trample on you here, or cats serve you a scratching.'

1384   "In peace and in security my poverty seems rich,
But wealth is penury to one whom fears and cares bewitch;
Uneasiness with opulence brings woes that burn and itch,
But happy poverty is wealth raised to the highest pitch.

1385   "I'd rather in my convent eat sardines preserved in salt,
Accompanied by honest dames (whose lives may God exalt)
Than sell my tail for roasted quail, to one who would not halt,
When I had lost my soul for him, to spurn me for my fault."

1386   "My lady," quoth the pious crone, "can you not see the error
In spurning luxury and joy for some fantastic terror;
Your choice is worse than was the cock's, your wit is no whit rarer—
There lies a moral in that tale and you may be its sharer."

# The Fable of the Cock Who Found a Sapphire in a Dung Heap

1387   "A cock was strutting near the river o'er a pile of dung,
      And, being hungry, 'gan to scratch, when lo, he found among
      The relics of digestion there, a sapphire which he flung
      Away, though none was better seen—he cried, by anger stung.

1388   " 'I'd rather have a grain of wheat, or one pit from a grape,
      Than hold within my hands a hundred baubles of your shape.'
      The sapphire answered, 'Let me tell you this, you jackanape,
      That if you knew me better you would bow to me and scrape.

1389   " 'If only some one found me who deserved to have the find;
      If only one held me who to my merits was not blind,
      I'd scintillate, instead of being daubed by dung unkind,
      But ah, my wondrous qualities can't penetrate your mind.'

1390   "So many people read a book, and hold it in their hand
      Without perceiving what they read—they cannot understand,
      Although the matter there is precious, subtle, deep, or grand;
      And hence they fail to honor what should great esteem command.

1391   "When God sends luck to any one who doesn't want to take it,
      Or doesn't see the profit hid, or doesn't want to make it;
      Then let distress, and want, and toil, seize on his heart and break it—
      He's like the cock who found the gem and wanted to forsake it.

1392   "Thus even so, Garoza, 'tis with you, though I deplore it,
      For rather in your cell you'd have a water jug and pour it,
      Than to be served in silver cups and with this gallant whore it,
      Reviving thus your failing youth (a means that will restore it).

1393   "You munch sardines and prawns within a cheerless monastery,
      Chew garden truck, and tough old steaks of shark, in portions chary,
      While shunning quail with which your lover wants to make you merry—
      You wreck your lives by shunning men, you wretched dames contrary!

1394   "With noisome victuals like sardines, besoaked in bitter brine,
      You give your bellies punishment—you wear coarse shirts of twine,
      And scorn your lovers' trout and capons, partridges and wine,
      Besides the flouncy gowns they offer, made of fabrics fine."

1395     Then Dame Garoza answered her, "I'll talk no more today,
But I shall well consider all that I have heard you say,
So if you come tomorrow, I shall give you aye or nay—
And be advised, I'll gladly choose what seems the better way."

1396     Upon the morrow, to the convent scurried off the crone,
And found my nun attending mass, as silent as a stone.
"Hi, yi!" she cried, "God choke that priest, the dull, long-winded drone.
Why do I find you every day attracted by his moan?

1397     "I find you singing hymns or prayers (it's always either one)
Unless it's caterwauling with some other pious nun;
But never I behold you gay, or frisking in the sun—
Indeed, my master told me I should see just such things done.

1398     "You nuns stir up more bedlam with your consecrated crowing,
Than ten geese squawking in a pond or ninety cattle lowing—
Come lady, I've a secret which is surely worth your knowing—
The mass is over anyway—it's time we should be going."

1399     So gaily saying that she tripped with her into the rectory,
And gaily, after praying, skipped the priest to his refectory;
The nun went off to learn she had a lover quite delectory,
The priest went off to guzzle his intestinal trajectory.

1400     Outside, my trollop said to her with many a hem and cough,
"I hope that you and I won't find ourselves in the same trough
As were the fabled ass and dog—my dear, if you won't scoff,
I'll tell you what the story is, and you can laugh it off."

## The Fable of the Ass and the Lap-Dog

1401    "There was a little lap-dog once who frolicked with his miss
    And gave her oft, with tongue and mouth, a wet but loyal kiss
    While much he barked and wagged his tail from that side and to this,
    Most eloquently telling her that love had brought him bliss.

1402    "Before her friends this dog would stand upon his hinder paws
    And entertain the company who rendered their applause
    By throwing bits of what they ate into his begging jaws,
    Which sport a certain ass beheld and marvelled at its cause.

1403    "Then like the silly ass he was, he pondered to himself,
    Till finally, between his teeth, thus spoke the assy elf,
    'I cannot figure why my lady puts me on the shelf
    When her I serve more than a thousand mongrels of that pelf.

1404    " 'Look how I bear upon my spine her galling loads of wood
    And carry from the mill the flour for her whole sisterhood—
    Well now, instead of standing on these four legs where I've stood,
    I'll prance on two to see if that will do me any good.'

1405    "Thereat with dulcet braying voice he bolted from the stable
    And like a stud-ass in a harem, raised a deafening babel,
    Cavorting, snorting, and disporting hard as he was able,
    Until he came to where his lady sat beside the table.

1406    "Then rearing up, he placed his hoofs upon the lady's shoulders,
    But she, half crushed in his embrace, screamed out to the beholders,
    Who mercilessly beat the ass with stones and planks and boulders,
    And left him in that place to die, where now, indeed, he moulders.

1407    "Well so, you see, no one should ever do a reckless act,
    Nor undertake improper things, nor say what's not a fact.
    What God and nature both forbid should no sane man attract,
    And therefore wise men never dare their dictates to infract.

1408    "When asses fancy that they utter wisdom fit and meet,
    Or think they render service when they do some garish feat,
    They only say improper things too silly to repeat—
    'Twere better that their mouths were shut in silence quite complete.

1409 "Now inasmuch as yesterday I was so sorely chided
Because I argued for your good and for it was derided,
I scarce dare ask for your opinion on what I confided—
However, still I beg of you, tell me what you've decided."

1410 The lady answered, "My good dame, did you get up today
So early just to tell the same old lies I heard you say?
I tell you, I will not consent to act in such a way,
Nor take the part that you advise in this dishonest play.

1411 "I feel just like the fox who told the surgeon where to stand
When he proposed a cardiac removal with his hand—
I'll tell you what the story is by way of reprimand,
Then if my meaning's still obscure, I shall on it expand."

## The Story of the Fox Who Ate Chickens in the Village

1412   "It happened that within a town well circled by a wall
    A nimble fox was wont to come and pay a nightly call.
    Between the bolted gates she found somehow a way to crawl,
    And thence, from every hen-house there, she made a wondrous haul.

1413   "But since on her account the townsfolk felt that they were mocked,
    They closed the windows, shut the doors, and every passage blocked,
    Whereat the fox cried, 'Let the pullets whom my raids have shocked
    Laugh at me, though they do not know what ruse I shall concoct.'

1414   "Accordingly she stretched herself before the city gate,
    And feigning death with gaping mouth, with legs up-sticking straight,
    And visage blotched, did patiently the passers-by await,
    Who seeing her cried, 'Here's the time this robber met her fate!'

1415   "Now that same morning hobbled by a man who fashioned shoes,
    'Oh such a tail as this,' cried he, 'I'd not for money lose;
    The hide I'll cut in laces which for my light boots I'll use.'
    He cut it off, but like a lamb the fox lay for a ruse.

1416   "A barber surgeon, coming from some patients he had bled,
    Espied the fox, 'This vixen's eyetooth is a cure,' he said,
    'For anyone who has a pain or toothache in his head.'
    Whereat he pulled it out, but still the fox pretended dead.

1417   "An aged beldame passed that way, whose hens the fox had caught,
    Quoth she, 'This eye will cure whate'er the evil eye has wrought,
    Besides all wenches whom the mother sickness has distraught.'
    Out came the eye, yet e'en that loss the fox esteemed as naught.

1418   "At last a great physician walked adown the street; quoth he,
    'A fox's ears are excellent, authorities agree,
    For ills auricular, I'll try this sovereign recipe.'
    He clipped them off, but still the vixen lifeless seemed to be.

1419   " 'And I recall,' the doctor said, 'though it may seem fallacious,
    The foxes' hearts in cardiac collapse are efficacious.'
    The fox exclaimed, 'To Hell with you, kind sir, but you are gracious!'
    And taking to her legs she fled to regions safe and spacious.

[201]

1420  "Said she, 'A man may suffer every accident and pain,
      Save having someone get his heart, since thus he would be slain.
      To that he never should consent—lost life can none regain;
      In evils irreparable, repentance is in vain.'

1421  "So therefore," said Garoza, "one with prudence should enquire
      Into the thing one wants to do in case one might desire
      Before it's done, at sudden danger, safely to retire—
      It's nice to have some refuge even if it's in the mire.

1422  "When man grows tired of woman, though she thought their loves
              were fast,
      His loathing waxes towards her 'spite of what has been their past.
      Then even God against her turns; by all is she outcast,
      And loses honor, loses fame, yea, loses life at last.

1423  "Through these foul arguments of yours in Hell I should be tossed,
      My body, soul, my life, my fame, all I hold dear, were lost—
      Be off! I say, without delay; by you I'll not be crossed,
      But if you stay I shall repay your merits to your cost!"

1424  At this brave declaration much my trollop grew afraid
      And cried, "Be moderate, my lady, spare the bastonade;
      Perchance some services to you through me may still be made,
      Just as unto a lion when a mouse came to his aid."

## The Story of the Lion and the Mouse

1425   "A tawny lion used to sleep out in the mountains cold
      Where, in a thicket dense, he owned a subterranean hold—
      There likewise gathered in that place a noisy, sprightly fold
      Of mice, who used with roistering to wake this lion bold.

1426   "One day the lion caught a mouse, but as he went to slay him,
      With wheedling voice the terror-stricken beastie 'gan to pray him,
      'Why should our king devour a mouse? My carcass would not stay him,
      Nor would the glory of the deed sufficiently repay him.

1427   " 'What honor is it for a lion—powerful, strong, secure—
      To kill the little, kill the weak, the timid and the poor?
      That is a deed contemptible, almost beneath a boor—
      Let him who triumphs o'er a mouse be of his laurels sure.

1428   " 'To conquer is an honor which all manly men should seek,
      But it's a vile and sinful thing to overthrow the weak;
      The prestige of the vanquished does the victor's prowess speak,
      And just as much as his was great, so is the other's eke.'

1429   "The lion with such arguments felt duly satisfied
      And let the little mousie go, who being loosened, cried
      That he was deeply grateful and would feel a special pride
      In paying back his majesty whene'er it might betide.

1430   "The mouse then went into his hole, the lion to his hunt;
      But as he scoured the wilderness as e'er it was his wont,
      He stumbled in a trapper's net, which caught him rear and front,
      So that he could not move but only rage and roar and grunt.

1431   "He therefore let his feelings out, which noise the mousie heard
      And promptly ran to him exclaiming, 'Lord, upon my word,
      I have a knife, these teeth of mine, behold, when they have stirred
      You'll have a hole whence you can fly as featly as a bird.

1432   " 'Just stretch your paws out through these cords which I have
            gnawed in twain
      And with your powerful arms tear up the net with might and main;
      Behold, but for my tiny teeth your highness might be slain;
      You spared my life, and now through me your own life you regain.'

[203]

1433 "You who are rich and powerful, don't spurn the poor, nor cast
Away from you impoverished folk by misery harassed,
Because a man who cannot pay a penny tax, at last
May render, when you need it most, some service unsurpassed.

1434 "It happens oft a trifle or a thing of small esteem
Turns up a profit for a man beyond his wildest dream,
And men without nobility, or power, or coins that gleam,
Have in their heads ability to plan some cunning scheme."

1435 With such an explanation was this lady more than pleased,
"Old woman," said she to my trot, "fear not, I am appeased,
But you must realize no dame should be by rashness seized,
And I am much afraid to slip upon some counsel greased.

1436 "These beautiful enticing words, and these seductions sweet,
Might turn to bitterness and gall if I of them should eat,
Just as those promises the crow exchanged for honest meat
The time a crafty she-fox overcame him with deceit."

## The Fable of the Fox and the Crow

1437    "One day, it seems, a hungry fox, while prowling ill at ease,
     Beheld an inky crow who perched above him in the trees,
     And held within his bill a goodly piece of fragrant cheese;
     Straightway with flattery began the fox this crafty wheeze.

1438    " 'Oh most aristocratic crow, oh handsome, knightly don,
     Your white and lordly garb proclaims your kinship with the swan;
     Much sweeter than all other birds you sing orison,
     Indeed, for just one song of yours I'd give a score anon.

1439    " 'Your voice the golondrina cannot match, nor popinjay,
     Nor even still the nightingale, nor thrush, nor skylark gay—
     Oh how a song of yours would soothe my aching heart today;
     You need only to ope your mouth to drive my grief away.'

1440    "The crow was quite convinced at last that by his raucous hawking
     He might give pleasure to the world and every creature walking.
     He thought that his vociferous interminable squawking
     Delighted people more than any kind of chant or talking.

1441    "He therefore opened wide his mouth and started saying, 'Caw,'
     When lo, the tasty bit of cheese slipped downward from his jaw.
     The fox devoured it suddenly and laughed a long, 'Haw, haw!'
     Which left the injured crow with naught but rancor in his craw.

1442    "False pride, vain glory, hollow honors, smiles that cheat and charm,
     And yield but sadness, grief, and woe, and work no end of harm.
     How many people think the owner really guards the farm,
     Whereas it's just his scarecrow which produces the alarm.

1443    "One never can with certainty rely on flattery sweet,
     Because such rations always yield a bitterness complete.
     That sin you'd have me do is not for any nun discreet,
     And nuns who are unchaste are worse than filthy, rotten meat."

1444    "My lady," quoth the trollop, "you need never dread that here,
     Nor shun the man who loves you with a passion most sincere—
     I wonder why all women have this silly, baseless fear,
     Particularly nuns—you have the hearts of rabbits, dear."

[205]

# The Fable of the Rabbits

1445 "A group of timid rabbits once upon a forest lighted,
But there, at every little sound, the creatures grew affrighted;
The very waves upon the lake which passing winds excited,
Distraught the fearful rabbits 'till in terror they united.

1446 "They glanced about on every side, too frightened to keep still,
And whispered it were best to find some crevice on the hill
In which to hide, when lo, they spied some frogs plunge in a rill,
Because those frogs, at sight of rabbits, likewise boded ill.

1447 "At that, one valiant hare upspoke, 'Stand fast, let's wait awhile;
It seems we aren't the only ones who tremble in this style;
Look how those cowards at our coming in their brooklet pile,
Methinks that both those frogs and we should at vain terror smile.

1448 " 'You should restrain yourselves much more whene'er the outlook's good,
Because those things still panic you which never really should;
Your hearts aren't stout, my friends, you're quick to scamper
      in this wood—
Now as for dreading baseless fears—men like me never could!'

1449 "As he waxed hot in his harangue, some hares began to run,
Which scared him 'till the fear he showed, stampeded every one.
So thus, my dear, the dread of death makes pious many a nun,
Who being timid, cheats herself from all this worldly fun.

1450 "A very cursèd thing is fear, it saps aggressive might,
But hope and courage overcome and win in every fight;
Base cowards die whene'er they cry, 'Our only hope is flight!'
But soldiers stout live when they shout, 'In God's name, comrades, smite!'

1451 "What happened to those rabbits happens to you, dear, and all
You nuns who take up monkery and into cloisters crawl.
Whene'er some hapless woman takes a stumble or a fall,
You sheep go headlong after with a pious caterwaul.

1452 "Take heart, and cast aside your fears, and such unworthy things;
Take this good lover and enjoy the good love which he brings;
If not, at least bestow on him the courtesy one flings
To boors, when one says, 'How de do.' Then let your cares take wings."

1453 "Old woman," cried the lady, "like the evil one you seem
     Who brought misfortune to his friend by counselling a scheme
     Whereby he stuck his friend and let him on a gallows beam.
     List to the tale and plot no more against my good esteem."

### The Story of the Thief Who Made a Pact
### with the Devil for His Soul

1454 "There was a land where laws were slack and robbers went so free,
The people to the king complained with many an earnest plea,
Until he sent his alguacils, his guards, and cavalry
To hang the knaves, for small offenses, on his gallows tree.

1455 "Then up there spoke a gallant rogue, 'Already I'm engaged
To wed the rope—you see my ears? For what I've last outraged,
They're cut, and for my next offense, if I am caught and caged,
The widow with the wooden legs will have her lust assuaged.'

1456 "But ere that precious gallows bird was frightened to repent,
And consecrate his life to God, the Devil to him went
And struck a bargain in this wise, that for his soul Hell-bent,
He'd help him steal without the dread of being gallows-sent.

1457 "The rascal signed away his soul in writing black and white,
And swore he'd follow every line and clause with all his might
(So does the Evil One devise for us some cunning plight);
Then at a fair the robber stole a chain of gold one night.

1458 "But caught he was and braceleted with heavy ball and chain,
So straightway for his counsellor he called with might and main.
The Devil came to him and said, 'Well, here I am again,
Just trust in me, I'll set you free without the slightest pain.

1459 " 'Now listen, when they talk about your party with the noose,
Reach for your purse and give the judge the wink all fixers use;
A friend I'll put inside which you won't have to introduce—
Give it to him, and by the saints, you'll skip the calaboose.'

1460 "So when they brought the prisoners out to give each man his jolt,
The rascal winked the judge aside, nor did his honor bolt,
For he was used to bribes like that, and hence did not revolt,
But said 'No bird is ever caged whose golden feathers moult.'

1461 "Then quietly he gave the justice what would change his sort,
At which the judge said to his sergeants, 'Friends, this august court
Finds innocent this worthy man—there was a false report—
Release him, sergeant, he stands cleared of any charge of tort.'

1462 "The thief was freed at once without the slightest reprimand,
And far and wide his arts he plied through that unhappy land;
Whenever he got caught he worked the same old sleight of hand
Until the Devil had to pay out more than he could stand.

1463 "The thief was caught, and as his wont, he bellowed for his friend,
But Satan came and said, 'Look here, you nag me without end;
Still, never mind, do what you did—I'll find some way to mend
Your difficulty if you give the judge just what I send.'

1464 "The rascal took the judge aside, as he was wont to do,
And searched his pocket, but, alack, when out his hand he drew,
Not money but a gibbet rope the robber brought to view,
'You brazen rogue!' the judge exclaimed, 'I'll have that dangle you!'

1465 "Then while they dragged him off to hang he spied the Evil One
Regarding him from some high tower as if he thought it fun.
The robber cried, 'Oh loyal friend, help me or I'm undone!'
The Devil said, 'Don't you have legs, why is it you can't run?

1466 " 'Yet hold your water, I'll be with you sooner than a preacher
Can mix a poultice of hot guts upon some pretty creature;
I did but just deceive a knave who might deceive his teacher—
The gallows is your widow now, stretch out your neck to reach her.'

1467 "Again right at the scaffold's foot the wretch began to cry,
'Oh help me, help me, loyal friend—if I'm strung up I die!'
The Devil called, 'What's that to me? Though you hang high and dry
I still can help you even then if I've a mind to try.

1468 " 'Just climb upon the death-woods—when they kick you off in space
I'll get beneath, and both your feet upon my neck I'll place;
I'll hold you up from choking so, and thus I'll save your face
As I have done my other friends who've met with like disgrace.'

1469 "The hangman kicked the robber off, the gibbet gave a jerk,
The crowd who looked on thought him dead and all returned to work,
But Satan kept his word that time and proved he would not shirk
Although the robber weighed a ton and did him muckle irk.

1470 " 'A thousand tons,' the Devil cried, 'You weigh, or very near—
These stupid escapades of yours have cost me mighty dear.'
'Your dirty trick,' the man replied, 'is what put me up here—
By God, for spite I'd like to make you hold me up a year.'

1471 "Then spoke the Evil One, 'Now friend, before I let you go,
       There's something full of interest which I've a mind to show;
       Just cast your eyes about and tell me what you see below.'
       'I see your feet,' the thief returned, 'and something I don't know.'

1472 " 'Yet stay, I see some worn out shoes and boots upon the ground,
       And lousy, filthy, tattered clothes, heaped up in one high mound;
       But viler still I see your hands with hooks set all around,
       A-dangling the most putrid cats that ever could be found.'

1473 " 'That's right,' the Devil said, 'all that you see and ten times more,
       And every foul and filthy thing I keep in noisome store
       Came to me from the likes of you—no wonder I am sore;
       I've stood about enough from you—now dance with your wooden whore!

1474 " 'Those hooks you saw upon my hands are tricks whereby I snatch
       The souls of men, and that explains those cats, my latest batch;
       The reason why you saw my feet torn up with many a scratch
       Is that I've trod some thorny ways ere I could make a catch.'

1475 "Then, having made his little speech, the Devil gave a jump
       And let the robber settle in the gibbet with a thump;
       Who trusts the Devil soon will feel his hooks upon his rump
       And in a little space will reap his troubles in a lump.

1476 "Be warned in time, let every man from Satan stand aghast
       Nor share with any friend of his a secret of his past,
       For slow though his undoing come, 'tis sure to come at last
       And in the falsities of friends calamities are massed.

1477 "The world is like a tissue where the rich man stands aloof,
       The warp he is, while round about him weave the poor, the woof;
       He may have friends and relatives like lice beneath his roof
       But just let him beg them for help, what will he get? Reproof!

1478 "You make your friend your all in all, to him your heart unbends;
       Your trust, your love, your very soul, within his being ends;
       But should there come an evil time, perchance you think he lends—
       You ask—he's broke—then where's the joke? God save us from
           our friends!

1479 "Above all, flee the lying friend who gives you counsel ill:
       You may have fearful enemies, he is more fearful still
       Because his tongue betrays your soul—he kills what none can kill,
       He is a viper in the grass—destroy him with a will."

1480   "Oh lady dear," the trull replied, "you who are wise and good
      Should know I don't mean what you think—you have misunderstood—
      I only meant to do for you what your own mother would
      In bringing him to speak with you in some place where you could—"

1481   "Oh yes you'd serve me," said the lady, "I can truly state,
      Exactly just as I have told you Satan served his mate;
      You'd leave me all alone with him and then you'd close the gate,
      The whiles he clipped and stript and pipped me—that would be my fate."

1482   "Your cruel talk," the hallion muttered, "pierces like a dart—
      To think how much I love you, child—you wound my poor old heart;
      But this I swear, if you but come, from you I ne'er will part,
      Not even though you wished me to and begged with all your art."

1483   The lady answered in this wise, "Does not the law say whether
      The gallant first should state his case when lovers are together?
      What must I do?" The trot exclaimed, "No dog can hunt at tether,
      Nor can a bird that keeps his perch know aught of outside weather."

1484   "Well then," Garoza answered her, "I'll give you one small chance;
      See if you can describe this man, his gait, his countenance,
      His figure, manner, everything, but mind you don't enhance
      And stuff me full of pretty lies, for I take all askance."

# The Appearance of the Archpriest[30]

1485   "My lady," then replied the crone, "I've seen him much about;
      His figure is uncommon tall, with members large and stout;
      He's hairy, with no little head; his bull neck bulges out
      Although it's short; his hair is dark, and long ears from him sprout.

1486   "His eyebrows do not join, and they're as black as charcoal smut,
      He walks erect with chesty gait just like a peacock's strut,
      Yet poised and certain is his stride, its length by training cut,
      But what deforms him is his nose which does so far out jut.

1487   "His gums are bright vermilion hued, his voice is deep and grave,
      His mouth not little, but his lips are like the average knave,
      More full than fine, yet colored with a red the coral gave;
      His shoulders are exceeding broad, his wrists are likewise brave.

1488   "The eyes he has are little ones and somewhat of a brown,
      His chest is full and to the front, his arm might win renown;
      Small feet he has with ample thighs, and legs well tapered down;
      That's all I saw, but here's his hug, 'twill more description drown.

1489   "He's lively, gallant, spirited—a youth but yet mature
      Who plays on instruments and knows all things of minstrel lure,
      Why by my shoes, a wooer gay he'll be to you, I'm sure;
      Such men as he aren't running loose, my dear, on every moor."

1490   How exquisitely was this nun persuaded by my whore!
      Said she, "You may distrust the bargains vended in a store,
      But here's an article that God is peddling at your door—
      Oh love such men as I describe—oh love them evermore!

1491   "You cooped up nuns are passionate, and burning up with lust,
      But sporting monks desire to be with gayer women trussed,
      Howe'er as all things like to swim, they'll wriggle where they must;
      For people starved a month will hunger for a week-old crust."

1492   Said Dame Garoza, "I shall see, just let me think awhile."
      "Nay," cried the crone, "Love doesn't like to dally in that style;
      I want to tell this to my priest, ah how I'll make him smile—
      Tomorrow I shall have him come to this sequestered aisle."

1493   "God save me, trollop," quoth the lady, "from the traps you fix;
       Well, bid him come, but say I must at least have five or six
       Good women with me, nor must he in any nonsense mix,
       Nor utter any obscene jest, nor prate about your tricks."

1494   Then came my loyal trot to me, delighted, smiling, sweet,
       But 'stead of saying, "God's with us," this message did she bleat,
       "A man who sends a wolf to hunt is sure of getting meat,
       And by my chastity, I've pimped your nun into a heat.

1495   "Now God will prosper you, my friend, go to it, have your fun;
       She said tomorrow you might come if with her were some one.
       But watch you don't crack filthy jokes before this pretty nun,
       For archpriests who are impudent these timid sisters shun.

1496   "Yet what may consummate your passion, that be sure to say,
       And what you'll speak tomorrow, plan with utmost care today;
       Go early to her church, and while God's holy mass you pray,
       Incite this nun to burn for you, and she will come your way."

1497   I answered, "Convent-trotter, let me beg you, dearest friend,
       To take this letter to my nun ere one word I expend,
       And afterwards if she says naught to you that may offend,
       Then if I speak, perhaps my love will have a happy end."

1498   She gave that letter to my lady, during mass at primes,
       And brought a happy answer back to what I'd put in rhymes.
       Yet guards she had more than my sword, but guards can't ward off crimes
       And pleasant conversation oft results in merry times.

1499   So in the name of God, next morn, I said my masses there,
       And Lo, I saw the lady kneeling, beautiful in prayer;
       Her girlish neck was slim, her face was flowerlike and fair—
       Whoever made her put on sackcloth did her wrong, I swear.

1500   So help me, Holy Virgin, but I raise my hands, alack,
       Who gave a rose as white as she that ugly habit black?
       'Twere better that a radiant girl should never children lack
       Than take the veil of chastity and fight her yearnings back!

1501   Though God considers it a crime which should all men repel
       To have a bride of Christ's within one's solitary cell,
       I would to God I might have done that sin so sweet yet fell,
       For I would bear my punishment with joy, e'en though in Hell!

1502    She gazed on me with eyes that shone like altar candles bright,
'Till like a prayer my spirit rushed out towards her at the sight;
She spoke to me and I to her as though from some far height,
And then she loved me with a kind of tremulous delight.

1503    Still she received me only as her loved retainer true,
And always loyally I did whate'er she'd have me do,
With clean and chastened love my spirit close to God she drew
So that as long as she still lived, that God I loved and knew.

1504    Through many prayers to God for me she did her life exhaust;
She helped me too by abstinence, though passion paid the cost;
She yearned for God, and in His love her spotless soul was lost—
Ne'er in this frenzied world's delights her being was engrossed.

1505    For loves like that are holy women (of both sexes) made,
That is, for praying God and bringing pious persons aid.
The lusty passions of this world, of those they are afraid,
Hence in some convent they withdraw to pray, lie, and upbraid.

1506    But ere I got converted, such was luck, two months ago,
My blessed lady left this life and leaving, left me woe.
Alas, all men are born to die—a shrewd God made them so—
Then, God, forgive her soul, and us, our sins down here below.

1507    Now being stricken down with grief, I made a little song,
But from the weight of woe I felt, it may have something wrong.
Still, everyone can understand, who does for good love long,
Since faults can't stop good resolutions, be they e'er so strong.

### How the Convent-Trotter Spoke to a Mooress on Behalf
### of the Archpriest and the Reply She Gave

1508    In order to forget this woe, I begged my best of nurses
        To hunt me out the sort of wench a preacher's care disperses.
        She therefore pimped a Mooress but the girl replied with curses
        Which showed her head was full of sense while mine was full of verses.

1509    'Twas thus in my behalf the crone did to the Mooress speak,
        "My friend, it's long since we have met, how are you, dear, this week?
        How comes it is so hard to find a girl whom preachers seek?
        A gallant new sends love to you." Said she, "Who is the Sheik?"

1510    "A man it is from Alcalá, and greetings warm he sends;
        You'll find within this note of his the offer he extends;
        I see the great Creator all your leasings comprehends,
        So take this letter." Quoth the girl, "Let Allah send no friends!"

1511    "Why daughter, if the good Creator sends you health and peace
        You shouldn't scorn it—what I bring will happiness increase
        Because this man will shake the moths from under your pelisse
        Unless you skulk away alone." The Mooress answered, "Cease!"

1512    Then when my trot found out she couldn't bring the girl about.
        She cried, "Whate'er I said to you is wasted, there's no doubt.
        So since you will not answer me I'll no more play the scout!"
        The Mooress tossed her head and screamed, "Get out, you bitch, get out!"

## What Instruments Are Not Suited to Moorish Songs

1513    Now after that I wrote a lot of jigs and dancing twirls,
For understanding nymphs of joy who specialize in churls,
For instruments, for Jewesses, and Arabs dear as pearls—
If e'er you want to learn a tune, just seek out dancing girls.

1514    I next made several blind men's songs for those who'd lost their sight,
And songs for student roisterers who prowl about at night,
And songs to grid from door to door for many a beggared wight;
Ten folios full of mocking songs and others full of spite.

1515    But know that there are instruments, each with its proper sound,
Appropriate in certain ways for whate'er songs abound,
So therefore, I shall here describe the ones which I have found
Most fit and for what instruments they will the best resound.

1516    First, Moorish songs are never good for fiddle nor for bow,
Nor do they seem with symphonies much sympathy to show,
While bagpipes, zither, and guitar hate Arab measures low,
But love the tipsy tavern airs and with barn dances go.

1517    The flageolet, the shepherd's flute, the triple stringed bandore,
Hate Moorish airs as much as we the Bolognese abhor,
And any one who wants with them to play a Moorish score
Deserves to pay full costs and bear the shame forevermore.

1518    Yet some philosopher has said (just where I have forgot)
Within his works, that sorrow irks and cares make one a sot;
Well, I must here confess to you that I can't write a jot
Because my convent-trotter now can neither plot nor trot.

1519    She has just died—oh hellish fiends!—she's dead, that loyal nurse,
She died while she was serving me (a thing that grieves me worse).
I know not what to say because the girls she could coerce
Now slam their doors on me and bar the ways I would traverse.

### How the Convent-Trotter Died, and How the Archpriest Makes Her Lament, Cursing and Reviling Death

1520    Ah Death! My Trotter, are you dead, sped off with foul dispatch?
You, Death, have killed my hoary whore ere you at me can snatch;
You enemy of all the world, no specter has your match,
And none there is who does not dread your cruel, grievous scratch.

1521    Ah Death! The one that feels your claws, you snatch at by the shirt,
Both good and bad, both lordling rich and villain poor as dirt,
All men, no matter who, receive alike your summons curt;
For popes and kings you would not give the value of a wort.

1522    You have no care for friends or kin, or what men hold of worth,
But keep an everlasting hate toward all the wide, rough earth;
Of moderation, love, or pity, you have only dearth
While cruel grief and pain and woe you bring with bitter mirth.

1523    No man can hide himself from you or from you hope to fly;
No man has ever been who could against your onslaughts vie.
Your grievous visitations none can tell when they are nigh,
And when you call, you will not wait 'till man's resigned to die.

1524    Man's body you leave lifeless, save for maggots in the marrow;
His soul you speed as swiftly on as arbalasted arrow;
No man can tell when he must tread your darksome pathway narrow,
But this I know, to talk of you does all my being harrow.

1525    Such great abhorrence to mankind your transformations bring
That though unto a living man a hundred loved ones cling,
No sooner on that selfsame man do you, unthought of, spring
Than all draw back from him aghast as from a rotten thing.

1526    To ones who liked the living man and loved near him to range,
Abominate him, being dead, as something foul and strange;
Both friends and kindred, all with loathing, look upon his change
And shun him as they would a being with repulsive mange.

1527    By father, mother, by the sons in whom his love is stored,
By all his male and female servants, faithful to their lord,
Yes, even by the very wife who shares his bed and board,
As soon as ugly death arrives, is he by them abhorred.

[217]

1528    Large men of wealth you force to lie in circumstances strait
        Where not a copper they can hold of all their riches great;
        A man who, living, is admired for all his pomp and state,
        When dead is but a stinking thing, a lump of filth men hate.

1529    In all the world of manuscripts and books that men have read
        There never has a single word of good for you been said,
        Nor has there been one benefit to any being shed,
        Save to the black and surly crow who battens on the dead.

1530    You tell the crows that every day you'll fill their carrion craws,
        No wonder men can't tell just when or where they'll feel your claws;
        Let them do good who can today, and do it without pause—
        The crows of death may come tomorrow clamouring with caws.

1531    My masters, do not try to be companions to the crow,
        But fear his threats, and do not heed when he would have you go;
        The good you've in your hands to do, that do and be not slow—
        Tomorrow you may dice with death, and life hangs in the throw.

1532    How quickly health and precious life are in the void interred,
        And vanish in a moment's time, almost ere men have stirred;
        Tomorrow's good intention is a naked, shameless word—
        Go dress it up today with works before Death's voice is heard.

1533    Whoever plays 'gainst loaded dice, is sure to lose the game,
        For though he thinks to win a stake, he forfeits all his claim.
        Dear friends, take thought to do good works in God Almighty's name,
        Because, as soon as Death arrives, he comes to quell and maim.

1534    When people think that they can win, they cry, "I stake it all!"
        But when they make a hapless cast they lose a mighty haul;
        Men scrape up treasures hoping they can build up mansions tall,
        But soon comes Death to strike them down—then in the mud they sprawl.

1535    Then speech and consciousness and wit, they lose forevermore,
        And from their treasure's infinite accumulated store
        Cannot a farthing take away or rightly will it o'er;
        The winds of death with evil breath blast all they labored for.

1536    A rich man's relatives foregather when he takes to bed,
        Expecting his inheritance as oft as he is bled.
        Should they ask, "Doctor, will his fever cure itself or spread?"
        And he say "Cure," with grief made sure they curse the quack instead.

1537    The brother and the sister, yes the kin who closest dwell,
Can hardly wait 'till they shall hear the surly, sullen bell,
Since relatives much more respect the heritance they smell
Than their white whiskered relative who waits for them in Hell.

1538    No sooner does a rich old sinner's soul start off for bliss
Than, loathing his foul carcass, friends dump him in some abyss.
Then all pounce on his property and rob now that, now this,
While only he steals the least, holds things to go amiss.

1539    Dear relatives have much to do before their kin they bury;
Some one may break his treasure chest (a fear that makes them wary);
They therefore haven't time to go to mass nor pray to Mary,
While as for spending of his wealth on grave clothes, they are chary.

1540    No sum they spend on charities; they raise to God no prayer;
What though his soul's in Purgatory, they will leave it there;
The most a dead man can expect from any grateful heir
Is that in his deaf ears the wretch will insults curse and swear.

1541    Men show their thanks as soon as they have dumped him in a hole,
By coming late to church to hear the mass's rigmarole;
Why should they worry any more—life's merry farce is droll—
They have his property and now the Devil has his soul.

1542    Perhaps he leaves a woman who is rich and young and pretty—
Men plot for her before the priest has sung his funeral ditty.
Then in a twinkling, she has coupled someone young or witty,
And without grief but much relief, since mourning seems a pity.

1543    This wretched scoundrel, Death, arrives yet no one knows for whom,
And though it happens every day he sends men to their doom,
There is no one who will the care of testaments assume
Until in his own eye he sees Death standing at the tomb.

1544    Oh Death, I must compel my heart to utter more again
Because you give no strength nor comfort to the sons of men
But leave their bodies to the toads in their sepulchral den;
You're bitter as the cress which grows within a stagnant fen.

1545    The man who crams his belly much, you make his head to ache—
Your minion, pain, no sooner comes than for your cursèd sake
Upon the head he strikes the wretch, until the strongest quake—
The frightful sicknesses you send, no medicines can break.

[219]

1546    Those eyes that once were beautiful, now in their bony house
        You blind and shutter up, the while their inner light you douse;
        You clog the throat and make the voice grow squeaky as a mouse;
        In you is every ill and woe, and every swindling chouse.

1547    The sense of taste and that of touch, of hearing and of smell,
        Yes, each of all the senses five, you come to snatch and quell;
        There is no man indeed who can your meanness frankly tell,
        For if you ever were exposed—say, Death, where could you dwell?

1548    You sacrifice all sense of shame and every handsome trait,
        You take away all grace and scoff at moderation's gait,
        You weaken strength and manly vigor, gentleness you hate—
        The sweet of life you turn to gall with bitterness innate.

1549    The gallantry of lovers you despise, and gold you shun,
        You unmake works and cast a gloom across joy's glorious sun;
        You spatter cleanliness with filth, with courtesy you've done;
        Oh Death, you conquer life and hate this world and every one.

1550    There is no person you can please, though you are pleased with much;
        That is, I say, with those who slay, with murderers and such;
        There is no thing of beauty which your mace won't smite and smutch,
        Nor being born, your net won't catch as soon as them you touch.

1551    You enemy of every good, you friend of every ill,
        Your nature spreads the dropsy, gout, and painful dying chill,
        So that the places you frequent, though vile, grow viler still,
        While those acquire the best repute which seldom feel your will.

1552    Your dwelling place forever is Hell's bottomless, dark pit;
        You are the primal cause of ill, the second, too, you're it.
        The world you e'er depopulate—'mid infamies you sit,
        And unto every one you say, "Life's bowl alone I split."

1553    Oh Death, on your account were made the murky depths of Hell,
        For if a man in this fair world might here forever dwell,
        Of you he ne'er would stand in fear, nor of your darksome cell,
        Nor would our mortal beings dread your terrifying knell.

1554    You waste great towns and populate the cities of the dead,
        You tear to pieces empires vast and build up graves instead;
        From fear of you, saints mumble prayers, from fear are scriptures read;
        Save possibly great God Himself, your power all beings dread.

1555   You, Mighty Death, depopulated heaven and its thrones,
And made the cleanest ones as foul as your own filthy bones;
You turned God's angels into devils, uttering mad moans—
For your wild orgies dearly paid the Father and His Crones.

1556   The very Lord that gave you birth was even by you slain,
That Man-God, Jesus Christ Himself, how you gave Him a pain!
The One that heaven fears and earth, the None-such-suzerain,
You scared so badly that you changed His nature once again.

1557   Hell was afraid of Him, yet you before Him showed no fear,
His flesh before you stood in dread—you scared Him with your gear—
His human side alone from fright was miserable and drear
But not His parts divine, for such you could not then come near.

1558   You did not then behold that side, He looked on you and saw
A cruel death approaching Him of which He stood in awe,
But afterwards He shattered you and also Hell's foul maw;
You slew Him for an hour, but now fore'er you're in His law.

1559   When you were conquered, Him you knew—of that there's no denying,
And if you scared Him once He gave you fears more terrifying,
And if you pained Him you received much greater cause for crying,
For He, the one you put to death, gave life to us by dying.

1560   The saints you kept imprisoned in your hellish dwelling place
Were given life when Jesus died by His infinite grace;
His holy death depopulated all that city base
You stocked by killing men but which He wholly did efface.

1561   Our father Adam He delivered whom you held in pain
And Eve our mother with her children Abel, Seth, and Cain,
Then Japhet and the patriarchs, and Abraham, good swain,
And Isaac and Isaiah, nor let Dan He there complain.

1562   He took Saint John the Baptist with full many a patriarch
Whom you kept locked up in the tortures of your coffins dark;
He freed the leader Moses whom you prisoned in your bark
Besides a lot of saints and prophets in your dungeons stark.

1563   I can't recall by name who were the worthies whom He freed
Nor yet how many first rate saints your Hell contained, indeed,
But anyway the ones He took were saints long pedigreed;
He left you nothing but the worthless ones of common breed.

1564  His favorite ones He took aloft with Him to paradise
      Where in eternal idleness they praise the great All-wise.
      Thus He who died for us will likewise take us to the skies;
      Let us not be the mock of Death but his demesne despise.[31]

1565  But all those wretches whom our loving Saviour Christ disclaims,
      In Hell's eternal furnaces are tortured by your flames;
      You fry them crisp and thus fulfill God's altruistic aims;
      Their brief, presumptuous life of sin your endless anguish tames.

1566  Oh may it please Almighty God to fend us from your foils!
      Yes, even He who cares for us but cares not for your coils;
      Because, however long we live, unto the end Death toils,
      And then at last your anguish comes which all the world despoils.

1567  Such is your nature, Death, you have no good of any kind,
      Why e'en the tenth part of your ills I cannot call to mind;
      I must commend myself to God since no one else I find
      Who can defend me from those steps which close on me behind.

1568  Oh damned, insatiable Death! Would you yourself had died!
      Why did you steal my faithful pimp to be your grizzly bride?
      You killed her, Death, but Jesus Christ will certainly provide
      For her with His own precious blood! She shall near Him abide!

1569  Alas, my Convent-trotter! Oh alas, my trusty bawd!
      Alive you lay with many men, now lie alone with God!
      Why is He taking you from me in that far land abroad
      Whence none who journeys e'er returns to show what path he trod?

1570  Dear whore, of very surety you sit in Paradise,
      And with the purest martyrs are attended in the skies
      Because on earth great God Himself your flesh did martyrize;
      'Twas He who made you be a whore and filled your life with sighs.

1571  I shall demand of God in prayer to set you up in glory
      For never in the mind of man was pimp so leal and whory.
      I'll make an epitaph for you containing all your story
      So those who can't behold you now can read your record gory.

1572  I'll set some pence aside for prayers—I'll pray a long oration;
      I'll have some masses sung for you and I shall make oblation;
      My Convent-trotter, then let God give you His consecration,
      For if He saved the world it seems He must give you salvation.

1573 And you, my ladies, don't reprove the author of this book,
    Nor call him fool—you too would weep if death your servant took;
    Yes, well, dear dames, you might lament, for what her subtle hook
    Once fastened in, she straightway caught and pulled out from the brook.

1574 Were it a woman short or tall, close-locked or careful hidden,
    My trot was ne'er thrown off until the wench was broke and ridden.
    I can't conceive a man or maid who, if death came unbidden
    And snatched as good a friend of theirs, would for their tears be chidden.

1575 I therefore made an epitaph, as small as great my grief,
    But from my heaviness of heart its rhymes were crude and brief;
    Let all who hear it for the sake of God, our Lord and Chief,
    Pray for this saintly bawd who brought our passions such relief.

[223]

1576   "I am Urraca, here beneath this sepulchre I lie,
      But while I trod the merry earth I passed no pleasure by,
      I yoked up many a buck and wench, but fought of nonsense shy.
      Now I have fallen underground and miss the happy sky.

1577   "Death crept up on me unawares and caught me in his net;
      Dear kin and friends here would you come to get me pimping yet;
      Ah well, do good works while you live and Jesus won't forget—
      Remember, just as I have died you, too, must pay the debt.

1578   "May God Almighty bless the man who muses o'er the dead,
      May God requite him with good love to bring his girl to bed.
      Oh, reader, pause, and for a sinner let a prayer be said,
      But, if you will not pray, don't curse the ones whose souls have fled."[32]

*Concerning the Arms With Which Every Christian*
*Should Arm Himself in Order to Conquer*
*the World, the Flesh, and the Devil*

1579   Hark, gentlemen, and meditate on this advice I offer;
       Put not your trust in any truce your enemy may proffer
       Because you cannot tell what hour he'll pack you in his coffer,
       Then if you see I lie to you, I'll let you be my scoffer.

1580   From Death we never should feel safe, but rather of him sure;
       He is our natural adversary, valiant, strong, and dure;
       Hence, since, my friends, we cannot flee to any place secure
       We ought, each one of us, take up arms against that boor.

1581   If any one of us should have to fight tomorrow morn,
       Or enter in the field to smite an enemy forsworn,
       We each would search to find what arms and armour could be worn
       For without arms no one would risk a peril so forlorn.

1582   If thus 'gainst living men like us we'd arm ourselves so well,
       How much more we should take up arms 'gainst enemies so fell
       And numerous and merciless as those who love to yell,
       "Come, knaves and scoundrels, down you go to everlasting Hell!"

1583   Already you have heard about those fearful, mortal sins;
       'Tis they that daily wage us wars that no one ever wins;
       'Tis they that would destroy our souls when they have pierced our skins—
       So let us be completely armed from muzzle to the shins.

1584   Three foremost champions 'gainst us stand prepared for war's alarms.
       They are the world, the flesh, the Devil, whence come mortal harms,
       And after them all other hurts, so let us take up arms
       Whereby they can be overcome—some weapons have great charms.

1585   For instance, there are deeds of mercy, doing pious work,
       The gifts the Holy Spirit gives to lighten earthly murk,
       Besides the seven sacraments entrusted to the kirk,
       And acts devout which stab our foes as deep as any dirk.

1586   Against all longings covetous, baptism helps us fight,
       (That gift the Holy Spirit sent from its omniscient height
       To help us not to want what is another man's by right)
       And justice, by whose virtue we see folly in true light.

[225]

1587    By clothing naked persons with the pious expectation
        That God, for whom we do those things, will make remuneration,
        With that cuirass we may harass foul envy's penetration,
        And oh may God protect us from both envy and damnation.

1588    By speaking much humility we crush o'erweening pride—
        'Tis good that we fear God for there does majesty reside—
        Then temperance, honesty, restraint, will certainly provide
        A sabre strong, wherewith full sure, we can our fate decide.

1589    Again through much compassion, giving lodging to the poor,
        While trusting pious works from God will large rewards secure,
        And through not stealing others' goods, nor forcing damsels pure;
        By means like these is arrogance torn out, though rooted sure.

1590    Against the sin of avarice let's keep a heart devout,
        By giving pennies to the poor and grieving at their drought,
        And then with native justice weighing humbly every doubt;
        With such a mace as that we'll knock our avarices out.

1591    The holy sacrament enjoins the sacerdotal crew
        To urge on God's authority (as clear as crystal new)
        That marrying poor orphan girls will piety imbue[33]
        Whereby we'll conquer avarice—so help us, spirit true!

1592    We can to lewdness easily administer chastisings;
        Through conscience and through charity we 'scape its agonizings;
        The Spirit full of constancy will help through exorcisings;
        This triple plated cod piece then will quell our lewd uprisings.

1593    Put on the greaves, thigh plates and groin strips of the Holy Writ
        Which God devised in Paradise to keep young people fit,
        That is, the marriage sacrament. To marry some poor chit
        Is thus a blow at lechery which always conquers it.

1594    Now anger is an enemy which many quickly kills,
        But with the gift of understanding, plus what love instills,
        This peril's seen and grows as light as flour ground fine at mills;
        With patience then we well can smite this chief of all our ills.

1595    Then through the virtue that is hope, through patience in addition,
        Through visiting the sorrowful, through practice of contrition,
        Through shunning all unseemly things, through loving good largition,
        We'll conquer ire and get from God His love and ben-volition.

1596     Another sin is gluttony—full many it can slay,
              But abstinence and fasting will its danger take away;
              A scientific spirit, wisely moderate, will pay,
              While eating little, leaves the poor wherewith their guts to lay.

1597     Moreover, importuning God by holy sacrifice
              (Because the bread is Christ's Own flesh—a veritable slice)
              And fighting in His service, minding how He paid the price,
              We can through grace o'ercome our greed which is a wicked vice.

1598     Now envy killed a number of the prophets of the best,
              Wherefore against this fiend who shoots his arrows at our breast,
              Let us put on the stout and blazoned shield where is expressed,
              "The Spirit of Good Sense" which serves as motto 'neath the crest.

1599     It is the unction's sacrament which we as priests take round
              Through pity, for God's sake, to help the faithful underground;
              Then if we harm not simpletons nor yet the poor confound,
              With these God-given arms we'll drive our envy out of bound.

1600     Yet let us, too, be armed against ill sloth, an evil which
              Of all the seven sins attains the most deceitful pitch;
              Where'er the Devil dwells this vice bespawns in every ditch:
              It has more evil whelps than has a rabid mastiff bitch.

1601     Wherefore 'gainst sin and all her brood that drag us basely down
              Let us long pilgrimages make, let prayer each moment crown;
              Let us think loftly thoughts which come from works of high renown;
              Thus doing holy deeds, our God need ne'er on folly frown.

1602     From all the pious works we do, from every good desire,
              Let us construct a pike or lance, but let us never tire
              'Till with its holy steel we smite our sins and they expire,
              Since fighting with these arms we shall command of them acquire.

1603     Against the three outstanding ones, unless they all join in,
              With charity we'll fight the world, with fasts strike fleshly sin,
              And with pure hearts our war against the evil one we'll win
              Whereby no trace of them shall rest in children, sires, or kin.

1604     All other sins (the mortal ones besides the venal string)
              From these three run as rivers do from perennial spring;
              They are, indeed, the sum and source of every evil thing;
              From parents, children, nephews, all, may God forfend their sting.

1605     Dear God, oh give us strength enow, and aid and health of heart
That we may conquer in the fight, and save us from its smart.
The Day of Judgment is at hand, and in that fearful mart
May Jesus say, "Ye blessed come, and ne'er from Me depart."

## Concerning the Qualities Which Little Women Have

1606    But now I want to put an end to all this windy preaching
Because I like a sermon brief with even terser teaching,
I also relish women short as much as pithy speeching
Since little maids like little words are handier for reaching.

1607    Men laugh at those whose speech is long (though only fools will giggle)
But little girls are great in love and muckle love to wiggle;
All loutish sluts I'd gladly trade for wenches chic who wriggle
Though as for trading short for long—'gainst that I long would higgle.

1608    The good about these little maids Love makes me here proclaim,
And hence I want to spread abroad their talents and their fame,
Wherefore I'll have you understand, if you would know the game,
That women short seem cold as snow but burn you like a flame.

1609    That is to say, they're cold outside though raging hot with passion—
In bed they slosh and wallow it in wild hilarious fashion—
But dressed, you'd think their lives were just a bread and water ration;
Indeed, you'll find out other things if you are keen to dash in.

1610    Within a little jewel lies a rare effulgent splendor,
Within a little sugar lies a sweet naught else can render,
Within a little woman lies great love surpassing tender,
And here's a case where little words suffice to recommend her.

1611    A pepper grain is wondrous small, but how it burns the snout,
And dries the body's humors up like sun in summer's drought;
'Tis that way with a little wench, if only she puts out;
You'll find no pleasure in the world she doesn't know about.

1612    Just as the smallest bud will have the full blown rose's hue,
Just as from tiny coins of gold much value will accrue,
And from a bit of flagrant balm exotic scents ensue
So you will find a little maid unsurpassed to woo.

1613    A little ruby can possess a worth within which shine
Its color and nobility, its price and virtue fine,
Thus likewise little women have a beauty so divine
That grace and charm and loyalty within them all combine.

1614    That skylark is a little bird, the nightingale is small,
But more than larger birds their songs and carolings enthrall;
Think not because a maid is short she has no worth at all,
For when it comes to loving she is like a honey ball.

1615    The oriole and popinjay are both of them petite,
But more than any other bird their jargoning is sweet
With Latin so melodious expressed in rich conceit;
So little girls bring ecstasy to love's enchanting feat.

1616    Short women have no peers among the female congregation;
They make an earthly paradise where men attain salvation
With pleasures, bliss incontinent, and every consolation—
You'll find their pudding is the proof, not just their salutation.

1617    I never saw a chit but what I hankered to possess her,
But as for big—'tis no disgrace to flee a large aggressor—
"Between two evils choose the least," proclaimed a wise professor,
So when it comes to sinful girls, the little one's the lesser.[34]

## Concerning Sir Weasel, the Archpriest's Boy

1618    When February passed and March brought Springtime back to life,
The father of all sin began to use his crafty knife
Until with archpriests, priests, and abbots his whole lap was rife;
Besides he took some cuttings choice from many a liquorish wife.

1619    Those days I had no go-between, and since my luck was limp,
I got to do my dirty work a most rapacious pimp
Whose name was Weasel, and I swear he was a clever imp,
Indeed, save having fourteen faults, I ne'er saw better shrimp.

1620    He was a liar, drunkard, thief, a sempiternal jangler,
Card-sharper, glutton, brawler, sot; a dirty, lousy, wrangler;
Soothsayer, exhibitionist, a pervert and a dangler,
Crack-brained, and lazy—save for that a very perfect angler.

1621    Two times within a week, perforce, he celebrated fast;
For instance, when there was no food the wretch skipped one repast,
Then when he had no wherewithal, he starved and groaned aghast,
Wherefore, you see, twice every week went hungry this outcast.

1622    But there's a grain of truth this saw expresses with a quip,
"A balky ass is better, even though you use the whip,
Than carrying the load yourself upon your either hip."
Thus from great need I had to use this pimp on many a trip.

1623    I said to him, "Friend Weasel, hunt me up some doxy pert."
"By God," said he, "I'll get you one or else my name is dirt,
And I will bring her quietly as quick as I can spurt;
Oft times an evil hound can smell the bottom of a skirt."

1624    Yet since he could but slowly read and read that litte wrong,
He said, "If you would get big game, do let me have some song,
And then, although I hate to boast, you'll see ere very long
That when I start on any course, I always finish strong."

1625    I therefore gave some songs to him (God damn the wretch to Hell),
He sang them through the market place as loud as he could yell,
'Till Lady This and Madam That cried, "Hush, you brass tongued bell!
Don't think we'll answer your behest, it's advertised too well!"

## How the Archpriest Says This Book of His Should Be Understood

1626    Now inasmuch as Holy Mary, as I've said, indeed,
Is start and end of every good, according to my creed,
I wrote four hymns to Her by which I quickly hope to speed.[35]
My book to its conclusion, yet mark this ere I proceed:

1627    My poem has this powerful charm, that whoso it peruses,
If he's a man whom night and day some filthy slut abuses,
Or yet a love-starved woman with an ugly man who boozes,
Its lofty moral tone will straight lead them to heavenly cruises.

1628    'Twill make them want to go to mass, to offer up oblations,
Give food and drink to needy ones in humble, abject stations,
Or else eructate loud in prayer almost divine orations,
And thus, my merry gentlemen, God's served by these ovations[36]

1629    But hark, whoever has a mind if he can featly rhyme,
May alter what he thinks will make this volume press and prime,
So let my book from hand to hand be flung from clime to clime
(As 'twere a lady's shuttle-cock) by all who have the time.[37]

1630    Now since this book's about Good Love, why lend it out right gladly
So that you won't belie its name nor advertise it badly;
Don't sell nor rent it out for gold, for that were trading madly
As without gree nor Grace, Good Love, when purchased, goes on sadly.

1631    I've made my text quite short for you, but oh the notes and glossary
Which pedants shall append to it may fill a monstrous ossuary;
The reason is, I gave each word some subtly writ embossery
To furnish letters for the dull but erudite cognossori.

1632    The holy portions in my book have wisely been extended;
Its jokes and jibes, howe'er, are brief, and scarcely cracked ere ended,
So therefore, let me close my chest, and as I've recommended
You'll find in short and simple words both wit and morals blended.

1633    I've served you, merry gentlemen, although with little learning,
And I have tried in jongleur's verse to please your every yearning;
I ask but this, that in God's name, where'er you are sojourning,
You'll say a prayer or two for me—'twill be my only earning.

1634    In thirteen hundred eighty-one this old romance was writ
To check the wrongs and injuries which persons ill commit
Whereby they oft through trickeries and plottings benefit;
Also 'twas made to teach the simple, stories told with wit.

[Here ends the Toledo Manuscript.]

# The Joys of Holy Mary

## I

1635
Oh Mother, who to God gave life,
  Thou Holy Virgin Mary, pure,
Both daughter leal and loyal wife,
  My Lady, Thee I now adjure
    To send on me perpetual grace
    That I Thy service may embrace
And in it evermore endure.

1636
Because to serve Thee I aspire,
  Although a sinner, I shall bring
This service which Thou mayest desire—
  Wherefore I shall Thy praises sing;
    Of those, the first
    That on Thee burst
    Was when an angel herald versed
The Holy Spirit's offering.

1637
With God in Thee Thou didst conceive
  So that there came a second joy
When Thou gavest birth, as we believe,
  And without pain, unto a boy,
    Yet by that birth
    Of greatest worth,
    A Virgin Mother still on earth
Thou didst remain without alloy.

1638
Thy third joy came when by a star
  The kings were guided through the night
To bring their treasures from afar
  To give Thee that divine delight.
    Those kings adored
    Their new-born Lord
    And gave the Child a noble hoard,
With gold and myrrh and incense dight.

1639 Thy fourth joy came upon the time
  That Martha's brother gave to Thee,
While sorrowing, the news sublime
  That He who died on Calvary,
   Thy son so sweet
   Was risen complete
   For though Thou sawest his death defeat,
  Him they again alive did see.

1640 Thou hadst Thy fifth in His ascent
  To paradise. Thy sixth befell
When down the Holy Spirit went
  As comforter, Thy woes to quell.
   Thy seventh one
   Did all outrun
   For then there came to Thee Thy Son
  To bring Thee up in heaven to dwell.

1641 I beg Thy grace, oh joyous Queen,
  That Thou mayest show, forevermore,
To me a happy, joyful mien,
  Full merciful, with smiles wreathed o'er;
   And when I stand
   At God's command
   As Jesus comes to judge the land,
  Be Thou my kind solicitor.

# The Joys of Holy Mary

## II

1642
    Our blessings we extend
      To Thee, oh Holy Maid;
    To Thy joys let us bend
      And tell how life was laid
    For Thee. Let us depend
      For this on what's portrayed
      By Scripture's aid.

1643
    The twelfth year of her age
      To that young damsel came
    God's own angelic page
      To greet with much acclaim
      That beauteous dame.

1644
    She gave the world a child
      (Oh what supreme delight!)
    And when thirteen, there smiled
      Upon that blessèd sight
    Those kings, who on them piled
      Strange presents to requite
      God's grace that night.

1645
    When Christ was thirty-three
      Near Him the Virgin stood.
    Her fourth joy came when He
      Rose from the Cross's wood.
    The fifth one came to be
      When she in holihood
      Saw Jesus good.

1646
    Her sixth delight was passed
      When with that blessèd One
    And His disciples massed,
      This miracle was done;
    God straight from heaven cast
      His shining Ghost upon
      Her like the sun.

1647          Then after life had gone
             From that messiac man,
          Nine long years more were drawn
             To Holy Mary's span,
          But then there came a dawn
             Which saw Her in the van
             Of heaven's clan.

1648          Her joys of seven were
             And forty told the years
          With four more numbered Her
             (This truth each one reveres)
          Protect us lest we err,
             Sweet Maid, in Satan's gears,
             And fend our fears.

1649          Oh Christians, let us call
             Most joyful, glad and gay
             That holy, blessèd day
          When Christ was born for all—
             Of Virgin born, I say,
             To smooth our earthly way.

# How Scholars Beg in the Name of God

## I

1650    Kind sirs, give something to the scholar
Who comes for charity to holler.

1651    If you will give me some oblation,
I'll make for you a long oration
To God, to get you His salvation;
    For God's sake, give me then a dollar.

1652    Much good for God you'll be achieving
For what you give He is perceiving
And when this world you must be leaving
    His recompense is sure to foller.

1653    And when you make to God excuses
For hoarding what your rent produces,
A gift will cancel your abuses
    Although you scarce could give a smaller.

1654    For every red and unfelt penny
You give, God will return you many.
You'll get to heaven as well as any
    And just because you helped my squalor.

1655    If you look round you'll see good doing
Is never lost. It fends the ruing
You'd make if you in Hell were brewing
    And paying Satan for his choler.

[237]

## II

1656    Kind gentlemen, we scholars two
        In poverty beg aught of you.

1657    The Lord of heaven, by name Christ Jesus,
        So loved us that He tried to please us
        By suffering death just to appease us,
            And He was murdered by a Jew.

1658    Our Lord He died, but shall attend us
        And as our Savior will defend us,
        Then for His loving sake befriend us
            As He saves every mortal too.

1659    Keep ever in your minds His story;
        Give for the sake of His death gory
        If you would have Him give you glory,
            Give money for God's sake anew.

1660    As long as you have life remaining
        For His sake give without restraining,
        Thereby you'll miss the awful paining
            That Hell reserves for all but few.

## On the "Hail Mary" of Saint Mary

1661    Hail Mary, glorious as the sun,
        Hail Virgin, holy, precious one,
        How wide Thy blessèd mercies run
            On us for aye.

1662    Thou full of grace and spotless being,
            Mine advocate,
        In mercy work, most gracious Queen,
        This miracle before my seeing
            With kindness great;
        Do Thou with kind and gracious mien
        Protect me all unharmed, serene,
            From shameful death, so that I can
            Give unto Thee the praise I plan
            By night and day.

1663    God dwells with Thee, resplendent star
            Who art the balm and cure of woe,
            Thy features, beautiful and bright
        All glorious are;
            No stain of sin doth in Thee show.
            Then, in the name of each delight
                Thou hadst, to Thee I humbly cry,
                Oh spotless rose, guard me lest I
                In folly stray.

1664    Thou art most blest, and without peer,
            Who still a Virgin, gavest birth,
            By all the angels Thou art praised
        In heaven clear.
            By Him Thou broughtst into the earth,
                And by that grace where Thou art raised,
                Oh blessed flower, oh rose divine,
                Most pious one, I beg Thee, shine
                Upon my way.

1665    Among all women, set apart,
            Most holy mother, Thou dost dwell;
            Protector of all Christian men
        And help Thou art.
            The Father, Son, and Saints as well,

Show Thee respect, wherefore again
To turn aside from me the crowd
Of people, cruel, base, and proud,
To Thee I pray.

1666      Oh *blessèd be the fruit* that yields
Joy and salvation to the race
Of men, ay blest because from woe
And loss it shields,
And from that fell and foul disgrace
The filthy Devil doth bestow
Upon our way—he that with snares
A prison made where unawares
He can us slay.

1667      Of *Thy sweet womb* the holy flower
Was never touched, and I beseech
That Thy great holiness will fend
Me from the power
Of error, that my life may reach
In virtue its appointed end.
So may I merit equal place
Among the saints and see Thy face
Near me for aye.

# A Song of the Praises of Saint Mary

## I

1668    Full many miracles a virgin makes for she is pure;
She wards the pangs of grief from men, of sadness she's the cure;
And he who worships Thine allure
    Thou wilt not, Blessèd One, forget
    Nor let him suffer with regret
The penance for his sinnings dure.

1669    The innocent Thou helpest with love of infinite degree
And one that is Thy worshipper Thou wilt most swiftly free
For Thou dost never fail nor flee
    But bringest aid without delay,
    Nor dost Thou ever let one stray
Since Thy love lasts as does the sea.

1670    Thou art my refuge, Virgin Queen, and now I suffer fright,
Wherefore to Thee my blessings go—protect me in my plight;
Yea since I do to Thy dear light
    Send up my songs, for Jesus' sake
    Do Thou my succor undertake
And shield me from death's dreadful night.

1671    Here in this lonely city drear I pine in great distress,
Defend me, for I turn to Thee—save me from this duress,
And since I so devoutly press,
    Thou wilt my praying not disdain
    For I shall give Thee praise amain
And earnestly Thy bounty bless.

1672    I do commend myself to Thee, oh Mary, Holy Maid;
Restore me, guard me, fend my grief, and swiftly bring me aid,
Watch o'er my path in peril laid
    Because, most Holy Maid devout,
    Thy grace to such extent goes out
It doth the farthest bournes invade.

# A Song of the Praises of Saint Mary

## II

1673
Blest Virgin, chosen by the hand
  Of God, Thou mother whom we love,
  Enthroned in heaven high above,
The health and life of every land.

1674
The health and life of every land
  That death dost with a death requite,
Whose grace doth everywhere expand,
  The guerison of grievous blight;
  Yea, wilt Thou not from this despite
    Of prison undeserved, where long
    I languish under cursèd wrong—
  Wilt Thou not fend it with Thy might?

1675
Wilt Thou not fend it with Thy might
  Nor take account of my past sin
And penance I should do by right,
  But let Thy bounty now begin;
  I must confess I did give in
    To wickedness and went astray,
    But Thou wilt be my help today
  And let Thy virgin power win.

1676
And let Thy virgin power win
  Which has not anywhere a peer
Or even aught beside it kin
  In purpose or in work sincere
  Which benedictions full endear;
    But I, although without desert
    Still come to Thee, that without hurt
  Thou mayest my petition hear.

1677
Thou mayest my petition hear
  E'en as Thou heardst another's plaint,
For I, within temptation's sphere,
  Endure a sorrowful restraint.
  But Thou hast strength, Almighty Saint,
    And Thou wilt guard me in Thine hand
    And haste to let me understand
  Thou wilt me with Thy love acquaint.

# A Song of the Praises of Saint Mary

## III

1678    I would that I might follow Thee, Thou flower among the flowers,
I would that I in praise of Thee might ever fill the hours,
          Nor would I swerve
          If I could serve
The best which all my best embowers.

1679    I pour my confidence in Thee, mine heart entire I pour,
For Thou, my Lady, art mine hope and life forevermore;
          From sorrow's sway
          Without delay
Come, free me, Virgin, I implore.

1680    Oh Sainted Virgin, stricken here I pass mine hours in grief,
Yea with such pain I think my torment ne'er can find relief;
          In Thee I hope
          Although I grope
And grapple with Sin's highest chief.

1681    Oh changeless star upon life's sea, oh quiet port of peace,
Oh blessèd Goddess, give, I pray, from agony surcease—
          Come, set me free
          And comfort me
If God from heaven grants Thee release.

1682    Thine ample mercy, may it ne'er in my misfortunes fail,
Thou healest always misery—Thou dost the sad avail,
          Thou wilt not let
          One die nor fret
Who in Thy worship ne'er grew stale.

1683    Here innocent I suffer wrong, in woe I make my bed
And know that yet a little while and I'll be with the dead;
          Oh succor me
          For none I see
To free me from this awful dread.

## IV

1684
> In Thee mine hope resides,
> Oh Mary, Holy Maid;
> 'Tis right that in such aid
> Our confidence abides.

\* \* \* \* \*

1685
> Oh fortune, evil starred,[38]
> Vexatious, cruel, hard,
> Thou catiff, spiteful wretch,
> Low born, and bastard-barred,
> What doth thy stern regard
> On me intend to fetch?

1686
> One thing can ne'er be writ
> Nor can men speak of it;
> I mean this strange distress
> That Thou dost on me fit
> To which I must submit,
> Though tortured to excess.

1687
> Up to this very day
> By leading me astray
> Thou madest my life a hell;
> Now have the grace, I say,
> To turn the other way,
> And kindly act, as well.

1688
> If Thou wilt take from me
> My woes and misery
> And tribulations great
> Or turn them into glee
> And help me willingly
> Thou'lt have here Thine estate.

1689
> But if Thou still dost strive
> And cease not to contrive
> To make my pains increase,
> Ere few more days arrive
> My miseries will drive
> Me into swift decease.

## A Ballad on the Holy Men of Talavera[39]

1690    In Talavera, yonder, while the month was April still
Some letters happened to arrive from old Archbishop Gil
Wherein there was an order which created quite a shrill,
And if it pleased some one or two, two thousand thought it ill.

1691    Then the archpriest whose task it was to be the law's recorder
Felt much more pained than pleased that he was its official warder,
Howe'er to court he summoned each ecclesiastic boarder;
They quickly came in hopes that he might read a better order.

1692    This archpriest then began to speak, and well he parlied thus:
"You needn't curse, this hits me worse than any one of us—
I who got grey by serving Gil—the old blackguardly cuss—
To think that I should live to see him stir up such a fuss!"

1693    Some tear drops started from his eyes, he spoke with great emotion:
"The Pope has done this just to make a show of his devotion,
So I must read this order out, though it's a bitter potion,
And I confess it's with duress, because I hate the notion.

1694    " 'Intelligence I have of sin, wherefore I put this stated,
That every priest or clergyman who has been consecrated,
Shall not have concubine or whore, nor wife already mated—
All those who disobey, henceforth are excommunicated!' "

1695    As soon as all the chapter did this information learn,
Young clerics flabbergasted were; old priests showed grave concern.
But several legates tabled it and motioned to adjourn,
Intending later to agree when business brought its turn.

1696    So when the matter came again to haggle and digest,
The deacon jumped up on his feet and eased this off his chest:
"Dear friends in Christ, let's all appeal against this papal pest
And carry to the king our case, for he will treat us best.

1697    "You see we are his subjects, notwithstanding that we're preachers;
We work for him as loyally as pupils for their teachers,
Besides he knows that priests are men and men are carnal creatures—
I know he'll sympathize and void this order's harsher features.

1698 "Why look, I gave my merry girl all that I stole last year,
So if I have to cast her off, the cost will be severe;
I gave a dozen yards to her of velvet brocade dear—
And by my shaven pate, last night she bathed to do me cheer!

1699 "I tell you I would sooner lose my prebend and my rent,
My dignity and pious graft before I would consent
To have my merry girl cast out like dirty excrement!
I think that many other minds are to this feeling bent.

1700 "I call on Christ's apostles, yea, all wielders of the pen,
Of sanctified authority who come within my ken
To justice us! With streaming eyes and grief I call again;
And now may God Almighty dwell among us saints—amen!"

1701 When he got done the treasurer delivered his harangue
(He was esteemed a most exalted brother by the gang),
"Kind friends," said he, "if that's true news which makes this sudden bang,
You may be pained indeed, but I endure a worser pang.

1702 "Of course, dear friends, your injuries concern me more than mine,
But there's Thérèse, my innocent and pretty concubine—
To Hell with Talavera! I'll to usury incline
Before I chase from bed and board a strumpet so divine.

1703 "White Flower ne'er loved her Flower as much nor in so leal a fashion;
Nor Tristran loved his Isolot with such a frenzied passion
As I Thérèse—her love sustains me more than any ration,
And if I have to leave her I will have my heart to gnash on.

1704 "They say a dog when he goes mad will sometimes bite his master
Because authority is void in moments of disaster—
Well, if I had Archbishop Gil, I'd kick that scoundrel pastor
With such a thump his filthy rump would always wear a plaster!"

1705 Next Sancho Muñoz took the floor (he was the chapter's chanter)
Said he, "Archbishop Gil can't tell which nag is his to canter,
He voids those privileges of which great God has been the granter,
And herewith I intend to take exception to the ranter.

1706 "Suppose I've some housekeeper or some maid to sweep and spin,
I can't see why Archbishop Gil should kick up such a din
Because she's no godmother nor a member of my kin—
The wench I keep an orphan was—now, truly, is that sin?

1707   "The Bible calls it pious work to give an orphan rearing,
        The same as keeping widows (which you know can be right cheering).
        Well, if old Gil holds that a sin both damnable and searing,
        Let's give up doing good and take to downright trollop-spearing!

1708   "Now Canon, Sir Gonzalvo, from your noisy, rude report,
        I guess it is the wench I keep which causes Gil to snort,
        Because the neighbors oft have told me how he would consort
        With her at home in bed all night though I forbade the sport!"

1709   But here it's time to close my tale—I'll haste its termination
        By saying all the clerks and clergy made an appellation
        Wherein they put unanimously this recommendation:
        That holy men should be allowed full rights to fornication.[40]

This Is the Book of the Archpriest of Hita Which He Composed While He Was
Imprisoned by Command of the Cardinal Sir Gil,
Archbishop of Toledo

*[Here ends the Salamanca Manuscript.]*

[247]

# A Blind Man's Ballad

1710
Good gentlemen and honored sirs,
    Incline yourselves to render aid
To these blind, sorry, wanderers
    By giving of the wealth you've made;
      For we are poor as famished curs
        And begging is our only trade.

1711
We never had the smallest share
    Of any riches in this earth,
We live in dread and hardships bear
    And much in life we suffer dearth
For, being blind, to us fore'er
      Are gone the shows and sights of mirth.

1712
Our Lady, Holy Mary, send
    Thy blessings down upon the one
Who does to us right now extend
    The first gift since the day's begun;
Give him salvation without end
      And bring his body lots of fun.

1713
Oh Holy Mary Magdalene,
    Beseech for us the one true God
That we may some first present glean,
    A silver penny or a quad,
To patch out our poor soup tureen
      When we with other beggars plod.

1714
He who today makes us first gift
    With coin mayhap or crust of bread,
May good Saint Julian send him shrift
    To do whate'er comes in his head,
No matter what from God he'd lift,
      See to it that it's freely sped.

1715
May God, our kind, paternal ghost,
    Preserve His children and His kin
From blindness, for it is the most
    Distressing ill to languish in.
Big barns and great four-footed host
    Saint Anthony will help him win.

1716     The one who gives to us a coin
       To show the love he has for Christ,
    Oh God, we herewith Thee enjoin
       Give tenfold what he's sacrificed,
    And round the region of the groin
       May Satan never have him spiced.

1717     Saint Michael wait upon the maid
       And man, with guardian angel's might;
    Yea, be their advocate and aid
       In whatsoe'er may be their plight,
    If some kind thought should them persuade
       To share their bread with us tonight.

1718     When Thou art busy sorting souls
       And them Thou hast in Thy right hand
    Who give us food and brimming bowls,
       Or otherwise help us to stand,
    Oh cast their sins upon the coals
       And lead them to the promised land.

1719     Thee, Lord, for mercy we entreat
       With lifted arms, may it suffice
    To yield pittance for our meat
       We ask Thy glory this small price;
    And whoso gives us aught to eat,
       Take up his soul to paradise.

## Another Blind Man's Song

1720
You Christians who are God's own friends,
To these blind beggars make amends
With crust or coin for what fate sends;
  Come, haste our help to undertake
  And do it for God's blessèd sake.

1721
If this we cannot get from you
We have no other help in view
  Or wealth wherewith to break our fast;
  We cannot earn because, aghast,
    Our famished bodies waste away
    So hence, perforce, poor beggars pray.

1722
Bestow on us your charity
And God will make the light you see
  To be a feast unto your eyes;
  Because you give in willing guise
    You'll have great pleasure from above
    Bide in the children whom you love.

1723
You'll ne'er see care nor shed a tear,
Your children God will let you rear
  So that Archdeacons will be some,
  Both hale and rich, and ne'er become—
    May God forbid it—stony blind
    But will leave poverty behind.

1724
May He give much of bread and wine
To those that hark when wretches whine,
  May they gain wealth and hoardings fond
  Who help a paupered vagabond;
    May clothes and costly robes adorn
    The man who gives to blind men shorn.

1725
And may your daughters whom you love
Be married into ranks above,
  To husbands who are lords and knights
  Or commoners with honored rights,
    Or merchants civil (granting such)
    Or burghers owning overmuch.

1726    Your fathers and your mothers-in-law,
        The mates your sons and daughters draw,
          The quick and those beneath the sod,
            May they be pardoned all by God.


1727    May God give you a rich reward
        And pardon for your sins afford,
          And may God's angel take your gift
          And it to Him as witness lift;
            Yea, Lord, hark to those sinners' prayers
            Because our lot was helped by theirs.


1728    Dear God, receive this song we sing
        And hearken to the prayers we bring
          Because we poor those prayers repeat
          For those who gave us aught to eat,
          And for the man who fain did give,
            Dear Christ, who died that we might live—
            Give paradise to him, we pray.


This Book Is Ended Thanks to Our Lord Jesus Christ;
This Book Was Finished Thursday the Twenty-Third Day of July of the Year
of the Birth of Our Saviour, Jesus Christ,
Thirteen Hundred And Eighty-Nine.

# NOTES AND
## SELECTED BIBLIOGRAPHY

# NOTES

1. Vulgate.

2. The eminent Spanish literary historian, Salceda Ruiz (Hist. 1, 339), exclaims, anent this and the following, "In our judgment this passage in the poem is the most beautiful, most humane, and most profoundly moral that literature has ever produced!"

It may surprise some to find the august author of the Aeneid figuring as a lascivious mountebank in a picaresque tale. The reason is as follows: In the first century B.C. in Mediterranean lands there was a vague belief in the coming of a sort of messiah. Some of these aspirations found their way into literature. Virgil, for example, in his sixth Eclogue predicts the coming of such a person. Christian mystics, more devout than enlightened, stumbling upon this passage, imagined, in their Ptolomaic conception of religion, that Virgil could be predicting nothing else than the coming of Christ. Hence Virgil was regarded as an inspired prophet-poet who saw through a glass darkly. Once accredited as a seer, the whole of the bard's works was subjected to minute scrutiny to discover other such profundities. As a result his verses, second only to the Bible, were taken as texts from which to draw the most extraordinary conclusions. From a prophet, Virgil's reputation was gradually extended to embrace the magical and a whole cycle of bizarre adventures was spun about his person.

3. Professor R. Schevill (*Ovid and the Renaissance in Spain*, p. 43) comments as follows upon Ruiz' stanza 274, "The lover after gratifying his passion experiences physical lassitude and mental depression mingled with regret." This bit of information the erudite professor, in a frantic search to find enough examples of Ovid's influence to warrant printing a book, concludes Ruiz drew from Ovid's lines, "At simul ad metas venit . . ." (Rem. Am. 413) although Galen said, "Quod omne animal post coitum est triste." But surely does not the dry professor know enough of life, love, and the pursuit of happiness to grant that Ruiz did not need to consult Ovid for his universal experience?

4. In the following stanzas the Archpriest intersperses his satire against the priestly Sir Love with scraps of liturgy (here printed in italic), using the divine words to profane purpose. Scriptural parodies, usually erotic as well as blasphemous, were popular pastimes for devout churchmen in the Dark Ages. By the twelfth century there are many complaints that bawdy tunes were being introduced into the church services to the increasing interest, if not edification, of the congregation. With the Renaissance the gusto for malicious parodies increased, finally reaching its height in the seventeenth century. There is, in French, a "Passion of Our Lord in Burlesque Verses" and a truly outrageous "Lord's Prayer of the Syphylitics" beside which Juan Ruiz' parody seems inspired by piety itself.

5. Cejador y Frauca, the incorruptible priest and erudite critic, has an illuminating note to this stanza. "Obscenity can go no farther; but our poet knows what

was going on, and describes it without nauseating the reader and yet without shearing reality of anything. As he himself has said, 'To describe evil well is a property of great poets. The 'Hail Virgin Queen' is the hymn sung at the end of the complines during Holy Week from the Purification to the 'In coena Domini.' The bloodiest stroke with which our poet could portray the blasphemous and felonious actions of those clerics, was to put this celestial salutation which is sung every day to the spotless Virgin, in the foul mouths of those who uttered it to their creatures in very moment of getting down upon them. The 'Hail, King of the Jews,' with which the Roman cohorts mocked Jesus in the Pretorium, is less grisly and infamous. Well indeed does he say, 'I never saw a curate who for souls said such complines.' They finished the prayer of the day by getting down on their women!"

6. Like the tale of the gallant who would marry three women, the Peter Pious episode has for its purpose the vilification of women, a favorite topic for churchmen of the dark ages. While satire against the sex can be found in the art of all times and climes, the Christian religion with its ascetic and monastic ideals is largely responsible for the enormous popularity of the anti-feminine cult of those dismal times. Earnest Christians could never forgive nor forget that it was a woman who was responsible for the loss of Eden, death, and worse, a life of sorrow and toil. With that in mind the indulgent Saint Tertullian kindly recommends that, "Woman, thou shouldst ever go in mourning and sackcloth, thine eyes filled with tears; thou hast brought about the ruin of mankind." Saint Ambrose devoutly asserts that, "Woman is not made in the image of God," while Saint Jerome gently observes that, "Woman is the gate of the devil, the road of evil and the sting of the scorpion." With real scientific inspiration Saint Thomas concludes that, "Woman is a mistake of nature, generated by accident, and is therefore a monster."

As the priests in the middle ages had to meditate on something between prayers, their minds hovered over the sexual extravagances of women as the most natural and efficacious method of counteracting any genuine sympathy and veneration for so depraved a sex. Practically all the lewd literature written at that time was composed by churchmen or by clerics who had been brought up in the sanctity of some monastery. Although few of their productions have much artistic merit they are interesting as illustrations of the baseness of certain ecclesiastical minds. One such work describes the effect which the mention of a man's unmentionables has upon women. A young girl hearing the unprintable word for the first time is more solaced than at the sound of God's name and wonders why she was not christened with so blest a name, while at the same word an old woman goes into ecstasies because of the sweet memories the sound evokes. More edifying is the account of the four irrevocable wishes given by the blessed Saint Martin to a married couple—the wife immediately wishes that her husband be covered with sexual organs from head to foot, the same ever to be in prime condition, for, she explains, a single organ counts for practically nothing. From this delicate situation the husband's wish and the conclusion of the story can easily be guessed. Another moral tale tells of two little nuns who find a man's genitals lying in the road. They quarrel so violently for its possession that the Abbess learns of it and confiscates it, much to the anguish of the whole sisterhood. At length the Abbess makes a holy relic of the precious member; it is enshrined in a high place and most devoutly worshipped by all her blessed nuns.

The Archpriest of Hita is by no means worse than his contemporary ecclesiastics. If he occasionally shares their lubricity and contempt for women he also champions the sex again and again. Though he may laugh at them he does not hate them, and when he dwells upon matters indelicate it is with the ribald gusto of unmorality rather than from a love of spiced obscenity.

7. One is very much surprised at Juan Ruiz' attitude on the temperance question inasmuch as wine and women are so intimately related. Perhaps, he thought, like the porter in *Macbeth*, "Lechery, sir, it provokes and unprovokes; it provokes the desire but it takes away the performance. Therefore much drink may be said to be an equivicator of lechery; it makes him and it mars him; it sets him on and it takes him off; it persuades him and disheartens him; makes him stand to and not stand

to; in conclusion, equivocates him in a sleep, and giving him the lie, leaves him" (II; iii). To Ovid's "Vina parant animos," Juan Ruiz merely answers that drinking fouls the breath which in turn nauseates women—certainly a very considerate and unselfish concession to the fair sex. Our poet is nothing if not gallant.

8. Of all the stories of the Bible which fascinated the chaste minds of the middle ages, the idyll of Lot's incest seems to have been the most popular, judging by its ubiquity. In English Literature the pious Langland refers to it in his *Piers Ploughman*:

> "For Lot in his lyf-days for liking of drinke
> Dude bi his douhtren that the devel louvede
> Dilytede him in drinke as the devel woulde
> And lecherie him lauhte and lay by hem bothe;
> And al he witede hit wyn that wikkede dede." (512; I; 27–31)

Chaucer, too, in the "Pardoner's Tale," has not forgotten the edifying incident:

> "The holy wryt take I to my witnesse
> That luxury is in wyn and dronkenesse
> Lo, how that dronke Loth unkyndely
> Lay by his daughters two unwitingly,
> So dronke he was he niste what he wrought."

9. Although many analogues to this tale were current in the middle ages, Juan Ruiz acknowledges pointedly the aphrodisiac effect of animals in *flagrante dilectu*, a well known prescription for 'failing vigor' at that time. A curious Arabic work by a high-minded sage, Sheik Nefzawi, *The Perfumed Garden*, possibly well known in Mohammedan Spain, has the following advice to men only: "Wise doctors have written that those whose members no longer enjoy their wonted force and are tinged with impotence, ought either to give themselves up to reading books discussing coition and study with care the manners of making love in order to restore their past vigor, or they ought to contemplate animals abandoning themselves to the act of coition for that is a sure means for procuring erections. But as it is not always easy to obtain the sight of animals coupling, books discussing the act of generation are of an incontestable value . . . they may be compared to the philosopher's stone which transforms base metals into gold."

10. Chaucer, too, in the "Pardoner's Tale," has substantially the same objection to the disgusting effect upon the breath of drinking wine:

> "O dronke man disfigured is thi face
> Sour is thi breth, foul artow to embrace." (13966–7)

11. This is the book on *Tafurerias* written by Maestro Roldán in 1277 by order of Alphonso X.

12. Juan Ruiz shows a marked predilection for widows—if there were no other evidence this preference would be sufficient to prove that he was a priest.

13. Lady Venus gives much shrewder, picturesque, and unprincipled advice on seducing women than Sir Love. Evidently the Archpriest realized that even among gods and goddesses the female of the species is more deadly than the male.

14. There are many references in mediaeval literature to the eye and smile as indications of the unchaste woman. The Archpriest of Talavera, who inherited Ruiz' mantle, describes the eye of a wanton woman in his *Corbacho* as follows, "There are many different meanings they convey through their eyes, by looking at a man they mock him, flatter him, infatuate him, and ruin him; by looking at a man they show spite and anger when they roll their eyes to one side. A woman can play more tricks with her eyes than a juggler with his hands." There are also numerous Italian proverbs, too vile to quote, associating movements of the eye, mouth, *et*

*alia* with lewd habits. Dante, in *Purg.* XXXII; 149, *et seq*, says, "A shameless harlot appeared to me with roving eyes and, as though she should not be taken from him, a giant I saw erect at her side, and from time to time each kissed the other; but, because she turned her lustful and vagrant eye upon me that fierce paramour did scourge her." Chaucer, too, in his " Miller's Tale," 3244, describes a wanton thus, "And certeynly sche hadd a licorous eyghe."

15. The apostrophe of the lover to his lady has many analogues in literature, the most famous, perhaps, being that in *Romeo and Juliet* (I; v):

"Oh, she doth teach the torches to burn bright!
It seems she hangs upon the cheek of night
Like a rich jewel in an Ethiop's ear."

Dante, too, in a sonnet in his *Vita Nuova* (XXVI), has the following:

"When meeting friends she knows upon her ways
Such humble kindness doth my lady suit
That sudden every tongue grows trembling mute
And no eye on her beauty dares to gaze."

Pedants have squabbled over the vague reminiscences between Ruiz and Dante in these opening stanzas. Fitzmaurice-Kelly denies the connection by calling attention to the fact that Ruiz is merely glossing an older poem, the Pamphilus, which, however, in this particular instance, has absolutely no resemblance to Ruiz' invocation. If sources and influences, the happy hunting grounds for pedagogical goslings, must be invoked for Ruiz, it seems not impossible that Arabic literature has left its traces. There is an apostrophe in the Portress' *Tale of the Thousand and One Nights* which Richard Burton translates:

"Thou pacest the palace, a marvel sight, a bride for a Kisras' or Kaisar's night
Wantons the rose on thy roseate cheek, Oh cheek as the blood of the dragon bright
Slim waisted, langorous, sleepy eyed, with charms which promise all love delight
And the tire which attires thy tiaraed brow, is a night of woe in a morn's glad light."

16. The classical metaphor comparing women to wax seems to have been very popular. The Archpriest of Talavera repeats it in his *Corbacho* (cap. V): "Woman is as soft as wax in receiving new forms that are impressed upon her. Just as wax derives the form of a seal, whatever it may be, large or small, well or evilly engraved, so a bad woman, come what may, gets her evil reputation from her nature." Shakespeare uses the figure in his "Rape of Lucrece" (178):

"For men have marble, women waxen, minds,
And therefore are they formed as marble will;
The weak oppress'd, the impression of strange kinds
Is formed in them by force, by fraud, or skill;
Then cast them not the authors of their ill,
No more than wax shall be accounted evil
Wherein is stamped the semblance of a devil."

17. The old bawd's speech to the lover is vaguely reminiscent of the Nurse's to Romeo. In Act II; iv, she exclaims: "I anger her sometimes and tell her Paris is the properer man; but, I'll warrant you, when I say so, she looks as pale as any clout in the versal world."

18. Again note the vague similarity to *Romeo and Juliet*, II; v; ll. 18–45.

19. Professor George Ticknor, the historian of Spanish literature, says, "Of their (i.e., procuresses') activity in the days of the Archpriest, a whimsical proof is given in the extraordinary number of odious and ridiculous names and epithets accumulated on them." Certainly it would be ridiculous to deny the enormous activity of such women during the dark ages. About the eleventh century they began to organize themselves into prostitutes' unions with euphemistic names as

"The Itinerant Wives and Maidens," "Sisters of Mary Magdalene," or "Joyous Virgins." Devout churchmen were not wanting but justified the institution. The godly Saint Augustine has the following utterance to his credit, "Suppress prostitution and capricious lust will overthrow society." A later moralist avers that the prostitute is an "angel that spreads her protecting wings over the virtue of pure women." Nevertheless the Archpriest's curious list of names is hardly sufficient proof of itself. The "names of a whore" have been popular though rather stupid witticisms in many literatures. They figure in some of the tales of *The Thousand and One Nights* and crop out in the sprightly Latin poems of mediaeval students, the Goliards. In Spanish there are a few notable examples. Francisco Delgado, another saintly ecclesiastic, in his absorbing picaresque novel *La Lozana Andaluza* (1525) has a list of about seventy adjectives to the honor of prostitutes. The *Cancionero de Obras de Burias*, a scandalous collection of verses dating from the Renaissance through the Golden Age, contains an edifying ditty entitled "Other Couplets On Four Gentle Men Vilifying a Woman," which is as good—or rather as bad—as its word. Rabelais has transferred the same idea in his extraordinary list of adjectives describing the *membrum virile*, delicately known as the "cod." Mathurin Regnier also takes a fling at calling unfortunate women names in his charming "Ode to an Old Whore." The practice seems to savor of the folklore of curses, or of some crude conventional joking rather than constituting proof of the prostitute's popularity—which was, of course, enormous.

20. The folk divide the year in two seasons only, winter and summer.

21. Scholars have shed some ink over the question of the origin of Ruiz' mountain girl songs. Fitzmaurice-Kelly holds them to be clever parodies of Galician *cantos de ledino*. Ticknor sees their source in the *pastourelles* of Giraut Riquier, which indeed resemble Ruiz' closely. Puymaigre mentions, in addition, the possible influence of the stilted poetry of Thibaut de Champagne; Menéndez y Pelayo, however, claims that their prototypes are to be seen in the Gallo-Portuguese poems composed at the court of King Diniz. Not that it really matters, but we, too, might observe that although the complicated verse form and general pastourelle flavor do seem to claim Provence as their ultimate origin, the geographic realism and intense personal individuality of Ruiz' work mark them as original poems written about actual experiences. Quirós, with a somewhat Freudian leaning, suspects that Ruiz' escapades with ugly peasant girls, particularly the one described further on in number IV, are evidence of some disgusting sex perversion in the devout Archpriest. Dante, he notes, while in the Casentino Alps loved a rather uncouth, bearish wench. Verlaine experienced libido toward old, hunchbacked women, and inquisitive malice might multiply such examples endlessly.

22. The dragon or serpent that killed old Rando which Ruiz went to see has been conjectured to be the skeleton of some prehistoric mastodon or dinosaur, imbedded in the rock and, once discovered, invested with legend and set apart as a local curiosity. Just how these fossilized bones could have killed old Rando is not clear unless that, too, be ascribed to tradition, but the only objection to the ingenious dinosaur theory is that the Guadarrama mountains in that vicinity belong to the world's oldest formations, Archaean and Cambrian. The only fossil existing at such a time is the Trilobite, in size and shape resembling a horse-shoe crab.

23. Such grotesque caricatures as Ruiz' of the mountain girl are common enough in literature and seem to characterize the crude humor of unsophisticated peoples. The Archpriest of Talavera, in his *Corbacho*, puts the following description in the mouth of an envious woman concerning a pretty girl who has captured a man's fancy. "But, my death sir, you haven't seen her undressed as I have the other day in the bath. She is blacker than the devil, flabby as death itself, her hair is frizzly and black as pitch, her head is large and misshapen and her neck is fat and thick as a bull's, her breasts are all bony and her teats hang down like

a goat's, long and dirty. She is ungainly, her legs are as skinny as a crane's, her feet sprawl out like a hen's. The filth and the stench of her body made all those of us spew who were at the bath." In the tale of the Portress, of *The Thousand and One Nights*, Burton translates the description of the old bawd thus, "An old woman with lantern jaws and teeth sucked in, and eyes rucked up, and eyebrows scant and scald, and head bare and bald; and teeth broken by time and mauled, and back bending and nape nodding and face blotched and rheum running, and hair like a snake, black-and-white-speckled in complexion a very fright."

24. From his knowledge of foods and kitchen scullery one may guess that Juan Ruiz, like many devout Christian priests, spent much of his time in the kitchen.

25. Compare the above description of the pilgrim with Langland's in *Piers Ploughman* (Passus VI; 6-15):

> "They a man met
> Apparelled as a palmer, in pilgrims' weeds,
> He bore a staff bound with a broad fringe
> In woodbine wise twisted round.
> A bag and a bowl he bore by his side;
> A hundred vials on his hat were set,
> Signes of Sinai and shells of Galicia;
> Many a cross on his cloak, and the keyes of Rome,
> And the vernicle in front, that men should him know,
> And see by his signs whom he had sought."

26. Roncevalle, or Roncevaux, celebrated in the Cid and in the Roland; a gloomy pass through which pilgrims for centuries have journeyed on their way to the shrine of Saint James in Galicia. It was the scene of the defeat of Charlemagne's rear guard and of the heroic death of Count Roland, as told in the old French epic.

> "High are the peaks, the valleys dark and dim
> The stark rocks grey, the district strange and grim."
> *Chanson de Roland: 814-815*

27. Even as the disciples of Jesus, when He appeared to them after His resurrection, constrained Him to abide with them at evening, so these nuns, the professional "brides of Christ," greet the lord of love with the same salutation and invite him to their beds.

Ticknor says, "It is not quite easy to see how the Archpriest ventured some things in the last passage. Parts of the procession come singing the most solemn hymns of the church or parodies of them, applied to Don Amor, like the *"Benedictus qui venit."* It seems downright blasphemy against what was then thought most sacred."

Parodies of sacred works began, according to Paul Lehmann, about the seventh century although their prototypes existed much earlier. During the late Empire coarse Roman playwrights burlesqued various Christian rites and sacraments, even going so far as to force Christian men and women to play the disgraceful parts, thereby arousing in the primitive church that bitter antagonism toward the drama that it still feels. In the early Middle Ages, strolling mountebanks and players, descendants of the Roman mimes, travestied divine services. Later, the Ass's Mass and other juvenile blasphemies of things sacred, were carried right up to the altar of God itself.

In Spain, during the Renaissance and the Golden Age, obscene songs and parodies interspersed divine services. A familiar of the Holy Inquisition, writing about 1663, makes the following official report of the abuses: "It is a public and notorious thing that in many of the churches of these realms, and especially in the convents of religious women, not only during the festivals of the birth of our Lord and of the Magi kings, which are the ones which most provoke unusual demonstrations of jubilation, but also in many other festivals of the year, and even before the very altar during the holy sacrament, there are chanted certain bawdy verses in the vulgar tongue, commonly sung in the farces of the theatre which they mix with divine services . . . and they are wont to sing some verses with words which are ambiguous and have double meanings, the most evident being the profane, and these words are applied to Christ our Redeemer and to His saints . . ." (Inquisitional papers, no. 41.)

An example of one of the bawdy verses, referred to above, intoned by these devout creatures during divine services, runs as follows:

"I call to mind a time gone by,
My lady, sweet and well beloved,
When darkness found me in your arms
And morning fair still saw me there,
And in the midst of these delights,
Though glories they were better called,
I mixed the tulips of my mouth
With that red rose which is your lips
And while two tongues found out the way
To creep inside each other's mouth,
We spent that unforgotten night
In silence utterly profound.
Oh how a love augments itself,
And how desire refines itself
Between soft sheets on pillows sweet
Among deep shadows in the dark . . ."

The rest of the poem is too grossly physiological to admit of translation.

28. This is, of course, a double entendre between the hair shirt or cilix put on by a nun to chasten her nature and that other hairy thing put on by nature to chasten a nun. The witticism was a favorite one in the middle ages, and Cejador smacks his priestly lips over it with infinite gusto. But as Rabelais said, "Folle à la messe, molle à la fesse."

The unchastity of nuns, as before remarked, was a favorite subject for devout persons. Friederich's *Garichtlische Psychologie*, mentions a number of curious examples: "Blankebin, the nun, was constantly tormented by the thought of what would have become of that part of Christ which was removed in circumcision. Veronica Juliana, beatified by Pope Pius II, in memory of the Divine Lamb, took a real lamb to bed with her, kissed it, and suckled it on her breasts. Saint Catherine of Genoa often burned with such intense inward fire that in order to cool herself she would throw herself upon the ground, crying, 'Love, love, I can endure it no longer!' At the same time she felt a peculiar inclination toward her confessor. One day, lifting his hand to her nose, she noticed a peculiar odor which penetrated to her heart, 'a heavenly perfume that would awaken the dead.' Saint Armelle and Saint Elizabeth were troubled with similar longings for the infant Jesus. The temptations of Saint Anthony of Padua are known to the world. Of significance is an old Protestant prayer, 'Oh that I had found thee, blessed Emmanuel, that thou wert with me in my bed, to bring delight to my body and soul. Come and be mine; my heart shall be thy resting place.'"

29. The three knights are symbolical of the three winter months: November, December, January. The space between the last of one month and the first of the following month is so small that a coin's edge could not pry into it, yet inasmuch as all months have from twenty-eight to thirty-one days, that long distance prevents one month from encroaching upon another.

30. This description of the archpriest is usually regarded as a bit of authentic self-portraiture. Although it is quite likely that it may indeed be so, still it is possible that a certain erotic symbolism lies beneath what seems to be a faithful and realistic portrait. Nearly all the details mentioned have a subtle, hidden,

sex meaning. The nose, for example, is supposed to indicate by its length the size of the male member; the depth of the voice, size of neck, and darkness of hair indicate sexual vigor, and so on. For a fuller study of this interesting subject see the article, "The Personal Appearance of Juan Ruiz," by E. K. Kane, in *Modern Language Notes*, February, 1930.

31. An interesting comparison with Ruiz' attitude toward Hell is to be seen in a thirteenth century anonymous romance, *Aucassin and Nicolette*. The hero, Aucassin, after having been threatened by the ward of the girl he loves that he will lose Paradise and roast in Hell if he seduces her, replies:

"Paradise? What have I to do with Paradise? I don't want to get there unless I have Nicolette, my dear sweetheart whom I love so much. For the only kind of people who go to Paradise are such as I shall tell you. Old priests go there and old crippled and lame people who grovel before altars and old crypts, and people with old worn out cloaks, dressed in ancient rags and tatters, who are naked and without shoes, whose shanks are bare and who die of hunger and thirst and cold and misery. Such like go to Paradise; I won't have anything to do with them—I want to go to Hell. For in Hell are the gay clerics and proud knights who died in tournaments of glorious wars; there are lusty sergeants and noble men at arms. I want to go with them. And there also go kind and beautiful ladies who have two or three lovers besides their husbands. And there go gold and silver and costly furs of precious color; and there go the jongleurs and music makers and those who are the kings of this world. With them I will go, provided that I have with me my Nicolette, my dear sweetheart."

32. It is rather disappointing that one with Ruiz' gift of sardonic irony made so little of the opportunity afforded by this epitaph. Satiric epitaphs are comparatively rare before the Renaissance. A number, to be sure, were written at the court of Charlemagne and many more in the twelfth and thirteenth centuries when parodies became popular. Clever, epigrammatic epitaphs, however, really came into their own with the Renaissance. Some famous ones might be quoted by way of contrast with Ruiz'. There is the epitaph of Pietro Aretino:

> "Qui giace l'Aretin, poeta tosco
> ["Here's Aretin, of many a Tuscan poem]
>
> Che disse mal d'ognun, fuor che di dio
> [Who slandered every one excepting God]
>
> Scusandosi col dir, non lo conosco."
> [But that can be explained—he didn't know Him."]

A famous epitaph upon a Jesuit brother:

> "Ci-gît un Jésuite,
> ["Beneath this stone does a Jesuit lie]
>
> Passant, serre les fesses et passe vite."
> [So tighten your buttocks and run quickly by."]

One epitaph, translated or paraphrased in nearly every language of Europe:

> "Ci-gît ma femme—ah quelle est bien
> Pour son repos et pour le mien."

Dryden has inscribed with great gallantry to his wife in the following form:

> "Here lies my wife, here let her lie;
> She's now at rest and so am I."

33. The church held it a pious act not only for a man to marry an orphan but even a prostitute. Anatole France advised that men should exercise common sense in all things save in matters of faith.

34. There are a number of aphorisms in Spanish, and more particularly in Italian, which connect intensity of passion with small stature in women. Such sayings naturally reflect a folk belief to which Ruiz quite evidently must have subscribed.

35. The Spanish scholar, Puyol y Alonso, believes that the four hymns to the Virgin mentioned in stanza 1626 are those beginning with stanza 1635 and following.

36. François Rabelais, in the prologue of his second book, *Pantagruel*, makes claim for analogous curative properties for his book.

37. Another Spanish scholar, Menéndez y Pidal, says that in stanza 1629 Ruiz, like a popular jongleur, intended his work to be common property for any one to add to or to change. The great French poet, François Villon, in his *Greater Testament*, stanzas CLX–CLXI, makes the same invitation.

38. Concerning the discrepancy in tone and subject between stanza 1684 and the following, Menéndez y Pidal rightly observes, "There has even been added a certain poem on the complaints to Fortune which in codices, editions, and anthologies is inexplicably lost and confused with one of the hymns in praise of the Virgin." *Poesia Juglaresca y Juglares*, page 273.

39. Many believe that Juan Ruiz was imprisoned by Archbishop Gil because of his disrespectful references to him. Don Gil de Albornoz was certainly stern enough to throw the Archpriest into prison but the fact cannot definitely be proved or disproved. Indeed if much, if not all, of *The Book of Good Love* was written in prison, and the above verses also, it is obvious that Gil would hardly have put Ruiz in prison for what he later wrote in prison. The argument savors of a sort of *cherchez la femme* desperate attempt to explain a mystery upon insufficient remaining evidence.

Menéndez y Pidal believes this ballad is "taken directly from the *Consultatio Sacerdotum*," a mediaeval Goliardic satire, and cites little scraps of verbal reminiscences to prove his case. Ruiz' ballad has the individuality of a historical narrative despite the pattern he may have copied.

40. So outrageous was the conduct of these eminent divines and their prostitutes that in 1351 the courts of Valladolid complained to Pedro I (The Cruel) about the luxury and arrogance of the concubines of churchmen. The king ordered the dress of such women to be regulated under a sumptuary law and required them to wear a red cloth under their wimples so that people might be able to distinguish them outwardly from honest women.

# SELECTED BIBLIOGRAPHY

## Books

### Editions

Alvarez de Villa, A. *Libro de Buen Amor*. Paris: 1910.

Brey Mariño, María. *Arcipreste de Hita, Libro de Buen Amor*. Madrid: 1964.

Canales Loro, Clemente. "Libro de buen amor versíon moderna," *Anales de la Universidad de Chile*. Santiago: 1941.

Castro y Calvo, J. M. *Libro de Buen Amor: Selección y Notas*. Saragossa: 1940.

Cejador y Frauca, Julio. *Juan Ruiz, Libro de Buen Amor: Edición y Notas*. Madrid: 1913.

Corso, Felix F. *Libro de Buen Amor*. Buenos Aires: 1939.

Criado de Val, Manuel, and Eric W. Naylor. *Arcipreste de Hita, Libro de Buen Amor: Edición Crítica*. Madrid: 1965.

Ducamin, Jean. *Libro de Buen Amor, Texte du XIV^e Siècle: Publíe pour la première fois avec les leçons des trois manuscrits commus*. Toulouse: 1901.

Janer, Florencio. *Libro de Cantares de Joan Roiz, Arcipreste de Hita*, in *Biblioteca de Autores Espanoles*. Madrid: 1864.

Malkiel, María Rosa Lida de. *Juan Ruiz, Arcipreste de Hita: Selección*. Buenos Aires: 1941.

Reyes, Alfonso. *Arcipreste de Hita, Libro de Buen Amor*. Madrid: 1917.

Sánchez, Tomás Antonio (ed.). *Colección de Poesías Castellanos Anteriores al Siglo XV*, IV. Madrid: 1790.

### Vocabularies

Aguado, José María. *Glosario sobre Juan Ruiz, Poeta Castellano del Siglo XIV*. Madrid: 1929.

Richardson, Henry B. *An Etymological Vocabulary to the Libro de Buen Amor of Juan Ruiz, Arcipreste de Hita*. New Haven, Conn.: 1930.

Amador de los Ríos, José. *Historia Crítica de la Literatura Española*, IV. Madrid: 1863.

Ambles y González, Rafael. *Juicio Crítico del Arcipreste de Hita.* Guadalajara, Spain: 1888.

Benito Durán, A. *Filosofía del Arcipreste de Hita.* Madrid: 1946.

Brenan, Gerald. *The Literature of the Spanish People.* New York: 1957.

Canales Toro, C. *El Libro de Buen Amor: Interpretación y Versificación.* Santiago, Chile: 1959.

Castro, Américo. *España en Su Historia, Cristianos, Moros y Judíos.* Buenos Aires: 1948.

————. *The Structure of Spanish History.* Princeton, N.J.: 1954.

Doddis Miranda, Antonio, and German Sepúlveda Durán. *Estudios sobre Juan Ruiz, Arcipreste de Hita.* Santiago, Chile: 1956.

Green, Otis. *Spain and the Western Tradition*, I. Madison, Wisc.: 1963.

Hart, Thomas. *La Alegoría en el Libro de Buen Amor.* Madrid: 1959.

Keller, John E. *Motif-Index of Mediaeval Spanish Exempla.* Knoxville, Tenn.: 1949.

Lecoy, Felix. *Recherches sur le Libro de Buen Amor de Juan Ruiz, Archiprêtre de Hita.* Paris: 1938.

Malkiel, María Rosa Lida de. *Two Spanish Masterpieces, The Book of Good Love and the Celestina.* Urbana, Ill.: 1961.

Martín Recuerda, José. *¿Quién Quiere una Copla del Arcipreste de Hita?* Madrid: 1966.

Menéndez Pidal, Ramón. *Poesía Juglaresca y Juglares.* Madrid: 1924.

————. *Poesía Arabe y Poesía Europea.* Buenos Aires: 1946.

Puyol, Julio. *Las Fábulas de Juan Ruiz, Arcipreste de Hita, Restauradas.* Santiago, Chile: 1898.

————. *El Arcipreste de Hita: Estudio Crítico.* Madrid: 1965.

Valbuena Prat, A. *Historia de la Literatura Española.* Barcelona: 1959.

Zahareas, Anthony. *The Art of Juan Ruiz, Archpriest of Hita.* Madrid: 1965.

## Articles

Alonso, Dámaso. "La Bella de Juan Ruiz," *Insula*, VII (1952), 3–11.

————. "La cárcel del Arcipreste," *Cuadermos Hispano-americanos*, XXX (1957), 165–77.

Babillot, F. "Le 'Libro de Buen Amor' de l'Archiprêtre de Hita," *Bulletin Hispanique*, XXXVI (1934), 500–2.

Barra, Eduardo de la. "Las fábulas de Juan Ruiz, Arcipreste de Hita," *Anales de la Universidad de Chile*, CI (1898), 371–86 and 391–408.

Battaglia, S. "Saggio sul libro de 'Buen Amor,' dell'Arcipreste de Hita," *Nuova Cultura*, IX (1931), 721–35.

Bernaldo de Quiros, C. "La ruta del Arcipreste de Hita por la Sierra de Guadarrama," *La Lectura*, III (1915), 145–60.

Bonilla y San Martín, A. "Antecedentes del tipo celestinesco en la literatura latina," *Revue Hispanique*, XV (1906), 372–86.

Buceta, Erasmo. "La 'Política de Aristóteles fuente de unos versos del Arcipreste de Hita," *Revista de Filología Española*, XII (1925), 56–60.

Capecchi, F. "Il *libro de buen amor* di Juan Ruiz, Arcipreste de Hita," *Cultura Neolatina*, Nos. 1–2 (1953) and 59–60 (1954).

Castro, Américo. "El *Libro de Buen Amor* del Arcipreste de Hita," in *Comparative Literature*, IV (1952), 193–213.

Castro, Guisasola F. "El horóscopo del Rey Alcaraz en el *Libro de Buen Amor*," *Revista de Filología Española*, X (1923), 39–98.

———. "Una laguna del *Libro de Buen Amor*," in *Revista de Bibliotecas, Archivos y Museos del Ayuntamiento de Madrid*. Madrid: 1930. Pp. 124–30.

Cirot, Georges. "L'episode de D.ª Endrina dans le 'Libro de Buen Amor,'" *Bulletin Hispanique*, XLV (1943), 139–56.

Clavería, Carlos. "*Libro de Buen Amor*, 699c: esas viejas troyas," *Nueva Resista de Filología Hispánica*, II (1948), 268–72.

Crawford, J. P. Wickersham. "El horóscopo del hijo del Rey Alcaraz en el *Libro de Buen Amor*," *Revista de Filología Española*, XII (1925), 184–90.

Fotitch, Tatiana. "El *Libro de Buen Amor*, 869c," *Studies in Philology* (1958), 464–71.

Garcia Blanco, Manuel. "Sobre un pasaje del *Libro de Buen Amor*," *Miscelánea Griera*, I (1955), 257–63.

Gibbon-Moneypenny, G. B. "Autobiography in the *Libro de Buen Amor* in the Light of Some Literary Comparisons," *Bulletin of Hispanic Studies*, XXXIV (1957), 63–78.

———. "Estado actual de los estudios sobre el 'Libro de Buen Amor,'" in *Anuario de estudios medievales*, III. Barcelona: 1966. 575–609.

Gilman, Stephen. "The Juvenile Intuition of Juan Ruiz," *Symposium*, IV (1950), 290–303.

Green, Otis. "On Juan Ruiz's Parody of the Canonical Hours," *Hispanic Review*, XXVI (1958), 12–34.

Hamilton, Rita. "A Note on Juan Ruiz," *Modern Language Review*, L (1955), 504–5.

Hanssen, Frederick. "Los metros de los cantares de Juan Ruiz," *Anales de la Universidad de Chile*, LXV (1957), 234–55.

———. "Un himno de Juan Ruiz," *Anales de la Universidad de Chile*, Nos. 107–108 ((1957).

Hatzfeld, Helmut A. "The *Libro de Buen Amor*," *Romance Philology*, I (1948), 323–24.

Henríquez Ureña, Pedro. "El Arcipreste de Hita," *Sur*, CIX (November, 1943), 7–25.

Jaimes Freyre, Ricardo. "El *Libro de Buen Amor* (Introducción a un estudio sobre Juan Ruiz)," *Revista de Letras y Ciencias Sociales*, VI (1907), 197–213.

Jiménez, J. O. "Los seiscientos años del Arcipreste de Hita," *Boletín de la Academia Cubana de la Lengua*, IX (1960), 97–115.

Kane, Elisha K. "The Personal Appearance of Juan Ruiz," *Modern Language Notes*, XLV (1930), 103–8.

————. "A Note on the Supposed Foreign Residence of the Archpriest of Hita," *Modern Language Notes*, XLVI (1931), 472–73.

————. "The Electuaries of the Archpriest of Hita," *Modern Philology*, XXX (1933), 263–66.

Kellerman, W. "Zur Charakteristik des *Libro del Buen Amor* del Arcipreste de Hita," *Zeitschrift für Romanische Philologie*, LXVII (1951), 222–54.

Lang, Evelyn. "El tema de la alegría en el *Libro de Buen Amor*," *Revista Hispánica Moderna*, XXII (1956), 1–5 and 13–17.

Lázaro, Fernando. "Los amores de D. Melón y D.ª Endrina: Notas sobre el arte de Juan Ruiz," *Arbor*, XVIII (1941), 210–36.

Leo, Ulrich. "Zur Dichterischen Originalität des Arcipreste de Hita," *Analecta Romanica*, VI (1958), 1–131.

Malkiel, María Rosa Lida de. "Notas para la interpretación, influencia, fuentes y texto del *Libro de Buen Amor*," *Revista de Filología Hispánica*, II (1940), 105–50.

————. "Nuevas notas para la interpretación de *Libro de Buen Amor*," *Revista de Filología Hispánica*, I (1959), 17–82.

————. "Una interpretación más de Juan Ruiz," *Romance Philology*, XIV (1960–61), 228–37.

Martínez Ruiz, José [Azorín]. "Juan Ruiz," in *Al Margen de los Clásicos*. Madrid: 1915. Pp. 20–22.

Menéndez Pidal, Gonzalo. "El arcipreste de Hita," in *Historia General de las Literaturas Hispánicas*, I. Barcelona: 1949. 473–90.

Menéndez Pidal, Ramón. "Título que el Arcipreste de Hita dió al libro de sus poesías," *Revista de Archivos, Bibliotecas y Museos*, II (1898), 106–9.

————. "Nota sobre una fábula de Don Juan Manuel y de Juan Ruiz," in *Homenaje a Ernest Martinenche*. Paris: 1938. Pp. 183–86.

Menéndez y Pelayo, Marcelino. Prologue to the *Antología de Poetas Líricos Castellanos*. Madrid: 1924. Pp. v–lxxxvi.

Miro Quesada, Garland A. "La Trotaconventos: Origen latino del célebre personaje del Arcipreste de Hita," *Letras*, IX (1943), 408–14.

Moffat, Lucius G. "The Imprisonment of the Archpriest," *Hispania*, XXXIII (1950), 321–27.

———. "The Evidence of Early Mentions of the Archpriest of Hita or of His Work," *Modern Language Notes*, LXXV (1960), 33–44.

Morreale, Margharita. "*Libro de Buen Amor* 869c.," *Hispanic Review*, XXIV (1956), 232–34.

Oliver Asín, Jaime. "La expresión *ala ud* en el *Libro de Buen Amor*," *Al-Andalus*, XXI (1956), 212–14.

Reckert, Stephen. "Avras dueña garrida," *Revista de Filología Española*, XXXVII (1953), 227–37.

Reyes, Alfonso. "El Arcipreste de Hita y su *Libro de Buen Amor*," in *Obras Completas*. Mexico: 1955. Pp. 15–21.

———. "Viaje del Arcipreste de Hita por la Sierra de Guadarrama," in *Obras Completas*. Mexico: 1955. Pp. 22–24.

Rodríguez, Julio. "Juan Ruiz, Arcipreste de Hita: Su *Libro de Buen Amor*," *Revista de las Indias*, XVII (1943), 55–67.

Rothberg, Irving P. "Juan Ruiz and Literature," *Hispania*, XXXVIII (1955), 44–58.

Sánchez Cantón, Francisco X. "Siete versos inéditos del *Libro de Buen Amor*," *Revista de Filología Española*, V (1918), 43–45.

Sandoval, M. de. "Los pretendidos endecasílabos del Arcipreste de Hita," *Boletín de la Real Academia Española*, XVII (1930), 659–63.

Schultz, A. H. "La tradición cortesana en dos coplas de Juan Ruiz," *Nueva Revista de Filología Española*, VIII (1954), 63–71.

Serrano y Jover, Alfredo. "Un ensiemplo de Juan Ruiz: De la pelea que hobo Don Carnal con la Quaresma," *La Ilustración Española y Americana*, LXXVII (1904), 238–39.

Solalinde, Antonio G. "Fragmentos de una traducción portuguesa del *Libro de Buen Amor*," *Revista de Filología Española*, I (1914), 162–72.

Spitzer, Leo. "Zur Auffassung des Kunst des Arcipreste de Hita," *Zeitschrift für Romanische Philologie*, LIV (1934), 237–70.

Ward, Humphrey. "A Medieval Spanish Writer," *Fortnightly Review*, XV (1876), 809–32.

Webber, Edwin J. "Juan Ruiz and Ovid," *Romance Notes*, II (1960), 54–57.

Willis, Raymond. "Two Trotaconventos," *Romance Philology*, XVII (1963), 353–62.

*Text set in Palatino Linotype*

*Composition, printing by*
*Heritage Printers, Inc., Charlotte, North Carolina*

*Binding by*
*Kingsport Press, Kingsport, Tennessee*

*Sixty-pound Olde Style laid paper by*
*S. D. Warren Company, Boston, Massachusetts*

*Woodcut figures from*
*Hartmann Schedel, Liber Chronicarum,*
*(Nürnberg: Anton Koberger, 1493)*
*Used by courtesy of*
*Rare Book Collection, Library,*
*University of North Carolina at Chapel Hill*

*Designed and published by*
*The University of North Carolina Press, Chapel Hill, North Carolina*